Si   e his wife died on 9/11, Jon Reznick has worked hard

    eep his shadowy world hidden from his eleven-year-old

    ghter. But when he's ordered by his handler to assassinate

    in in an exclusive Washington DC hotel, he discovers the

    et is not at all who he at first appears to be.

    uickly ensnared in a web of murder, extortion and

tre   hery, Reznick finds himself fighting to outwit not only

the clandestine group intent on hunting him down, but also

FF Assistant Director Martha Meyerstein, who's determined

to   pture him as well.

    s not only Reznick's survival that's at stake. A terrifying

    y a foreign government to bring the United States to its

    s is underway. And Jon Reznick is the only man who can

    t.

J B TURNER

HARD ROAD

EXHIBIT A
An Angry Robot imprint
and a member of Osprey Group

Lace Market House,
54-56 High Pavement,
Nottingham NG1 1HW
UK

www.exhibitabooks.com
A is for American Heroes!

An Exhibit A paperback original 2013
1

A catalogue record for this book is available
from the British Library.

UK ISBN 978 1 90922 345 5
Ebook ISBN 978 1 90922 347 9

Cover photo © Dylan Kitchener/Trevillion Images; design by Argh! Oxford
Set in Meridien and Franklin Gothic by Epub Services.

For my late father

ONE

The call came from a man he knew only as Maddox.

Jon Reznick was sitting on his freezing deck as darkness fell over Maine, nursing a bottle of beer, staring out over the ocean. He let his cell phone ring a few times, knowing what lay ahead. The ringtone was incessant. It had been ten long weeks. He pulled his coat tight and watched his breath turn to vapor.

He sighed long and hard before he picked up the phone.

"We gotta delivery problem in Washington," Maddox said.

Reznick said nothing.

Down below in the cove, the Atlantic breakers crashed onto the rocky headland with a deafening roar, sending salt water into the winter air. The silhouettes of the tall oaks and maples in the garden, shorn of their leaves, which his late father had planted when he was a boy, bent and creaked in the wind. Away in the distance, out on Penobscot Bay, Reznick could see the lights of the lobster boats as they headed back to Rockland with the day's catch.

Maddox finally broke the silence. "They want to know if you can ensure the safe transfer of a consignment."

"When?"

"You must leave tonight."

Reznick said nothing.

"Is this inconvenient for you?"

"Kinda short notice."

"Are you available?"

"Tell me, how's the weather where you are?"

A long pause. "It's wet."

The word "wet" said it all. "Someone must want this delivery real bad."

"Will you do it?"

Reznick said nothing.

"This has got to happen. This is an important customer."

He let out a long sigh. "Tell them I'm in."

"Smart move, Reznick. Pick up your tickets at the airport."

"Where am I going?"

"You'll see."

The line went dead.

Just before midnight, Reznick's plane landed at Dulles. He wore a black leather jacket, a grey T-shirt, and dark blue Levi jeans and scuffed cowboy boots. He slung his bag containing a shaving kit, fresh boxer shorts, two T-shirts, a clean pair of jeans and his running gear over his shoulder and headed over to the Avis lot. Then he picked up a black Chevy Camaro. In the trunk was an envelope with a fake credit card and two thousand dollars in cash alongside a three-night reservation receipt for the Omni Shoreham Hotel in northwest Washington.

Reznick knew the city well. He headed onto the airport toll road and drove due east on Route 66, over the Roosevelt Bridge and exited onto Constitution Avenue. The traffic was still heavy, despite the late hour. His mind flashed back to the time he first visited the city with his father. It was the fall of 1982 during the first of many trips to see the Vietnam Veteran's Memorial. He remembered his father cursing the snarled-up traffic in his rental car. But most of all he remembered what his father wore. A dark suit, white shirt, Marine Corps tie and black shoes polished to a glassy shine. Without fail, his father always touched the names of the young men carved into the black granite wall the moment he arrived. Reznick would stand in silence, arms by his side, as his father fought back the tears.

The blaring siren of a fire truck in the distance snapped him out of his reverie as he drove over the historic Taft Bridge and past the two imposing concrete lions guarding either side. Eventually he took a left onto Calvert Street, the hotel up ahead.

He pulled up outside a traditional eight-story building and tipped the valet ten dollars.

Reznick walked through the grand, sprawling lobby. Marble floor, ornate columns and chandeliers. A young man on the desk took his details as he signed in under a false name, Ron Dixon.

"Three nights. Good to have you with us, Mr Dixon. Do you mind me asking if you're in town for business or pleasure, sir?"

Reznick managed a smile. "A bit of both."

"Excellent. Can we help you with any bags?"

"No, you're OK, thanks."

His fake credit card was swiped and he took the elevator to the sixth floor.

Reznick used the card to open his door and flicked on the lights. He hung a "Do Not Disturb" sign outside before he locked the room.

The room was too warm, but spacious. A huge TV was on one wall, a welcome message across the screen. The décor was the *classic* look, green floral patterned carpet and king-sized double bed with a couple of rosewood dressers. The drapes matched the carpets.

He peered out of the window over the upscale Woodley Park neighborhood; a good base, well away from downtown. He turned down the climate control switch to cool. He showered and wrapped himself in the white terry dressing gown. Then he lay down on the bed and stared at the ceiling, waiting for Maddox to call.

The next morning, Reznick ordered a freshly squeezed orange juice and black coffee from room service, before he got changed into his jogging gear – navy T-shirt and sweatpants with well-worn Nike sneakers. He headed over to Rock Creek Park under a flawless December sky, for his daily run. When he arrived at the water-powered Peirce Mill near the entrance, he did some stretching and warm-up moves although the temperature was in the low 60s. A handful of joggers were already pounding the trails.

He switched on his iPod, blocking out the outside world, helping him focus on the task in hand. The thunderous riffs and beats of a Led Zeppelin song got his blood flowing. He checked his watch, 8.48am precisely. He headed north towards the Western Ridge Trail, the smell of dead leaves and pine trees in the mid-December air.

After about a mile, he passed a young Hispanic woman sitting on the curb of a parking lot near Broad Branch Road. She grimaced as she rubbed her knee.

Reznick ran on by. No need to engage in unnecessary conversation with a stranger. Being anonymous was best. He knew the rules. The list was endless. Do not wear loud clothes, talk too much, appear distracted or lost; in fact anything that meant you were no longer blending in. The appearance was crucial. Greys, navy tracksuits and business suits were good. Black shoes, also. But you had to fit into the surrounding environment.

The way you spoke, the way you carried yourself, your accent, dialect, they all gave off signals. The moment a concierge thought your luggage looked too flashy or too beaten-up; it all painted a picture. If you're in a top-end hotel, wear top end clothes and carry smart cases.

The small things matter. Be attentive. Logos are easy to remember. Better without them. The trick was to be anonymous. But don't try too hard. Don't shun eye contact. That in itself will attract attention. What has he got to hide?

The senses had to work overtime. And tactics had to be changed, depending on the circumstances. Move to another hotel, change into new clothes, ditch a car and get a different model.

He headed along Beach Drive as he ran through the park. Heart rate steady. Deeper and deeper through a verdant urban sanctuary in America's capital city.

Slowly the endorphins kicked in as the sun flickered through the branches of the leafless oaks and maples. The sweat ran down his back and stuck to his grey marl T-shirt.

On and on he ran.

Up a hill and down a ravine, and back on the trail along Beach Drive, passing a small stone police substation in the center of the park, two officers leaning against a cruiser, drinking coffee. He gave a polite nod and they nodded back.

Heart pumping harder as his head became clearer. This was his routine ahead of every job and it passed the time. Kept him focused.

Along the northern section of the park, he passed Rolling Meadow Bridge and doubled back along a trail by the public golf course. On past the amphitheater and across Bluff Bridge to where he'd started.

He checked his pulse. Only slightly raised.

Ten minutes later, Reznick did some cool down stretching exercises against a park bench, when his cell phone in his waistband vibrated. He switched off his iPod and saw the familiar caller display.

"How you feeling today?" It was Maddox.

"I'm fine."

"So, any questions?"

Reznick wiped some sweat off his brow with the back of his hand. "You got a name?"

A beat. "All I know is that he's an American. OK?"

"On home soil? How come?"

A long pause. "Look, they wanted to keep it in-house. That's all I can say. This is a sensitive one."

"Tell me, where is the subject now?"

"Walking the national mall with his son."

"What kind of monitoring?"

"Electronic. Far safer."

Reznick stayed quiet, knowing he was right.

"How about we speak later today?"

"When?"

"I don't know. But stay close to your hotel."

Reznick shielded his eyes against the sun. "Why?"

"Why what?"

"Why stay close to the hotel?"

Maddox sighed. "Look, I've not had any confirmation, but I've heard from someone higher up the chain that we might have to move very quickly on this particular delivery."

"Timescale?"

"Sooner rather than later. Bear that in mind."

The rest of the day dragged as Reznick waited for Maddox to call.

It could be a matter of hours. He dialed 12 and ordered a late brunch of scrambled eggs, black coffee, buttered toast and more freshly squeezed orange juice. After a warm shower, he channel hopped between CNN, Fox News and the Weather Channel. Bombings across Kabul and Helmand Province as the Taliban launched a coordinated series of attacks to destabilize the Afghan government and instill fear in the population. He could see the way the wind was blowing there and it was all bad.

Early evening, he ordered a club sandwich and a Coke from room service. Afterwards, he went for a walk, keeping within six blocks of the hotel. He returned to his room, lay down on his bed and fell into a fitful sleep.

When he awoke, he checked the time. It was 8.09pm. And still Maddox hadn't called. Had there been a delay? Perhaps a last minute change of plan?

The thought of delays depressed him. He was asked to do a job; he wanted to get it over with. Then move on. He couldn't abide the long-drawn-out ones.

Feeling groggy, Reznick headed down to reception, bought a pair of swimming shorts and swam forty lengths of the empty pool, leaving his phone on his towel, on top of a lounger.

He headed back to his room and changed into a fresh T-shirt, jeans and sneakers. He paced the room, stopping occasionally to do push-ups and sit-ups, trying to keep sharp, not knowing when the call would come or if it would come at any moment.

Eventually, he slumped in the room's easy chair and watched an old black and white Jimmy Cagney film with the sound down.

His cell phone vibrated in the top pocket of his T-shirt.

"You're on the move." The voice of Maddox.

"Where?"

"Go to the Park America garage, 3000 K Street Northwest, and leave your car on Level 2."

Reznick made a mental note.

"Proceed to Level 5 where you'll find a black BMW convertible. Your keys can electronically open it. Proceed to the St Regis Hotel, and book in under the name, Lionel Fairchild. New ID and documents are in the passenger's jockey box, and a tan Louis Vuitton travelling bag with overnight essentials is in the trunk."

"What's in the bag?"

"The usual kit. Laptop, delivery equipment; it's all there."

Reznick said nothing.

"After you check-in, head straight to your room, which has already been allocated, and await final instructions."

Reznick did exactly as he was told.

First, he checked out of the Omni taking time to thank them for such a pleasant stay but sorry he had to cut short his visit for family reasons. He picked up his car from the valet and drove to the nearby parking garage as instructed. He left the vehicle on Level 2 and climbed the stairs. A rather smart BMW with tinted windows was parked at the far end of Level 5. He popped open the trunk, the monogrammed designer men's travel bag was inside. He picked it up, got into the car and clicked the fob to centrally lock the doors before he unzipped the bag.

Inside was a metallic thirteen-inch MacBook Pro laptop, a specially modified cell phone, a 9mm Beretta handgun and sufficient ammo to kill a small town, an electronic anti-jamming device, a military issue stun gun, a powerful muscle relaxant drug in a syringe disguised as a ballpoint pen and five thousand dollars in cash.

Reznick zipped up the bag and slid it under the passenger seat. Then he drove straight to the deluxe hotel in downtown Washington to await final instructions.

TWO

The St Regis Hotel on 16th Street was known as one of Washington's smartest hotels, two blocks north of the White House, its impressive limestone façade only hinting at the grandeur inside.

Reznick pulled up shortly after 10pm and handed the keys over to the Hispanic valet, careful to pick up the Louis Vuitton bag.

A concierge opened a door as he strode into the lobby. It was like some Italian renaissance dream. Chandeliers hanging from coffered ceilings, gold gilt-edged paintings, oriental rugs on the marble floor and antique and dark wood furniture.

Reznick handed over his fake driver's license and credit card to a young woman behind the desk. "Good evening," she said. "Nice to have you at the St Regis, sir." She brought up his details on the computer. "Is this your first time with us?"

"Yeah."

"Well, we hope you enjoy your stay." She handed over a swipe card as a smiling uniformed bellman approached. "This is Andy, the butler for your floor. You need anything, don't hesitate to ask."

Reznick smiled and was escorted to the sixth floor by Andy, tipping him twenty dollars. "I'll get it from here."

"Are you sure, sir?"

"Absolutely."

The butler gave a polite nod and headed back to the elevator. Reznick waited until the guy was out of sight before he carefully swiped the card. Inside, the deluxe room was decidedly upscale. A king-sized bed, large flat screen TV, dark wood antique-style writing desk, chair and sofa, gold-framed octagonal mirror, Bose radio, iPod sound dock, mini-bar stuffed with Krug and Rolling Rock beer, original artwork on the walls, chandeliers setting the scene. In the bathroom, brass fittings and earth tones of mosaic tiles, a large mirror which doubled as a 15 inch "intelligent" TV, two marble sinks and a fluffy white St Regis bathrobe hanging behind the door.

The first thing he did was hang a "Do Not Disturb" sign outside his room and lock the door. Satisfied he wasn't going to be disturbed, he opened up the luxury bag and placed the pre-configured MacBook Pro on the writing desk. He opened it up and within a matter of seconds it was up and running.

Reznick sat down at the desk and punched in his allotted password – *coldbracelet1* – into the keys of the laptop, scanning his inbox. A soft beep and there was one encrypted message with an attachment.

He clicked on Decrypt Message to view the file and was prompted to confirm two unique passwords. He keyed in *OfwaihhbTn*, initials from the first line of the Lord's Prayer, followed by *DNalKcOr*, his hometown spelled backwards. Then three personal questions – his grandmother on his father's side's maiden name: Levitz; his father's birthplace: Bangor; his blood group: Rh negative.

He typed in the security protected keys and the email displayed in the browser. He clicked on the "Reply" button and the attachment was returned securely.

A two-page dossier and six black and white photos appeared before his eyes.

The man he'd been sent to kill.

Reznick's stomach knotted as he scanned the screen. Tom Powell, aged fifty-nine, described as an "imminent security risk".

He lived with his second wife and two school-age children, in a quiet cul-de-sac in Frederick, Maryland; his oldest son away at university. According to the file, he had checked into the St Regis the previous evening, Room 674, three doors down. It didn't say why exactly he should be neutralised.

He pondered on that. Usually, when he did a hit, the reason was made quite clear. It could have been spying, terrorism or a whole host of threats to the country. Invariably they had an explanation.

So, why not now?

Reznick read on. The file said Powell had to be a "suicide". No other options.

This was the first time that Reznick had been asked to kill an American citizen on American soil. He knew that it would have been impossible if he was still within Delta because of the Posse Comitatus Act, which prohibits under federal law the military being used in operations within the United States. But he was no longer constrained.

In the past he'd taken out a Saudi military attaché in New York, a billionaire Arab banker in London funding Hezbollah, a Russian spy in Vienna, a host of Jihadists across the Middle East and a smattering of Islamic fundamentalists, living and working in America.

It was business. Realpolitik. The stone cold reality of politics based on realities and material needs.

He studied the picture of the man, including one with his eldest son – John, a law student at George Washington University – playing football in a local park in Frederick, and committed them to memory. A good-looking kid. Clean-cut, short blonde hair, preppy clothes.

He looked again at the photo of Powell until he could remember the smallest detail. The dime-sized mole on his left cheek, the greying sideburns, the bushy eyebrows, and the small scar above his right eyebrow caused, according to the file, in a schoolyard fight.

Reznick's training at the Farm in Virginia, all those years ago, had stressed the importance of knowing the subject inside out. The little details. This enabled an appropriate plan to be drawn up and executed.

Maddox and his team would have explored Powell's lifestyle habits as well. His sleeping patterns and any health problems. The file noted that he was a keen golfer, not on prescription medication, led a clean life; a glass or two of expensive French red wine over dinner on a Friday and Saturday evening, his only vice.

He finished reading the dossier, shut down the computer, and waited for Maddox to call.

The waiting was always the worst part of the job. Endless hours spent hanging around motels, hotels, safe houses, halfway houses, flop houses, apartments and all myriad of places, before the final phase.

The end game.

Reznick was not the judge. Nor the jury. He was the executioner. Except he didn't sit in on the trial, because there was no trial. This was summary justice, as practiced by every government in the world. Sometimes the dirty work was sub-contracted to a foreign intelligence agency or their contractors. But this was in-house.

Just after midnight, Reznick's cellphone vibrated in his pocket. He switched on the TV, showing a Redskins game, to drown out his voice.

Maddox said, "Are you in place?"

"Yes."

"This is a wet delivery. Do you understand?"

"Absolutely."

"OK, run-through time. Our guy is a creature of habit. He's in his room, fast asleep."

"How do you know?"

"GPS on his Blackberry and bug in his room's smoke detector."

Reznick made a mental note.

"Hold back until five minutes *after* oh-two hundred hours when the video camera in the corridor will be remotely switched off until oh-three hundred and the lights dimmed. You have a copy of his room swipe. Assume you have fifty-five minutes to make this delivery."

Reznick said nothing. He had enough time.

"Do good."

"Need to get rid of my wet bag and case. Won't be needing any of that."

"We're ahead of you. Your room will be cleaned as soon as this delivery has been made. A maintenance uniform is hanging in your closet with a matching navy bag." A long pause elapsed. "Sit tight. Then it's just you and him."

With less than one hour to go, Reznick was sitting in his darkened hotel room, primed to carry out the delivery. He had changed into a pale blue short-sleeved work shirt and black pants, gold wire-rimmed glasses, shiny black shoes and metallic nametag on his lapel: Alex Goddard, service engineer, a small holdall at his feet. He pressed a tiny audio device into his right ear for communication, whilst the nametag concealed a hidden microphone.

Everything in place. No diversions. No TV, radio, music, magazines or newspapers to sidetrack him. The way he always worked during the crucial last hour.

The pale blue LCD display on his digital watch showed 01.21.

Not long now.

Reznick's earpiece buzzed and he tensed up.

"Reznick, do you copy?" The voice of Maddox was a whisper. "Reznick?"

"What?"

A small sigh. "OK, we have two room service types – a guy and a woman – one dropping newspapers outside doors, the other pushing a room service trolley with food and drinks. They're in the elevator, and they're heading your way."

Reznick could hear his heart beat.

"OK," Maddox whispered, "now they're on the sixth."

On cue the ring of the elevator doors opening and dull footsteps padding down the carpeted corridor. The faint tinkling of metal against glass, accompanied by a low male voice. Thuds as the papers are left outside each room. The sound of a door opening.

Three long minutes later, they were gone.

"OK, buddy, sorry about that. You all set?"

"How's our guy?"

"Sleeping like a baby. Slam dunk, Reznick. You've got a clear run."

The line went dead at 1.23am.

When his watch hit 02.05, he peered out of the peephole. No movement or sound. He lay flat down on the floor and pressed his left ear – the one without the earpiece - to the carpet, listening for elevator vibrations, footsteps or sudden noises, anything.

He heard the faint sound of water pipes creaking. Perhaps the merest hint of laughter somewhere below.

Apart from that, all quiet.

Reznick got up and stood holding the bag. He took half a dozen slow, deep breaths.

Just breathe.

His breathing even, he was ready.

Slowly, he turned the handle and stuck his head out of the door and peered down the dimly lit, carpeted hallway.

Not a soul.

Slow is smooth, smooth is fast.

The military dictum of the Marines kicked in. It meant moving fast or rushing in was reckless, and could get you killed. If you move slowly, you are less likely to put yourself at risk.

He edged out and closed the door as slowly and softly as he could. The metallic locking system sounded to him like a rifle reloading.

Reznick looked around and took the short walk to the man's door. Slowly he swiped the card, the metallic clicking noticeably softer. He cracked the door. The sound of deep snoring. He kept the door ajar for a few moments as his eyes adjusted to the semi-darkness. The room smelled of stale sweat and old shoes.

Underneath the window, the crumpled silhouette of the man lying in bed, facing the wall, duvet on. Softly he shut the door, barely making a noise as it clicked into place.

Reznick crept towards the sleeping man. Closer and closer, careful not to trip on any objects lying around.

Standing over him Reznick saw the dime-sized mole on his left cheek. Suddenly, the man groaned and turned over onto his back. The springs on the bed creaked.

Reznick froze, not daring to breathe. A deep silence opened up for a few moments as he wondered if the man was really awake. He stood still and waited. One beat. Two beats. Three beats. Eventually, on the fourth beat, the snoring continued as before, rhythmic and deep. He let out his breath slowly. Then he reached into his trouser pocket and pulled out the lipstick-sized Taser.

He leaned over and pressed the metal device hard against the man's temple. Electric currents provoked convulsions for three long seconds. His eyes rolled back in his head; the sound of gurgling and groaning. Then nothing.

Unconscious.

A standard first-step procedure. Eight minutes, maybe ten, before the man came to.

Reznick rummaged in the bag and produced the auto-injecting syringe disguised as a ballpoint pen, containing succinylcholine chloride, which he knew as "Sux". The drug was a skeletal muscle relaxant used as an adjunct to surgical anesthesia and had been employed as a paralyzing agent for executions by lethal injection. A twist of the nib and a quick stab into the man's skin would deliver seven milligrams of the drug. But only five milligrams was necessary for death. The victim would be paralyzed within thirty seconds. The muscles, including the diaphragm, would shut down, with the exception of the heart. He would be unable to speak or move, although his brain would still be working. Then he had three minutes until his breathing ceased, unable to scream out for help.

The beauty of the drug for assassinations was that enzymes in the body begin to break down the drug almost immediately, making it virtually impossible to detect.

Powell was to be injected in the buttocks with the drug, knowing most medical examiners would suspect a heart attack as the natural cause of death, in the absence of evidence of foul play.

He pulled back the duvet and switched on his penlight, examining the paunchy unconscious man lying before him. He wore pale blue pajamas, white vest underneath. He had a cheap watch with a frayed brown leather strap. The last moments in his life, and the poor bastard didn't know anything about it. He never usually felt anything when he had to kill a raghead or billionaire terrorist bankroller. But in this case it did feel strange, knowing that this was an American.

The penlight picked out something round the man's neck, tucked inside his vest. He looked closer and thought it looked like an aluminium dog tag. Then he held it in his hand, turned it over and saw an inscription in Hebrew.

The name Benjamin Luntz, date of birth, 1.29.71, and a seven-digit identification number. *Israeli Defense Forces*.

He stared at the dog tag for a few moments.

Why the fuck had Tom Powell got an IDF dog tag of an Israeli soldier around his neck? It didn't make any sense.

The doubts began to set in. He needed certainty.

He had to wait more than eight long minutes until the man came to with a low groan.

Reznick pressed the Beretta to the man's forehead. The man gazed up, confused and scared.

"Shut up and listen," Reznick snarled, hand covering the man's mouth.

The man nodded with a blank expression.

"This gun has a suppressor attached. Any sound, and you die. Got it?"

The man nodded again.

Reznick removed his hand from the man's mouth. "All right," he said in a low voice, "gimme your name, date and place of birth. Right now."

The man gulped hard and Reznick pressed the cold metal of the gun tight to his sweaty brow. "Please, take whatever you want."

Reznick pressed the gun tighter to his skin making a small indentation as the guy began to tremble. "This is the second time I will ask. I don't ask a third time. Now, give me your name, date and place of birth. Failure to comply will result in the maids cleaning your brains off this wall in six hours time. Got it?"

"My name is Frank Luntz, born New York City, October 12, 1953."

Reznick's mind went into freefall for a split second. The target's name was Powell. Something was badly wrong. "Tell me about the dog tag around your neck."

"It's my son's."

"What's his name?"

"Benjamin Luntz."

Reznick's wondered whether to believe the man or not. Something wasn't adding up. Was he being played? "Are you Israeli?"

"No. My son emigrated. He had joint citizenship."

"What do you mean had?"

"He was…he was blown up by a suicide bomber at a checkpoint in the West Bank three years ago."

The man made a sudden movement and Reznick pushed him back down into the pillow. "Don't even think about it."

"I want to prove it to you."

The man reached under his pillow and pulled out a silver photo pendant. A faded color picture of a young man in combat fatigues, rifle slung over his shoulder, sitting atop a Merkava tank.

The man pointed to the bedside cabinet. "The top drawer. Check my wallet if you don't believe me."

Reznick reached over and opened the top drawer. Empty. No driving license or credit cards to establish the man's true identity. "There's nothing there you lying bastard."

"That's impossible. Perhaps Connelly has it next door."

Reznick was tempted to kill the fucker there and then. "Who's Connelly?"

The man began to cry.

"Answer me. Who's Connelly?"

"He's a Fed. He's in the adjoining room. He's looking after me."

Reznick's stomach knotted. "What the hell are you talking about?"

"He has the adjoining room to this." He pointed a shaking finger in the direction of a door next to the dresser.

"Are you lying to me, because if you are, you die, here and now?"

The man began sobbing. Reznick placed his huge hand over the man's mouth to muffle the sound.

"One more peep out of you and I will rip out your wiring. Do you understand?"

The man nodded, tears spilling down his cheeks.

"Hands on your head."

The man complied. Reznick pulled a sock out of a drawer and stuffed it in his mouth, before tearing up strips of the bed sheet and tying it around his head to secure the sock. Then he tied the man's wrists and ankles to the four corners of the wooden bed, crucifixion style.

Reznick shone the penlight directly into his eyes. The man blinked away more tears. "Don't even think about fucking moving."

The man nodded quickly. Reznick walked across to the adjoining door and pressed his ear up against it, listening for several seconds for any sounds. Creaks. Groans. But he heard nothing.

Slowly he turned the handle. His eyes adjusted and he scanned the room. The bed was made, wooden blinds and curtains shut, as if awaiting the next hotel guest. Perfect order. Empty. Or so it seemed. The hint of sandalwood in the air told another story. The room had been occupied.

Reznick sensed something was wrong. He shone the penlight towards the bathroom and opened the door. Opulent white marble sinks, bath and floor. White towels neatly stacked on a metal rack above the bath. A slight smell of damp pervaded the air, as if from a recent shower.

That again didn't add up to an unoccupied room.

Reznick went back into the bedroom as the penlight strafed the high quality navy blue carpet beside the huge wardrobe. His gaze wandered round the room, past a small flaxen sofa, until he fixed on a white painted louver door. He saw it wasn't shut properly. Perhaps half an inch ajar.

He moved closer. Kneeling down, he shone the light through the slatted openings. Inside, he saw what looked like tousled blond hair.

He held his breath.

Then slowly, he reached out and felt the wooden handle, before yanking open the door.

Reznick's heart jolted as the penlight picked out the dead eyes of the crumpled, semi-naked body of a blond-haired man, staring back at him. Telltale purple bruises around the neck and throat, hemorrhaging around the eyes. Reznick had seen this sort of thing before. Many times. The man had been manually strangled.

This was so fucked up it wasn't real.

His mind was racing when he returned to the darkened bedroom. He leaned down beside the man strapped and gagged to the bed. The man's eyes stared up at Reznick like a terrified child, afraid of his fate.

Reznick untied the bed sheet around the man's mouth and pulled out the sock. Then he pressed his face right up against the man's, smelling the sweat and fear. "Who the fuck are you?"

"I already told you."

"Why do people want you dead? Who do you work for?"

Again Reznick pressed the gun to his head.

"I work for the government. Look, please tell me who you are. What've you done to Connelly?"

"Forget about him. Forget about me. What about you? What exactly do you do?"

"I told you, I work for the government."

"Doing what?"

The man closed his eyes and shook his head.

"Answer me."

The man said nothing.

Reznick stuffed the sock back into the man's mouth. He walked over to the window and buzzed Maddox on his lapel microphone, giving him the lowdown. The discovery of the murdered man's body – perhaps a Fed – and the possibility that they had the wrong guy.

Maddox listened in silence before he said, "Gimme two minutes and I'll get back to you."

In less than a minute, the earpiece buzzed into life.

"The subject is to be protected and brought in. Make your way with the subject to a motel, the Clarence Suites, six blocks away on N Street NW, due southeast, and sit tight. Room 787. You are booked in under Ronald D Withers. He is your brother, Simon Withers. Clear?"

"Then what?"

"We are sending two of our guys, Bowman and Price. They'll take him off your hands."

Then the earpiece went dead.

THREE

"Get dressed," Reznick snapped, as he untied Luntz.

He needed to get them both out of the hotel. And fast. But he couldn't just walk out of the lobby as he was, dressed as a fucking maintenance man.

He rifled through the chest of drawers and found a dark blue cashmere jersey. He pulled it on but the sleeves were too long, so he rolled them up a couple of inches.

"One word out of place and you and your family will die," he said, picking up his delivery bag. "Do you understand what I'm saying?"

The man nodded and licked his lower lip.

Reznick shoved the gun into the back of his waistband. The cold metal felt reassuring against his warm skin. He cracked the door, saw the coast was clear and grabbed the man's arm and marched him down the thickly carpeted corridor towards the stairs. They passed a fire alarm. He punched the glass with his knuckles and pressed the red button.

The sound of ear-splitting alarms shattered the calm.

Got to keep moving.

He hustled Luntz through the fire exit doors and down the stairwell. Luntz appeared bewildered and groggy, eyes heavy. Behind them, some shouts and instructions to "get a move on".

Luntz asked, "Please, where are you taking me?"

"Shut up and do as I say."

Reznick pushed through doors at the bottom of the stairwell and emerged into the huge lobby. Scores of frightened guests in nightgowns and pajamas were filing out towards the main doors. He found it easy to blend in and leave the hotel. They emerged into the cold night air as doormen and valets handed out blankets. In the distance, the sound of fire truck sirens.

His mind replayed the grid of streets he'd walked the previous night as he got his bearings. They headed along a still busy K Street, the main east-west artery through Washington's business district, past anonymous redbrick and concrete office blocks. It was home to powerful lobbying firms, think tanks and numerous advocacy groups, wanting to be close to the levers of power. But at that ungodly hour, the street was busy with groups of young revelers and professionals heading to nearby hip lounges and clubs.

Reznick was glad to cross over the road and up 17th Street NW, away from the main drag. Past the Pot Belly sandwich shop and the YMCA.

He pulled out his earpiece, lapel microphone and nametag, dropping them down a storm drain. He hurried on along the sidewalk and across the street, squeezing between two huge SUVs parked beside each other.

"Quicker!" he said.

The man nodded furiously.

Reznick hustled the man as they turned left and headed west along N Street NW, a broad, tree-lined street full of elegant row houses, past the Hotel Tabard Inn until they came to the redbrick Clarence Suites. He took a few moments to gather his thoughts.

His mind flashed to the dog tag around the man's neck. Was it genuine? Was it a ruse?

He turned to the man. "Not a word."

The man nodded, fear in his eyes.

Reznick held Luntz's arm as they climbed the stone steps and through the hotel doors. The night desk guy looked very young, but was clean-shaven and sported a maroon waistcoat and matching tie.

"Good evening," the kid said. "You guys booked a room?"

Reznick forced a smile. "Sorry we're so late. We got delayed with a connecting flight. My name's Withers and this is my brother. We've booked a room."

The kid smiled back. "Not a problem." He checked the computer in front of him, going down a list of names with a pencil. "OK, Room 787." He handed over the swipe card. "You guys in town for a convention or something?"

"Yeah, something like that," he said.

"Any luggage?"

"Got lost at the airport, I'm afraid."

"Oh, I'm sorry. Do you want me to try and contact your airline?"

"Don't worry; we've already been on to them. Should arrive later today. But thanks anyway. Appreciate your help."

The night desk guy smiled. "Anytime."

Reznick looked at the kid's badge, which read, "Steve Murphy, Night Desk". He was clean-cut, polite and doing a thankless job for what probably amounted to minimum wage. He looked sixteen, if that. The kid reminded Reznick of himself when he was that age. Having to work shitty jobs on weekends and vacation time to help his dad make ends meet. "Hey Steve, tell me, have you got a room nearby which is free?"

The kid shrugged and checked the register. "Room 788 is vacant. Across the hall. You want to change rooms?"

"No, I'd like to book room 788 as well, if that's OK. I'm a light sleeper and my brother the opposite. And it'll be the only way I get some shut-eye."

The night desk guy grinned. "No problem, Mr Withers. We've already got your card details, so that's all been taken care of. Will you be requiring a wake-up call?"

"No, I think I'll have a lie in. Long flight."

"Enjoy your stay," he said, and handed over the other swipe card. "Coffee machine and cable on demand in both rooms. So we've got you down for staying one night."

Reznick smiled and nodded. He took Luntz by the arm and they rode the elevator to the 7th floor in silence. It was a long walk down the carpeted corridor. He swiped the card for Room 788 and went inside. He sat Luntz down on the bed.

"Why the room change?" Luntz asked.

"Never you mind."

The truth was he didn't like the set-up. Not one bit. This didn't happen. So why this time? And how long until the handover?

The questions were stacking up as he paced the warm room while the man he should have killed sat with his head in his hands. He needed to think this through without having to babysit this guy.

Reznick reached inside his back pocket and produced what looked like a nasal spray and calmly sprayed the highly concentrated sleeping drug into Luntz's left ear.

The man's eyes rolled back in his head and Reznick had to stop him collapsing onto the floor. He picked him up and placed him on the bed. The drugs would knock him out for at least four hours, leaving Reznick without that worry ahead of the handover.

The minutes dragged.

Reznick checked his watch repeatedly as he paced the room. He made himself a black coffee. Then another. The more he thought of the sequences of events, the more it didn't make any sense.

Maddox wouldn't have fucked up so badly. His preparations were meticulous. Which posed the question, was it people higher up the chain that had fucked up? But to compound matters, a dead Fed.

Shit.

He ran through the events in his head one more time. The encrypted message and accompanying document were received in the usual way prior to an assassination. The target was Tom Powell. He had the right room. He had followed instructions. But something had gone seriously wrong and someone had to take responsibility for this.

The best solution was, as Maddox said, for Luntz to be taken off his hands so Reznick could disappear back into the shadows. Maddox always made the right call at the right time. He'd lost count of the number of times that Maddox had got Reznick or one of the contractors out of a jam when an operation became problematic. But as of now, Reznick was in the middle of a fucked-up operation and needed to get out of Washington.

He switched off the lights and sat in the dark, unable to relax. He checked the luminous dial of his watch. It showed 3.33am.

What was keeping the handover team so long? It was more than an hour since he'd called Maddox and still no sign of them. He wondered if Maddox had tried to contact him with an update to the plans. But since he'd ditched the microphone and earpiece, he had no way of being contacted.

He gulped down some of the cheap coffee and looked out of the window towards an apartment with lights on, curtains drawn. Shadows moved inside. He tried to open the bedroom window to let in some air but it wasn't budging.

Damn.

Upstairs, the sound of a TV, the vibration carrying through the ceiling. Down below, a strained woman's voice. Outside, the drone of an air con unit.

The waiting continued.

He made his third coffee.

The sound of the drugged man's deep breathing reminded Reznick of his own father lying in a drunken stupor in a crummy Washington hotel room, all those years ago. His mind flashed a picture of his father lying face down on the bed at the end of the day, exhausted and drunk, his best suit still on, the room stinking of booze. His father hated his job at the sardine-packing factory in Rockland, hated his life and was haunted with the memories of the war. It was plain for all to see. The moment his father, a man he revered, stood to attention in front of the Vietnam Veteran's Memorial and saluted the names of his fallen or missing comrades, there was a terrible pain in his eyes. It was as though he was reliving the horrors again. His father had never spoken of what he'd witnessed or what he'd done. He didn't have to. The war had left him hollow. The scars etched on his craggy face and burned into his shattered mind. Some part of his father had died in Vietnam, left behind like the young comrades who had given their lives in the jungles of a foreign country.

A soft moan from the sleeping man lying sprawled on the bed snapped Reznick out of his reverie. The waiting dragged on and on.

Eventually, just after 5am, the sound of padded footsteps in the corridor outside.

Finally, they were here.

He peered through the peephole. A well-dressed white couple that looked like Mormons were walking down the corridor. They stopped outside Room 787, directly opposite.

Strange. Maddox said it was an in-house job. So who the fuck was this?

Reznick moved closer to the door and softly pressed his left eye up to the glass, eyelashes brushing off the metal surround. He held his breath and stood statue still. Into view came a second man. He was stocky and wore a dark suit and forensic gloves.

This was no pick-up.

The three of them said nothing, not even looking at each other. The woman stepped forward and knocked four times on door 787 as the two men stood hidden either side of the door, guns now drawn.

Rat-a-tat-tat.

She waited a second before she knocked again. A few moments elapsed. Then the stocky man swiped a plastic room card through the door's locking system and the three of them went inside, shutting the door quietly.

Reznick stepped back from the spyglass and let out a long, slow breath. He felt trapped in the suffocating room. His mind raced. Who were they? The more he thought of the situation the more it didn't make sense.

Eventually, more than five minutes later, they all emerged stony faced. The stocky guy remained outside Room 787, but the couple walked towards the elevator.

Shit.

Reznick knew the couple had gone to speak to the guy at the desk. He figured he had only four, maybe five minutes, tops, before the couple returned.

The stocky man stared straight at Room 788's peephole for a few moments. The room he was in with Luntz.

He wondered if the man had seen him. Impossible. Then the man turned away and faced Room 787.

Fuck it.

Reznick stepped away from the door and slowly pulled his 9mm Beretta from his waistband. Then he padded like a tomcat across the room and got his Trident 9 suppressor from his "delivery" bag. He slowly screwed the silencer into the gun. Then he carefully clicked off the spring-loaded safety lever with his thumb.

He was glad he had already racked the slide of his gun, knowing the sound would alert the man.

Reznick walked silently back to the door and stared back through the peephole. The stocky man had walked five yards down the hall. But then, slow as you like, he turned and walked back until he was standing stock still outside Reznick's door.

He held his breath as the man moved closer until his face became distorted, as if through a fish eye lens. He seemed to be paying far too much attention to the door Reznick was standing behind.

Suddenly, behind Reznick, Luntz let out a loud moan in his sleep.

Reznick winced at the sound. The man outside stopped chewing his gum and stared long and hard at the door.

Reznick did not move.

The man began to chew his gum again, eyes unblinking. Then he leaned forward and pressed his left eye up against the glass.

Reznick raised the suppressor to the peephole, turned his face away and squeezed the trigger. It made a muffled "phutt" sound. A small jaggy hole – less than an inch in diameter – had been blown out of the chipboard door.

The adrenaline flowed. He opened the door wide enough to drag the man's body into the room. The bullet had torn into the man's left eye. Blood oozed down his cheek from the gaping wound.

Reznick bent down and pulled the man in by the feet and laid him on the bedroom floor before he could bleed out onto the corridor's carpet. He checked outside the door and quickly picked up the wood and glass splinters lying in the corridor before closing it.

Then he pulled Luntz off the bed and replaced him with the huge stranger. Reznick felt sweat beading his forehead. He rifled in the dead man's pockets and found an iPhone, but no ID or wallet. He quickly went to the bathroom, picked up the hotel toothpaste and twisted off the cap. Then he went back to the door and wedged it into the small hole so at a quick glance from the outside it appeared intact.

Reznick grabbed his bag, picked up Luntz and slung him over his shoulder. He weighed around ten stone. Comparatively light compared to the stocky guy. He cracked the door. All clear.

He edged into the corridor, closed the door quietly, turned left down the corridor to a fire exit sign, and down a stairwell.

He reached into his pocket and switched on the anti-jamming device that would nullify the hotel's door alarms, before leaving through a basement emergency exit.

Reznick emerged with Luntz at the rear of the building. He walked nearly half a block until he came to a narrow side street where he saw a Mercedes parked up. He used a new fob that deactivated the car locking system, the immobiliser, and the alarm system and opened the door. He laid Luntz on the ground for a few moments. He checked underneath the car and felt a magnetic box attached to the under side of the car.

Reznick pulled it out, prizing it open with a knife and found the spare set of keys. He opened the car's back door and lifted a sleeping Luntz into a seat, before strapping him in. He climbed into the driver's seat and checked inside the glove compartment. Nothing.

Reznick pulled away slowly, not wanting to attract attention, and punched in Maddox's secure number on the dead man's cellphone.

"I'm on the move," he said. "The delivery has been compromised. Someone or something has left us wide open. I repeat we have been compromised."

Maddox stayed quiet for a few moments. "Is the target safe?"

"Yes, he's safe. I got a visual on a crew of three. Two men and one woman. One of the guys is down. I'm calling from his cell."

"Jesus."

"Do you want to download the data from the phone?"

"We're already doing it."

Reznick pulled out the anti-jamming device and switched it on so no one could track the GPS on the phone. "So, what happened to the two guys you sent?"

A long sigh. "They've been taken out. The whole thing's fucked up. Head to the safe house."

Then the line went dead.

FOUR

The Gulfstream jet was cruising at forty thousand feet as it entered American airspace on the Eastern Seaboard. FBI Assistant Director Martha Meyerstein, in charge of the Criminal, Cyber, Response and Services Branch was the only member of her team awake. She looked around the cabin. The rest were getting some shuteye after the long flight home from Dubai.

Meyerstein speed-read the first email of the day on her Blackberry from the Director wanting a progress report into an ongoing investigation into public corruption involving a Californian Senator, Lionel Timpson. She'd have to reply by the end of the day. Something else for her in-tray. She put down her phone on top of a pile of intelligence briefing papers in the adjacent empty seat. Then she reclined and stared out of the window at the white strobe light on the wing tip.

Her mind hadn't shut off after the cyber-security conference.

Waves of tiredness swept over her. She tried to remember the last time she had had a proper vacation and realised it had been over two years. She was killing herself, but she didn't know any other way. This was the job she had craved for so long, after all. Her father, a top Chicago attorney, thought she was mad for embarking on a career with the FBI when she could have sailed into corporate law, with a high six figure salary. She was currently earning $157,000 with $20,000 extra in bonuses, for reaching her targets. A great salary. She had a lovely house in Bethesda, Washington DC, round the corner from Fox pundit John Bolton; she sent her kids to private school and was pretty happy with her lot. But she knew, deep down, her father would much rather she'd have entered the rarefied atmosphere at a top city law firm.

Maybe he was right. Her privileged upbringing in the upscale North Shore suburb of Winnetka, an elite private education at the city's Latin School, and then Harvard Law School, had led to numerous offers from law firms from New York to Los Angeles. But instead of following in the footsteps of her three brothers, she had embarked on a fast-track career with the FBI after attending a lecture by an inspirational woman, a Dartmouth graduate, who headed up the Boston field office. She found she loved Quantico. And she loved the Bureau. It became her life.

Meyerstein had eclipsed that woman. She was now the highest-ranking female within the FBI structure, which she was very proud of. But it had come at a steep price.

She stared at her wedding-ring-finger. The white band where her gold ring used to be, her finger slightly indented from wearing it for more than a decade. The only sign of her old life. The only visible sign she had once been happily married; before her husband James, a Professor at the Center for Peace and Security Studies at Georgetown University, had left her for one of his students, a French girl he was mentoring.

She should have seen the signs. Goddamnit, how could she have been so blind?

The ringing of the secure phone on her armrest snapped her out of her reverie. A couple of her team around her stirred.

"Martha, sorry to bother you, but we've got a problem like you wouldn't believe." It was Roy Stamper, who headed up the Criminal Investigative Division that she was responsible for.

Meyerstein closed her eyes and sighed. "What kind of problem?"

"How long till you touchdown?"

"Half an hour. What's going on?"

"Violent crime unit got a call from the Washington field office a few minutes ago. Luntz is missing."

"He's what?"

"We think he's been kidnapped."

"Wasn't someone watching over him?"

Stamper sighed. "Yeah, Special Agent Connelly. He's dead."

Meyerstein felt her insides go cold.

"He's been strangled."

Meyerstein remembered a fresh-faced young special agent at a briefing just over a fortnight ago. "The rookie from Seattle?"

"Right."

She closed her eyes for a moment. "Shit."

"Washington field office has a team over at the St Regis, as we speak."

"So what are the indications as to whom or what is behind this?"

"Too early to say. But I've spoken to Stevie." Stamper was referring to Stephen Combe, the Special Agent in charge of the Washington field office. "He said it had the hallmarks of a professional job. But we've also got what appears to be a separate hit on a guy at the Clarence Suites, nearby. We think they might be linked."

Meyerstein listened in stunned silence as Stamper gave a summary of what had happened. When Stamper had finished talking, she gulped down the last of the cold coffee still left in her cup.

"The guy at the Clarence Suites was shot through the eye from behind a door."

"What are the police saying to this?"

"They aren't happy and are asking a lot of questions."

"We need to button this up. This is on a need to know basis. Who's the lead detective on the scene?"

"Maartens. I've spoken to him already and we're getting full cooperation."

"OK, we need to stand up SIOC for this." Meyerstein was referring to the Strategic Information and Operations Center on the fifth floor at FBI HQ. It was the global watch and communications center providing round-the-clock information on emerging criminal and terrorist threats to the US. "But first I want everyone in the briefing room in two hours."

"Leave it with me."

The massive office of FBI Director, Bill O'Donoghue, overlooked Pennsylvania Avenue on the seventh floor of the Hoover Building. It was located in a secure wing, three doors down from Meyerstein's own office, sealed off behind electronic doors with security cameras; a keypad code was required, which only the most senior FBI agents had access to.

Meyerstein was ushered through the glass door etched with the silver FBI seal and into his huge office by Margaret, his PA, who had worked for the Bureau for nearly twenty-five years.

"Take a load off, Martha," O'Donoghue said, not lifting his head. He was sitting behind his oversized mahogany desk, reading a raft of briefing documents, ahead of his meeting with the Director of Intelligence at 10am. Probably why he was so preoccupied.

"Thank you, sir."

She sat down in a deep leather chair and looked around the office. His desk contained two phones neatly placed beside each other – one for internal calls and the other for the President – two gold lamps and three framed family photos. The pictures all showed a proud O'Donoghue pictured wearing a smart dark suit with his wife and only son Andrew, taken at his son's recent Princeton graduation.

Behind O'Donoghue was a floor-to-ceiling mahogany bookcase – flanked by an American flag and an FBI flag – with a huge TV in the middle. Political biographies of Roosevelt, Rockefeller, Churchill and Truman; history tomes; law enforcement awards and photos took up most of the space. The prints adorning one of the walls looked like Rembrandts while on an opposite wall were black and white photos of the San Francisco and Washington DC offices.

To Meyerstein's right, an oval conference table with six burgundy leather chairs. On the wall in front of the table, a plasma TV with a video teleconference feed camera, used primarily for video conferencing with the President, the Attorney General or any Special Agent in Charge of the fifty-six FBI field divisions.

To her left, in the far corner of the room, a new blue and burgundy pinstriped sofa with three burgundy wing-back chairs beside a mahogany coffee table stacked with FBI books and magazines. Adjacent to where she was sitting, a mahogany credenza that had mementos received from visiting dignitaries.

O'Donoghue continued to read the document as Meyerstein shifted in her chair. She cleared her throat, but still he didn't let on. He was always first in each morning just after 6am and rarely left before 10pm. He had served in the military as a navy pilot in Vietnam before he joined a powerhouse Washington legal firm, eventually making partner. He even knew her father from his high profile court cases. He was scrupulously polite, occasionally asking how her father was. She invariably smiled and said he was the same old lovable curmudgeon, which made the Director smile, knowing her father's fearsome reputation in court.

O'Donoghue, like herself, lived and breathed his job. He had been recruited to the FBI six years earlier as Deputy

Director – before his latest promotion to Director two years later – and had transformed the organization ensuring a seamless flow of information to all the field divisions, HQ and other government agencies, making it fit for the twenty-first century.

He was comfortable with broad-brush strategy documents or mission statements, but also meticulous with detail, hauling anyone over the coals for not following correct procedure. He was that sort of guy. But she had always found him to be a very professional, unfailingly polite, perhaps not on this occasion, albeit a slightly aloof, by-the-book kind of man.

O'Donoghue let out a long sigh, leaned back in his seat and fixed his gaze on Meyerstein. "OK, down to business. I've got the bare bones so far of what happened at the St Regis. What's your take on this?"

Meyerstein cleared her throat. "This has all the hallmarks of a professional assassination. To take down a Federal agent in such circumstances indicates planning and backup, either military or special ops. Perhaps, if I'm to speculate, we may be talking about a foreign government."

He went quiet for a few moments before he spoke. "Any intel?"

"Not so far. But this is a bespoke job, not off the peg."

"Foreign governments, eh? Got any in mind?"

"Take your pick from any number of countries which hate America at this moment."

"What about Iran? They hate America."

"Well, they fit the bill. We foiled the Iranian plot to kill the Saudi ambassador in 2011. Is this payback? I don't know. So, they can't be ruled out. But the National Counterterrorism Center is working the problem as we speak."

O'Donoghue sighed. "Look, I'm meeting with the Director of National Intelligence. He will want some detail. He will also want to know how this is possible. How could this happen?"

"That's what I intend to find out."

"Then again," O'Donoghue said, shaking his head, "is it possible there's a problem in our ranks?"

Meyerstein saw where this was going. "I hear what you're saying."

O'Donoghue shrugged. "Just playing Devil's Advocate."

"I agree we can't discount such a possibility."

O'Donoghue leaned back in his seat and stared across at her. "I'm intrigued you think a foreign government might be behind this. What's your rationale?"

"Luntz's area of expertise makes him valuable to any government. But the fact that he specifically asked to speak to the FBI so urgently makes me think something else is afoot – and that's why they want to silence him."

O'Donoghue nodded. "Taken from right under our nose. Very audacious. And dangerous."

Meyerstein nodded.

"Tell me more about Connelly. Is he new?"

"Just a few months with us, sir. Was based in Seattle for a couple of years, before being posted here."

"Is he married?"

"Young wife, two kids."

O'Donoghue turned and stared out of his window over the Washington skyline. "I want the bastards who did this, Martha. And for once, I don't give a shit about cost or overspend. You have whatever resources you want."

"Sir, my team will also be alive to the possibility another story is playing out. I'm of course talking about national security. We can't rule that out."

O'Donoghue nodded. "Indeed. OK, won't keep you any longer."

Meyerstein got up out of her seat.

"Oh, Martha?" he said.

"Yes, sir?"

"Let's do this right. And let's nail those responsible."

"Count on it, sir."

Meyerstein walked out of the office and took the elevator down two floors to where Roy Stamper was standing waiting for her, unsmiling. He was wearing his customary navy suit, white shirt, navy blue silk tie and highly polished black leather shoes. He had been in the FBI since he was headhunted after graduating from Duke, coming top of his class at law school. They had both started training at the FBI's academy at Quantico at the same time.

He wasn't a great mixer. Never had been. He was quiet, but, unlike her errant husband, he was a great family man. Her own father, despite being a workaholic like her, was the same, trying to take time out of his punishing schedule to meet her mother for lunch or supper. He was devoted to Meyerstein's mother. He liked being with her. He liked being around her. She could see that. They looked relaxed in each other's company. She never felt that with her own husband. He never wanted to share a glass of wine with her when she got home. He never wanted to go to the park with their children. He didn't want to do anything with the kids. It was as if they were an inconvenience to his academic life, getting in the way. She herself didn't have a great work/life balance, but when she was home her family was the be all and end all.

That's what she admired so much about Stamper as a man. He loved his wife and his three kids with a passion. He was teetotal, and had once told her he was truly happiest when he had his family around him. He was that sort of guy. He didn't talk about women, he didn't chase women and he simply got on with doing his job. He rarely raised his voice. But apart from being one of the good guys, he was also a good listener.

They had worked their way up the ladder together. But whilst she was his boss, Meyerstein had always used him as a sounding board, knowing him to be discreet, offering wise counsel when the job threatened to swamp her.

"What a mess, Roy," she said.

"Tell me about it."

"So, have the schedules been created to ensure we will be fully manned for the duration of this case?"

"Yeah, crisis management guy with SIOC – Guy Stevens – has sorted it out. We've been allocated OPSD." It was the main operation room for major cases. "The Rapid Deployment team has created logs from the Washington field division, so we're all up to speed. They're setting up boards in our SIOC room as we speak."

They headed straight along the corridor as her heels clicked on the beige tile floor, then straight into the windowless and radio-secure Strategic Information Operations Center (SIOC) – pronounced "sigh-ock" - on the fifth floor and into their allotted briefing room. A huge full size wall screen on one wall, which could be manipulated to show twelve different screens for showing the news channels or video teleconferencing, was currently showing a live feed from the St. Regis Hotel.

A young male agent greeted her with a "morning ma'am", and handed her a fresh cup of black coffee when she entered the room.

"Thanks," she said, as Stamper went to the far end of the room to speak to one of his team.

She felt mentally exhausted and jet-lagged, having only napped in the last forty-eight hours. Now she had virtually no chance of catching up on her sleep until Luntz was found.

A quick glance around the briefing room. Most of the faces were familiar and she had worked with them for years on numerous investigations. The task force pulled together the finest investigative and analytical brains from numerous government agencies. They each brought their own areas of expertise into a large pool.

There were two agents from Stamper's criminal investigative division who specialised in kidnapping investigations; a profiler, Jan Marino, from the national center for the analysis of violent crimes; four agents from the critical incident response group including behavioral and tactical; two critical incident and intelligence analysts; three members of the Computer Analysis Response Team who would be responsible for laptops owned by Luntz or at his place of work; a member of the Cyber Division to run down whether a threat was made electronically, and to see if computer systems were hacked; and a handful of counterterrorism specialists.

In addition, she recognised representatives from Homeland Security, the police and the CIA dotted around the briefing room.

Meyerstein sipped the steaming-hot coffee as she stood at the lectern taking a few moments to gather her thoughts.

"Alright folks," she said, leaning over to put down her cup on a nearby desk, "we've got three problems. Firstly, a government scientist has gone missing. We need to find him and we need to find him quick. Secondly, one of our colleagues babysitting him is dead. Strangled. We need to find the people responsible. Thirdly, the specter of a major security threat to this country."

The men and women all nodded solemnly. A few scribbled notes on pads of paper, while others worked on iPads.

She turned and faced the huge plasma screen. "I must warn you, this will not be pleasant viewing." She pointed at Stamper. "OK, Roy, let's roll it."

The huge screen showed graphic forensic pictures of the body of Special Agent Connelly, stuffed into the base of a wardrobe in the adjoining room to Luntz. His face was grey-blue, distinctive marks around the neck.

"OK, freeze-frame the picture. Roy, what are we talking about?"

"Manual strangulation, but with a twist."

Meyerstein closed her eyes, feeling a headache coming on. "Meaning?"

"Initial toxicology reports were clean, but we retested the body fluids which show traces of succinylcholine in the brain."

Meyerstein nodded. She knew all about the properties of the quick-acting, depolarising, paralytic anesthetic drug that could render a person incapable of resisting any intruder. It was the drug of choice for intelligence services the world over. She looked around at the grim faces of her team before turning to face Stamper again. "This is a hit, right?"

"This has all the hallmarks of a neat job." Stamper was using "neat job" as a euphemism for a professional kill. "The drug's immobilised Connelly, and then he's been killed by someone's bare hands. He would've known what was happening to him but would've been helpless to do anything."

"Fingerprints? Cameras catch anything?"

Stamper pointed the remote control at the screen. "Grainy CCTV pictures of a white man in his thirties checking into a hotel."

"Freeze it there, thanks," Meyerstein said. "We got any idea who this guy is?"

Stamper cleared his throat. "Face recognition has confirmed this is highly likely to be a guy called Reznick. Used to be involved with the Agency."

Meyerstein looked over the assembled faces towards Ed Hareton who had been seconded from Langley. "What's Langley saying, Ed?"

Hareton paused for a few moments as if thinking out his answer. "He's not on their books. Then they just give us the usual spiel, 'we don't do that shit'."

Meyerstein shook her head. "Does that strike you as a likely scenario, Ed?"

Hareton shook his head as the briefing room became deathly quiet, all eyes trained on him.

Meyerstein stared at Hareton for a few moments, letting her withering gaze linger. "So, that's it?"

"No, I've made some calls. He once did work for us. But he hasn't worked for us in an official capacity for three and a half years."

Meyerstein sipped some more coffee. She felt her anger grow. Why did she need to wheedle the information out of him? What happened to post-9/11 inter-agency cooperation? "Does he now or has he ever worked for the CIA in an unofficial capacity? Sub-contracted, so to speak."

"There are indications—"

"I don't want indications or some agency doubletalk, Ed. We are looking for a missing government scientist and one of our colleagues has been murdered. Now I'm going to ask you again: has he now or ever worked for the CIA in an unofficial capacity?"

Hareton shifted in his seat. "He once did wet work for the government. What he's doing now, no one knows."

Meyerstein's senses had switched on despite her tiredness. The phrase wet work was a euphemism for murder or assassination, alluding to spilling blood. She gazed again at the footage. "OK, now we're getting somewhere," she said sarcastically.

Hareton flushed a deep red, embarrassed in front of everyone.

It wasn't Meyerstein's style to humiliate individuals in front of their peers. But she needed answers not prevarication. She turned to face the freeze-framed footage. "Well, he's certainly not retired. So, has he got any links to private security firms? Sub-contracting assassinations for foreign governments?"

Hareton shook his head. "He only ever worked for the American government."

Meyerstein looked across at Stamper. "What else, Roy?"

"Reznick checked in under a false name only hours before this happened. His fingerprints are all over this."

Stamper picked up the remote control again and played more footage. It showed Luntz and Reznick caught on camera outside the St Regis Hotel in the middle of the night after a fire alarm had gone off. He froze the image of a white guy – average height – wearing a dark jacket. "We're scouring the hotel's internal CCTV as we speak."

Meyerstein stood up and studied the image, hands on hips. The man was ruggedly handsome, a day or two's growth, short dark hair, an impassive expression. "Tell me more about Reznick."

Stamper shrugged. "The guy's a ghost. Black ops. No one knows or is admitting whose responsibility he is, but like Ed says, we believe he's carried out countless assassinations on behalf of the American government for the best part of fifteen years. Former Delta Force. The unit is also known as CAG, short for Combat Applications Group, for those familiar with Fort Bragg. This guy, Reznick, is something else. Been there, done that, got the T-shirt. Also got a major beef with authority, according to his file."

Meyerstein sipped the coffee. "You want to elaborate?"

"It was noted by Colonel Gritz at Fort Bragg, who incidentally personally invited Reznick for the Delta assessment following glowing reports, that Reznick didn't like officers and was openly hostile during the Delta Selection phase. Apparently despised nearly all the officers he ever met."

Meyerstein put down the coffee and folded her arms. "Anything else?"

"Highly decorated. A bit of a legend amongst the Delta cadre, by all accounts."

"And then?"

"And then… then he disappeared into the clutches of what we assume to be the Agency, working across the globe."

Meyerstein noticed Hareton shift again in his seat.

"The files note that Reznick was directly responsible for killing Hamas commanders, Al Qaeda operatives hiding in Pakistan, and he has advised friendly governments on assassination for the last decade."

Meyerstein looked at Hareton. "Special Activities Division?"

Hareton shook his head. "CIA has issued a denial, but I think we can take it as read that he was at one time known to Langley."

"Full name?"

Stamper continued, "Jon Reznick. Lives alone in a house on the outskirts of Rockland, Maine. He pays his taxes. On his IRS return describes himself as management consultant. He has two bank accounts."

"How much has he got in them?"

"Three hundred and forty thousand dollars in the main one. He has no stocks, but he owns his own home, estimated to be worth eight hundred thousand dollars outright."

"What about the second account?"

"That is topped up each year to the tune of fifty thousand dollars. It goes on tuition fees at Brookfield boarding school for his daughter Lauren Reznick, which comes in at $43,800 per year, and the rest on piano lessons, vacation money, that kind of thing."

"Is he married?"

Stamper sighed. "He was. Elisabeth Reznick was a partner for a law firm, Rosenfeld & Williams Inc, who had their offices in the Twin Towers. She… she died on 9/11. Pulverised to dust. No body found."

Meyerstein's mind flashed back to the day the world fell in on America. She remembered watching the nightmare images on the big screen in her office. The dust cloud over Manhattan.

"Tell me about his medical history."

"He was shot in the leg in Afghanistan, but he made a full recovery. Tough as hell."

"Has he been involved in anything high profile?"

"Textbook stuff. We believe he headed up a CIA team that went into Afghanistan, to help the Northern Alliance topple the Taliban. He led Task Force 121, a Special Forces group answerable to no one, assembled from Delta, Navy Seals, CIA paramilitary operatives and others, into Fallujah to assassinate some hardline Baathists. Then they had to fight their way out, street by street, for nearly six hours, after two Black Hawks were downed during the rescue mission."

Meyerstein pointed to an NSA guy, Kevin Warwick. "So, Kev, what about Reznick's phone records? Has Fort Meade unearthed anything?"

"Untraceable number made a call to a cell phone which is registered in his name. GPS pinpointed his home in Maine. Someone called him a matter of hours before he appeared in Washington. We're still trying to pinpoint who it was."

Meyerstein turned and stared long and hard at the "ghost" on the screens. "So where is he now?"

Stamper blew out his cheeks. "We know he took Luntz to the Clarence Suites, close to the St Regis. Night desk guy said a man matching Reznick's description checked in under the name Withers, with a man who matched Luntz's description. The body of what we believe to be an unidentified foreign national, without any ID, was found in one of two rooms booked under the name Withers. Forensics are on the scene. We're checking surveillance cameras in the street as we speak. Still drawing a blank."

Meyerstein let her gaze wander round the room. "Luntz is top priority. We must get him back. But to do that, we must find Reznick." She went quiet for a few moments as the assembled agents scribbled or punched in notes on their iPads. She faced Stamper. "What about Luntz's wife?"

"Two agents speaking to her right now."

"What's she saying?"

"She said he didn't talk about his work."

"That doesn't seem credible. Are you telling me he didn't mention anything about why he was heading to Washington?"

"Apparently not."

"Check out his computers, files, records, everything on Luntz. I want to know about him from his friends, neighbors, people at the lab, I want to know about him. I also want Bangor field office to go over Reznick's home, from top to bottom. We need to get into his life. Are there are cellphones? Laptops? Phone books, anything. I want to know everything there is to know about him."

Stamper nodded in agreement. "I believe he's got cousins that live in South Carolina. He's also got relations in Nova Scotia."

"Good. Let's get onto the Canadian Security Intelligence Agency. We need to build up a complete picture of Reznick. Has he been in contact with anyone he knows?"

Meyerstein sighed as she looked at Stamper and knew both would be away from their families until the investigation was resolved. She hated that part of her job. She turned to face the assembled agents and sighed. "I want to make one thing clear. There must be no mention of our missing scientist or a murdered Fed. Am I making myself clear?"

The agents and specialists nodded. For the next fifteen minutes, the analysts gave their take on what was happening, sharing and sifting any trends, the log boards being updated all the time with a plethora of information on the case.

"OK, people, I want calm heads on this. Let's get to it."

FIVE

It was still dark as Reznick headed off the freeway at Exit 24 and into Annapolis, Maryland, Luntz still out of it in the back seat. The car hit a pothole and it jolted Luntz from his slumber.

"Where are we?" he asked.

Reznick said nothing as he glanced in the rearview mirror as Luntz's head lolled like a rag doll.

"I said where are you taking me?"

"Never you mind."

Luntz began to dry retch.

"What the hell's wrong with you?" Reznick said.

"I don't feel too good."

"Are you shitting me?"

"No, I'm not."

He dry retched again.

"Better keep it in."

"I'll try."

Reznick sighed. He got onto Rowe Boulevard and drove on for a few blocks. He couldn't wait to get shot of Luntz and let Maddox figure out what to do with him. A short while later he pulled up at the deserted parking lot at Gate 1 in the shadow of the Navy-Marine Corps Memorial Stadium. He opened up Luntz's door. "This is as good a place as anywhere to be sick," he said.

Luntz stumbled out of the car. Then he fell to his knees and heaved the contents of his stomach on the asphalt. He retched a few more times before he wiped his mouth with the back of his sleeve. "I'm sorry."

"You finished?"

"I think so."

"You sure?"

"Yes, I'm sure."

He had a ghostly pallor that wasn't surprising in the circumstances.

"Please... can you tell me what you're going to do with me?"

"You're gonna be fine, trust me."

"Why don't you answer my questions? Why were you sent to kill me?"

"It's nothing personal."

"Who hired you?"

"Too many questions."

Reznick buckled him back up and slammed his door shut, before he drove off towards the safe house.

"Why didn't you kill me when you could?" Luntz asked from the back seat. "What stopped you?"

"You're starting to bug me now. Like I said before: too many questions."

A few minutes later, Reznick was driving through a near-deserted downtown Annapolis, past the floodlit Maryland State Capitol Building and over the King George Street Bridge.

The dead man's cell phone rang.

He picked up. "Yeah," he said, expecting to hear Maddox's voice.

A long pause. "We need to talk, Mr Reznick." It wasn't Maddox.

Reznick realised it had to be an accomplice of the guy he had taken out. The last thing he needed was to get into a discussion with *them*. "I think you've got the wrong number."

He ended the call and dropped the phone onto the passenger seat. But a few minutes later, only half a dozen blocks from the safe house, the phone rang again.

Reznick sighed and picked up. "I thought I told you–"

"You have something we want."

"Not interested, thanks."

"Don't be so hasty, Mr Reznick. You need to hand him over."

"I think we're done."

The man let out a long sigh. "We have something of yours, Mr Reznick. Do you want to know exactly what?"

Reznick felt his insides go cold. "What are you talking about?"

"Do you recognise this woman?"

A few seconds elapsed before a familiar voice came on the line. "Jon? Jon, is that you?"

Reznick's chest tightened and a feeling of dread washed over him. He was listening to the fragile and frightened voice of his late wife's mother. His thoughts were in free fall. He took a few moments to gather his thoughts. "Beth, what the hell's going on?"

"Jon, I'm so sorry…"

"Sorry, what do you mean sorry?"

Silence.

"Beth, what's wrong?"

A deep sigh before she spoke. "Some men… some men took me from the house and–"

The man's voice came back on the line. "I have a gun pointed at your mother-in-law's head as we speak. You give me what I want and you'll see the lovely Beth again. But you must listen very carefully to what I have to say."

"Who the fuck is this?"

"Wrong answer. Maybe this will focus your mind."

A shot rang out down the line as Reznick drove on in stunned silence.

The man came back on. "Do we have your attention now? I hope so. OK, Jon, hopefully you realise that we are serious people. So, I'm going to come straight to the point. It's not just Beth that we took. We also have your daughter."

Everything seemed to slow down as he tried to comprehend what was happening. The word *daughter* sent Reznick spiraling into a private hell. His beautiful daughter. How could this be happening? Wasn't she still at school? The chain of events was swamping him and he realised he'd gone into shock.

"She's very pretty. But if you want to see her again, you need to do exactly as I say. I will call you back in two minutes."

The line went dead as an unbearable emptiness opened up inside Reznick.

He pulled over on a tree-lined residential street four blocks from the safe house in the pre-dawn darkness. His heart raced as a black anger began to build deep within him, ready to devour him at any moment. Part of him wanted it to. But then, slowly, it subsided, as his training kicked in.

He began to think and reason, moving beyond a visceral reaction as he tried to figure out exactly how to respond.

The questions began to rain down. How on God's earth had they kidnapped Beth and Lauren? She boarded at an exclusive school in western Massachusetts. But then it slowly dawned on him that she must've stayed over in New York with Beth for a day or two – which she did occasionally – before she was due to meet up with Reznick on Christmas Eve in Maine.

So, was she being held in New York? But that didn't explain how those guys knew about his family.

He wracked his brains. He'd only had a handful of friends over the years, and they'd drifted from him since Elisabeth's death.

No one, not even among his oldest friends in Rockland – guys he'd grown up with throughout the late nineteen seventies and into the nineteen eighties, when his hometown was a tough fishing port struggling with boarded up shops on Main Street and motorcycle gangs with their dogs running amok in the bars – had any inkling of Lauren's whereabouts. He'd deliberately tried to shield her from his shadowy world. Even Davie McNeish, his closest friend since High School – who he used to drink beers with on the Rockland harbor breakwater when they were both fifteen – was kept in the dark. Davie, who now ran Radio Free Rockland, the only guy he felt he could trust with anything – who he'd called at crazy hours to talk about Elisabeth and who he used to occasionally hang out with at the Myrtle Street Tavern when he was back home – was none the wiser about Lauren. He'd kept it that way since Elisabeth had died. He wanted her to be away when he came home from a job. He was always in a black mood, and wanted to be alone. She didn't need to see him like that.

The bottom line was that he didn't want his daughter anywhere near him or his world.

His mind flashed back to an evening at the Myrtle. The only time the subject had been openly broached by someone out with his tightknit circle. Danny Grainger, a lobsterman and obnoxious High School classmate, who hated his life and liked to drink himself into oblivion six out of seven nights a week, approached Reznick and asked about his daughter. He had heard that Reznick was in the military. Reznick knew he was spoiling for a fight and would have gladly obliged. But he just smiled and said his daughter was fine, and thanks for asking, and left it that.

The answer'd seemed to placate Danny and he'd smiled his best drunk's smile, put his arm around Reznick and proceeded to talk at length about how he didn't recognise the working class town of Rockland these days. The once tough waterfront of fish-packing and commercial docks now transformed, especially downtown around Main Street and the harbor, with countless art galleries, museums, fancy restaurants and the North Atlantic Blues Festival. But Reznick hadn't given him or anyone, that or any night, a clue about where his daughter was.

He knew that in his line of work, the best way to get to people is to get to their family. Easy targets.

Luntz cleared his throat loudly in the back seat, snapped Reznick back to reality. "What the hell is going on?" he said.

Reznick turned round and pointed a finger in Luntz's face. "Not a fucking word."

Luntz looked close to tears as he shook his head.

A few moments later, a chime tone on the dead man's iPhone signaled a message. He opened up the inbox. A short video clip. His mother-in-law was lying tied to a pillar in a dingy basement or warehouse, hands behind her back, blindfold over her eyes. He noticed the emerald stone round her neck, the one her late husband had given her as a fiftieth birthday present. He watched her bony shoulders begin to shake, then her lip, before the gun was pressed to her head and her brains splattered onto a steel pillar.

He closed his eyes as revulsion swept over him. He shut down the message as his breathing quickened.

Reznick needed to get control back. Focus. He thought of Lauren. She was only eleven. He couldn't be sure they had her. But deep down he sensed they weren't bullshitting.

He needed to contact Maddox.

Reznick picked up the cell and punched in his number. Then, just as he was about to press the green phone icon to dial, he stopped. He didn't know why but he just did. He needed to take things slow. He needed time to think.

The more time he thought of it the more it began to dawn on him that he couldn't entrust anyone else on this. The less people who knew the better. He had to do this his way. This was his daughter. She was priceless. He couldn't allow one false move that could jeopardise her. All it would take would be a phone call to Maddox, which they would be monitoring.

The cell phone rang again.

"If you don't want the same thing to happen to your daughter, listen and listen good. You will take what I want to Miami. You will drive him there so as to avoid any problems at airports or trains. In just over twenty-four hours' time, we will contact you on this number, and talk about an exchange. If you speak to the police, the Feds or anyone, you will receive the same video image of your daughter getting a bullet in the head. Don't disappoint me, Jon."

Then the line went dead.

The call was the beginning of a nightmare for Reznick, the voice like a dark whisper that echoed in his head.

Terrifying emotions clouded his shattered mind as he started the long drive south on I-95, the beginning of a fevered journey. What if they were about to kill his daughter? What if she was screaming for her life at that moment?

He imagined his beautiful daughter being pulled by her auburn hair and then slapped. Was she being humiliated?

He began to burn up inside. Nightmarish images seared into his psyche as if by a hot poker. His mind flashed back to Beth's dreadful final moments. A woman who had suffered so much with the loss of her daughter, Reznick's wife, on 9/11. A woman who had tried to rebuild her shattered life, despite not having a body to bury. A woman who had looked after Lauren in the years after her mother's death. What a terrible end to a fine woman.

His mind flashed back to the first time Reznick was introduced to Elisabeth's parents. It was dinner at the Café Carlyle in the Carlyle Hotel on the East Side, half a block from their townhouse. A pianist played jazz standards as the wine flowed, and Elisabeth draped her arm around him as Beth smiled.

Waves of guilt swept over him. He alone was responsible for Beth's death and his daughter's kidnapping. His shadowy world had encroached on his family.

He drove on as his mood darkened further. The anger coursed through his blood and veins, developing like a cancer, threatening to eat him alive. On and on he drove south.

Reznick pulled over four times during the sixteen-hour journey. Deeper and deeper, closer and closer. The man in the back seat, Luntz, tried to make conversation. But Reznick was too busy trying to figure out what the hell to do.

The hours dragged. He wondered if he was making a monumental mistake going it alone. Was he doing the right thing? Wouldn't Maddox have been the guy to call? It wasn't too late.

On and on as doubts filled his head.

He drove on, tormented as he headed down through the Carolinas. Eventually he pulled off I-95 and drove into Florence, South Carolina. He still had blood relations that lived nearby although he had never met them. His mother's bloodline could be traced back to Scots who had been forced off the land during the Highland Clearances in the nineteenth century. They had immigrated first to Nova Scotia before they crossed the border, stopping off in Maine. His mother could trace her roots back to one Jimmy MacKinley, who had moved his family to Maine in the late nineteenth century, where he became a fisherman. The rest of the MacKinleys headed down to the Carolinas. Poachers, trappers and outlaws, unable and unwilling to be tamed. They lived on the land. Backwoodsmen. Renegades. It was their home. Wild people.

He pondered on that as he found a parking garage and stole a black Lexus with tinted windows. Afterwards, they went to a diner and ate in silence, before Reznick got back onto the freeway, headed for Florida. But as the day drew to a close, as he crossed the Florida state line, a plan had begun to formulate in his mind.

Simply turning up and handing over Luntz wasn't an option. *They* held all the cards. What he needed was someone he could trust to keep Luntz safe and someone who could help him out.

He knew such a man. A man he'd trust with his life.

Just before midnight, Reznick turned off I-95 and headed into Fort Lauderdale, South Florida. Luntz was out cold in the trunk, and had been for the last hour, trussed up like a chicken. He pulled up half a block from the neon-lit and spray-painted entrance of the Monterey Club. The bar was located south of downtown, close to the commercial bars of Las Olas, next to a tattoo parlor, part of the same complex that sold classic bikes.

The owner of the bar was an old Delta operator, Harry Leggett, his best man at his wedding. Tough, funny and a complete nightmare after ten bottles of Heineken. Leggett was the only one from Delta his late wife, Elisabeth, had liked.

It was Leggett's sister Angie, who worked alongside Elisabeth, who'd introduced her coworker to Reznick.

His mind flashed back to their first date. It was imprinted on his mind. He was home for two weeks' leave and Angie had suggested they meet up as a foursome for a drink at McSorley's Old Ale House, a spit and sawdust dive in the East Village. Elisabeth talked fast about everything under the sun from running the New York Marathon to fighting off a mugger in Central Park with pepper spray to her expensive education at the Chapin School. He'd surprised himself by liking her immediately. They just clicked. He had never entertained the thought of settling down until he saw her. She was beautiful, neurotic, open, relaxed in his company and, he noticed, quick at self-deprecation. She was from a different world. She talked of Cubism and modern art. He hadn't had a clue what that was all about. But there was an immediate connection.

He'd listened to her go into minute detail about the distinction between tax avoidance and tax evasion. They'd drunk warm beer in half-filled mugs and ate a cheese platter with raw onion and hot mustard. When she'd asked him about his work, he didn't tell her about Delta, but said he worked overseas a lot for the government. She hadn't pressed him further. He'd liked that, but guessed that Angie might have filled her in on the details. Then he'd talked of Rockland and how it was a great town these days. He'd told her about new art galleries popping up almost overnight and how it was changing the image of his hometown. He'd talked of the calming nature of the sea, the smell of the fresh fish that had just been landed and of the crowded Main Street, thronged by visitors in the summer months. He'd told her that when he smelled the sea, he knew he was home. And that he was safe. She'd listened intently. She'd said she always wanted to live by the sea; work was in Manhattan, but she could see herself giving it all up for a less stressed life.

The possibilities seemed endless.

He'd felt like a different person. The following day they'd met up again and walked in the park. Within a few months, and quite out of character after returning from the Gulf, he'd found himself proposing to her at the Crystal Room at the Tavern on the Green overlooking Central Park. The following year, 1999, they'd got married. The wedding reception had been at the Plaza on August 14, 1999, a blazing hot day. Twenty Delta operators wearing impeccable grey morning suits turned up and sat in the corner of the main ballroom, guzzling beer and laughing uproariously as the band played Carpenters covers. Elisabeth's family, blue bloods who gave large donations to the Met and the Museum of Modern Art, had looked aghast; although Beth seemed to enjoy it more than her husband. The highlight of the evening had been an inebriated Leggett attempting to mimic the moonwalk of Michael Jackson as the band played "Billie Jean", before collapsing in a heap, leaving the Delta crew in stitches.

The sound of thrash metal from Leggett's bar snapped him out of his reverie for a few moments. The tiredness was starting to swamp him. He popped a couple of Dexedrine.

Reznick closed his eyes and his mind flashed back to 9/11. The news footage of the collapsing towers. The smoke. The dust cloud. The twisted metal. The mayhem.

The world of Reznick and Leggett were inextricably linked that fateful day.

Elisabeth and Angie were both tax attorneys and worked in the same law firm in Tower One of the Twin Towers and both perished on 9/11. Leggett's sister was one of the jumpers, trapped by the flames, jumping alone from the eighty-ninth floor to her death. The downward spiral of his old friend Leggett had begun on that day.

They both had the same coping strategy: they cut themselves off from the outside world. They found solace in their own ways. The first thing Reznick did was ask Beth to look after Lauren. He couldn't cope with looking after a baby. There was no body to bury and he wasn't sleeping. And he'd wanted Lauren to be safe in Beth's Manhattan townhouse as he wasn't able to cope, consumed by anger and grief. He couldn't provide the stable family home she needed. He'd retreated back to the solitude of his home outside Rockland. He sat on the beach where he'd sat with Elisabeth and Lauren for hours at a time. The memories haunted him. Plagued him. He would sometimes climb down onto the rocky shoreline when it got dark, and listen to the waves crashing onto the beach. But then he was engulfed by a black mood and screamed in a burning rage until his lungs nearly burst.

It was like it would never end. He drank too much and he didn't see a soul for months. He didn't want to.

Then one day, out of the blue, he'd called Leggett. They'd met up in New York and they'd hugged and they'd cried and they'd talked about their losses.

It had been clear that Leggett was drinking insane amounts. He knocked back two bottles of Scotch a day, interspersed with numerous beers. But it didn't end there. By the start of 2002, Leggett had begun to self-harm, cutting his wrists and arms, until he was hospitalised. Eventually he seemed to have sorted himself out and got back with Delta, but by 2004, he had had enough, and retired to Florida.

The raucous laughter from the bar snapped Reznick back to the present. He stared across at Leggett's bar. Standing outside in the fetid Florida air, the kids were wearing black, smoking cigarettes, drinking from bottles of beer, arms draped around some burlesque bar girls.

The night air was warm and sticky. He checked his rearview mirror and side mirrors, but he didn't detect any tails or cops. He was running a risk with a stolen car with South Carolina plates. He decided he would take that risk. But his major concern just now was that he couldn't take Luntz into the bar. That would be asking for trouble.

He weighed up his options and realised he didn't have any. He decided to leave the car where it was as he was only going to be gone for a couple of minutes. He shut the window and stepped out into the sultry night. Pressing the car's central locking fob, he walked up to the entrance.

A tattooed skinny guy with tousled blond hair wearing a black T-shirt stepped forward and smiled, partially blocking his way. He was holding a cigarette in one hand, a bottle of Bud in the other. "Sorry my friend," he said. "We're closed."

"I'll bear that in mind, son," Reznick said, as he brushed right past him and headed inside to the cool of the bar.

A crazy old hippie was belting out some punked-up blues standards on an old guitar, as stoned college kids lounged around on sofas, drinking beer and laughing loud.

Reznick walked up to the bar and ordered a Heineken. He handed the tattooed, muscle-bound barman with chiseled features a twenty-dollar bill and told him to keep the change.

The kid took the money and Reznick took a long drink. The cold beer quenched his thirst. "I'm looking for Harry Leggett," he said.

"Who's asking?"

"Name's Reznick."

"You got a first name?"

He gulped the rest of the Heineken. "Tell him Reznick's in town."

A smile spread slowly across the barman's chiseled features and he handed Reznick back his twenty-dollar bill. "Your money's no good here, man. It's on the house." He extended his hand. "Pleasure to meet you, sir. Ron Leggett. Remember me? We met a few years back, up in New York."

Reznick shook his hand. "Christ, Ron. I didn't recognise you. How's your father these days?"

"A pain in the ass, if you must know." He asked a barmaid to hold the fort for a few minutes. The girl nodded sullenly as Ron opened a couple more Heinekens and joined Reznick at the other side of the bar.

Ron pulled up a stool and sat down. "Man, dad's gonna freak when he sees you," he said, taking a large gulp of beer. "I take it you're not here for the music."

"Is your dad around?"

The kid pulled out a packet of Winston from his shirt pocket, tapped out a cigarette and lit up. He inhaled half an inch of cigarette before he flicked ash on the floor. "Yeah, he's around. Just not here. An old buddy turned up this morning and they went out fishing this afternoon. He likes to kickback a couple of times a week. But he's probably sleeping it off on his boat."

Reznick's gaze was drawn to a faded color picture behind some whisky optics of Leggett that showed some guys drinking in the bar. He didn't recognise any of the faces. "Your dad's got a boat?"

"Yeah, a brand new fifty-foot Cabo," he said. He took a deep pull on the cigarette and crushed it in the ashtray. "It's awesome. Pure teak inside. Man, my dad loves that boat."

Reznick smiled but said nothing.

"Real pleasure to meet you again." He leaned closed, voice low. "My dad once told me that you were the only man he truly trusted. Said you never made a wrong move. You always made the right call. And you never, ever let him down."

Reznick averted his gaze. "I don't know about that." He looked at the boy's rippling physique. "So, how's life working for your dad?"

"I work all the hours here, and he spends most of his time on his boat."

"I hear you."

The kid fired up another cigarette, dragging hard. He blew the smoke out of the corner of his mouth, away from Reznick. "It's a job." He slugged back some more beer. "But my heart's set on becoming a Marine. An officer."

"You any idea what it entails?"

"A bit."

"You know the motto at the Officer Candidates School at Quantico?"

"No, I don't."

"*Ductus Exemplo*."

The kid shrugged.

"Look it up. It's Latin."

Ron smiled blankly.

"I really need to speak to your dad, now. Is his boat nearby?"

Ron shrugged. "Yeah, he's gotta nice new berth down the marina. Walking distance. Man, he'll freak when he sees you."

Reznick drove the Jeep – with the man he should have killed still in the trunk – to a parking garage, three blocks away. He popped open the trunk. Luntz was still out of it and probably would be for a few more hours. Locking the car, he headed down to the beachfront.

A short while later, he walked past the Elbo Room bar on the corner of Las Olas Boulevard and South Atlantic Boulevard, the sounds of whoops and cheers and thumping music from the bar spilled out into the warm, humid air.

He walked on for a couple of hundred yards, the lights of the yachts and restaurants at the marina in the distance. A few minutes later, along a wooden gangway to Dock E beside the Intracoastal Waterway, right beside the dock master's office and the fuel dock.

An old black guy, cigarette at the corner of his mouth, hosing down the decks of one of the boats nearby, nodded to Reznick.

"You down to do some fishin'?" he asked. "If you are, you're too early. But I'm taking my boat out at first light if you wanna come back and do some serious fishin'. Snared fifteen marlins yesterday alone."

The smell of fish bait, kerosene and barbecued meat hung in the muggy air. It reminded him of night fishing with his father when he was a boy, his father reminiscing about Nam, the Mekong and his buddies who hadn't made it home, trying not to think about his next shift at Port Clyde Foods sardine cannery. He'd always hated his factory job. He'd wanted Reznick never to work in any of the Rockland fish packing plants. He'd once invited him in to watch him work. The smell made him sick. He remembered watching the dead eyed expression of his father – so different from his pictures back from Vietnam. He'd worked at the packing tables using a pair of sharpened knives to cut the heads and tails off the fish coming in, and packing them in cans, being bellowed at by a weasel foreman. His father could never answer back as he'd never work in any of the plants in Rockland again if he did. It was piecework, so the faster he went, the more money he made. He'd worked from 7am until 10pm straight every day, with hardly any breaks. It was there and then that Reznick vowed he'd never do that job.

Reznick saw the lights from a nearby yacht partially illuminating the dock. "Maybe next time."

"You got a boat here?"

"Looking for a friend of mine. Harry Leggett."

The black guy pointed to the pristine fifty-foot yacht berthed nearly twenty yards away. "That's Harry's boat. Damn fine it is too. Went out fishing with one of his friends around noon, cooler full of beer. But I was gone when they must've come back. Harry and his friend probably sleeping it off."

"Thanks for the tip."

"Any time," he said, mopping the deck of his boat.

Reznick walked further down the gangway and climbed on board the yacht, using the aluminum rails to help him on. The slight swell made him feel sick. He never did have good sea legs.

Bait tanks and tackle storage boxes lined the cockpit. In the center, a fighting chair mounted on an aluminum-reinforced plate for marlin fishing.

Reznick knocked on a small window on the cabin's doors. He got no answer. He tried a couple more times but still nothing. He peered through the window and looked around a modern galley, granite surfaces and best teak.

"Hey, anyone home?" Reznick said. "Harry, you in here, you old boozehound?"

No reply.

Reznick opened the door and switched on the lights. Ron was right. The yacht was teak everywhere. Two single berths made up, and a small settee. On the wall, a large flat screen TV with DVD player.

"Hey, Harry, you wanna shake a leg?"

The sound of the water lapping against the side of the yacht and the heavy brush strokes on wood of the old black guy outside. But he also heard the sound of a TV.

Reznick knocked hard on the door to the main stateroom and went inside. It was dark except for the huge plasma screen TV blaring. The place stank of liquor and cigarette smoke. "Fucking hell." A Fox News anchorwoman shrilly talked about the costs of health care. He reached over and flicked on a light switch.

A half empty bottle of Tequila lay on its side, its contents soaked into the thick beige carpet, an empty bottle of Scotch on a bedside table.

Reznick slumped on a sofa and looked around. He couldn't believe he had missed Harry. He must've headed out for a late night bar crawl with his buddy. Waves of tiredness washed over him. His body was telling him to close his eyes. But that wasn't an option. He reached into his pocket and pulled out a packet of Dexedrine and popped two more.

Within a few minutes, he felt his senses sharpen. The drug was in his blood stream. "Shit."

He felt anger gnaw him. He was running out of options fast. He needed Harry to take Luntz off his hands, no question. But as he looked around the detritus of his Delta buddy's broken life, he wondered if Harry was indeed the man to help him.

The more he thought of it the more he got angry with himself for even considering his old friend, a burned-up alcoholic, as suitable to watch over Luntz or anyone for that matter. He couldn't even look after his own life.

The newsreader droned on. *America would have to make some hard choices.* His heart sank as he began to face up to the consequences of his own hard choices. The real prospect that the only positive thing in his life, the only thing he lived for and gave a damn for, his daughter, was going to be murdered by some crazies he'd never met. And all because of what he did. What he was. It was eating him up from the inside. The bottom line was that he was responsible. He would have to deal with that. He would also have to deal with the fact that they held all the cards. He knew that. They knew that. And they were going to kill her if he didn't show up with Luntz, of that he had no doubt.

Reznick closed his eyes, head in his hands. He listened to his heavy breathing as he could barely hear himself think over the braying voice on the TV talking of repercussions about the size of the US debt. *There would be a price to pay some day.* "Gimme a break, for chrissakes."

He sat up and stared again at the empty booze bottles. "Where the fuck are you, Harry?"

He thought of all the crazy times they'd had. The night missions in Somalia. The surveillance in the desert. Then blowing off steam when they got home, letting rip for days, sometimes weeks at a time. The comedown was long and slow. But sometimes, it was impossible to return to a normal life.

The drudgery and pettiness of day-to-day living was too much for Harry. Deep down, it was clear he missed living on the edge. Waiting for the call. All the time waiting for the signal.

It was a closed world to outsiders. No one would understand how they felt about each other. The tightness. The blood bonds which tied them.

He knew Harry would have given his life for him. He would have done whatever it took to help Reznick find Lauren. He remembered the time when he'd visited his home in Maine one Thanksgiving, when Lauren was around nine. Harry managed to tone down his drinking, only partaking of a couple of glasses of wine with his meal, talking politely and in measured tones, unlike his usual raucous profanity-laden utterances. But when Lauren had gone to bed for the night, his old buddy couldn't stop the tears running down his face, talking of his sister. He was a wreck, broken down by booze and scarred by terrible memories, unable to move on with his life.

The newscaster's booming voice talking of a Taliban resurgence in Helmand Province in Afghanistan, snapped Reznick out of his reverie. He leaned over and picked up a remote control, turning off the TV. He sat in contemplation for a few moments. He thought he heard something. It was like a tap running. He cocked his head and wondered if it had begun to sound like a shower.

He looked over towards a recessed door which was partly concealed by old cardboard boxes. He got up, stepped over the empty bottle of Scotch, kicked aside the boxes and opened the door which revealed a huge en suite shower room and bathroom. The room was steamed up. "Harry are you drunk? You in here all this time?"

Reznick walked over to the shower and yanked back the curtain.

His heart nearly stopped. Lying in the fetal position inside the shower cubicle was Harry, familiar crewcut. He bent down and recognised the familiar tattoo on his left forearm. The Delta insignia. A black dagger and the word Airborne above it. He remembered the night they'd both decided to get tattooed, after completing the Operator's Training Course.

He turned the body over. The dead blue eyes of Harry Leggett stared back at him. He edged closer and smelled the booze. His skin was bluish-grey. His gaze was drawn to his firing hand, his right, and a large callus in the web of the thumb. The telltale sign of a former Delta Assault Team member even after all those years. He had the same.

Then his attention was drawn to something so small and insignificant, it could and most certainly would be missed by the cops when they eventually found the body.

Behind Harry's left ear was the tiniest of pinpricks.

Reznick felt his throat constrict. It was a telltale sign he was all too familiar with. Someone wanted those who discovered the body to think Harry had overdosed on booze and pills. But Reznick could see with his own eyes.

His blood brother Harry had been suicided.

Reznick began to shake. He thought his heart was about to burst. He fought back the tears as he slid his hand under Leggett's head, cradling it like a baby, as the shower poured down. He felt a volcanic anger take hold as he stared at the lifeless eyes. The same eyes that'd shed tears of joy and laughter. The lines more pronounced, almost like claws around the skin surrounding the eyes. He pulled Leggett's head to his chest and he began to weep. Unashamed. "Who did this, Harry?" He clutched him tight to his beating heart. "Who did this to you? Tell me!"

He felt numb as dark thoughts began to cloud his head. Someone had got to him. Not so long ago. Perhaps within the last few hours. Just ahead of Reznick. He wondered if he had been followed south. The whole thing was so fucked up it wasn't true.

He felt conflicted. He didn't want to leave him. But he knew he had to go.

Reznick carefully lowered Leggett's head down onto the plastic floor of the shower room. Water cascaded into Leggett's open eyes. His mind flashed images of Leggett's sparkling eyes as they'd touched down in Black Hawks. A man who'd radiated courage. The old American values. Honour. Sacrifice. He sighed. "I've got to go, Harry. I need to leave you here." He stared down, a lump in his throat. "I'll be seeing you." He touched his cheek. Cold.

He felt the raw anger inside begin to subside. He zoned out as he had been trained to do.

Reznick looked around the teak paneled cabin trying to figure out his next move as he gathered his thoughts. His prints were all over the place. On the rails, on the handles and in the cabins. The body would be eventually discovered. And they would have him pegged for killing his old buddy.

This was a cute operation. But how did they know about Leggett? Reznick hadn't called ahead.

Reznick took another look at Harry's pathetic, naked body. He thought of the operations they'd been involved in. The firefights. The training. The killings. The secret missions. It made him desperately sad that the once invincible Harry Leggett, his closest comrade, had ended up like this.

He looked again at the faded tattoo, turned and headed back to the bar.

SIX

Reznick took Harry Leggett's son into a back room at the bar, locking the door. The boy had the same sunken eyes as his father. He sat the kid down and told him the news straight. He watched as the kid went a ghostly white before he broke down in tears.

"I don't fucking believe you, man. Are you kidding me?"

Reznick draped an arm around the boy's broad shoulders. "Ron, look at me. If I could turn back the clock, son, I would. Your father meant the world to me."

The kid was sobbing hard.

"Let it out, son."

Reznick remembered the wretched emptiness the day his own father died. He remembered watching them lower his coffin into the grave, former Marines looking on. He'd been a young man himself and had put on a strong face. A mask.

The boy's body was shaking and quivering as he sobbed his heart out.

"I don't have the right words, Ron. But I want you to know that your father loved you."

The kid wiped away the tears with the back of his hand. "What happened?"

Reznick leaned in close and sighed. "Listen to me Ron," he said, keeping his voice low, "what I'm about to say is difficult to get your head around."

"What do you mean?"

"There were no visible signs of injuries. But I believe it was made to look like it was an accident, as if he's fallen over and banged his head in the shower, drunk."

"I don't understand."

"I can't go into it... but I know the signs. He might have been jabbed by an anaesthetic type drug, one that paralyses, makes it look like a person has collapsed and had a heart attack. It's a method of assassination."

The kid looked at him aghast.

"Is this related to your work or people you know?"

"Maybe."

"Maybe? What does that mean?"

"It means I don't really know."

The kid shook his head, tears streaking his face. He stared at Reznick. "You caused this, didn't you?"

"Ron, you've every right to be angry. I'd be angry too."

"Someone is after you, is that what it is, and got dad instead?"

Reznick said nothing.

"My mum always thought something like this would happen. The people you work with get tangled up in your personal lives; she always worried about shit like that."

"Ron, you said a guy turned up here yesterday morning, asking to speak to your dad. I need you to tell me about this guy."

He wiped his eyes with the back of his hand. "You think he did this?"

"I don't know. Maybe."

The kid shrugged. "What do you want to know?"

"Have you seen the guy before?"

"No."

"Did he have a name?"

"Chad... I think he said his name was Chad."

The name sent alarm bells ringing with Reznick. "Chad?"

"Yeah, Chad. Fucking huge guy."

"Ron, look, I know this is tough, but can you describe this guy to me?"

The kid dabbed his eyes. "Long blond hair, dark tan, mean looking dude."

"Mean-looking, right. Did he have a pronounced accent at all?"

"What do you mean by that?"

"I mean, did it stand out in any way?"

"Yeah. He sounded like a big Texan boy."

Reznick nodded. "I know this isn't easy, but is there anything else you can remember about this guy? I'm talking physically."

"He had a fuck-off scar on his face, if that's what you mean. Nasty looking motherfucker."

Reznick's blood ran cold. The description was a perfect match for a guy he knew. A guy Leggett knew. A guy called Chad Magruder. A former Delta crazy who had been on countless missions with Leggett and Reznick, before he was found guilty of raping a woman after breaking into her home in Fayetteville, near Fort Bragg.

Had that sick son–o- a-bitch killed Leggett? And if so, why?

"Listen, Ron, this is very important, is there anything else you can remember about this guy, Chad? Did he arrive by car? Think very carefully."

"Yeah, the dude's car was right outside, half blocking the entrance. Look, Mr Reznick, I don't want to talk about this anymore. Don't you understand that?"

"I understand that absolutely. But just try and think for a minute what kind of car was he driving?"

"I don't know… Look, I think it was maybe a black SUV."

"How do you remember that?"

"Surveillance cameras out front. I distinctly remember him pulling up. He stood out."

"Can I check if they caught anything?"

"I don't understand… This is crazy. What difference will that make? My dad's dead and you…"

"I know that, Ron. I wish he wasn't. But he is." He held the boy by the hand. "I need your help, Ron. I need to know what this guy knows, do you understand? So, I would really appreciate it if I could look over the footage."

The kid stared blankly before averting his gaze and getting to his feet. "Follow me. It's out back."

Reznick felt sick and soiled as he followed Ron through to a small windowless room near the rear of the bar. A keyboard and two small monitors on a table. One was blank and one showed the exterior of the bar, some kids still goofing around, smoking and laughing. He punched in the approximate time the guy called Chad arrived. Scrolling through the footage, minute after minute, he got to 9.04am with a black SUV pulling up, partially visible from the camera. The car reversed into view.

"Let this section play," Reznick said.

A few moments later into the view of the camera walked a tall and wiry man, long blond hair, shades on, pale blue Cowboys baseball cap, black shirt, jeans and cowboy boots.

Magruder. Fuck.

"Freeze that!" said Reznick.

He looked long and hard at the grainy still image. It was Magruder all right.

"OK, I think that's the guy you told me about," Reznick said. "Can you back up to when the car arrives? I'm sure there's something on the rear windshield, a big sticker, when he reverses."

The kid scrolled back and froze the image.

Reznick peered at the screen. "Ryan's of Weston?"

The kid scrunched up his face. "Yup."

"What the hell's that?"

"Rental company based in Weston."

"Where's Weston?"

The kid blinked away the tears. "On the edge of the Everglades. Not far. Maybe twenty miles or so."

Reznick looked at the boy before hugging him tight.

The kid began to sob into Reznick's chest. "Why did he kill my dad?"

Reznick sighed. "God only knows."

As he headed back to the parking garage, his mood darkened. Having Magruder on the scene was bad. He crossed a busy intersection and took a right and saw a blue neon sign for the parking garage.

What the hell are you doing, Reznick? Stuck in the middle of Fort fucking Lauderdale, walking around in the middle of the night, when your little girl needs you. Goddamn, why hadn't he gone straight to Miami and focused on playing along with those guys, and getting his daughter back?

He balled his fists tight as he strode along the sidewalk, anger coursing through his veins.

Lauren was somewhere out there, alone. Probably terrified at the hands of God knows who. An innocent, staring into the abyss. And all the time he was pissing around, trying to get help from a psychologically damaged former Delta operator and lumbered with some fucking scientist he should have capped.

You idiot, Reznick. You fucking idiot.

His mind flashed back to the image of the man on the surveillance camera. The shades. The wiry physique. The scar. It was *him*. Why had that crazy fuck Magruder turned up at Leggett's bar? And what were the chances of both Magruder and Reznick turning up within a day of each other?

Zero, that's what. This was no coincidence.

Reznick's gut instincts told him Magruder had killed Leggett and the thought unsettled him.

Suddenly Reznick heard the low growl of a car engine not far behind him.

"Hey, buddy, you lost?" a man's voice said.

He turned around as a cop car pulled up beside him, the arm of the officer in the passenger seat hanging out of the window.

"Just looking for a bar, officer."

The officer chewed gum as the driver talked into a radio. "Yeah, what bar you looking for?"

"Any bar'll do."

The officer smiled chewing hard on the gum. "You not from around here?"

"No, sir. From out of town."

"Out of town, huh? Where you staying?"

"Supposed to be staying on a friend's boat. But he's gone out night fishing instead. So, you know how it is, a man's gotta pass the time some way."

The car pulled up beside him and the officer stepped out of the car. "Sir, do you have any identification on you."

Reznick reached into his back pocket and handed him his second fake ID driver's license. The cop chewed his gum as he scanned the license before nodding.

"Long way from Burlington, Vermont, Mr Laird."

Reznick smiled but said nothing.

The cop shrugged. "Seems OK. But I'll need to check these details over on our computer, sir. Won't take a minute, OK?"

Reznick nodded. "Take your time, officer."

The officer got back in the car and called in the name. A couple of minutes later, the radio crackled into life. "Yeah, it's clean."

The officer stared at Reznick. "What do you do up in Burlington, Mr Laird, if you don't mind me asking?"

"A bit of this, a bit of that. Maintenance mostly."

The officer handed his ID back to Reznick. "Sorry for keeping you, sir. A routine check, I'm sure you'll understand."

"Not a problem, officer."

The officer nodded to the driver and they drove off, taking a right at a set of lights.

Reznick let out a long sigh at the close call. If the cop had stopped the car, he'd have had had to take the cop down. Not ideal in any circumstances. He walked on for a few minutes, before he headed down a side street and founds his way back to the parking garage. He popped open the trunk and Luntz was breathing hard. Reznick untied him and undid the gag. "Let me out of here," Luntz said, sweat beading his forehead. "Please don't lock me in there again."

Reznick stared down at the blinking, terrified scientist. "It all depends if you behave yourself. Do you understand?"

Luntz blinked away more tears and nodded.

Reznick yanked Luntz out of the trunk by his T-shirt and stood him up. He looked unsteady on his feet. "You OK?"

Luntz shook his head. "No, I'm not OK." He was breathing hard, eyes glazed.

"Do what I say, and we're gonna get through this, do you understand?"

Luntz stared blankly at him but said nothing.

"OK, let's go," said Reznick, and marched him across the concrete second floor parking garage towards a Volvo.

"Please, where are you taking me? Please, I'm scared. I'm scared you're taking me somewhere to kill me."

"That's not gonna happen. Just trust me." Using a high tech fob, Reznick disabled the alarm and the immobiliser system. Then he opened the passenger seat and strapped a disorientated and blinking Luntz in. "Don't move a fucking muscle."

Reznick went around and opened the driver's door. Pulling out a knife, he bent down and popped the plastic cover around the steering wheel. On the left hand side was the ignition. He got out his Swiss army knife, unscrewed the two bolts that held a metal cover in place, and jammed the smallest knife into the slot. The engine purred into life.

He slid into the driver's seat, pulled on his seat belt and revved up the engine a couple of times.

Where to now? Should he follow up the Magruder lead to the town of Weston on the off chance of getting lucky?

His thoughts turned to Magruder's name. Unusual. Rare, even. So, how many Magruders could there be in a provincial town in south Florida?

Reznick pulled the iPhone out of his back pocket and punched in 4-1-1 for directory assistance.

"Good morning, what number are you looking for?" a woman's voice said.

"Hi, looking for a number in Weston, Florida. Is there any for Magruder?"

"How are you spelling that, sir?"

"Magruder. M-a-g-r-u-d-e-r."

"Hold the line, sir." Vivaldi's Four Seasons started playing for what seemed like an eternity. It was probably only a couple of seconds. Eventually the woman came back on the line. "Yes, sir, I've got one in the town of Weston, Florida."

"One number, that's great."

"Yeah, we've got a Shelley Anne Magruder, 2387 Lake Boulevard, Weston. Number is 954-384-7272."

He ended the call as he made a mental note of the address and number. He buckled up, switched on the satnav and punched in the town of Weston as the destination.

The woman's voice on the satnav directed him out of Fort Lauderdale, onto the I-95 ramp towards Miami and the Port Everglades Expressway towards Weston.

Reznick screwed up his tired eyes, dazzled by the oncoming lights. His mind drifted. He thought back to his daughter playing in the rock pools as a little girl, down in the cove on the rocky Maine headland. She was paying the price for his life in the shadows. He willed himself to focus.

Make haste slowly.

He needed to slow down his thought processes to prepare properly. The adrenaline rush that was making him nauseous would eventually burn off. But until then, he needed to focus.

He cranked up the air con and the blast of cold air began to refresh him. Then he switched on the radio and some country station was playing.

He turned it up and his mind flashed back to the first time he'd met Magruder.

It was a cold spring day in 1995; snow still on the ground, during the Selection and Assessment for the 1st Special Forces Operational Detachment – Delta – in Camp Dawson, West Virginia. It started with the same bullshit eight-hour standardised psychological tests. Do you like brunettes? Do you have black, tarry stools? Do you think people are talking about you? Do you hear voices? On the whole, do people understand you? Do you think of yourself as a serious person? Are you introspective? That kind of lame pseudo psychobabble talk.

They wanted to screen out the crazies. But they must have been asking the wrong questions that spring morning.

Magruder, a tall wiry man, was clean gone. He also had insane amounts of nervous energy. He stood out as an obsessive, even amongst the obsessives of Delta. He had a stellar reputation for marksmanship even amongst the Delta crack shots, and practiced religiously. He attended shooting competitions across America and beat everyone out of sight. He'd practiced magazine change and dry firing, time after time. And he'd read his Operator's Training Course manual, religiously keeping abreast of tradecraft and explosives. Everything was an opportunity to improve. To get better. He carried more weight in his rucksack; he studied martial arts to the highest level, beating the shit out of some of the best fighters in America.

But what no one knew at the time was that Magruder was damaged. Unlike Reznick, who had enjoyed a typical outdoor childhood in Maine – hiking, hunting and fishing with his dad – Magruder had endured a torrid, violent childhood. His father, a trucker, had physically abused him for years. Beatings bordering on torture, which initially toughened him up, had then sent Magruder spiraling into his own dark hell.

Whilst other Delta guys drank like maniacs when off duty, Magruder, who wasn't married and lived alone in a trailer, had been content to nurse a bottle of beer for hours and then retire quietly for the night.

He didn't talk about sex at all and seemed embarrassed as Delta watched porn, drank beer and talked about women.

Then, in the mid-1990s, a succession of violent rapes occurred in Raleigh, including at North Carolina State University, by what police thought was a lone stranger. The hooded man had climbed into their windows, dressed in black, and at knifepoint raped the women.

Police arrested Chad Magruder who was reported to have been deferential to the detectives when he was charged with three counts of rape. He was convicted and most people, including Reznick, who'd read about the case in the newspapers, had thought the key would have been thrown away.

The truly terrifying thing was no one ever thought Magruder was mad. A bit quiet, obsessive sure, but one of them.

"Why are we heading in this direction?"

"Never you mind. Look, I don't want to hear any more from you. I'm having a really bad day."

"Please, can't you just drop me off and let me go?"

"Knock it off and we'll get on a whole lot better."

Reznick let out a long yawn and popped two more Dexedrine, washed them down with a can of Coke. He began to feel more switched on. Alert.

Up ahead a sign for Weston. With six miles to go, Reznick's thoughts again turned to Lauren.

Where the hell was his girl? Who the hell had her?

He thought back to when she was a baby, cradling her in his arms at the hospital. The smile on her tiny, pink face as she stared up at him: her protector, her father. The way Elisabeth had held her in her arms, then broke down and pulled Reznick towards them both; a family.

Reznick felt a rising anger within him. He thought of Magruder again and what his role was.

Up ahead, the turn-off sign for Weston. He headed into the town, past silent lakes, surrounded by million dollar homes.

The satnav guided him down a dark and near-deserted street towards a huge house overlooking the lake, partially hidden behind a trim hedge. Blinds drawn. The number 2387 on the gate, a metallic silver Mercedes convertible in the drive. But no sign of the black SUV caught on cameras outside the Monterey Club.

He stopped outside for a few moments.

A police patrol car came into sight at the far end of the lake.

Reznick drove on as the police passed in the opposite direction. Neither of the two officers glanced out of their window. He drove on for another half mile before he turned around and headed back towards the house.

He pulled up behind a BMW, about a hundred yards away from the house, but with line of sight to the front door and asphalt driveway. Then he switched off the engine and lights, before letting out a long sigh.

"Why are we stopping here?" Luntz said.

Reznick turned and sprayed the sleeping spray into Luntz's ear for a second. A moment later, Luntz's eyes rolled back in his head.

He was out cold, leaving Reznick to focus on the Magruder house.

SEVEN

Fifteen miles southwest of Baltimore, Thomas Wesley was driving past block after block of soulless glass and steel towers in a sprawling business park. His nighttime drives were becoming a routine, killing time until he returned to his job as a night shelf-stacker at Walmart. He yawned and checked the luminous orange clock on his dashboard that showed 3.47am, thirteen minutes until he was due back. It had only been three months since he'd taken the minimum wage job. But already the mind-numbing hellishness coupled with the small talk of his coworkers about reality TV shows he didn't watch and fad diets of film stars he didn't know, made him hanker for his old life.

Up ahead, the office sign of Xarasoft – his old employer – glowed bright yellow, only a few lights on in the foyer of the mirrored glass tower. A company he had given twenty-one years of his life to.

Wesley gazed across the parking lot at the other monolithic towers that populated the business park. Cameras scanning everywhere. Most of the companies were technology firms and were contracted – like Xarasoft – to the National Security Agency.

He had had a good life.

A voice analyst who worked for the NSA as a contractor. Six figure basic salary. Huge bonuses. Foreign holidays. The works. Now he couldn't even pay his utility bills, he was so fucking broke and his wife had had to go back to work as a teacher.

His coworkers at Walmart had no idea what he used to do. They never asked. Even if they had he couldn't have told them the truth about his top-secret work. They probably wouldn't believe him anyway.

Wesley saw a light go on in the fourth floor of his old company. He wondered if they were communicating in *real-time* with the NSA, perhaps ingesting one or two intercepted bulletin boarding postings, instant messages, IP addresses or vital FLASH traffic that had been flagged up.

The more he thought of his old life the more depressed he felt.

His wife thought it was only the Prozac that was keeping him from being able to face the world. But there was something else which was keeping him going. The reason he wouldn't give up trying to get people to listen to what he knew.

A conversation he had begun to piece together from fragments of near-nigh-impossible-to-intercept scraps of information.

He listened to the voices. He played voice comparison technology and listened over and over again in the small booth in his home study, headphones on, stripping down to the core voices. He wasn't sleeping during the day. His wife worried about him. But she didn't know what he knew.

Two days ago he had uncovered a smooth and terrifying narrative amongst the disembodied voices.

The problem was no one was listening.

Wesley took out his Blackberry and set about composing the latest encrypted email to his friend, Lance Drake, a Republican Congressman on the House Intelligence Committee. He stared at the email on the screen for a few moments before he sent the message. He put away his Smartphone and closed his eyes, thinking of his fiftieth birthday party only a year earlier, when the Congressman and other close friends attended a barbecue in his back yard. But now those same people he thought were his friends, people he had a beer with on a Saturday night, guys who he went bowling with once a month, didn't return his calls or go out for drinks.

His cell phone rang and Wesley almost jumped out of his skin.

"Thomas, what the hell are you playing at?" It was Drake, his old Yale drinking buddy.

Wesley cleared his throat. "Lance, appreciate the call back."

"Do you know what time it is?" His voice was an angry whisper.

"Yes, I know what time it is. Did I wake you?"

"The buzzing of my fucking Blackberry on my bedside table woke me up."

"Lance, why haven't you answered my emails?"

"Why haven't I answered your emails?" The tone was heavily sarcastic. "Do you want me to level with you?"

Wesley said nothing.

"You've sent me precisely seven emails – all virtually identical – in the last forty-eight hours alone. And not to put to fine a point on it, I'm starting to question your state of mind."

"My state of mind, huh?" Wesley felt a knot of tension in his stomach. "There's nothing wrong with my state of mind."

"Thomas, they say you had two psychological evaluations before you were sacked and that you show certain personality traits."

"That's bullshit."

Lance let out a long sigh. "Thomas, look, I know how smart you are. But the fact of the matter is you screwed up before. You made the wrong call."

"It's that what they told you? That's bullshit."

"They say you were flat out wrong."

"They're lying."

"Listen, I've not got time for this, Thomas."

"OK, let's focus on the here and now. Forget about that. What I'm about to tell you is something that sounds a bit far-out there, I understand that."

"Thomas, please, it's late."

"Just bear with me. I've been busy working on developing a new bit of software. It helps achieve tight bandwidth compression of the speech signals like you wouldn't believe. Have you heard of MELP?"

Drake sighed. "No, I've not."

"It's enhanced Mixed Excitation Linear Prediction."

"What the hell is that?"

"It's a speech voding standard used mainly in military applications and satellite communications, secure voice and secure radio devices. Vastly improves the previous quality. I'm talking primarily speech quality, intelligibility and noise immunity, whilst at the same time reducing throughput requirements."

"Thomas, I don't understand this technical stuff you're throwing at me."

"My technology is a major leap forward even from MELP. I began to piece something together before my security clearance was taken away. It's not related to the reason they fired me. This is something bigger and far more troubling. Lance, all I ask is that you take heed of what I'm saying. I believe there is a very real threat to America."

A long silence opened up for what seemed like an eternity.

"Did you hear what I said, Lance?"

"What did you say?"

"There is a very real threat. I can't tell you the ins and outs on the phone."

"Why haven't I heard of this?"

"Good question. But that's just half of it. There's more I've discovered recently. I've been listening to the voice again. I think I've identified the person. You wanna know who it is?"

"In the name of God, Thomas. You don't work for the NSA or Xarasoft anymore. Are you telling me you've taken secret recordings off site?"

"I'm not going to say. What I will say, Lance, is that if you just meet up with me and put me in front of that committee, then they can decide. I swear you have to listen to what I've got."

"I can't believe what I'm hearing. Look, why don't you take what you've got to the NSA?"

"I have. I sent them the details anonymously, but I haven't heard back. Nothing."

Drake sighed again.

"Lance, I did over two hundred hours of speech data tests, and I know I'm correct. The cover audio I picked up was an innocuous pop song, but underneath was an encrypted conversation. I stripped away all that shit. But Lance, it's not just the conversation I've decrypted. I believe a covert message has been embedded within the digital audio signal."

"What?"

"I'm still working to decode that side of things. America needs to wake the fuck up."

"I can't believe what I'm hearing. You were sacked for wrong analysis."

"I told you that was lies. Do you really think I don't know what I'm talking about, is that what it is?"

"I've spoken to people at the NSA and you know what they're saying about you?"

Wesley closed his eyes, knowing what was to come.

"They're using words like paranoid and deluded. Look, maybe it's best if you don't email me anymore."

Wesley shook his head. "They've got to you, haven't they? Someone has told you that this guy is nuts, and for your career, leave him alone. Is that what's happening?"

"Thomas, I think we're going round in circles. OK, let's assume for a moment that what you're saying is the truth."

"It is!"

Lance sighed heavily.

"Look, I'd like to meet you at your office, and let you know everything."

"That ain't gonna happen."

"Why?"

"There are procedures for doing things. The right way of doing things."

"Lance, what's more important? To do things the right way, or do the right thing?"

"Look, this is getting us nowhere."

"So, what do you suggest I do with what I've got? No one is listening."

"Thomas, we're done. I'm sorry. Don't bug me again with this."

Then the line went dead.

EIGHT

The ranch-style house in Weston appeared algae green as Reznick peered through night vision glasses. He was slouched down low in the car, watching and waiting, with Luntz still out cold in the back seat.

His mind flashed back to the green tinged landscape of Fallujah at night.

Blinding lights. Screaming and pleading. The smell of the open sewers. The dust. The filth. The Black Hawks flying low, strafing the neighborhood. The green smeared vision through night sights as Task Force 121 scoured the warren of streets and alleys in the darkness, looking for insurgents.

He'd lost count of the number of kills. He'd become desensitized until he almost didn't care. They'd trained him that way. It had become second nature. But somehow, he still managed to keep a small part of his soul intact. Even when his team had killed an insurgent, and cut off his blood-stained clothes to check for tattoos to help identify the person, Reznick always remembered what his dying father – haunted by memories of Vietnam – had once said when he said he was going to join the Marines. "Never be blasé about death. Don't forget, every man you kill is somebody's son."

The words stayed with him. Echoed down the years. He always clung to that even as he felt his soul was turning black. Even when they were scanning the dead man's iris and fingerprints with a portable biometric scanner. It was always *somebody's son*.

The front door opened and Reznick snapped out of his thoughts. A woman in her thirties emerged wearing a smart jacket, dark slacks and kitten heels, speaking into her cell phone.

Reznick watched as she locked the door, turning the handle a couple of times. She climbed into the driver's seat, slamming the door shut. Then she reversed out of the driveway and drove off past the lake.

He had a split second decision to make. Follow or fold? Was Chad Magruder inside? He felt conflicted.

"Fuck," he said, feeling himself grinding his teeth.

He hung back for a few moments until she was nearly out of sight. Then he started up the engine but kept his lights off. Time to see where she led him.

He pulled away slowly and waited for a couple of minutes before he switched on his lights. A few moments later he caught sight of her car further along the north side of the lake. He hung back as much as he could as he negotiated the quiet residential, palm-lined streets before they skirted downtown Weston. It was like a Mediterranean village, all pastel colors and low-rise buildings.

Then she took a right at some lights and drove down Racquet Club Road, past the Hyatt.

A few moments later, she pulled up outside a low-rise motel overlooking another lake.

Reznick drove on and took a left into a parking lot on West Mall Road. It had a clear line of sight over to the motel's car park a couple of hundred yards away. He picked up his night vision glasses and peered into the darkness towards the deserted motel parking lot. The woman was sitting in her car, lights on, engine running, cell phone pressed to her ear, occasionally nodding her head.

The woman then ended the call, got out the car and walked into the reception of the motel.

Reznick edged the car around the corner and back on Racquet Club Road, then got himself into a position at the far end of the motel's parking lot, shielded by an island of shrubs and palms. He switched off his engine and lights, slouched in his seat. Then he picked up the night vision glasses.

Did she work there? Maybe she was an innocent. But what if… what if his daughter was being held there? Was that too far-fetched? The thought triggered an adrenaline rush to his heart. His breathing quickened.

The seconds ticked by, then the minutes.

Just as he was about to get out of the car and head into the motel, the woman emerged alone. She got in her car, switched on her lights and pulled away, oblivious to Reznick.

What now? Follow her or sit tight? He couldn't barge into the motel and go room to room. The cops would be called and he would be taken in. And then what?

"Goddamn."

Reznick decided to sit tight. He wondered if the woman had taken a message to someone inside. Was that it? Was Magruder holed up inside?

His mind flashed back to news footage of Magruder being led away in handcuffs from the courtroom, impassive, eyes dead.

The time dragged like a chain at the bottom of a sandy seabed. He waited. And waited. And still he waited. More minutes being eaten up. But no one left or entered the motel.

"Fuck," he said.

He turned the car around and drove back into Weston town center. He stopped to pick up some sandwiches and provisions from an all-night deli to keep them going for the next few hours, intending to head back to the ranch house to find out who the woman was or see if Magruder turned up.

The plan changed.

As he headed along affluent residential streets, he took a right at the lights into Main Street. As he drove by, his gaze was drawn to a Jeep, parked diagonally opposite a Starbucks under a huge palm. He checked the plates. It was hers.

Reznick drove on for a couple of hundred yards, pulled a U-turn and parked fifty yards behind the Jeep with a perfect view of the coffee shop on the corner. The clock on his dashboard said it was 5.31am. He switched off his lights and picked up his binoculars, switching off the night vision facility as the lights were on in Starbucks.

Scanning the inside of the shop, he saw the Magruder woman sitting at a table with a couple of coffee mugs. His instincts told him she wasn't having her morning coffee alone. But a few minutes later the woman walked out of the Starbucks alone. Her clothes looked expensive, well cut.

"Who are you?"

He slouched down in his seat as she walked towards her car, opened the Jeep with a fob and drove away down Main Street.

Reznick felt torn again. Should he follow her or sit tight? But there were two coffee mugs on the table. He decided to stay where he was and peered through the binoculars into the interior of Starbucks. A young woman was wiping down the tables.

A couple of minutes later, the Starbucks door opened. A lean white guy in his mid-thirties walked out. He wore faded jeans, cowboy boots and a black T-shirt, long blond hair, thick scar on his face.

It was Chad Magruder.

Reznick felt his flesh crawl.

He watched as Magruder lit a cigarette and walked further down Main Street and then disappeared up a street to the right. Reznick switched on the ignition and headed the same

way. A few moments later, he saw Magruder climb into the
black SUV – the same one Reznick saw on the surveillance
tape at the Monterey Club.

"OK, you bastard," Reznick said to himself, "where are you
going?"

Reznick drove on past at the same time as Magruder was
getting into his car. Five hundred yards up ahead, Reznick
pulled into a space at the curb outside a deli and switched
off his engine and lights. He checked his wing mirror and
a minute later Magruder drove on past, oblivious, cigarette
dangling from the corner of his mouth.

Reznick waited a few moments before he pulled out and
followed Magruder's car. He was about one hundred yards
back and it looked like he was heading for the freeway. Five
minutes later, he was heading up a ramp and onto I-75S. The
traffic was heavy even at that ungodly hour. He was now four
cars back.

Reznick crossed lanes for a couple of miles to try and stay
out of his rearview mirror. They were headed in the pre-dawn
darkness towards the Dolphin Expressway. Then Magruder
changed lanes, and slowed down, only two cars ahead,
glancing in his rearview mirror.

Counter surveillance move.

Reznick stayed in lane, knowing not to dart off in another
direction. He stayed calm as Magruder continued to check his
rearview mirror for tails. Then he turned round and stared at
the car behind him.

The bastard was cute.

A few minutes later, a sign for Miami and Magruder
changed lanes again, took the Miami Avenue Exit 2.

Reznick was about one hundred yards behind and followed
Magruder towards the huge skyscrapers of Miami's business
district. All the time, Reznick kept his distance. Glass and steel
office towers loomed over Brickell Avenue.

Then Magruder hung a sharp left and headed into an underground parking facility. Reznick drove on by and went round the block twice, before he headed into the basement car park.

Reznick caught sight of Magruder's car parked in a disabled space right beside the elevators. His left arm was out of the window, cigarette dangling from his fingers, cell phone pressed to his right ear.

Reznick passed within fifty yards and took a ramp to the upper level parking. He drove around the deserted car park for a couple of minutes and then headed down to Magruder's level.

Cruising past, he stole a quick glance in his rearview mirror. At that moment, Magruder stepped out of his car, dropped his cigarette and crushed it with the heel of his boot. Then he placed his cell in his back pocket and headed towards the steel elevators.

Reznick drove into a space straight ahead beside a massive concrete pillar, engine still running. He looked in the rearview mirror and saw Magruder press an elevator button. He picked up the binoculars and turned to see Magruder get into the elevator. Then he trained the binoculars on the light indicating which floor. It eventually stopped at the forty-second floor.

Reznick switched off the engine and got out of the car. He checked on Luntz who was still out of it, centrally locked the car and then took the elevator to the forty-third floor. From there, he headed down a flight of stairs. A metal sign on an outer door for Norton & Weiss Inc.

He looked around the outer lobby. A camera strafed the entrance with the locked glass doors and metallic password keypad beside the handle. He headed back down to the car park and popped a couple more Dexedrine.

It wasn't long before Reznick felt wired. He waited, grinding his teeth as the pills kicked in big time and the adrenaline flowed. He no longer felt hungry.

Did Magruder kill Leggett? He pondered on that for a few moments. But he had to have. He was asking for him. Then Leggett is found dead. So it meant someone had hired him? But who?

The more he thought of it, the more Reznick began to realise that someone knew far more about his life that they should have done. They knew about his daughter. They knew about his friendship with Leggett.

But who was that someone? They knew that Reznick would turn to Leggett, a man he had trusted since the day they met at training.

His thoughts switched to Lauren.

He had shielded his daughter all these years from his secret world. He visited her at Brookfield once, maybe twice a year, taking her out for pizza. She didn't know what he did, content to believe her father was a security consultant for US embassies abroad. Deep in his heart he had believed he had everything under control. But that was then, not now. A government scientist he was supposed to have suicided was lying out of it in the back of a stolen car, while Lauren's life was in the balance.

What a monumental fuck-up. How the hell had it got so crazy?

Half an hour later, Magruder appeared, running his hands through his hair. Nothing like a vain psycho, Reznick thought. But instead of heading towards the car in the disabled bay, Magruder walked over towards a Suburban with blacked-out windows. Why the change of car? Then he used a key fob to open the driver's door. Had Magruder just been given a new job? And how did Norton & Weiss fit into it?

Reznick slunk down low and waited until Magruder had left the garage and then he turned on his engine. He caught sight of Magruder driving fast through the dark downtown streets before he headed across the Macarthur Causeway to South Beach.

He needed to hang back and not get too close but nearly lost him not wanting to run a red light on Washington Avenue. Eventually, he caught sight of the Suburban, one hundred yards up ahead, cruising down Lenox Avenue, then onto 19th Street, past the Holocaust Memorial Museum and past the rundown neon-lit Sunset Motel.

Magruder parked one block away, with a clear diagonal line of sight to the motel.

Reznick drove on to Dade Boulevard and double-backed onto Alton Road, before pulling up in West Avenue. He was out of sight, but now less than seventy-five yards from Magruder, whose car was facing the opposite direction.

A panhandler came into view. He was walking the near-empty pre-dawn streets wearing a filthy jacket and Yankees baseball cap and some fancy shades, taking the occasional slug from a bottle of Nightrain.

It was then Reznick had an idea.

NINE

Reznick switched off his engine, got out of the car and walked up to the panhandler who smelled of piss, rancid booze and cigarettes. The old guy's eyes were wild and bloodshot.

"You wanna make an easy fifty bucks, old man? he asked.

The panhandler gave a nonchalant shrugged as if he was used to getting such offers every day.

"Gimme your jacket, hat, shades and your bottle, and this fifty is yours," Reznick said, flashing the bill.

The man grinned, exposing nicotine-stained stumps for teeth. "Why would I do that?"

Reznick took another fifty-dollar bill from his pocket and shook his head. "A hundred bucks."

The panhandler nodded as he took off his jacket, hat and shades, before he handed over his bottle of booze, snatching the money from Reznick's hand in one movement. "Nice doing business with you, my friend."

Reznick put on the stinking coat, the hat and the shades. "Get some soup in you, for God's sake," he said, but the panhandler was already sauntering down 19th Street, straight for the nearest all-liquor store. Further down the street, Reznick caught sight of the black Suburban parked up.

Magruder's window was down, phone in his left hand pressed to his ear. His voice was low and raspy from the cigarettes.

Reznick shuffled across the road and headed slowly in the direction of Magruder. He was within ten yards.

Magruder turned around, phone still pressed to his ear, but ignored the sight of the panhandler approaching.

Reznick ambled up to the Suburban's open window, hand outstretched, as if for money.

"Get the fuck away from me," Magruder said.

Reznick punched him hard on the side of the head and Magruder's eyes rolled back in his head. His cell phone fell out of his hand, but Reznick caught it before it hit the ground. Magruder was out cold.

He leaned over and rifled in Magruder's waistband where he retrieved a Berretta. Then he patted down his jeans and discovered a serrated hunting knife taped to the back of his left calf.

Leaning into the car, he pulled out the plexicuffs he had in his back pocket and tied up Magruder's hands and feet before pushing him over on to the floor of the passenger seat.

Reznick dumped the stinking coat, shades and hat at the side of the road before he slid into the driver's seat and drove off. He headed round the dark South Beach streets for a few minutes, away from the main drags of Ocean Drive and Washington Avenue, looking for the right spot. Past empty parking lots, small art deco hotels with neon-lit signs and dimly lit side streets. Then on down palm-fringed residential streets until he saw a Realtor sign outside a boarded up house on Michigan Avenue between 12th and 13th Street, adjacent to Flamingo Park. It was painted a sickly yellow and looked like an abandoned house.

He looked across and considered if it was suitable. It didn't look bad at all. A rusty chainlink steel fence with flaking black paint surrounded the property including the padlocked driveway. He waited until a couple of pedestrians walking by were out of sight. Then he reversed back onto the sidewalk until the car was pressed up against the padlocked gates, leaving the engine running. He got out and unpicked the chain, opened the creaking metal gates and got back in the car, reversing back up the driveway. Then Reznick hauled the deadweight of Magruder up the overgrown driveway, before kicking in a wooden panel on the ground floor.

Dragging him inside, he took a few moments for his eyes to adjust to the darkness, only the glow from the street lights filtering in. It looked like a ransacked kitchen and smelled as if an animal had died there.

A pile of rotten blankets lay on top of a mattress. Strewn on the tile floor were cigarette ends, old crack pipes, empty cans of beer and bottles of wine, as if some panhandlers had used it recently as a flophouse.

He placed Magruder onto the mattress and then ripped up the filthy rags. Then he stuffed part of a rags into Magruder's mouth.

Reznick picked up a half empty bottle of wine, poured out the contents, and went over to the sink and filled it up with water. Fixing a suppressor to his Beretta, he kicked Magruder in the back.

The bastard came to. Eyes crazy. He tried to stand, but the blow to the head and the fact that he was trussed up meant he was immobilised.

Reznick leaned close and pointed the gun at his head. "Time to answer some questions, Magruder."

"Reznick?" The rag muffled his voice. "What the fuck, man?"

"Shut up."

"What've you got me tied up like a hog for, man?"

Reznick slapped him hard on the face. Blood spilled through the rag from Magruder's mouth. "I said shut up. Now, listen to me very closely, I want some answers."

"What's this all about?"

"Leggett. What did you do to him?"

"I don't know what you're talking about, man."

Reznick slapped him hard on the other side of the face. More blood spilled from his mouth. "I think you do. Now, you're gonna tell me, or you're gonna taste some water, do you know what I mean?"

The fear in Magruder's eyes was real. Reznick knew from their days training, he had a phobia about water, although he had tried to overcome it.

"Hey look, I don't know what you're talking about, man. I swear. Reznick, what's this all about?"

Reznick pressed his right foot hard down on Magruder's chest as he writhed on the floor. He tipped the water from the bottle through the rags and into Magruder's mouth. The water glugged through the cloth and into Magruder's throat, down into his stomach. Veins in his neck were nearly bursting through his skin, eyes wild with terror. They had both been trained to withstand waterboarding. They knew that it was just a simulated drowning. But he knew Magruder would buckle because of his phobia.

He stopped pouring after ten seconds.

"I want to know what you were up to. Were you ordered to do a job? Were you asked to neutralise Leggett?"

Magruder shook his head furiously, tears streaming down his face.

"What did you do to him?"

He was crying and half choking.

"What about my daughter? Tell me what you know."

Magruder shook his head and closed his eyes. Reznick poured more water from another wine bottle into Magruder's throat. He flailed again and thrashed as Reznick pressed his foot into his chest.

He stopped and gave Magruder a few moments to try and recover. This time the terror had become blind panic in his eyes. "I'll ask again, where is my daughter?"

Magruder shook his head.

Reznick pulled the soaking rag from his mouth as Magruder spluttered and coughed. "Answer, you fuck."

He coughed up water and retched for nearly a minute before he spoke. "Please, believe me, Reznick, man, I didn't have a choice. I was told to do Leggett and turn up in Miami today."

Reznick felt the anger rise inside him. "Turn up for what today?"

Magruder began weeping. "Man, I'm sorry."

"Tell me what you know or you will die, right here and now. I'll ask again, who gave you the orders?"

"The guys..."

"What fucking guys? The guys in that tower in downtown Miami?"

Magruder nodded, sniveling and sobbing hard. "It's a front. Jon, believe me I would never–"

"A front for what?"

"I don't know. I've done various jobs for them. Russian oligarch. An Arab woman. They pay me a lot of money. A lot of money. In cash. I need the money, man. I owe a lot of people."

"I asked what kind of front is it."

"The front is that it's a legal firm."

"How did you get to hear about them?"

"They approached me in jail about a year ago and said they could get me out, if I went to work for them."

"Who's 'they'?"

Magruder began coughing, hacking up water and phlegm. "I don't know."

"You must know. Who is in fucking charge there?"

"All I know is that I get a call, and I head there, and I speak to a guy called Vince. White guy. Real intense. And when I mean intense, I mean real intense, you know what I'm saying?"

"All I need to know is where my daughter is."

"I know nothing about that."

Reznick's mind was racing. "What were you parked on 19th Street for?"

He closed his eyes and shook his head. "They wanted me to acquaint myself with the area, that's all."

"Were you told to kill me?"

Magruder closed his eyes, retching and coughing at the same time. "I was just told something was going to go down, get to know the area, that's all, and then await instructions."

Reznick stuffed the rag back into his mouth and poured the rest of the water from the second bottle. He stared down. "Where is my daughter?"

Magruder was bug eyed with terror, spluttering. Reznick could see he was close to the edge. He took out the rag as Magruder coughed and brought up water.

"I swear, I don't know about your daughter."

"You fucking liar. You piece of shit. You know about her, don't you? Where is she? Tell me!"

Magruder eyes were turning in his head, nearly unconscious.

Reznick pressed the gun up hard to his head. "Last time, what do you know about my daughter?"

Magruder shook his head as he spluttered some more. "Absolutely nothing, I swear, man. I did Leggett. And I was going to be given one hundred thousand dollars cash to kill you."

Reznick stared down at the former Delta operator. For a split second he felt pity for a man who was tougher than anyone he had ever met. By now Magruder was shaking but saying nothing.

Reznick went over to the sink and filled up a bottle full of water again. Then he stuffed the rag back into Magruder's mouth. "You want some more?"

Magruder shook his head.

"One last chance, where is my daughter?"

He removed the rag.

"I don't know your daughter or where she is."

Reznick rammed the rag back in and poured the rest of the water over Magruder's mouth.

Magruder's face scrunched up as if in pain and he clenched his teeth. Then he groaned and moaned, mouth open, before shaking uncontrollably.

"Don't pull that shit with me, do you hear me?"

There were gargled gasps for air, chest heaving up and down. Time seemed to slow.

Reznick stared down at Magruder for a few moments.

He leaned over and slapped him hard in the face. "What the fuck is wrong with you?"

No breathing. No sound. No movement. Reznick lifted Magruder's right hand and felt his wrist for a pulse.

He didn't feel a pulse.

Reznick turned away and kick over a chair. "Goddamn you." He felt sick to the pit of his stomach. He paced the deserted house, head in hands. He hadn't meant to kill Magruder, despite him taking down his friend Leggett. He'd just wanted to make him talk. But he'd gone too far. Way too far.

He turned and took one final look at Magruder's lifeless body, rag stuffed in his mouth.

And he knew that image would be burned into the darkest recesses of his mind forever.

TEN

It was still dark when Lt Col Scott Caan's alarm clock rang at his rented home near downtown Hagerstown, Maryland. He groaned and leaned over to switch it off after a fitful sleep. He wasn't a morning person. Never had been. He took a few moments for his brain to adjust to a new day before he got up and headed to the bathroom. He splashed some cold water on his face and looked at it in the mirror. Toned, lean, eyes clear. He felt in the best shape of his life. But he was still waiting to hear from them.

He didn't dwell on that. It wasn't his role to worry about them. He had to focus on his part. He pulled on a T-shirt and running shorts and laced up his Adidas sneakers. Then, like he always did, he headed downstairs to his gym in the basement and did five miles on the running machine, twenty minutes pumping iron, ten minutes on a rowing machine, and topped it off with fifteen minutes hitting a punch bag, jabbing and hooking until he thought his heart was going to pack in.

He checked his pulse. It was within acceptable limits for aerobic workouts. He was in great shape. He was ready. Had been for weeks.

Afterwards, sweating profusely, endorphins running round his body, he took a long, hot shower. He closed his eyes and wondered if he needed more sleep. He reckoned he'd managed, at best, four hours sleep.

Caan enjoyed the warm water pummeling his skin. He knew it wouldn't be long. Any day now. He wondered if his coworkers were asking why he hadn't been in work. He thought of the eight long years he had given to the company. The sacrifices. The hours. The time he could never get back. But he also knew it would all be worth it.

The more he thought of it the more he realised how well he had done, concealing his secret life from his coworkers. He was playing a long game. They thought he was just the quiet guy who was diligent and liked to go for runs at lunchtime. The guy who worked long hours and never complained, or bitched or made any trouble. The guy who did his job and never, under any circumstances, attracted attention. But they didn't know him. They didn't know him at all.

He turned off the shower, dried himself and put on a clean set of clothes that had been carefully chosen for him. The pale blue checked button-down shirt, the dark blue jeans, thick blue jumper and the Timberland boots. After cleaning his teeth and combing his short dark hair, he put on his black puffa jacket and clipped on his pager. Then he headed to a diner, three blocks away.

Outside, the cold air nearly took his breath away, a sharp frost on the ground. The forecasters had warned of a serious cold front heading down from Canada, perhaps bringing snow. He had been keeping an eye on the forecast for days, checking the weather in New York and Washington DC.

He was glad to get into the warmth of the diner where he ordered a hearty breakfast of waffles, bacon and poached eggs with his black coffee. The chubby black waitress brought him his meal and coffee and said, "Enjoy your breakfast, sir."

Caan just smiled but said nothing as he tucked into the meal and ate alone.

It had been ten days since he had moved to Hagerstown. It was the largest city in western Maryland with a population of nearly forty thousand. It was a semi-rural setting which had a nice, friendly feel to it. He enjoyed leisurely lakeside walks at City Park, then visiting the Washington County Museum of Fine Arts. The sort of things his dad was interested in and that he'd encouraged when he was growing up. He particularly loved gazing at the Norman Rockwell painting, *The Oculist*, showing a red-haired boy with a baseball glove, being fitted for a pair of glasses by a middle-aged man. It was classic Rockwell. The symbolism of a supposed American golden age. An America vanished.

He had always been entranced by the Rockwellian mythology of small town America. The idealised and sentimentalised world of friendly faces, white picket fences and impossibly blue skies that evoked nostalgia for simpler times. The world he had grown up in, in the small upscale town of Skaneateles in central New York State.

His mind flashed back. He remembered the biting cold winters. The colonial house overlooking the water. The family round the dinner table at Thanksgiving. Huge snowfalls. The ice-skating on the frozen lake with friends, the hockey and the snowball fights with his two brothers and sister. His mother and father arm in arm. He felt safe and happy. The seasons changed, and the village was awash with color. The village teemed with visitors in the summer who descended on the lake – one of the famous Finger Lakes. Boat trips. The smell of hot dogs. The daily summer concerts at the Presbyterian Church where they heard recitals during the Skaneateles Festival.

The water was so pure the city of Syracuse used it unfiltered. Then it was the fall. The smell of the damp, red leaves falling.

A waitress shouting an order snapped Caan out of his reverie.

He sipped some coffee. He felt alive for the first time in years, perhaps since his childhood. He had a purpose. A purity of purpose, like a Rockwell painting. Most of all, he had been given a plan.

He only received coded instructions. But in the last year, they had begun to talk specifics: a timescale, methodology, resources.

It had all been formulated and thought through.

He knew what was at stake.

His pager bleeped and he felt his stomach lurch. The last time it had bleeped was a week ago instructing him to go to Baltimore. Was this the day? Unclipping the pager from his belt he read the coded message he had been waiting to hear. It read simply: "Blue skies in Madrid."

This was indeed *it*.

"Want a refill, sir?" the waitress asked, seeing his mug was empty.

Caan clipped his pager back on and smiled. "I'm good thanks. Gotta dash."

"You have a good day, now."

Caan smiled back and left a five-dollar bill under his empty mug of coffee. Then he paid the tab at the counter and left for the short walk back home. He went to the spare bedroom and picked up his suitcase that was already packed and lugged it downstairs and then popped it in the trunk of his beat-up Datsun. Then he got in the car and headed up I-95 N to a state-of-the-art storage facility on the outskirts of Baltimore.

The traffic was heavy as he switched on a Bach CD. His mind drifted, thinking back years earlier to the time his father took him, his brothers and sister to an open-air summer concert, beneath the stars, given by the New York Philharmonic on Central Park's Great Lawn. He remembered his father explaining the importance of Bach in classical music, and how the composer pulled together the strands of Baroque period, creating an enriched form of music with unheard of texture. More than anything, he felt his heart swell, as the music washed over them, his father wrapping his arm around them. That was a year before his father and mother died. The crash. A dumb drunk driver in a pick-up, loaded with cheap liquor. He often thought of that night and wondered if things might have turned out differently if they had lived.

He remembered the heated political discussions between his parents – his father was a leftist, his mother a Republican. But most of the time, it was good stuff. The trips to musicals in Manhattan, up to the upper west side to the American Museum of Natural History where they saw a full-size model of a blue whale, the music of Bach and Mozart wafting out into the balmy Skaneateles night, and staring over the lake from his bedroom window of their home on East Lake Road, watching the snow fall.

The sound of a car horn snapped Caan back to the present. He checked in his rearview mirror for signs of any tails. But there was nothing. The journey was uneventful.

He drove off the freeway and into the quiet streets of a business park. He saw the sign for the I-Store facility he had visited less than a week earlier.

The guy behind the reinforced screen was chewing gum. Caan showed the fake ID and took the elevator to the third floor and punched in the four-digit pin code, before pressing his thumb up against the biometric scanner. Then the sound of mortise locks clicking and he opened the locker. Inside was the sports holdall he had deposited seven days earlier.

He carefully picked up the bag and headed to the exit.

"You get what you were looking for?" the guy at the desk asked politely.

"Yes, thank you."

"Have a good day, sir."

Caan opened the trunk of his car and placed the bag inside, before slamming it shut. And so began the near two hundred mile journey to New York City.

As he headed along I-95 N into Delaware, he checked again for any tails in his rearview mirror.

He changed lanes a few times, but nothing.

He afforded himself a smile. Not long now, he thought.

ELEVEN

A pale orange sun was peeking over the art deco rooftops as Reznick returned to the car on 19th Street in South Beach. He felt wired. He couldn't believe Magruder had gone so quickly. That wasn't how it was supposed to work. Magruder was the only one who might have had information about his daughter's whereabouts. It seemed inconceivable that he knew nothing.

Fuck.

The whole thing had descended into a living nightmare.

He popped open the trunk. Luntz was lying in the fetal position, eyes screwed up against the sun.

"Get the fuck out," Reznick said.

"Why?"

"Just do as I say."

Luntz clambered out. He looked unsteady on his feet and Reznick helped him into the passenger seat, before strapping him in. "This is insane."

"Get in and stop whining." Reznick fired up the car. "You hungry?"

"I don't think I can eat. I feel sick."

"Too bad."

Reznick drove to a nearby 7-Eleven on 6th Street and took a subdued Luntz in with him. He ordered two hot English muffin breakfast sandwiches, black coffees and picked up some donuts for later. They wolfed the sandwiches in the car, washed down with a strong coffee.

"Feel better?" he said.

Luntz nodded as he chewed his food.

The sun was edging higher in the sky and Reznick squinted, using his left hand to shield him from the glare. Suddenly the iPhone rang. He didn't recognise the number.

"Dad…Dad, it's Lauren."

Reznick's heart missed a beat at the sound of his daughter's voice. "Lauren, are you OK? Talk to me, honey."

Silence.

"Lauren! Speak to me!"

More silence.

"Lauren! Lauren!" Reznick closed his eyes tight. "Lauren! Are you there?"

"Yes, she is," a man said. The same voice he'd heard before. "And she's alive. For now, anyway."

"Listen to me, if you harm her in any way, and I mean in any way, I will hunt you down and rip out your fucking heart."

"Shut up! We're running the show. So, here's how it's gonna work. You hand over the scientist and you get Lauren back. Any attempt to call in the police or Feds will result in Lauren being killed. Are we clear?"

Reznick sighed. "Crystal."

"I don't want to harm her. But I will if Luntz is not handed over. I'll call you in an hour with the delivery point."

Then the man hung up.

Reznick felt sick. His daughter's life was hanging by a thread. All alone and at the mercy of God knows who. But she was alive. That was something. But where the hell was she?

Luntz broke the silence. "Was that them?"

"Was that who?"

"The people who want me?"

Reznick said nothing.

"They have your daughter, don't they?"

"You talk too much."

"You're going to hand me over, aren't you?"

"Just be quiet."

Luntz stared straight ahead. "I'm a family man too. My wife and two other kids need their dad back."

"So does my daughter."

Luntz looked away.

"Someone wants you dead, real bad. Why is that?"

"I know things."

"Stop playing fucking games. Why do people want you dead?"

Luntz went quiet for a few moments before he spoke. "I need to speak to the FBI."

"About what?"

"I believe lives may be at stake. American lives. And that's why you need to hand me over to the FBI."

"Not while they've got my daughter."

Reznick was running out of time and options. He knew he couldn't just sit and wait for them to call and bounce him all over Miami. But he couldn't give up Luntz, as he was the only bargaining chip he had.

There was only one real option.

He had to take the fight to them. The problem was that the only lead he had was the downtown tower where he'd followed Magruder to. Norton & Weiss.

Luntz said, "Please, don't hand me over to those people. You've got to believe me. I'm begging you." He clutched the photo pendant tight and pressed it to his chest. "I swear on my son's grave that I'm telling the truth."

Reznick looked into Luntz's sad blue eyes and could see he wasn't lying. He started up the car and headed away from the beach and back across the causeway into Miami. He saw a sign for Brickell Avenue and headed into slow-moving traffic, the towering skyscrapers either side.

He recognised the green sign for the parking garage he had followed Magruder into and pulled up beside the elevator doors.

"Where's this?" Luntz asked.

Reznick turned and sprayed another dose of sedative in Luntz's ear. His eyes rolled back in his head and he was out of it again. "Sorry, Frank. I'll tell you later." He got out of the car, popped open the trunk and shoved him inside, knowing he was going to be out of it for quite a while.

Reznick looked around the parking garage. At the far corner, he saw a brown UPS truck, its engine was idling. The driver was sitting filling out a log sheet, one arm out of his window. He walked over and knocked on the driver's window. The man wound down his window.

"Think you got a flat, buddy," Reznick said.

"You gotta be kidding me." The man got out of his truck frowning and cursing under his breath. Reznick pressed a gun to his head.

"Hey, what the fuck?!"

"In the back of your truck. Now!" He hustled the man into the back of the truck, alongside parcels and boxes. The man was shaking and terrified, cowering in the corner of the van. "I'm not going to hurt you. But I need your clothes."

The guy didn't protest. He just stripped off and threw his clothes towards Reznick. He was then tied up with duct tape. "Not a sound for half an hour. If I hear a peep out of you, you get a bullet in your head." The man nodded furiously, sweat beading his forehead.

Reznick took off his top and pulled on the brown UPS shirt (which was a bit tight, but would do) matching baseball cap. He picked up a parcel and the delivery clipboard. "Not a fucking word." He stepped out of the truck and carefully locked the door. Then once he had made sure that there was no one around, he walked on over to the elevator and punched in the button for the forty-second floor.

He stepped into the empty elevator. The door closed and less than twenty seconds later he was on the forty-second floor. He walked up to the glass doors in the outer lobby. On closer inspection, the black metal buzzer on the metallic silver keypad had the name Norton & Weiss Inc engraved in small writing.

Behind the huge glass doors, a small bespectacled young man wearing a suit looked up from his computer.

Reznick pressed the buzzer as he smiled through at the guy.

The kid inside got up from his chair and ambled across to the intercom. "I'm sorry, sir," he said. "Our firm doesn't accept visitors."

"It's a delivery from Washington. Urgent."

The man shook his head. "I'm not expecting any deliveries today."

"Look, I need a signature, man," Reznick said. "I've not got all day. Real urgent."

The kid bit his lower lip as if he was thinking it over.

"Look, I ain't got all day, pal. You wanna sign?"

The kid cracked open the door.

Reznick barged inside and pressed a gun to the startled young man's temple. "Be very quiet."

The kid stumbled backwards as the door clicked shut.

TWELVE

The outer office was mostly open-plan, a cool grey-blue interior, laptops and iPads on half a dozen desks. Reznick could see there were two other offices inside, their doors closed.

"Where's everyone else?"

"Please... I'm the only person in just now."

Reznick pushed him back into one of the wood-paneled inner offices. Legal tomes and journals lined along the walls.

"What do you want?"

Reznick pressed the gun to the man's head. "Tell me about your company."

"We're a law firm. What the hell is this?"

Reznick pulled back the slide of his Beretta. "Don't take me for a fool, son."

The kid flushed crimson. "I work the back office stuff. That's all I can say."

"What was Magruder doing here earlier?"

"I have no idea what you're talking about."

"Stop bullshitting me, son. If you want to do this the hard way, that's fine."

"Please, we're a law firm. There must be some terrible mistake."

Reznick slapped the man hard on the side of the face. Blood poured from his mouth, just like it had with Magruder. Then he pressed the gun to the man's head. "Now, if you don't tell me what you know, you'll be checking out of this world earlier than you thought."

"Please! Please!"

"I want some fucking answers. Do you understand?"

"Please, don't…" He composed himself. "Please believe me, I have nothing to do with this."

Reznick shook his head. "Wrong answer." He pressed the gun hard up against the kid's forehead.

"Christ almighty!"

"He's not going to help you. No one is. Now tell me what Magruder was doing here."

The kid began to whimper as he cowered. "I am… I am not what you're looking for."

"Why can't you answer a simple fucking question? Tell me about Magruder."

A long silence opened up before the kid spoke. "All I know is that he did a job for us. I don't get involved in that. Look at me. Do I look like I get involved in that end of things? I'm an analyst, OK?"

"So, what's this setup?"

"We are a private company. We receive commissions to do security consultancy for the government."

"Stop the bullshit. What do you really do?"

The kid closed his eyes. "We sub-contract web jobs, satisfied? I'm logistics."

"Who funds this operation?"

"I don't know anything about that. My boss does. He runs the show."

Reznick grabbed the kid by the throat, gun still to his head. "Where's your boss?"

The kid's eyes were screwed up tight with the pain. "He's out of town."

"I don't believe you."

The young man's eyes filled with tears as he shook his head.

Reznick pressed his face right up to the kid's and smelled the fear. It was as if it was seeping through his pores. "I just killed Magruder." The look on the kid's face was that of sheer terror. "Now I am not in the mood to discuss matters at length. I want answers. And I won't stop until I find my daughter. So, where is she?"

"I swear: I don't know anything about your daughter."

Reznick stared down at the kid. "Magruder said he was going to kill me. So, how was he going to carry this out?"

"All I know is that you were going to be directed to the Sunset Hotel."

"And then what?"

"Magruder was told to await instructions. You would then…"

"I would then what?"

"You would then receive a call saying to phone a cab. And Magruder would then be dispatched to pick you up before the official cab company and kill you. He was then to take the guy you have to the rendezvous point where they would be waiting."

"Where's the rendezvous point?"

"Not a clue."

Reznick kneeled down beside the young man. He lifted his gun and the kid recoiled. "Who's running this show?"

"Brewling. Mr Brewling."

"Does he work for the *Company*?"

The man shook his head. "Used to. A lot of contacts there."

"So, you sub-contract the dirty work?"

The man nodded.

"Will Brewling be at the rendezvous point?"

"I don't know. I just sit in this office all day. That's what I did at Langley. I never worked out in the field."

"Figures. Who does Brewling use, apart from Magruder? Any Miami crew involved?"

"Some Haitians. I think they're all FRAPH."

Reznick knew all about the feared paramilitary group, The Front for the Advancement and Progress in Haiti, set up in 1993 by the CIA. He was the operations chief for a Special Forces A-Detachment, which spearheaded Operation Restore Democracy in Haiti in 1994.

He saw first-hand what FRAPH were capable of. They broke into homes and tortured and killed their political enemies. Thousands were slaughtered. They left faceless bodies strewn in the back streets of slums. It was known as "facial scalping', in which a victim's face was peeled from ear-to-ear with a machete. In voodoo mythology, it was believed to be a way of torturing people in the afterlife, the mutilation denying them a proper burial.

Many of FRAPH were former members of the Tonton Macoutes, the infamous Duvalier gang, named after a child-snatching bogeyman from Haitian fairy tales.

Was that who had his daughter?

Reznick pressed his face up to the young man's. "How do you know for sure they were Haitians?"

"Look, that's what I know."

"You got a name for these Haitians?"

The man shook his head and said nothing.

"Tell me where they are."

"I think…"

"I don't want think or maybe, I want a precise location where they are."

The man closed his eyes. "Somewhere in Miami Beach."

Reznick stared out towards the outer office. At the desk where the young man had been sitting there was a Blackberry with a flashing red light. A recent message had been received. He went over to the desk and pulled the weeping kid with him. A trail of blood was left behind him.

He picked up the Blackberry and scrolled down. Nothing of any interest. But he was curious. So he scrolled through the applications and saw apps for Smart Wi-Fi, eOffice 4.6 and e-Mobile Contacts. Then he saw an app he didn't recognise or know anything about, Dexrex SMS.

"What the hell is this?"

He opened it up and saw it required a screen name and password.

The young man blinked away the tears as he stared at the Blackberry screen.

Reznick pressed his gun to the kid's head. "Screen name and password now, fucker!"

The kid began to shake. "Screen name is Lemonheart, password is Genesis. As in the Bible."

"As in the shitty rock band," Reznick spat.

Reznick pressed in the letters onto the tiny Qwerty keyboard. Then an extra security question was asked. "Childhood nickname."

"Please… I am not authorised to–"

"Childhood nickname!"

"Droop."

"Droop?"

The man flushed crimson. "I walked around with droopy drawers as a toddler."

"Jesus Christ. And you used to work for the CIA?" Reznick shook his head as he keyed in Droop. Suddenly a huge archive of de-encrypted instant messages, which had been sent from the Blackberry, was downloaded.

The last message sent caught his eye. It said:

Proceed to 5131 North Bay Road for safe delivery of cargo after pick-up.

Reznick showed the message to the man. "What's this address? I thought you said you didn't know."

The man stared at the screen for a couple of seconds. He scrunched up his face as if trying to remember what the address meant, before he clutched his bloody knee. Then he reached out underneath the nearest desk.

"What the fuck are you touching?" Reznick said, pulling the kid back.

Reznick crouched down and saw a silver switch, underneath the table. The little bastard had set off an alarm.

Suddenly, the kid was scrambling across the floor to his jacket slung over a chair and reached inside. He pulled out a pistol and turned to point it at Reznick.

Reznick was already one step ahead. He stared down at the kid and fired two shots into his chest. He watched, as if in slow motion, as the kid crashed to the floor. Blood oozed out of the dead kid's chest, through his shirt and seeped into the carpet. He stared long and hard at the dead young man. He'd given Reznick no choice.

His mind was in freefall. He committed the North Bay Road address to memory. Then he headed down the stairwell for three floors, rode the elevator to the first floor, and then raced down the stairs to the basement garage to get back to Luntz.

Heart pounding, he pushed through the basement door and froze.

A huge black security guard was pointing a gun straight at him. "Don't move, motherfucker!"

THIRTEEN

In the control room of the FBI in Miami, Assistant Director Martha Meyerstein was staring grim-faced at a bank of screens all showing real-time CCTV footage from the Brickell Avenue tower, as the drama unfolded. Standing at her side was the Special Agent in Charge of Miami, Sam Clayton. His arms were folded and sleeves rolled up.

Her team was on phones either chasing down leads or reaching out to other intelligence agencies. But it was clear that the ongoing police incident, which had thrown up red flags as it matched Reznick's description, was the breakthrough her team needed.

She recognised Reznick's features as he stood, hands on head, with an ill fitting brown UPS uniform. The middle-aged black security guard was speaking into the radio attached to his shirt, gun fixed on Reznick.

"We've got the fucker," Clayton said.

Meyerstein ignored the comment as Reznick was ordered to turn around to face the guard. He was now staring straight into the security camera. The dark circles around his eyes made it look like he hadn't slept in days. A heavy growth on his face, mouth turned down.

"What's the ETA?" she said, turning to look at Clayton.

"Approximately two minutes."

"You mind me asking why it's taking them so long?"

Clayton sighed. "Some hip-hop convention. Miami-Dade police have to help out Miami Beach police who are swamped with calls. Tens of thousands of them are flooding the city hogging the beach, Ocean Drive, Washington Avenue. But there are two cars already downtown, and should be there real quick."

Meyerstein stared at the screen as the guard wiped sweat from his brow. "I don't like it. And what's happened to Luntz?"

"Our guys are scouring the footage in the parking garage as we speak."

"Good. What about our two Fed teams?"

Clayton blew out his cheeks. "North Miami Beach to downtown. Ten minutes if they're lucky."

"They need to get a move on."

Meyerstein couldn't take her eyes off Reznick. He was staring into the camera and it felt as if he was staring straight at her. As if he knew she was there. She pushed the thought from her mind. "What about the guy Reznick killed inside this building? And what about his company, Norton & Weiss?"

"Don't know the identity of the kid who ran into Reznick. All we know is that Norton & Weiss Inc is a law firm, run by a former CIA guy, Brewling. He wasn't on our radar. We had him down as retired. Name ring a bell?"

"Brewling? Didn't he work under Buckley way back in the 1980s?"

"Was his sidekick in Beirut no less. Led the covert operation to free Buckley when he was kidnapped by Hezbollah. It was a fuck-up and, as you know, Buckley was killed. Brewling retreated back to Langley."

Meyerstein didn't take her eyes off the screens. "That figures. Does he live in Miami?"

"Just north. Very upscale area. Indian Creek Island. But he's not there."

"Well let's find him. We need to speak to him."

"We're working on it."

Meyerstein felt frustrated just watching pictures. "Why is there no sound? Can't we hook up to this guy's radio through his security company?"

"We're still trying. Shit, he's making his move."

Meyerstein watched as Reznick took a step forward. She knew what was coming. In an instant, Reznick grabbed the man's gun and used his left hand to redirect it away from his body, before he slammed his right fist hard into the guard's jaw. It was a Krava Maga move Meyerstein herself had been taught by the Israeli military. The guard was out cold.

"Oh Christ, what the hell?"

She watched as Reznick headed out of view. "Is it possible to get some other camera angles, people?"

A computer guy shouted across, "That's all we've got."

Her cell phone rang and she recognised O'Donoghue's caller display. "Damn, that's all I need."

Meyerstein hooked up with O'Donoghue who was taking charge of the emergency secure video teleconference from inside his huge office on the seventh floor at the FBI's HQ in Washington. She quickly brought him up to speed with developments down in Miami.

The FBI Director spoke first, "Martha, we have begun discussions with the President's National Security Staff, the Director of National Intelligence and the Department of Homeland Security, on this ongoing investigation. We are all very concerned that this is resolved ASAP. How did you let him get away?"

Meyerstein felt herself flush momentarily and took a few moments to compose herself. "With respect, sir, this is not an ordinary Joe. Jon Reznick is trained to cope with almost anything. Look, I don't think this is a time for pointing fingers. This is a very complex investigation."

"Miami is not a big city. Why can't we trace Reznick and in turn our scientist?"

"The signals are being jammed, pure and simple. We just cannot pinpoint where he is."

The bright red light on the phone on the conference table began flashing. "Bear with me a second, sir, I'll turn this on to speakers so we can all hear."

She pressed the speaker's button so O'Donoghue and everyone in the FBI's Miami conference room could hear. "Martha, we got something."

It was Kate Reynolds, a bright up and coming young FBI Special Agent in her late twenties – a political science graduate signed up at John Hopkins – who had been seconded to the Hoover building from the Kansas City field office and was now at the lab Luntz worked at. She reminded Meyerstein of herself at that age. Fresh, eager and not worn down by the pressures of the job. But Meyerstein also detected a toughness and no-nonsense approach which she could relate to.

Meyerstein said, "Kate, we're in the middle of a teleconference with Director O'Donoghue, just so you know."

Reynolds gave a nervous cough. "I'm working alongside the lab's senior management team. We're going through the records of everyone who's worked there in that lab, and we have three members of staff who have left in the last three years. Two have been accounted for, tracked down to new jobs. But there is one guy who worked with Luntz and who seems to have dropped off the radar."

Meyerstein said, "Kate, you got a name?"

"Lt Col Scott Caan, a US army scientist. Hasn't been seen in the last couple of weeks."

Meyerstein spoke first, facing the screens. "That's great work, Kate. OK, let's find out everything about him. Phone records, medical history, friends, coworkers, let's get into his life and see what we can find."

Special Agent Reynolds said, "Sure thing."

O'Donoghue was nodding, taking notes. "You lead on this, Martha. And no more excuses."

The screens from O'Donoghue's office went blank.

Meyerstein cleared her throat and turned to her team in the Miami conference room. "A guy disappears from a government lab. No word from him. Luntz contacts us and is under FBI protection before he is due to meet us about his concerns. There are red flags here. Agreed?"

Everyone nodded.

"Kate, are you still there?"

"Yes, ma'am."

"I'd like a full report in in hour. The bare bones will do. Get me a picture of Caan and send it now." Meyerstein turned again to her team. "As soon as the photo arrives, I want it run through face recognition software. I want it analyzed in-depth and then let's get Caan's picture to every field office in the country. He's out there somewhere."

The phone on the conference table rang. Meyerstein picked up and the caller display told her it was Roy Stamper.

"Martha, I've been following up a couple of leads with Miami Beach police," he said, loud traffic in the background. "We've got something real interesting."

"Where exactly are you, Roy?"

"A back street in South Beach. The body of a forty two year-old white male. Look's like he's just been water-boarded."

"You gotta be kidding me."

"Nope. Not exactly an everyday occurrence."

"You got a name of this guy?"

"We got a name and a direct connection to Reznick."

"I'm listening."

"The dead guy is called Chad Magruder. Ed has got back to me with confirmation that he was Special Activities Division.

Has a sister who lives out in Weston, nice town on the edge of the Everglades."

Meyerstein felt her stomach knot. "Tell me all you've got on this connection."

"You're gonna love this. Magruder and Reznick were in Iraq together. Black ops. But it doesn't end there."

Meyerstein glanced up at the screen as medics attended to the unconscious security guard at the Brickell Tower. "Yeah, I'm listening."

"Four hours ago, a suspicious death was called in from Fort Lauderdale."

"Go on."

"Local police found a dead guy on a boat. Guy named Leggett. Old Delta operator, just like Reznick. Best man at his wedding."

"Good work, Roy."

She ended the call and looked around at her team, relaying the news. "I don't believe in coincidences. It's obvious Reznick is the common thread. Two dead former Delta buddies of his. A dead young man who worked in Norton & Weiss. And a missing scientist. And let's not forget, one of our colleagues, Special Agent Connelly from Seattle, is also dead."

She detected a renewed sense of determination amongst her team. "We might've let Reznick slip through our fingers. But that's the first and last time it's gonna happen. I want to find both Reznick and Luntz. I want everyone on it. I want all agencies brought up to speed. And I want results, not excuses."

FOURTEEN

The first thing Reznick did after speeding away from the Brickell Tower was to dump the car in an underground garage. He hauled Luntz out of the trunk and moved him into the passenger seat of a dark blue Chevrolet Tahoe with blacked-out windows. Then he headed across the causeway to South Beach.

He glanced at Luntz who looked clammy and pale, clearly not well. Probably exhausted as well as traumatised. Tiredness was also beginning to cloud Reznick's head. His thoughts seemed to be slowing down. Even the amphetamines couldn't kill the creeping mental fatigue. But he knew he had to try and head across to 5131 North Bay Road.

Was his daughter being held there?

The cold reality was that she could be anywhere.

The satnav showed North Bay Road was on the north side of South Beach, overlooking Biscayne Bay.

"I feel unwell," Luntz said. "I feel a migraine coming on. I can't go on."

"Just hang in there."

Reznick groaned. He could see that driving around with Luntz was asking for trouble. Sooner or later a cop would pull them over. It was getting too risky having him around. The bottom line was that he needed to dump Luntz. Get him somewhere safe.

His mind raced realising he was clean out of ideas. He needed someone who knew the area. But who?

He racked his brains, desperately trying to think of ideas. The more he tried to conjure up an idea the more his mind clouded over.

Think, damn it, think.

He drove on for a couple of more blocks.

Think man.

Suddenly, out of nowhere, a name sprang into his head. Tiny. Ex-Delta operator, Tiny. That's right.

Reznick began to remember back to a telephone conversation he'd had with Leggett, a year or so earlier. He said he'd bumped into Tiny in a bar. Tiny was working the door. But what was the name of the bar? And where exactly? Had to be relatively close to Fort Lauderdale.

He took the cellphone from his jacket and punched in the number of Leggett's bar. A young woman answered.

"I need to speak to Ron Leggett right away," Reznick said.

"Who's this?"

"Just put him on. I'm a friend."

A few moments later Ron came on the line. "I'm sorry, things are–"

"Ron, don't hang up. I think your phone will be bugged, so I want you to go to someone in the bar and ask for their cell number. I'll call you back in ten seconds on that number."

"I don't understand."

"There's no time to explain. Just do it."

Leggett came on the line and gave Reznick a cell phone number. Then he hung up and Reznick punched in the number.

Leggett answered immediately. "What do you want?"

"The man who killed your father has been taken care of."

A long silence opened up as if the kid didn't know how to react. Was he in shock? "Are you sure?"

"Positive. Now listen. I need a little help. Your father mentioned to me that he visited and had bumped into an old friend. Big guy. We called him Tiny."

Ron sighed. "I know the guy. Met him once. I was with my dad. The guy was working the door."

Reznick said, "Which bar? Where?"

"South Beach. 14th Street."

"You sure?"

"Yes. I got it. Ibar. It's open twenty-one hours a day. Just off one of the main drags."

The line went dead.

That's all Reznick needed. It was nearby. He headed half a dozen blocks down Collins and turned left on Espanola, turned back onto 16th Street and then cruised down Washington Avenue and past The Playwright Irish Pub. A prowl car was parked outside a tattoo parlor, the cops drinking coffee, the window down, watching a group of five black guys fooling around with a couple of scantily-dressed Hispanic girls.

He doubled back down Washington again and pulled up at some lights. A crowd of young white girls, wearing short skirts and tight tops and impossibly high heels, swayed past. Then he took a right down 14th Street. Up ahead on the right, at the front of a queue of kids, a huge black doorman stood outside a dive bar. Reznick slowed and wound down the window. He looked across the street and saw the familiar diagonal scar on the guy's left cheek.

Charles "Tiny" Burns. It had been more than ten years since they'd worked together in Special Forces, but he recognised him immediately.

Reznick turned right and parked down an alley round the corner from the bar. He hustled Luntz out and threw him in the trunk again. Then he headed round the corner.

"Charles," Reznick said, "how the hell you doing?"

Tiny turned around and took a few moments to twig who it was. His face broke into a broad smile. "You gotta be kiddin' me? Jon, what the hell are you doing here?"

"You don't wanna know, believe me."

Tiny roared with laughter and gave Reznick a hug that nearly crushed the wind out of him. "Goddamn, man, you've no idea how good it is to see you."

Tiny gripped Reznick's hand tight. "Man, how the fucking hell are you?"

"Better for seeing you. Look, I've got a problem. And I need help. If you can do this, you need to leave right now."

Tiny shrugged and nodded. "Jon, what do you want?"

"Where do you live?"

"What?"

"Do you live here on the beach?"

"No, man, a former Delta operator, Bobby Sloan, you know him?" Reznick shook his head.

"Well, he loaned me his trailer. It's shit, but it's a home."

"Does anyone know where you live?"

"I don't have any family. Parents dead, no brothers or sisters, I keep myself to myself. I live from day to day. This job pays well. The owner of the bar, Mac, is a great guy. He gives me work whenever he can. But even he doesn't know where I live."

"Perfect. I need you to look after someone for me. I've got business here in Miami. But it has to be right now."

Tiny nodded but said nothing.

"I need someone I can trust. I need someone that I can trust, just like you trusted me. You remember Fallujah?"

"Every night I fall asleep I remember Fallujah."

"Who got you out of that hole?"

"You did."

"I'm calling in my favor. I'm not gonna sugarcoat it. I'll also give you one thousand dollars to look after this guy for twenty-four hours."

Tiny stared down at the ground for a few moments.

"Will you do it?"

He looked up and smiled. "Goddamn right I will. I'd do anything for you, man."

"Gimme your trailer plot and the address."

"Pitch 87, Del Raton trailer park, up the coast at Delray Beach."

Reznick pulled out a wad of cash from his back pocket and handed it over. Tiny didn't count it but merely put it in the side pocket of his jeans.

Reznick handed over the keys to the car he'd just stolen and they went around the corner. "Got a guy in the trunk. I want you to drive back home and look after him with your life."

Tiny slid into the driver's seat and fired up the engine. "Nice ride. Do you want my car just now?"

"I'll find my own."

Tiny clasped his hand firmly and pulled him close. "I always wanted to try and repay you, Jon. Guess what I'm trying to say is–"

Reznick's phone rang interrupting Tiny mid-sentence. He didn't recognise the caller display. "Yeah?"

"Mr Reznick," a woman's voice said, "this is the FBI. We need to talk."

Reznick said nothing. He knew the phone was unable to be traced because of the jamming equipment. But it was clear the Feds were starting to close in. It was the absolute last thing he needed.

"I am Assistant Director Martha Meyerstein. I am based in FBI headquarters in Washington, but I'm here in Miami. I need to know if you still have a government scientist."

"I don't know you."

"You do now. Now, I want to talk. But first I need to know if the scientist is alive and with you. Look, you must trust me."

"I don't trust people I don't know."

"I'm asking you to trust me. We have reason to believe that there is a serious plot underway, and you must return him into the custody of the FBI. This is a matter of national security. Do you understand?"

Reznick looked at Tiny who shrugged back. "I'm listening."

"Firstly, we would like confirmation that he is alive."

"Yeah, he's alive."

Meyerstein let out an audible sigh. "Can I call you Jon?"

Reznick said nothing.

"Jon, can I speak to the scientist?"

"Not possible."

"Jon, as an act of good faith, we would really appreciate it if you could let the scientist confirm that he is alive. That's all."

Reznick stifled a yawn.

"We just want to have him tell us his name, date of birth and his wife's name."

Reznick's gut instinct told him to end the call. But the two words – national security – bothered him. He had served his country over the years. And he was loyal to the flag.

He popped open the trunk and shoved the phone's mouthpiece beside Luntz. "FBI wants you to confirm your name, date of birth and wife's name. Go right ahead."

Luntz blurted out, "14th and Collins!"

Reznick yanked the phone from him and ended the call. "Not smart." He slammed the trunk shut. "Tiny, get this guy the fuck out of here. Take him to your place. Keep him safe and sound. I'll be in touch."

He turned and walked north down 14th Street and hailed a cab, eager to get as far away from the bar as possible. He knew the cops and Feds would be descending on the place. The cab driver was a young Brazilian woman who looked like a model.

"North Bay Road," he said, climbing into the back seat.

She nodded and sped off, headed west away from the crowds thronging the main drags of Washington Avenue and Ocean Drive, past fading pastel colored art deco apartment blocks. She didn't talk but glanced occasionally in the mirror. Then past Flamingo Park and onto Alton Road.

His cell rang.

"Don't hang up, Jon." It was the Fed woman again, Meyerstein.

Reznick said nothing.

"The longer this goes on, the harder it will be for me to try and help you. I want to try and help you find your daughter. We know about her. And we know what happened to her grandmother. I know that's what's driving you on this."

"Keep talking."

"Jon, I have scores of people working to try and track down Lauren."

"Don't bullshit me. You want Luntz."

"We want them both back safe and sound. Jon, you've got to trust me on this. It's the only way."

Reznick let out a long sigh.

"Jon, as I said before, national security is at stake. This is a very grave situation."

"What about my daughter?"

"We will find her, I promise. But we're dealing with a highly–"

Reznick ended the call. He knew they had either managed to track the cellphone or were close to pinpointing his location, despite the jamming. And he also knew that they would have swamped the area with cops, looking for suspicious vehicles, cars and people.

They drove on down Purdy Avenue beside the waterfront and then along 20th Street, which led to upper North Bay Road.

The huge palms, hedges and foliage nearly shrouded the huge mansions behind their high walls, along the narrow road. Past West 45th Street as the houses seemed to get bigger. He was half a dozen blocks from the house.

"Just drop me off here," Reznick said.

The driver pulled up and turned around. "Five dollars, please," she said, smiling broadly.

Reznick pulled out two one hundred dollar bills. "Gimme your phone and I'll give you two hundred dollars and this shiny new iPhone for your trouble."

The driver shrugged. "Yeah, whatever," she said, taking the money and the phone and handing her Sony cell phone over.

"If someone calls within the next hour, give them the number of your phone, can you do that?"

"You kidding me? For two hundred dollars? Absolutely."

She smiled as Reznick slammed the door shut. Then he watched her drive away, knowing he had bought himself some time, as the Feds tracked the phone in the cab.

FIFTEEN

With his gun tucked into the back of his waistband, concealed by his jacket, Reznick walked along North Bay Road on the shaded side of the street for a handful of blocks. He knew it wasn't ideal walking around in the affluent neighborhood knowing every cop in Miami Beach would be looking for him with a full ID and photo. He had to get out of sight. And quick.

A man walking an overweight golden Labrador and an elderly lycra-clad male jogger passed by, his sunglasses glistening, earbuds from his iPod leaking bass-heavy dance music.

Reznick didn't make eye contact knowing he needed to get out of sight as soon as possible. Eventually, up ahead, he saw a large white mansion behind high wrought iron gates. Cameras with a small red light strafed the gate and part of the perimeter wall and surrounding street. He crossed to the opposite sidewalk to stay away from the prying cameras.

He knew there would be infrared motion sensors in the grounds of such a house and alarmed doors and windows. He stood under a huge palm tree diagonally opposite from the house as a gold Lexus passed by.

Reznick felt the sweat run down his back as he rifled in his front pocket and pulled out a lighter-sized military electronic jammer. He switched it on to "lock". Within seconds the red lights on the surveillance cameras had gone off.

He had created a forty-meter dead zone disrupting three main bandwidths and all Bluetooth and Wi-Fi signals.

Reznick slid the device back into his pocket and waited for a few moments to make sure the coast was clear. Then he crossed the road and went down a small deserted lane at the side of the house, before taking out the suppressor and screwing it into the Berretta. When it was all clear he climbed over the wall and dropped down the other side onto a stone path.

He moved towards the house.

Out of nowhere two Dobermans bounded towards him. They flew at him, teeth bared, salivating, their black eyes locked on him.

Calmly, Reznick took out his silenced gun, aimed and fired. A couple of muffled shots and both dogs were dead. Blood spilled down their dark coats and seeped into the lush lawn.

He edged across the lawn towards the side of the house and found an unlocked door. Inside, the house was bathed in an ethereal orange light coming through floor to ceiling bay front windows.

He stood still, listening for any movement. Silence. But that didn't mean anything.

He moved forward, yard by yard, through the ground floor. He scanned each segment of the space. He had been trained to visually "pie-off" a room – a military term for slicing up a room into sectors of fire resembling the triangular pie slice shape. It applied to a clearing team with each man having his own point of domination. But one-man room clearing was a different animal altogether. And the risks were far greater, no backup. Room to room, gun in hand.

Slow is smooth, smooth is fast.

The terrible thought crossed his mind that he had the wrong house.

Reznick headed down a highly polished hallway, which led to a spiral staircase. Gun drawn, his senses all switched on, he slowly headed up the flight of stairs, one step at a time. Again he went from room to room until he came to a room whose door was shut. He made sure to stay clear of the "fatal funnel", directly in front of each door, to prevent being shot from behind the door. He also made sure he opened the door from the non-hinge side.

He reached out and softly turned the handle, pushing open the door.

Scattered on the wooden floor of the room were voodoo dolls, feathers and paraphernalia. A large photo on the wall showed a handsome young black man shaking the hands of what Reznick thought looked like Baby Doc Duvalier, the Haitian dictator.

This was the place. This had to be the place.

Reznick had seen enough. He went back into the hall and stood stock still, not breathing. He listened. But again he heard nothing.

He walked along the hallway, which led to another spiral staircase. The wooden stairs creaked as he climbed to the second floor. He continued to pie off the space. The landing curved around and led out until he was on the bayside of the house with several rooms, all the doors shut.

One at a time.

The first room was a huge bedroom, bed perfectly made up, modern art on the walls, beige and cream throughout. The second room was a smaller bedroom and was painted a cool blue. He stood outside the third room. Then he turned the handle and pushed open the door. It was a study, overlooking the bay. Dark woods, leather chair, dark brown walls and the smell of sandalwood.

Reznick approached the fourth door side-on, gun in the air. He sensed something. He stopped. His stomach knotted as he crouched down low. Then he peered under the crack at the bottom.

A creak inside and a shadow moved.

Reznick froze. He could hear the beating of his heart.

Suddenly, shots fired through the door, narrowly missing Reznick. He hit the floor and fired five muffled shots through the top half of the door. The sound of a body falling the other side.

Reznick kicked in the door, gun drawn. A stocky black guy lay on the ground. Blood seeped from his mouth and two bullet wounds – one in his chest and one in the throat. The man's eyes were open. But he was dead and gone. *Goddamn.*

He turned, exited the room and headed slowly down the hallway towards one final door. He waited a few seconds before he kicked it open and looked around. It was a huge bathroom, floor to ceiling frosted windows overlooking the bay. He stood still.

The sound of whimpering. Close by. It was coming from behind a door within the bathroom.

He gently pushed open the door. Cowering in the shower room beside a washbasin was a trembling black woman.

"Please don't hurt me!" she implored.

Reznick walked over to her and pressed the gun to her head. "Who the fuck are you?"

The woman was crying, shaking her head. "Please, don't hurt me."

"Where is my daughter?"

"I don't know anything. I'm just the maid."

"Stand up!"

Slowly she stood up, hands on her head. From the cheap navy nylon slacks and plain cotton top, Reznick could tell she was indeed the domestic help.

"Who was the guy I just shot?"

"Bertrand. He looks after the security of the house when Claude is away."

"Who is Claude?"

"Claude Merceron."

"Where is he?"

"I have no idea. They don't tell me anything. I just cook and–"

"Shut the fuck up."

Reznick grabbed her by the shirt. "Who else is in the house?"

"No one. It's just me, now."

Reznick frog marched her downstairs to the main lounge with bay front views. He saw a large black and white framed photograph of two late-middle aged men shaking hands. "Who are those guys in the picture?"

"Mr Merceron is on the right," she said.

Reznick studied the picture. He noticed the dark, cold eyes. "Who's the other guy?"

"That's the Haitian Consulate General."

"So, what is Merceron?"

"Sir, he is a diplomat within the Consulate in downtown Miami."

"Is this a recent picture?"

"Yes, quite recent."

"Where was it taken?"

"I don't know."

Reznick stared at the photo, the chubby face with the black eyes imprinted on his brain. "I think you know more than you're letting on. Where is my daughter?"

The woman averted her gaze. "I told you I don't know."

"You're lying!" Reznick pressed the gun to her head. "Where is my daughter?"

"Please, I have two young children. I'm on my own. They need me."

"So does my daughter. Tell me where the fuck she is or your children won't have a mom to look after them."

"Please…"

Reznick pressed the gun tight to her head.

The woman wept. "I'm telling the truth. I haven't seen your daughter. But I do know something was happening here the night before last. I was told to keep to my room. I came down to the kitchen to make myself a sandwich and fetch a glass of milk. And Bertrand was angry to see me. So was Mr Merceron."

"Why?"

"I think they'd been down in the basement."

"OK, now we're getting somewhere. Tell me about this basement."

"I never go down there. Only Bertrand and Mr Merceron."

"You never went down there at all?"

"Never."

"Show me this basement."

The woman led Reznick through to a huge modern kitchen and pointed to a pine dresser in the corner adorned with cookbooks and small china ornaments. "Underneath there," she said.

Reznick pushed the dresser aside and a few ornaments smashed to the ground. A sealed iron hatch like a manhole was revealed. There were two rectangular holes either side, which would open the cover. "Where the fuck are the keys?"

"Bertrand has them. I swear I don't know where they are."

Reznick pressed a gun to her head. "Tell me."

She pointed to the huge freezer.

Reznick rummaged inside and found two large keys in the third compartment down beside packets of frozen fish and frozen fries. "You weren't being entirely truthful were you?"

The woman bowed her head and began to say a prayer, tears rolling down her face. She made a sign of the cross. "I'm sorry."

"Yeah, so am I."

He crouched down beside the hatch and carefully placed both keys into the small rectangular slots. Then he turned them both anti-clockwise.

Reznick lifted the hatch with the keys still inside the slots, revealing ladders leading to a hidden basement. He pulled out a penlight and the narrow beam of light strafed the darkness. A cavernous concrete space. He ordered the maid down first. She protested, but he pushed her down the ladders. He followed her and directed the beam of light around the empty space. He saw a light switch and flicked it on.

The basement was bathed in a cold, silver light and supported by four large concrete pillars. Reznick looked around and his gaze was drawn to an open hatch just behind one of the huge pillars. He shone the penlight down into a sub-basement.

Reznick forced the maid to lead the way into the darkness as she mumbled a prayer under her breath. He placed the penlight between his teeth and climbed down and found himself in a dank and dimly lit dungeon that had to be below sea level. A sickly smell pervaded the air. A rat was gnawing something in the corner. The damned thing didn't move when he shone his penlight directly on it. He saw the rat was tearing at a bone.

Reznick shone the light around. Attached to the ceiling were dead chickens hanging from meat hooks and voodoo dolls. He turned and shone the light towards the far end of the room. He saw what looked like a small shrine. A voodoo shrine. Unlit candles, wooden carvings of men and the blood and bones of dead animals scattered around the cellar floor. At least he thought it was animal bones.

Beside the shrine was a heavy wooden chair bolted to the floor with iron wrist and ankle cuffs attached.

Reznick felt sick. He checked the rest of the cellar, but it was completely enclosed. He headed back up the stairs with the maid and then up the next flight through the hatch into the ground floor kitchen. He shut the hatch and breathed the fresh air.

Inside he felt a mixture of anger and emptiness threaten to engulf him. He thought of Lauren in such a sickening place and wanted to scream. Had she been kept here? Was that it?

"What the fuck is all that about?"

The woman shook her head. "That's not me. I believe in Christ. I am a Roman Catholic. I follow God."

"What about Bertrand and Claude Merceron, what about them?"

The woman closed her eyes. "Their beliefs come from rural Haiti. Spirits. Supernatural."

Reznick stared out of the kitchen window towards a sleek sixty-foot-plus sports yacht tied up on the jetty at the bottom of the garden. The stainless steel rims glistened in the sun. "Tell me about visitors to this house. Have you had any visitors? White people in the past week?"

The woman nodded.

"Tell me what you know."

"There was one white man. I don't know his name. He came here to speak to Mr Merceron. I made them dinner and that was that."

Reznick pressed the gun to her head. "What did he look like?"

"Grey hair. Dark suit. Very expensive. He wore shades and didn't take them off, which I thought was unusual. I didn't really see much of his face. Very thin."

"What about a young woman? Was there a young white woman in here in the last week?"

The woman made a sign of the cross and mumbled a prayer. "I don't know about any girl."

Reznick stared at the woman not knowing whether to believe her or not. "Why haven't you a cross if you're so religious?"

"Mr Merceron wouldn't allow it. He thought everyone was subordinate to Bondye, the voodoo God. He wouldn't hear of anything else."

"Where is Merceron? Is this where he lives?"

"Two or maybe three times a week."

"Has he got another place in Miami?"

"I know he used to stay in the Setai."

"I want to know where he is now!"

"I don't know. He doesn't use this place as often as he did. Maybe to chat things over with Bertrand."

Reznick pointed to the cruiser tied up outside. "Is that his boat?"

"Yes."

He grabbed the woman by the arm and frog marched her out of the huge glass French doors and down the wooden jetty. He stepped onto the teak deck with the maid, holding her arm, and went down into the galley.

Reznick looked around. A walnut-paneled stateroom with cream sofas, mahogany furniture, African art on the walls and a huge TV. A wraparound mini-bar at the far end, bottles of Chivas Regal, Johnnie Walker and Cristal Champagne on show. It had every mod con. He checked the guestrooms. But it was empty, no sign of Lauren.

Reznick and the maid got off the boat and headed back to the house. As they approached the kitchen door, the cab driver's cellphone burst into life, blasting out an R&B ringtone.

"Hello, Jon. You've been busy, haven't you?"

Reznick's blood ran cold. It was the guy who had Lauren. "Cut the bullshit, I want Lauren. I want to meet up."

"Just want to say how cute that cab driver was who dropped you off. She was a real honey. You wanna know what happened to her, Jon?"

Reznick's heart sank. He stared out over the dark blue waters of Biscayne Bay, the towering skyline of downtown Miami in the distance and wondered where the hell they had Lauren.

"Let's put it like this, the same thing will happen to your daughter if you don't bring us this scientist tonight."

He closed his eyes. "Where and when?"

The man sighed. "I really don't know if I can trust you any more."

"I said where and when?"

"I will call you an hour before the exchange with the place and a time."

"I want to speak to my daughter. How do I even know she's alive?"

The man began to laugh. "You don't, that's the thing."

Then the line went dead

SIXTEEN

The interstate traffic heading into Washington DC was down to a crawl, as Thomas Wesley thought of the lunch date he was about to crash. He felt nervous and wondered how his old friend, Congressman Lance Drake, would receive him.

Hadn't Lance made it clear during the phone conversation in the middle of the night what he thought of them meeting up? And perhaps more importantly, why would Lance want to be seen with a disgraced loser who had been sacked from his high ranking job at the NSA? Lance was on the up, after all. He was a "star of the future" in Republican circles.

Wesley's mind flashed back to their college years together. He knew Lance then as a wild college boy who knocked back Tequila shots, washed down with bottles of cold beer. But now, when he turned on Fox, Congressman Drake was riffing on guns, God and "old-fashioned values". It was strange. Whilst at Georgetown, Lance had never expressed right wing or even liberal sympathies. He was apolitical. He was more interested in getting loaded on booze and fooling around with "hot chicks".

Wesley on the other hand was known as the college nerd. He reveled in all things technology, wrote software code through the night and never skipped class. Occasionally he would be dragged along to an on-campus party with Lance and his drunken friends. But more often than not it was to

The Tombs - a *Ratskeller* at the main gates of the university - for pitchers of beer and buffalo wings to watch Hoya basketball games. He didn't mind, as Lance and his friends were in general pretty hilarious and fun to be around. But smoking weed and hanging out with crazy girls seven days a week didn't hold as much appeal for Wesley as it did for Lance. For Wesley, the only girl who interested him was the one who became his wife. Lance thought that was weird. But despite their differences, they rubbed along well together and became good friends.

He looked at the photo of his wife, which hung from the rearview mirror. Her black hair cut in a soft bob; her head back laughing at a friend's wedding in DC. She was truly beautiful when she smiled. She didn't want kids and wasn't in the least bit maternal. She wanted her career as a management consultant. He accepted that. But over the years, as he saw his friends change and start families, he realised he desperately *did* want to start a family. Children to hold and love and cherish. To bring into the world and show them all the great things.

His hands-free car phone rang and he snapped out of his reverie. The caller display showed it was his wife calling from work.

"Hey, honey," he said, "I was just thinking about you."

"Hope they were good thoughts."

"Gimme a break, will you?" he smiled.

"Sorry I missed you this morning, but I had to get out the door before six."

"Don't worry. I managed to pour the milk into my cheerios without spilling anything on that beloved hardwood kitchen floor."

She laughed. He loved her laugh. "Are you driving?" she asked.

"Yeah, I'm heading to Washington."

"I thought you were working a dayshift today."

"I'm taking a day off from the delights of Walmart. I need to speak to Lance in person."

A long silence opened up. His wife spoke first. "I thought he wasn't interested."

The tone of her voice told Wesley she was annoyed. "I'm just going to turn up and speak to him. Hopefully change his mind."

"Thomas, what has got into you? You can't do that."

"Why not?"

"Why not? Because he's a powerful Congressman now and not a buddy from the old days. Thomas, you're not in his world anymore."

"Honey, he needs to know exactly what I know. I don't know what else to do. I–"

"Why can't you just let it go?"

Then she hung up, leaving Wesley to wonder if this was really such a good plan after all.

The Beaux-Arts façade of the Old Ebbitt Grill – opposite the White House – let Thomas Wesley know that he had found the right place. A cherished memory flooded back. He had visited the bar once when he attended Georgetown University. It had been his first drink with the girl who would become his wife, and he had deliberately picked the place to impress her. They drank champagne and ate grilled filet mignon with mashed potatoes, sautéed spinach and red wine sauce. They sat and drank and laughed and talked about nothing in particular for hours all through the afternoon.

He walked through the revolving doors clutching his briefcase and looked around. It was all dark mahogany and velvet booths, brass and beveled glass, just as he remembered it.

"Good afternoon, sir," the maître d' asked. "Are you joining us for lunch?"

"I'm joining Congressman Lance Drake for lunch in the main dining room," Wesley lied. "Has he arrived?"

"Absolutely," he said, picking up a menu. "Follow me, sir."

Wesley followed the maître d' to the main dining room. It was all wooden cross beams, starched white tablecloths, antique gas lamps and an air of refined decadence. At the far end of the restaurant, Lance was sitting alone at a table, wearing a dark blue single-breasted suit, maroon silk tie, hair slicked back and talking too loudly into his cell. A half empty glass of white wine was on the table, a chilled bottle of Chablis in a silver ice bucket by the booth.

Wesley sat down opposite Lance as the maître d' gave a respectful nod and handed him the menu.

"The waiter will be over to take your order in a few minutes, sir."

"Very good," Wesley said, as the maître d' disappeared into the melee of the restaurant.

Lance stopped speaking in mid-sentence and shot him a dirty look. "I'm sorry to cut short this conversation, Frank, but an old friend of mine has just turned up right this moment. Do you mind awfully if we catch up later today, is that OK?" He waited for a few moments and then said, "Frank, great idea. I'll see you then." He ended the call and put down his cell phone beside the half-finished glass of white wine. Then he leaned forward and Wesley smelled the drink and smoke on his breath. "What in God's name do you think you're doing here? I thought I had made my position clear."

Wesley smiled. "Good to see you too, Lance."

"Who told you I'd be here? It sure as hell wouldn't be my staff."

"Your itinerary on your phone laid out what you're doing for the next three months."

"Have you hacked into my phone?"

Wesley sighed. "You weren't listening to me, so I knew I needed to speak to you face-to-face. So, here I am."

An awkward silence opened up before a waiter approached their table and asked to take their orders. Wesley asked for a bottle of mineral water with two glasses, while Lance told the waiter that they weren't quite ready to order lunch and to come back in ten minutes.

When the waiter was out of earshot, Lance leaned forward. "I've a good mind to report you for this. You'd never work again. You'd be banged up for fucking years."

"Lance, does Christine know about this lunch with one of your Harvard interns?"

Lance took a long sip of his wine and smiled. "Is that what this is about? You're blackmailing me?"

"Absolutely not. But I feel like I'm banging my head up against a brick wall time after time on this. This is too important."

The waiter returned with two glasses and a large bottle of Evian. He poured the water into the two glasses and gave a respectful nod, before he left them to it.

"Look, I'm not interested in what you've got to say. Have you got that?"

Wesley shifted in his seat and his foot knocked into something. He looked under the table and saw it was Lance's briefcase. He took a sip of cool water. "Lance, how long have I known you?"

Lance rolled his eyes. "Look, what does it matter how long I've known you?"

"It matters because you know that I do things right, and I always do the right thing. You wanna cut me some slack?"

"Look, I'm sorry what happened to you. Really I am. But I'm not the person who can help you with this. What it sounds like you've got is classified. We'd be breaking the law."

Wesley reached under the table and out of sight, pulled the tiny blue i-Pod shuffle with white earpieces out of his jacket pocket. Then he opened up the briefcase and dropped it in.

"What did you do there?" Lance asked, glancing under the table.

"Check your bag. There's an iPod. Listen to track one."

Lance shrugged. "You better take it out right now." His voice was barely a whisper. "Do you hear me? If I listened to what you have obtained, that would mean–"

"Take it, and I'll be out of your face. I promise."

Lance let out a long sigh and finished the rest of his glass of wine. "OK, let's for argument's sake say that I agree. What does it contain?"

"It lasts about three minutes. It's been cleaned up. Digitally remastered, if you like."

"Why me?"

Wesley leaned forward, hands on table. "You have the clout. Pure and simple. I've tried and I got nowhere. I don't know where else I can turn." He leaned closer, his voice a whisper. "I think once you know the identities of the people on the conversation, you will call in the specialists at the NSA or FBI to try and decode the covert message it contains. On the surface, the message is undetectable. Which points to a highly sophisticated operation. And I'm convinced we're talking about an attack on America."

"OK. Let's be clear on this. I'll listen to it. But I'm only doing this because what you're saying concerns me. I care passionately about this country."

"And I respect that, Lance."

"But I want to be clear that I can't guarantee anything. I will listen to this when I get back to my office, and then I'll call you."

Wesley finished the rest of the water. "That's all I wanted, Lance. I appreciate that."

The waiter returned and poured out more wine. Lance waited until the waiter had finished and was out of earshot. "Who else knows about this?"

"Me, you and an inspector general at the NSA."

He went quiet for a few moments before looking towards the revolving doors and giving a small wave to a stunningly attractive twenty-something blonde intern. Then he fixed his gaze on Wesley. "Leave this with me and I'll get back to you. But if anyone asks, I don't know anything about it, OK?"

Wesley knew when it was time to leave. He stood up and patted Lance on the shoulder like old friends do. "Appreciate that."

Then he walked past the young woman who flashed a pearly smile before he headed out of the revolving doors into the harsh glare of the early-afternoon sun, knowing his old friend wouldn't let him down.

SEVENTEEN

Dark thoughts were starting to crowd Reznick's mind. He drove south along Alton Road heading away from North Bay Road in a BMW 650i convertible he'd taken from Merceron's huge garage in a state of flux. He was no nearer finding out where his daughter was. He felt empty, almost bereft as his anxiety mounted as the minutes ticked down. He hadn't felt this sense of detachment since Elisabeth died.

The problems were myriad.

He didn't know if the people who were holding her, perhaps Merceron's men, would keep their promise to kill her if he didn't deliver Luntz. He had to assume they would. He wondered how long it would take them to find out that Reznick had visited Merceron's house. He figured not very long. He had tied up the maid to some piping, attached to the basement hatch. And she would talk. The woman, he knew, would be discovered sooner rather than later. But that was more than could be said for his daughter.

She was still being held. And he knew Merceron was the key. Was it associates of his that were holding her captive? Was he under the control of Brewling and Norton & Weiss?

Got to find that bastard.

Reznick knew he was running out of leads to pursue. He felt increasingly isolated and angry at the sequence of events. And to compound matters, he had dropped off Maddox's radar for forty-eight hours without checking in, as he fought what was fast turning into a personal war in south Florida.

He needed help. Any kind of help.

The more he thought of it the more he was inclined to believe that only Maddox could provide the logistical help he needed. He figured that going it alone had only got him so far. He knew Maddox would find a way to get to a man like Merceron. That's what he did. That's all he did.

Reznick thought about it for a few moments. It was weird. He had never met Maddox. His voice was all he knew. It was a slightly detached, educated drawl. Maybe Louisiana. Maybe Florida. But he trusted him with his life. *With his life*. He more than anyone knew what made Reznick tick. It was as if he intuitively knew what he needed at any particular moment.

They were bonded by a mutual trust. Maddox trusted Reznick to get the job done. He assumed he knew all about his time in Delta. Probably what got him the gig. His mind flashed to the first call he received from Maddox on his cellphone. He remembered he was walking the beach outside Rockland late one summer evening. After a long silence on the line, the man he had never met opened up with the words, "You don't know who I am, and you probably never will, but that's of no importance. I'd like to talk about opportunities I may have for a man like you."

The monotone delivery added to an unsettling effect. Reznick listened as Maddox went on to outline the critical job Reznick could do on *special* jobs. "Off-piste", as he described it. Stuff that wasn't "on the grid". He said he would be the point man. And everything would come through him. Then he gave Reznick twenty-four hours to think about it.

He mulled it over and considered his options. His life at that point was a mess. He was drinking way too much and was considering leaving Delta. But suddenly, a shadowy new world opened up to him. A world of false passports, false identities, fake IDs and synthetic suicides. A world of surveillance and shootings. The more he did the less he felt. He got a call, he did the job. No questions asked. And the money was great.

He worked it out that, on average, he had to wait six weeks for a job. In between he kept himself super-fit. He ran with rucksacks loaded down with stones, swam in the sea until he turned blue and kept himself in fighting shape. He read historical biographies, researched the American civil war and became fascinated by Gettysburg, but most of the time, he just sat and stared out to sea, thinking of the old days. He didn't sleep much, plagued by recurring nightmares. The one thing he looked forward to was keeping in touch with Lauren using FaceTime, a video calling software, which he used with his Mac-Book. It was reassuring to see her beautiful face, smiling back at him from the safety of her study bedroom at the school. It was only for a few minutes at a time, as he didn't want to intrude too much. He wanted to keep that distance. But sometimes, if he found himself at a loose end and with the dark moods returning, he more often than not headed into town where he drowned himself in whisky and beer, before walking back home alone. He usually drank alone. When he did bump into friends he once knew, it was awkward. They had become like strangers. Forced bonhomie. It was as if they sensed he wasn't all he said he was. As if they knew he wasn't opening up.

The sounds of loud hip-hop from a passing jazzed up pimp mobile snapped Reznick out of his reverie. He knew he had to make the call. He punched in Maddox's number from memory.

Maddox answered on the second ring. "Who is this?" He hadn't recognised the number.

"Who do you think?"

"Where the hell are you?"

"Miami."

"I don't believe this. I gave you a simple job. We now have five dead. The Feds are after you and the target is missing.

Reznick, I know what this is about. I heard about Lauren and her grandmother. I'm sorry, Reznick, for that. But you have a job to do. You need to bring in the target in the next hour. Do you understand?"

"That might be tricky, Maddox. And it's six dead. I just shot a guy half an hour ago."

"Reznick, we need to draw a line under the whole thing. Look, I'm glad you finally called. We can help you get Lauren. Make no mistake about that. But you need to bring in the target. We'll work this out."

Reznick said nothing.

"There's something you need to know about the guy you were supposed to take down."

"What about him?"

"Did some checking of my own. The IDF dog tag is bullshit. His name is not Luntz."

"What?"

"We've been played. All of us. Our communication was compromised, you were right on that. But there is no such person as Luntz. He doesn't exist. He played you. He played us."

Reznick's tired mind tried to keep up.

"This guy runs a private bank which deals exclusively with the rulers of Saudi Arabia. He has tried to conceal the financial trail for 9/11. He tried to cover the tracks of the hijackers. And that's why his number is up."

Reznick felt as if an oncoming truck had hit him. His mind flashed images of the falling towers and the dust cloud. Free fall speed. "He came up with a credible story. How did you get this information?"

"I've said enough."

He felt sick. How was this possible?

"We need to bring him in, Jon. There are other elements at work. We need closure on this today."

"I need to think of my daughter. How does she fit into this?"

"Reznick, as far as we can ascertain, they have your daughter somewhere in south Florida, I'm hearing near Key West, but they just want to get this guy back and get him out the country. Those on high in a foreign government are protecting him. We can't allow them to succeed, Reznick. We need to get rid of this guy."

Reznick pulled up at a red light, car idling. His mind was struggling to take it all in. He felt conflicted. He didn't know what to believe. "Key West?"

"Here's what I propose. Hand the scientist over, and I will negotiate with these guys, to get your daughter back."

"Look, I don't know what the hell has gone down here, Maddox, but I feel like I'm closing in on them."

"Reznick, you need to focus. You can't go out on a limb. You can't do this by yourself. Look, I've flown down to Miami. Do you know The Tides on Ocean Drive?"

"I've heard of it."

"Let's meet up and we can run through our options. You call the shots how you think we go about getting your daughter back. But you need backup, Reznick, don't you see that? You need logistics. One man can't do this alone."

Reznick was beset by doubts. He knew he was close. Merceron was the key. But the contradictory information Reznick had been dealt made him fear the worst for Lauren. He was bombing around Miami trying to get a lead. Now Maddox and his team seemed to have got Key West in their sights. Was it really possible that Luntz had pulled the wool over his eyes? Was Luntz really a shadowy banker who had concealed the 9/11 money trail? None of it made any sense.

"Reznick, are you still there?"

"Yeah."

"Thank God. I thought I'd lost you again. Right, first things first. Is the target somewhere safe?"

"Sure."

"Good. We're in business. Bring him to The Tides within the hour. He'll be taken care of. Then our priority will be Lauren."

His mind raced as he turned onto Washington Avenue and headed south. Deep down in his soul something about Maddox's story didn't make sense. It wasn't because the explanation he gave was complex. The fact was that it just didn't feel right. But what if his own reading of the situation was wrong and Maddox was indeed right. Where would that leave him? And to compound matters, he had information that pointed to Lauren being held in Key West.

The more he thought of it the more Reznick didn't know who to trust and what to believe.

He thought of his daughter. All he wanted was her back. He didn't know for sure if she was even alive. But if she was, she couldn't be used as a bargaining chip. She was first, last and everything to him. She was all he had.

"Reznick, are you still there, goddamit?"

He saw a sign for Cybr Caffee, an Internet café, dark green awnings partially shading the sidewalk. His mouth felt dry and his stomach growled. "Maddox, I need more time on this. I've got to think this through."

"Reznick, you're out of time."

"Perhaps. Look, I'll call you."

"Wait. You need–"

"Speak to you later, Maddox."

Reznick ended the call and drove around for a couple of minutes until he found a deserted alley, garbage bins overflowing from nearby restaurants and hotels. His mind flashed back to what Maddox had said. Was the guy Tiny had really a 9/11 financier and had he been duped? Doubts were still lingering and his nerve ends jangling. He needed to focus. He needed to get back in the game. He locked the car and headed back round to the café. It was all whitewashed walls, modernist black and chrome chairs and circular glass tables, three computers per table. The place was nearly empty, some electronic music playing low in the background.

He ordered a bottle of still water, a double espresso and a large toasted cheese and tomato sandwich. He handed the girl wearing a Motorhead T-shirt in the cafe a twenty-dollar bill and asked her to keep the change, which brought a smile to her face. Probably just earning some money to pay her way through college. He had such high hopes for his own daughter despite not going on to college himself. It was something he regretted. He felt like he had missed out on something. He was a big reader, just like his dad. He envisaged Lauren attending an Ivy League college. Despite only being eleven, she talked about Princeton, the same school as her mother.

He thought back to when Lauren was just a baby. Elisabeth holding her tight, leafing over tax papers whilst breastfeeding their daughter. Reznick popped out for some Chinese food. And they would eat. Then Lauren would fall fast asleep. And he'd carry her to the cot, lay her on her back and gaze down at his beautiful little girl, sleeping like an angel.

But all that seemed so very far away just now, embroiled in a race against time with some crazy kidnappers. It might already be too late for all he knew.

He snapped back to reality.

Reznick drank his bottle of water and wolfed down the sandwich. He picked up his espresso and headed over to a table with no other users and sat down, back to the wall. He logged onto the Internet and Googled the name Claude Merceron. It pulled up six hundred and thirty-two entries. He double clicked the top entry and it showed Merceron's short biography, alongside a picture.

He moved the cursor to the images of Merceron and double-clicked. Twenty-five separate images were pulled up.

Reznick scrolled through them. They showed Merceron sitting at his desk in the Haitian consulate in downtown Miami in front of the distinctive Haitian flag, two horizontal blue and red rectangles and the coat of arms in a white panel in the center.

Shit, the guy really was a diplomat. This meant diplomatic immunity. Untouchable.

Four pictures showed him handing over a one million dollar check raised from the Haitian community in Miami for the disaster relief appeal.

He studied his profile. He looked around mid-fifties, short cropped hair with a peppering of grey. Those black eyes again. He was physically imposing and was obviously well-nourished.

He exuded quiet authority, perhaps even menace.

He thought back to the basement in North Bay Road. The voodoo symbols. The blood and bones. The smell of rotting flesh.

Reznick clicked back to open up a few of the articles written about Merceron. He read about his charity work and business interests. Then blogs from Haitian exiles came up, speaking about the fundraising efforts for under privileged children in Little Haiti.

The more he read the more he wondered if he had the wrong guy. But Reznick knew that charity work didn't mean shit.

Thirty minutes later, as Reznick felt increasingly jaded staring at the computer screen, he came across an interesting article. It was a *Miami Herald* article about Merceron's vision for Haiti following the January 2010 earthquake. He was pictured sitting on a roof terrace.

Reznick scanned the tagline on the roof terrace photo that just said "Consulate General Claude Merceron's birthday party, March 7, 2010, in Florida". But no indication of the location.

He stared long and hard at the image and wondered if the party was held at the Consulate in Miami. Was that where he could be found? Then he remembered a high-tech device that could help him.

He searched for the website for specialist software and tried to down the program Opanda IExif, which would perhaps help him find the location. But he wasn't in luck. Almost immediately an error message came up on the screen saying *Incompatible Extension.*

His heart sank. "Goddamn," he said, before he even had time to keep his emotions in check.

"You got a problem, sir?" He turned and saw it was the girl who had served him coffee.

"It's OK, I'll figure it out."

Reznick could feel her looking over his shoulder.

"The firewalls and security measures on all our computers will stop any new installations. And that includes the exchangeable image file format reader."

"I appreciate your help, thanks."

Reznick turned and stared back at the error message on the screen.

"Why don't you just download it to your cell phone?"

He leaned back in his seat and turned again to face the young woman. "Unfortunately, my phone is used for work purposes, and has been configured in a certain way. I know for a fact it won't accept that."

She smiled and shrugged her bony shoulders. "That's too bad."

Reznick groaned and shook his head. "I'll figure it out. Do you mind if I have another espresso and some of that carrot cake?" He handed her a twenty-dollar bill. "Appreciate your help. Keep the change."

"Thanks. You mind me asking what you need that program for? Not gonna case some joint through geotagging, are you?"

Reznick showed his palms, as in mock surrender. "You got me. Am I that transparent?"

She laughed.

"No, actually, I'm wondering where a picture was taken. I'm a location scout. Just curious where it is."

"You kidding? You in films?"

Reznick nodded.

She flushed crimson. "Oh wow, how cool is that?" She handed him her iPhone. "Hey listen, you're in luck. Download the program to my phone if you want."

Reznick smiled graciously. "Very kind, thanks. Are you sure?"

"Go right ahead."

For a split second, Reznick felt bad for spinning such a line. But what she didn't know wouldn't hurt her. Besides, Merceron was hiding his daughter, he was sure of it. And all bets were off.

He downloaded the program. Then he Googled the name Claude Merceron again, moved the cursor icon toward the image tab and then clicked enter. Then he scrolled through the images until he got to the one with Merceron being interviewed on the roof terrace.

Reznick opened the image. His heart hiked up a notch. Please gimme a break, he thought. Almost immediately the GPS longitude and latitude references and the time stamp came up. Then he opened a tab that said "Locate Spot on Map by GPS".

A Google map appeared before him with a red dot at South Ocean Boulevard, Palm Beach. The tag read The Palm Beach Club.

Reznick kept his feelings in check. He didn't want to get ahead of himself. It didn't mean a goddamn thing if Merceron wasn't there. But he sensed he was getting closer. A lot closer.

The website showed a liveried door man wearing a dark blue suit with gold braid, smiling outside a sprawling five-story white-washed mansion, its marble entrance shrouded by palms. It was founded in 1959 and drew its clients from wealthy businessmen and political leaders who had "made Palm Beach their home', including Florida Senator Jimmy Labrecq and Governor Collins and a smattering of retired hedge fund head honchos from Manhattan. The website showed the dark mahogany interior, the forty thousand dollars per annum fees, the health club, the cigar bar, the roof terrace, the three restaurants and the butterfly-shaped swimming pool.

He added the club's main number to his cell phone.

The girl arrived with his espresso and carrot cake and Reznick finished it in seconds.

"Appreciate your help," he said again.

"You got everything you were looking for?" she asked.

"Absolutely."

Then he headed out of the café into the blinding afternoon sun.

Reznick knew that the temptation was to get into the car and drive at breakneck speed up to Palm Beach and storm into the club, trying to find Merceron or anyone who knew where he resided. But that wasn't the smart way. The smart way was the slow way. The considered way. He needed a way to get into the club.

He strode down Washington Avenue, along Collins, all the time gathering his thoughts, before he got back into the car.

Reznick fired up the car and pulled up the club's number on the phone.

"The Palm Beach Club" a man said, "how may I help?"

"Good afternoon. My name is Bill Crenshaw, the Governor asked me to give you a call. He's sponsoring my membership of the club next month. I've just bought a place down in Palm Beach, and he thought it would be a good idea for me to have a look around the club first."

"That's not a problem, Mr Crenshaw. I can arrange for you to meet with Mr Symington, our general manager tomorrow."

"That doesn't work. I've got a flight first thing tomorrow morning and I'm pressed for time, so it would have to be later this afternoon or this evening."

"Very good, sir. Please hold the line, Mr Crenshaw, and I will check to see if Mr Symington is free later."

A few moments of Bach before the man spoke.

"Sorry to keep you waiting, Mr Crenshaw. That's not a problem. The general manager has set aside his diary for this evening, if that's alright with you, sir."

"Excellent. I look forward to seeing what you have to offer."

Reznick gave the false name and personal details, before he ended the call. The shadows were lengthening as he drove off and headed along Collins. Up ahead he saw Barney's, an upscale clothes shop. He parked the car nearby and popped inside to the second floor up a staircase and bought a pair of shades, a dark blue linen jacket, new expensive faded jeans and a pair of burgundy loafers.

Then he went into a convenience store and bought himself some shaving gel, a razor, a comb, shower gel and booked himself into the nearby art deco Stardust Apartments further up Collins, using a false credit card. He showered and shaved, cleaning himself up. He stared at himself in the mirror. His grey-blue eyes always reminded him of Lauren's eyes. The same grey-blue.

Elisabeth often remarked on that.

You will find her, he thought.

Reznick put on his new clothes and stared at himself in the full-length mirror. He looked like a different person. Hair short and groomed. Smart clothes.

He knew chasing down the Merceron lead was a long shot. It was risky as hell. But he believed Merceron held the key to where his daughter was being held.

He headed downstairs and dropped off the key card for his room at reception and got back to the car, popped a couple of

Dexedrine washed down with a bottle of water, punched the details of the club into the satnav and drove back over the causeway into Miami.

The dark orange sun was low in the sky as Reznick headed north out of the city. He got onto I-95 and sped on, past sun-scarred housing projects on one side, country clubs on the other. The lights of oncoming cars dazzled his eyes as the sky darkened.

A sense of foreboding swept over him like he'd never felt before.

EIGHTEEN

It was dark and the air warm and muggy when Reznick drove across the Southern Boulevard causeway onto Palm Beach Island. He hung a left onto South Ocean Boulevard. Huge palms swayed in the breeze, manicured hedges shielding the Mediterranean-style villas and mansions of the rich and powerful. Rock stars, royalty and assorted wealthy émigrés, including a few Russian Oligarchs.

Reznick knew the area quite well having done a job there three years earlier, made to look like a heart attack, on a Saudi Prince – a minor royal – who was funneling millions of dollars each year via secret Swiss bank accounts to bottom feeders used by the Taliban. It was a rather crude job, a jab in the ass with the nib of a syringe inside a Mont Blanc pen filled with Sux, in the middle of a crowded champagne bar during a polo match. The Prince went down within seconds, clutching his chest. Within minutes, he was pronounced dead, but Reznick was already gone.

He cruised past the upscale Four Seasons and then a couple of hundred yards on he saw a sign for the Palm Beach Club.

He drove on for nearly a mile before he doubled back. Driving past he slowed down as he approached the main entrance.

Reznick scanned the locale as he pulled up opposite the entrance. The club was sandwiched between two sprawling mansions, divided by huge, manicured hedges, poles with surveillance cameras scanning the grounds.

He pulled out a pocket telescope and stared down the well lit, gravel driveway to the huge red sandstone building. Three young valets, wearing white shirts, gold waistcoats, black trousers and shiny black shoes, standing ready to park members' cars. A couple of honks from a car horn and a flash of lights from a passing car, no doubt angry at where he'd pulled up.

He slouched down low as he watched the valets goof around in the driveway. Two cameras strafed the entrance steps.

He checked his watch and saw it was 6.38pm. For the next fifteen minutes, a handful of expensive cars – a couple of Jaguars, a Porsche and a Rolls – turned into the driveway.

Reznick watched as the men got out their cars, helped by the valets – some dressed in conservative business suits, others in chinos, blazers and pink shirts, à la Ralph Lauren. Old and new money. Traditional and nouveau riche. All white. No women in sight.

He waited another five minutes. No new arrivals.

He pulled away and drove down the oceanfront road, before pulling a U-turn outside a huge property, then heading back towards the club. He turned into the driveway. The sound of gravel crunching underneath the wheels as Reznick drove towards the valets.

He pulled up outside the ornate entrance of the club and switched on the mini-jammer. *No hidden cameras or alarms would detect anything.*

A young valet with a floppy fringe walked around his car. Reznick wound down his window.

"Welcome to the Palm Beach Club, sir. Can I take your car, sir?"

"Look after it, son," he said, tossing the keys to the kid.

The kid grinned and jumped into the car as Reznick was escorted inside. A huge mahogany-paneled lobby opened up before him, black and white checked tile floor. Recessed lighting. Hanging on the walls were oil paintings of American presidents down the years that had been members of the club.

Reznick was greeted by the club concierge and asked to wait in the dark brown leather chair in the lobby while he fetched the general manager. It was all rich wood paneling, grandfather clock in the corner, hunting scenes and plaid patterned carpets. He picked up the New Yorker magazine sitting atop a pile on a glass table adjacent to him and he flicked through it, trying to appear calm, but inside burning with anger.

Was this Merceron's haunt? If so, would he be able to get an address? He was being consumed by dread, but he had to keep up the façade of calm sophistication.

The course of action he was taking could already have resulted in his daughter's death.

He checked his watch as the minutes ticked by, ignoring the relentless ticking of the grandfather clock. A full seven minutes after he had arrived, an effete man flounced over to him, hand outstretched. He wore a single-breasted well-cut dark suit, white shirt, pale yellow tie and shiny black Oxford shoes. "Mr Crenshaw," he said, shaking his hand. He had a surprisingly strong grip. "Patrick Symington, General Manager. Lovely to have you here tonight. How was your journey?"

"Not a problem. Always good to be back in Palm Beach."

"Indeed. Are we staying for dinner?"

"Sadly no. It'll have to be a super quick tour. I've got a late night meeting in Miami, before my flight first thing tomorrow."

"Very good, sir, if you follow me."

Symington led the way through the dark paneled hallways and into a drawing room overlooking the ocean, wine red seats all around. A couple of members turned round and smiled, nodding in his direction.

"What sort of line of work are you in, Mr Crenshaw, if you don't mind me asking?" Symington asked.

"Hedge fund management."

A smile crossed his lips. "We have an eclectic cross section of Florida's business community. A couple of ex-presidents are members, too, as well as numerous senators and congressmen. I'm sure you'll feel most at home."

Reznick nodded as he was taken to the first floor where there was a swimming pool and a gym. Then the second floor where there was a huge library, and a twenty-five-seat cinema. The third floor had private rooms and apartments for members staying over and a couple of bars. Then finally the fourth floor where he was taken to a bar.

"Are you sure we couldn't fix you at least a drink, sir?" Symington asked.

"Actually, I think I will. Scotch. Single malt, please."

Symington signaled a waiter over. "A single malt whisky for Mr Crenshaw."

Reznick and Symington made small talk about the balmy December weather for a couple of minutes until his drink arrived on a silver tray. He picked up the glass and took a sip of the whisky. The warm amber fired up his belly. "Very nice. Is that everything in the club?"

"We have a cigar bar, at the top, if you are interested, sir."

"That would be great. Can someone take my malt there and I'll have a Montecristo to go with that. Can't think of a better way to relax before my meeting later tonight."

"Absolutely, sir."

Symington called over the waiter to take his whisky upstairs and asked him to fetch a Montecristo cigar. He led Reznick up the stairs to the next level as the waiter followed.

"It attracts a terrific clientele. Of course your membership application along with the Governor's nomination should go through on the nod, probably in a matter of days."

Symington turned and smiled before he escorted Reznick through a dimly lit corridor and opened a door into the cigar bar. The sound of easy-listening piano music filled the air. "A very popular spot later on in the evening," he said.

A wraparound walnut bar. A barman holding a tumbler up to the light to check that it was clean. Dark brown sofas and a wine red carpet, more oil paintings of people he didn't recognise on the walls. A vague smell of cigar smoke, the humidifiers probably taking out the worst of the smell. "Very nice place you have here."

Symington then walked through the bar and down another corridor and out more doors onto the terrace.

Reznick recognised Merceron immediately. His heart began to beat a bit faster. He was sitting at a table on the open terrace with an imposing figure in a white suit. They were both smoking huge cigars, drinking brandy. A gentle breeze blew in from the ocean, rippling a few napkins, and carrying the sound of the waves crashing on the beach.

Symington led Reznick past Merceron and the other man to a seat on the opposite side of the terrace. The waiter placed the drink on the table.

Reznick sat down and stared out over the dark ocean. "This is a perfect spot for me to take twenty minutes out. Been a helluva day."

Symington made a small bow. "I'll bring you your cigar."

Reznick shook his head and smiled, picking up his glass. "Actually, I think I'll pass on the cigar and stick with the single malt, if that's OK."

Symington again gave a small nod. "Very well, sir. I'll be back to see you in twenty minutes." He turned on his heels and headed inside.

Reznick waited for a few moments before he knocked back the Scotch in one go. The warmth coursed through his veins. He looked over at Merceron and the other man, but they were deep in conversation. Then he turned around and looked into the bar. The barman was still busy polishing the glasses. He didn't think Merceron's table was in line of sight of sight, which was good news.

Apart from Reznick, Merceron and his friend, the terrace was empty.

He took off his jacket and put it on his lap. Then he assembled the Beretta and the suppressor, under the table, away from the prying eyes of Merceron and the man. Satisfied it was screwed in securely, he flicked off the safety lever with his thumb and pulled back the slide.

Reznick looked over towards the bar and could see the barman who was wiping down the surfaces and had switched on the Bloomberg channel. The grating voice of a Wall Street analyst got louder. He watched as the barman headed out of the bar and through the doors downstairs.

This was his chance. He had a minute or two, if that.

He concealed the gun under his jacket and got up from his chair and ambled over to Merceron's table and smiled. He looked at the man sitting with Merceron. His neck was thick, veins bulging. "Mr Merceron and I have some urgent business to attend to," he said.

The man looked at Merceron who in turn shook his head. He stared at Reznick long and hard. Then he broke into a broad grin, exposing excellent white teeth. "And what's it regarding?"

Merceron raised his eyebrows at the remark and also grinned at Reznick as if he was stupid.

"None of your goddamn business."

That wiped the smile off their faces.

The bodyguard stared sullenly up at him, a sneer on his face. "Who the hell are you?" He began to reach into an inside pocket.

Reznick smashed his fist hard into side of the man's neck, just below and slightly in front of the ear. The bodyguard's head lolled forward like a rag doll. He had been rendered unconscious by the brachial stun to the carotid artery. The man would be out of it for a good ten minutes, maybe more.

He stared down at Merceron who wasn't grinning anymore. He dragged heavily on his cigar as if he didn't care, but a slight tremor in his hand betrayed his fear.

Reznick pulled up a seat and sat down at ninety degree angle to Merceron, his back to the bar. He pointed the gun under the table. "Hands on the table."

Merceron said nothing. He crushed the cigar in an ashtray and expelled the rest of the cigar smoke through his nostrils. Then he sat with his hands on his lap.

Reznick pressed the gun to Merceron's crotch. "I said hands on the fucking table."

"I don't think we've met. And you are?"

Reznick leaned over and struck a quick rabbit punch to Merceron's windpipe. He winced and clutched his throat, struggling to breathe.

"You will do as I told you. Hands on the table."

Merceron's eyes filled with tears after the shock of the blow and he placed his hands on the table as instructed.

"Where is my daughter?"

Merceron swallowed hard and took a few breaths before he spoke. "Do you honestly think you can get away with this? In my club?"

Reznick stood up and picked up a white cotton napkin, stuffing it into Merceron's mouth. Then he pressed the gun to his shoulder and shot him once. The screams were muffled. "Now, tell me where my daughter is."

Merceron yanked the bloody napkin out of his salivating mouth and snarled through the blood, "You're gonna die, my friend. The voodoo gonna get you."

Reznick pressed the gun to Merceron's throat. He leaned in close. "I don't care much for that superstitious bullshit. In fact, I don't care much about anything. But I do care about my daughter. And I want her back. Now where is she?"

Merceron began to laugh uncontrollably, tears streaming down his face. Then he spat at Reznick.

Reznick wiped the spittle with the back of his hand and wiped it on his shirt.

"Go fuck yourself."

That was the final straw. Reznick kept the gun trained on Merceron as he pulled the tan leather belt from his chinos.

"What the fuck are you doing?" Merceron asked.

Reznick wrapped the belt tight around Merceron's neck. Tighter and tighter until Merceron looked as if his eyes were going to pop out of their sockets. The leather was biting deep into the thick folds of skin, and Merceron's mouth opened wide as his breathing became constricted. "I'll tell you what I'm going to do," he said, teeth clenched. "I'm going to squeeze the life out of you, you fat fuck, unless you tell me what I want to know. You wanna know what that feels like?"

Merceron was gasping for breath, shaking his head frantically.

He had found Merceron's tipping point.

Merceron rasped, "OK, enough! Please!"

"Where is she?"

"My wife's boat, your daughter is on the boat!"

"Name of the boat? And where is it?"

"The yacht is called *Pòtoprens*, as in the Haitian Creole pronunciation of Port au Prince."

"I need the coordinates."

"It's anchored one mile south of Key West."

So, Maddox was right.

Reznick loosened the belt from Merceron's neck as he struggled for breath, coughing and retching. He stared down at him for several moments wondering if he was telling the truth. The problem was that if Merceron was telling the truth, he could easily call up the yacht and get them to move. "I don't believe you."

Merceron closed his eyes and held his throat as blood continued to spill from his bleeding shoulder wound. "I'm telling the truth."

"Who asked you to do this?"

"It was a favor."

"A favor for whom?"

"A guy. He works for the government."

"Name?"

"I can't give you his name. I've never met him. I do work for him. I do contracts."

The sweat was running down Merceron's brow and perspiring around jowly cheeks. He eyed the gun with bloodshot eyes. "Your daughter is on the yacht."

Reznick pressed the gun to his head. "How do I know that?"

"Check my iPhone. Open up the marine traffic application. It gives the co-ordinates of the yacht."

Reznick picked up the iPhone from the table and doubled clicked on the marine traffic app. It showed a map of the Keys and the real-time GPS coordinates of the yacht, *Pòtoprens*, with a red arrow, along with the speed and course it was taking.

"That's where she is. On my mother's life, I swear."

A beat. "I believe you."

Reznick stared down into Merceron's terrified dark eyes. He wanted him to feel what it was like. He wanted him to suffer. He felt a rage build deep within him. Then he pressed the end of the suppressor to his head and squeezed the trigger. A muffled "phutt" sound and brains and blood splattered all over the white starched tablecloth and napkins and glasses.

His adrenaline was pumping. Senses switched to the max. Seconds ticking by. He needed to clean up.

He hauled Merceron's body feet first through the empty terrace to behind the bar and left a trail of blood dripping onto the hardwood floor. He saw an open trap door, with beer lines leading down to a cellar full of kegs. And he shoved Merceron's hulking body head first down there, crashing into bottles and metal kegs. The same procedure for the bodyguard, spraying some anaesthetic spray in the guy's ear first, ensuring he'd be out of it for hours. Finally, he wiped down the floor and all surfaces with the bloody white tablecloth and the barman's wet rag which he dropped down into the cellar with the two bodies, before locking the hatch and putting the key in his pocket.

Jesus H Christ.

The barman still hadn't returned. If he was lucky, it would be hours before they were discovered. He needed to disappear.

He washed his hands behind the bar, put on his jacket, took Merceron's phone and headed through the cigar bar and headed down the stairs all the way to the huge lobby and out the doors where he picked up the keys from the valet, tipped fifty dollars and sped off in the stolen BMW.

Then he headed south out into the night, leaving the lights of Palm Beach in his rearview mirror. He drove hard down I-95. His mind was on fire. He had to get to Lauren. But as he got south of Miami, he realised the traffic was getting slower and slower.

Eventually it stopped moving. Traffic was gridlocked.

He wound down his window and looked across at a guy with his arm dangling out of his pick-up truck in the next lane. "What's the problem?"

The guy just shrugged. "Four car accident, apparently, buddy. Some kids racing each other."

Reznick closed his eyes, as the engines around him revved in the sultry evening air, hoping and praying his daughter was still alive.

NINETEEN

It was 2am and the wailing from a passing ambulance, coupled with the incessant drone of traffic noise in lower Manhattan, was starting to bug Lt Col Scott Caan. He stared down through the wooden blind slats in his third floor apartment in Tribeca to the icy cobbled street below. A boisterous group of young women wearing Santa hats, high heels and tinsel around their necks were hailing a yellow cab. One pulled up and they all piled in, laughing and screaming obscenities.

He hadn't ventured out of the rehabbed industrial building on the corner of Duane and Greenwich, since he'd arrived in New York. Within walking distance were trendy bars like the Knitting Factory and the fashionable Japanese restaurant Nobu and Mr Chow's on nearby Hudson Street. But the hustle and bustle wasn't for him.

His father, by contrast, had loved that. He remembered when his father headed into town to show a new selection of cartoons either to the *New Yorker* or the *Times*, he sometimes took along Caan, the youngest, for the ride. He remembered being fussed over by staff at the *New York Times*. His father was feted and swapped political anecdotes and stories with journalists and senior editors alike. It was the Nineties and Clinton was the man in charge. And for his father, it was like manna from heaven. How could you go wrong? His father rubbed up some of the numerous liberals on the paper with his close-to-the-bone drawings, showing Clinton as having no restraint or moral compass. But anything – left or right – was fair game for his father. Caan liked that about his dad. He didn't mind kicking the great and the good, but only if their actions or lofty position deserved it and needed to be deflated.

He felt slightly envious of how very much at home his father had been amongst the metropolitan elites. The world of lunches, networking, dazzling conversation. He would have liked to be a conversationalist, hogging the limelight at dinner parties. But that wasn't really him.

He preferred his own company. His sister and two brothers all lived on the West Coast, but they didn't see each other apart from Thanksgiving when they all met up at his sister's house in the Hollywood Hills where she was a music producer. He felt suffocated in their company. He couldn't be himself. Their material lives and that of their pampered children were of no consequence or interest.

Caan stared down at the street and sighed. He wanted to escape the apartment. He wanted to breathe the air. He missed his daily runs and walks. But he knew he was under strict instructions not to leave the apartment.

So he just stayed put, blinds down, doing hundreds of push-ups and sit-ups, waiting for the call. The apartment was all whitewashed walls, huge modern art paintings including a Warhol print that he abhorred, hardwood floors, high ceilings, all mod cons. But he was starting to get cabin fever.

He felt claustrophobic. He needed air. But *they* didn't want him to jeopardise anything at this stage. He understood the rationale and the need to maintain discipline.

He had time to kill for the first time. He occasionally turned on the TV and he found that he rather liked Fox News. It wasn't that it was fair and balanced. Clearly it wasn't. But it was compulsive TV. He missed Glenn Beck on Fox, looking teary-eyed as he talked of freedom and liberty and the Constitution.

Time dragged.

When he tried to read a book, he found he couldn't concentrate, so focused was he on the task at hand.

He had gone over the plan a thousand times in his head. He'd memorised the blueprints of the building and could probably give a tour blindfolded, if he had to. He was in no doubt. He was ready to give America its wake-up call.

His cell rang and his heart skipped a beat. Could this be it? At this hour? He picked up the cell from the coffee table and pressed the green phone icon.

"The time has come, my friend," a man said. "We have every confidence in you. *The job is yours if you want it.*"

The code words had been spoken.

Caan felt numb as if in a trance. He ended the call and stood and stared at the phone for a few moments, stunned. He quickly got himself together. He slipped the cell phone into his front shirt pocket and went over to the kitchen drawer where he pulled out an electronic screwdriver.

This was it. This was what he had waited so long for.

At the far end of the room, beside the bookcase, he bent down beside what looked like an air vent, six inches off the floor. He unscrewed the metal grill, which had covered the false air vent. Then he reached inside and pulled out the toolbox he had hidden inside when he had arrived. He carefully placed the toolbox on the coffee table. Then he went to the bedroom closet and took out the suit holder, which contained the blue maintenance uniform. He laid out the uniform on the bed and went back into the closet for the boots and overcoat.

Everything was ready for this moment.

He took off his shirt and pants and laid them neatly on a chair. Then he put on his uniform, laced up the black safety boots, put on the thick dark overcoat, dropping his cell phone into one of the pockets.

Caan looked at his reflection in the mirror and smiled. He was ready.

You're going to make history, he thought.

He took a deep breath before he headed into the living room, picked up the toolbox and walked out of his apartment, carefully locking the door. Then he headed down the three flights of stairs and through the building's lobby doors and out into the sub-zero streets. He sucked in the cold air, his warm breath visible in the early morning chill. It was good to breathe fresh air again.

He shivered as he headed across a striped crosswalk and past Puffy's Tavern, which was still open. Down Hudson Street and in the direction of the Civic Center, east of Tribeca. A doorman was hosing down a sidewalk outside a smart brick building with warm water, steam rising off the frozen street.

He did a zigzag route as he'd been instructed, past suited porters outside glass fronted apartment blocks, then past a wine shop, then opposite the Tribeca Performing Arts Center, and past Washington Market Park where he got a whiff of hash in the air. He looked through the darkness and saw a handful of kids smoking pot inside the park's gazebo.

Then he headed east along Duane Street and within a few minutes, he saw the forty-plus story structure of the Jacob K Javits Federal Office Building. It housed twenty federal government agencies where thousands of employees worked in the heavily guarded building.

But it also housed the New York City district field office of the US Citizenship and Immigration Services. He knew that in a few hours' time there would be a long line of immigrants already lining up along Worth Street, ready to go through the security checkpoint and enter the building.

Caan walked across Foley Square on the Broadway side of the building, towards the lights from the large ground floor windows, and knew security would be watching his every move on CCTV monitors and through the cable net curtains. The Federal Protective Service relied on low-wage contract personnel to provide security at federal buildings across America.

This was no different.

And it was a major weakness.

He had read the 2009 Government Accountability Officer report. It had cited frequent security lapses in incidents across the country, including investigators carrying weapons into key federal installations.

It was a no-brainer to pick such an installation.

His throat felt dry as he went through the glass doors to the airport-style security screening area. The lobby was high ceilinged, glass and very modern; bright glare from the intense lighting. Roped off areas to process the thousands of visitors every day.

The night security detail was as he'd been told. Four white guards, three of them morbidly obese. One was sitting monitoring an x-ray machine, one with an electronic wand and two others watching proceedings.

Caan stepped forward and swiped his fake plastic ID through a reader and a gate opened. A guard chewing gum checked his photo.

"Step right the way through, sir," he said.

Caan walked through the metal detector to the other side as his toolbox was put through the x-ray machine. No beeps. Then a supervisor stepped forward and ran an electronic wand across his body. Still no beeps.

"He's clean," the man said.

The toolbox was being opened up on a large table and a guard rummaging inside motioned him across.

Caan felt a knot of tension in his stomach.

"Can you explain to us what's inside, sir? It's showing five separate metal containers."

"Not a problem. I'm air conditioning maintenance." He picked up the aerosol container. "This is a bubble up leak detector. We spray this stuff onto refrigeration pipes to test for any leaks. Pain in the ass, but gets the job done."

The guard lifted up an electronic device from the toolbox. "And what's this?"

"Diagnostic equipment for temperature and air leakage."

The guard turned and checked a computer screen. "It says here on the call-out log you're doing five bits of maintenance."

Caan handed over the faked paperwork he had been given. "Old buildings always have these goddamn problems. Never a dull moment."

The guard nodded and looked at his superior who waved Caan through.

Caan nodded and smiled. "See you guys later."

The men nodded, expressionless.

Caan walked across to the elevators and headed down to the basement. He knew from the blueprints where he was going. He stepped off the elevator and headed down a long corridor, harsh artificial light illuminating the way, his footsteps echoing on the tile floor until he got to Maintenance Room 3. He swiped his card and went inside. Lockers and cupboards and the smell of diesel and disinfectant. He took off his coat, hanging it in an unlocked locker, and picked up a set of metal ladders from a cupboard. Then he took the ladders and toolbox and headed up on the service elevator to the twenty-third floor.

His heart was racing hard. So far, so good.

He watched the elevator climb. He counted off the numbers. Eventually a loud ping noise and the elevator opened. He got out and headed along a deserted corridor and opened out the ladder at the first designated location. He pulled a power screwdriver from the toolbox and climbed up two steps and opened up an air con grill. Then he got his toolbox and climbed up four more steps - his head inside the air vent – and took out one of the five aerosol cans, which looked like leak detection sprays, but were in fact primed to detonate their contents by radio signal.

He felt the cold metal on his warm, clammy hands, and smiled. Then he reached up and carefully attached the aerosol can to the roof of the air vent. The metal stuck to metal, first time.

Satisfied it was firmly in place, he carefully replaced the air con grill, climbed down the ladders, picked them up and walked down to the seventh floor. Over the next three hours, he did exactly the same on the seventh, tenth, twelfth and fifteenth floors.

When he finished, he took the service elevator back down to the basement and put the ladders back in place. He put on his overcoat and picked up the near-empty toolbox, before he headed for the exit.

"You all done, chief?" a guard asked.

"It's all sorted. Have a good night."

Then he walked around the corner and hailed a cab.

"Where to, buddy?" the driver asked, as he climbed in the back.

"Penn Station. And make it quick."

The maze of corridors inside Penn Station, the artificial light from the low ceilings, the throng of early morning commuters, the smell of cheap junk food, coffee, piss and crazy-eyed panhandlers straight out of a psychiatric unit shouting about God and Heaven and Hell, were making Scott Caan feel nauseous. He remembered the first time he rode on a train and arrived in New York. The sense of chaos and noise assaulted his senses.

As he rode a packed escalator up towards the Amtrak concourse, his nerve ends were twitching, scanning the huge arrivals/departures boards at the top. He saw that he had twenty minutes to board the 6.30am Acela Express to Washington DC, which was departing from the West Gate on the left.

Caan had been through the station numerous times before. It was a shithole and an embarrassment to the nation, tourists standing agog at the filth as the Long Island and New Jersey commuters flooded down the escalators after their early morning trains pulled in.

It was a relief to get to the Acela lounge for First Class passengers.

Caan saw for the first time the man who was shadowing him. He was clean-shaven, wore a dark blue fleece, dark blue jeans, Timberlands and was carrying a black Adidas sports holdall. He fitted the description perfectly. The man didn't make eye contact. He bent down to tie his shoes. *The sign.* Then he followed him into the empty bathroom.

The man placed the bag at his feet as he peed. Caan went over and picked up the bag and locked himself in a stall. He unzipped the bag and put on the fresh set of clothes that were inside. Then he left the toolbox in the stall for the man to dispose of, along with the discarded maintenance clothes.

Caan got a seat in the lounge and settled into a comfortable seat to read his *New York Times* with his complimentary latte and blueberry muffin. He had just over ten minutes before he had to board the train to Washington. A short while later came an announcement that his train was boarding and he followed a red cap and the other passengers to the train. He stepped on board and entered the first class compartment. The décor was all silvers and greys. He found his allocated blue leather seat and sat down, letting out an audible sigh.

He watched as his shadow took a seat four rows in front of him. The man didn't make eye contact. That was fine. That had been explained to Caan.

As the train headed out of the city – still cloaked in darkness – towards Newark, Caan was given a complimentary latte, his second of the morning.

He gazed out into the darkness as the train picked up speed. He had dreamed of this journey for the last twenty-four months since the planning started. He couldn't believe how well the New York side of the operation had gone. The mission could already be described as a success. What was to come would be the icing on the cake.

All the years he had lived a lie. He had concealed his true feelings about America. But now his wildest dreams were on the brink of coming true.

TWENTY

The first pink rays of the early morning sun could be seen on the horizon, as the traffic finally got moving. Reznick was headed south out of Miami towards Key West. Throughout the night all he could do was sit in stationary traffic after the horrific multiple-lane pile-up. The long hours were filled trying not to think of his daughter. He channel hopped from talk radio station to talk radio station.

They blasted out everything from Bible sermons to the dangers of big government. But all he could think about was Lauren. His little girl.

He pictured her lying gagged and bound, drugged, at the mercy of some Haitian crazies.

He felt a volcanic anger brewing within him, ready to devour him at any moment.

Reznick looked at his satnav which told him it was a one hundred and thirteen mile drive on Highway 1 from Miami to Key West. It would take the best part of four hours. And he would have to stick to fifty most of the way.

He pressed on south as the dawn broke finally on the sun-bleached road.

The blue-green Atlantic was on his left, the Gulf on his right. He kept an eye on his speed so as not to attract attention. His gut reaction was to hit the gas pedal and get out to the yacht Lauren was being kept on. But that was not

187

the way he was going to do it. He was too close now to blow it.

Reznick's mind drifted back to Lauren. He remembered the day she was born, nearly a year to the day after they married, and the way his wife held her so close. When it was his turn to hold her, he stared down into her soft pink face and she smiled back, blue eyes sparkling. The feel of her silky hair. The way she held his hand. He felt lighter that day. He felt something inside like he'd never felt before. A sense of calm. And of love.

But what if she had been killed? What if she was being tortured at that moment? What if…?

"Fuck!" he shouted to himself.

Reznick resisted the urge to put the foot on the gas. He passed through Key Largo and saw a small green mile marker sign indicating 102.5, the number of miles to the southernmost part of the Keys. He drove on ignoring the kitschy gift shops selling seashell necklaces, burger stands, dive shops, bait shacks and headed towards Islamorada.

The traffic seemed to slow with a slew of camper, rental convertibles and pickups hauling fishing boats, heading south.

Overhead pelicans swooped and then dived into the turquoise waters.

His mind flashed back to an old Special Forces friend, Frank Clements, who had sported a huge tattoo of a pelican on his back. The guy was a real family man who had four kids and was nuts on diving. He raved about the sports fishing on the Keys, although he also bemoaned the crappy restaurants and entertainment bars, which were springing up everywhere. When Reznick once asked out of curiosity why he'd got a pelican tattoo, Frank told him that in medieval Europe, the pelican was thought to be particularly attentive to her young, to the point of providing her own blood when no other food was available. The story always stuck with

Reznick. He would do the same. He would gladly give up his own blood for his daughter. He would die for her. He would kill for her.

Reznick drove on. The sky seemed bigger and the hamlets smaller. He passed roadside stops with sandy beaches and long shallows. Then it was past Little Duck Key, a couple of locals fishing from a bridge. The sky became a deep blue, not a cloud in the sky. He felt drowsy, losing track of time, not having slept properly in two or three days.

He cracked open the window and felt the warm breeze from the Gulf waters. It reminded him of Elisabeth, before Lauren was born, when he was on R&R from Somalia. They decided to catch a flight down from New York to Miami and then drive down to Key West for a few days. They stayed at the Hyatt-Sunset Harbor, which was close to Sloppy Joe's, where they kicked back most evenings. They walked the beaches, and he felt himself unwind from the flashbacks of atrocities he'd witnessed. They dived together. Elisabeth tanned easily and in her faded denim shorts and white vest, with her long legs and toned arms, she looked great.

It was hard to believe she'd been gone more than a decade. After a time he didn't feel anything.

He sometimes wondered how he hadn't gone under. Perhaps it was something to do with his Delta training. The desensitisation to trauma. The psychological profile that detaches at will. But then again, maybe it was because he was damaged. Maybe he didn't realise how far gone he was.

A loud blast of a car horn snapped him out of his reverie.

Reznick looked in his rearview mirror and saw a dark blue Lincoln tailgating him, desperate to overtake. Further back, he noticed a black Suburban. There were no other cars following. He let the Lincoln pass him as the driver shook his head.

Up ahead, Reznick saw a sign for an outdoor seafood restaurant, Mangrove Mama's, and decided to pull over, feeling empty inside. He parked the car and picked an outdoor table with a great view over the water.

He felt empty and realised he was famished. He ordered conch fritters followed by a crab sandwich, washed down by a large glass of Coke. The same kind of food his father liked. Afterwards, in the bathroom, he popped two Dexedrine, splashed cold water on his face, and was ready for anything.

He walked back to the car and turned the radio onto a rock station as he began the final leg of the journey.

Fifteen minutes later, he glanced again in his mirror and saw the same black Suburban as before. Same plates. Had they stopped in Sugarloaf Key when he did?

Reznick drove on. He looked again in his mirror. The black Suburban had dropped further back in traffic that was now building up as he approached Key West.

He drove down North Roosevelt Boulevard on his way into the historic "old town', shrouded in tropical foliage and bone-dry palms. The pastel painted bungalows, wooden-framed mansions, the peaked metal roofs, louvered shutters, covered porches and wood lattice screens. The feel of Key West was always something that appealed to him. And it held such precious memories for him. Moments of peace.

Reznick followed the P signs for a parking garage at the corner of Grinnell and Caroline. He drove to the upper level where he parked the car and switched off the engine. Then he got out, popped open the trunk and lifted out a small rucksack containing all his "work" gear. A couple of pistols, scope rifle, an electric stun gun and a selection of knives.

Reznick strapped on his rucksack, locked the car and strode towards the sign for the stairs. Out of the corner of his eye he saw a black car edge towards him. He stole a quick glance and saw the same black Suburban again.

Keep on walking.

He sensed the car was slowing behind him. It pulled up and the car door opened and then slammed shut. Reznick reached inside his belt for his gun.

"You're a long way from home, Jon," a woman's voice said.

Reznick stopped in his tracks. He was surprised to hear a female voice. He turned around and saw a strikingly attractive woman in her late thirties, wavy dark hair, standing beside the Suburban. She wore a dark blue suit, pale pink blouse underneath.

"I think you got the wrong guy, sorry," he said.

Reznick turned to walk away.

"We can help each other, Jon."

Reznick turned around again and moved towards her. Immediately, four dark suited guys stepped out of the Suburban in a casual manner and stared at him. He stared back at each one before he turned to the woman. "Look, you must've got me mixed up with some other guy, I get that a lot."

The woman stood her ground, before she took a few steps towards him until they were standing face-to-face. She was a few inches shorter than him. Her eyes were cobalt blue and her makeup was subtle and soft. "FBI, Jon. I'm Assistant Director Martha Meyerstein."

Reznick said nothing.

She reached into her jacket and held up a picture of Reznick and Elisabeth, arms wrapped around Lauren. The images seared into his head. His most prized possession. The last picture he had of her alive. The last picture he had of them as a family. Two weeks later *she* would be dead. He looked at his wife's eyes, smiling, oblivious to the fate that was about to befall her. He felt his anger rise, but kept his emotions in check. "If you're wondering, we got it from your screensaver. So let's cut the bullshit. We know everything about you, Jon. We know about your wife, Elisabeth. We know about your father. We know he served his country, as have you. And we also know he brought you up when your mother died. You want me to go on?"

Reznick stared back at her. His mind flashed back to the day of his mother's funeral. He was only four. His first memories. Snow was falling as they lowered her into the bone-hard ground. His father gripped his tiny hand throughout, as if scared he would be snatched away. He wanted to cry, but he didn't. He learned later that she had scrubbed and cleaned holiday homes in Rockland in the mornings and at night, for extra money. She'd scrimped and saved all her life.

"You live in the same house your father built when he returned from Vietnam. He was in the Marines. He was the reason you joined up."

Reznick said nothing.

"Look, there's two ways we can do this. There's the smart way and there's the dumb way. The dumb way, there's a fair chance you will be shot dead before you reach for that gun again. The smart way? Well, the smart way would be for us to talk."

"Look, this is all very interesting, but I've got things to do."

She looked him over with a steely gaze. "We know why you're here in Key West, Jon. We know what you've been up to since you drove down from Washington. And I've got a proposition for you."

"What kind of proposition?"

"I want you to get your daughter back. But in return, you've got to help us out."

The Schooner Wharf Bar on Key West's harbor walk overlooked a marina, scores of yachts and boats bobbing about in the swell. Dozens of people were drinking in and around the bar, knocking back lunchtime margaritas, beers and mojitos; country music playing loud.

Reznick headed to an empty upstairs deck and sat down under a huge umbrella. Meyerstein sat down opposite him and donned a pair of shades. He ordered a large Coke, she ordered an iced tea. The four suits sat at a table near the entrance with direct line of sight to Meyerstein and Reznick.

When the waitress was out of earshot, Meyerstein leaned over and spoke softly.

"OK, before we can get down to business, I need to get some answers," she said, curling her hair behind her ear.

Reznick said nothing.

"Jon, you need to help us."

"Look, let's cut to the chase and say what you've got to say."

"I want to help you get your daughter back. But we've got to trust each other, at least a little."

"You've got two minutes to make your point."

"Someone took your daughter. Why? Because you should have killed a government scientist. Now, I'm gonna level with you. Someone wants this scientist dead real bad. But we need him, Jon. And it's no word of a lie to say this man is vital to America's national security interests."

Reznick listened as he wondered who he could trust. Meyerstein or Maddox. He'd never met this woman, but she didn't seem like a bullshitter, much less a liar. He assumed she could lie if she had to. But something about her told him that she was giving it to him straight.

The waitress arrived with the drinks. "Enjoy!" she said cheerily.

Reznick looked away as Meyerstein gave a wan smile to the girl.

"Where is he, Jon? Where's Luntz?"

"He's safe."

Meyerstein blew out a sigh of relief. She looked over to the four suits before she stared straight at him. "We've also got a big problem, Jon. An additional problem. We have a trail of bodies, some I don't care about. But one of them was a Special Agent. We found him in a wardrobe. We saw the signs that he had been neutralised. Jon, do you know he was married? Had two young daughters. Now their daddy will never come home. They'll never see him again."

"Listen to me and listen good. That wasn't me."

"I want to believe you, Jon. But my colleagues beside the door–"

"This is bullshit."

A long silence opened up before Meyerstein spoke, leaning forward. He smelled a light citrus perfume. "No, this is not bullshit, Jon. This is as real as it gets."

Reznick jabbed his thumb into his chest. "I want my daughter back. She is a child. She's out there. And she'll be frightened out of her mind. On a fucking boat. Now are you gonna stop fucking me around or what?"

"I need answers, Jon. Did you kill Agent Connelly?"

Reznick said nothing.

"Your prints are all over the place."

"Aren't you listening? I didn't kill him. Got that?"

"So who did?"

"Probably the same people who took my daughter."

"OK, let's say for a moment that I believe this. Let's move to Luntz. Where is he?"

"I told you he's safe."

"Jon, here's what we have. We're up against the clock. You're up against the clock. But what I'm going to propose can help us both. But you must trust me, like I want to trust you."

Reznick knocked back his Coke and stared out again over the marina. "Can you help me get my daughter back? That's all I'm interested in."

"Yes, I can." Meyerstein finished her iced tea and stood up. "Let's walk as we converse."

They walked down the boardwalk past a line of shops, restaurants and bars, and on the other side yachts, catamaran, ferries and dive boats, vying for business. Then over to Mallory Square, a huge plaza on the waterfront, where jugglers, clowns, jewelry vendors, face painters and tourists mingled. A cruise ship was heading out of the port.

Reznick was aware of the Feds in suits walking about twenty yards behind them. Meyerstein led them over towards the big red building – Key West Museum of Art & History – and sat down on an empty bench.

Satisfied there was no one within earshot, Reznick leaned forward and spoke first. "You mentioned about a national security threat to America. What kind of threat?"

"We're talking mass casualties. A possible bio-terrorist attack. Do you understand what I'm saying?"

Reznick took a few moments for the information to sink in. This was totally at odds with what Maddox had told him. He wondered if he shouldn't just turn and walk away. But something deep within him sensed not only that she was telling the truth, but that she could be trusted. "That's not the information I have."

"Trust me, this guy is indeed a scientist. I don't know if your handler, or whatever you call him, is in control of this situation. He won't save you or your daughter. Only we can."

"OK, let's say for a minute that what you're saying is correct. So, how does the scientist fit into this?"

It was Meyerstein's turn to go quiet.

"Listen, we're either going to level with each other, or you better speak to someone else."

Meyerstein cleared her throat and sighed. "You've not got clearance for this."

"Fuck clearance. You either deal me in or I walk."

Meyerstein pinched the bridge of her nose for a moment. "We believe, we're not one hundred per cent sure, but we believe that the guy you were supposed to kill had concerns over a fellow scientist. That scientist has disappeared. Bottom line? Luntz is America's leading authority on this threat, and is close to coming up with ways to neutralise it."

Reznick held his head in his hands and said nothing.

"Jon, we need this scientist. Just like you need your daughter."

"So, what do you propose?"

"Before I run this by you, I need to know why you didn't kill Luntz."

Reznick looked down at his hands. He didn't want to elaborate.

"Look, if I'm putting my cards on the table, I want you to do the same. Don't shut me out."

"Let's just say there was a discrepancy."

Meyerstein sat in silence waiting for him to speak.

He sighed. "I had been given another name. The scientist was wearing an Israeli dog tag written in Hebrew."

"What?"

"Exactly my response. The tag was his son's. He worked for the IDF. It showed the name Luntz. Also had a picture of his son around his neck. But there was no ID to corroborate that. It had already been cleared out."

"Who by?"

"I don't know. Perhaps by the crew who did your colleague?"

Meyerstein blew out her cheeks and shook her head. "Are you saying this might have been compartmentalised into two separate jobs?"

"Think about it. Everything is compartmentalised in the military. Same with the government. You're given an order and that order – whatever it is – is carried out. It's operational level. But you don't know the big picture. What's really happening? This is how it's done on major jobs. You only know one piece of the jigsaw. The people higher up the chain know how it all fits together. Need to know, and all that jazz. The person or people who did the job on your colleague, were possibly staying in the same hotel as me, who knows?"

"OK, let's assume that what you're saying is correct. Then what?"

"I received instructions…"

"From whom?"

"I'm not going there."

"Why not?"

Reznick just shrugged, eyes dead.

"Oh…you got instructions. To do what?"

Reznick told her everything that had happened and how he had got down to Miami via Fort Lauderdale.

Meyerstein listened before she turned and stole a quick glance at the agents twenty yards away. Then she faced Reznick. "OK, this is how it's gonna work."

Reznick said nothing.

"You've opened up to me, just like I've opened up to you. We both want different things, though. Now, listen closely. Do you know where your daughter is being held?"

"I've got a fair idea."

"But do you know whose yacht it is?"

Reznick nodded. "Wife of a Haitian diplomat goon."

"As you can imagine, that poses us problems."

"So what are you saying?"

"I'm saying this is tricky."

"Listen, am I wasting my time? Are you or are you not going to help me get my daughter back? She is an American in American waters."

Meyerstein sighed. "We can help you, but not directly."

"Why the hell not?"

"Diplomatic immunity. Under the Vienna Convention, the diplomat and his immediate family is accorded full protection under international law. They're out of bounds."

"Oh, you're not gonna pull that bullshit are you?"

"It's not bullshit. It's the law. Whether we like it or not."

"Don't throw that crap at me. International law? This is America. I don't give a shit about international law."

"Well I do. And here's what I propose. You tell me where the scientist is, and I will give you free reign to get your daughter and provide any assistance required. No questions asked."

Reznick felt a burning anger inside as uncertainty reigned. He wondered if he could really trust her. He knew it would be the easiest thing in the world for the FBI to promise something but then renege on that. It was only business. He tried to size her up. She wasn't flustered or blustering or blabbering on. She was serious and it was direct. But he also got the impression that she wasn't fazed by him or what he did. "And then what?"

"We can come to that obstacle later. As of now, you either play ball, or it becomes a lose-lose situation."

"OK, let's say I agree to this. What guarantees are there?"

"There are no guarantees."

"So, if I manage to make it out of there and get my daughter, then what?"

Meyerstein sighed. "Jon, I've got two children of my own. I miss them like crazy every day I'm away from them. I know what I'd do for them. And I'd probably do what I think you're going to do. If you're smart, you'll take this offer. What I can say is that my number one priority is getting the scientist back."

"Look, if I agree, you must give me your word that my friend watching over Luntz, will not be charged, or anything. He was doing me a favor by looking after him. Can that be done?"

"Who is he?"

"Look, he's not in my line of work. He used to be in the Unit, like me. But whatever you do, don't creep up on him with a SWAT team. He'll take half of them out."

"If we get the scientist back safely, your friend will be fine. You have my word."

Reznick went quiet for a few moments. "I don't need the coastguard around. I need free access, in and out. I want radio jamming in and around that location. Can you arrange that?"

"Not a problem. Two mile exclusion OK for you?"

"That'll work. I also need to know who's on the boat. How many? What are they packing?"

"If this all goes sour, you're on your own. We will deny any involvement. Are we clear?"

"That goes without saying."

Meyerstein sighed. "There are two guys. Both with Uzis. Part of the former FRAPH crowd that still hangs around Miami. Maybe high. Not a good combination."

"Do you know anything about the condition of my daughter? Is she alive?"

"We believe she may be drugged. Some opiate, perhaps."

Reznick's stomach knotted and he clenched his fists tight.

"Jon, look at me." Meyerstein took off her shades. Her eyes were as blue as the sky. "I've been in this job a long time. And I've always played it by the book. But I'm going to go out on a limb for you if you give me an address. Can you help me out?"

Reznick's mind was racing. How could he trust her? Truth was he didn't have any cards to play even if he wanted to. "You're gonna need a cover story for some guy trying to board a diplomat's yacht."

"No one need know. It's out at sea. The coastguard will be kept out with an exclusion zone. All I need is a location. And I swear on my children's life, I will not fuck you over on this if you've told me the truth and keep your side of the bargain."

"I need something else from you too. To help my daughter. If she's even alive. If she's been drugged, I need an antidote."

Meyerstein nodded.

"I need three doses of Naloxone and a clean needle and syringe."

"To counteract the opiates?"

"Precisely."

Meyerstein curled some hair behind her ear. The way she did it reminded him of Elisabeth. "I'll get that for you."

Reznick closed his eyes for a moment and sighed. "Pitch 87, Del Raton trailer park, up the coast at Delray Beach. But play it gentle. Like I said, if you go in with SWAT, you better have the body bags ready."

Meyerstein made a call and relayed the details. She ended the call. "When are you going to do this?"

"As soon as it gets dark."

Meyerstein stood up. "I'll get what you need before then. We'll talk again, Jon. I hope to God you find your daughter alive, really I do."

Reznick looked at her and bowed his head. "Yeah, so do I."

TWENTY-ONE

The sky was pitch black six miles out on the Straits of Florida. Reznick saw a faint light in the distance and cut the outboard engine. He anchored the dive boat over a mile away from the target. The heavy swell was affecting his balance. Anxiety over the fate of his daughter wasn't helping. But he knew that he had to focus on the task in hand.

He checked the luminous dial on his watch which showed it was 6.28pm. He picked up the night vision glasses and peered through the darkness in the direction of the light. A luxury yacht was bobbing in the choppy waters. He scanned the yacht and could just make out the word *Pòtoprens*. This was it.

Reznick did a slow sweep across the yacht and saw a man sitting on the deck drinking from a can, feet up on the stern side of the boat. For the next five minutes, he just watched. But no sign of the other man or his daughter.

Damn. Ideally he wanted both guys on deck at the same time. Far easier to deal with.

Reznick quickly assembled his M24 sniper rifle, aligning the night sights, securely attaching it to a mobile tripod. He crouched down and pointed the rifle in the general direction of the yacht. Then he pressed his left eye up close to the rubber eyepiece and peered through the electronic green sights. Using the scope's cross hairs, he zeroed in on the man's chest. But

201

the heavy swell meant he only had the target in sight for a couple of seconds at a time.

The rifle had an optimum range of one mile. He recalled being on a patrol with a British unit in Afghanistan and their sniper had killed two Taliban machine gunners from one and a half miles away. The time it took for the bullet to leave the rifle and kill the target was three seconds. Reznick could factor in around two seconds, maybe a fraction less.

One man in range, the other out of sight. If he fired now, it would alert the other man and spell the end for his daughter.

The sniper option was too risky.

Goddamn.

He watched the man on deck finish his drink, before crushing the empty can with one hand. The man was oblivious to being watched in the middle of the sea, darkness all around.

Reznick turned to the neat pile of diving gear at the back of his boat. This was his Plan B. He remembered an exercise with Navy Seals ten years back when he had done one hundred foot per minute. But that was in inshore waters. And he was ten years younger. He reckoned eighty foot per minute would be a more realistic figure. So that would take him a full forty minutes or so to reach the boat.

"Fuck," he muttered to himself.

He kept on staring through the rifle's night sights. The man in the seat got up as the second man from below, holding a bottle, came up onto the deck and took his place.

Reznick put the rifle down and picked up the pile of diving gear on the deck, which the owner of the boat had personally checked before loading it on the boat. He had double-checked, just to make sure.

The guy had kitted him out with a night vision dive mask with his wet suit. Reznick had never dived at night. But that didn't faze him. He just rolled with it as he was trained to.

He pulled on the wetsuit, flippers and then the Draeger rebreather tank. The rebreather equipment didn't produce any bubbles and allowed a diver to breathe their own air over and over again. It was used by Seals and advanced divers because of its stealth-like capacity in not disturbing marine life. The tank was lighter as compressed air was seventy-eight per cent nitrogen, and rebreathers only need oxygen tanks. Also, decompression was not a problem as nitrogen, associated with the bends, was kept to a minimum.

He strapped on a sheathed knife to his left calf and one to his belt clip. Then he placed his Beretta and a medical kit in a waterproof LokSak Arm Pak and strapped it to his right forearm.

He checked the compass on the luminous dive watch, which placed the yacht one mile due south south east of his position. Then he put his mouthpiece in and put on his night vision diving mask. It had an LCD display showing depth but also used thermal imaging technology so he could swim in total darkness.

His world now had a green tinge.

Reznick slipped into the dark waters of the Florida Straits and dived to a depth of ten yards and headed in the direction of the boat.

He kept his arms at his side as he swam horizontal in the water, legs and flippers working hard. The underwater night vision world opened up before him. Shoals of fish parted.

The tranquility in the lime green was at odds with how he felt. Simmering anger coursed through his veins. He thought of his daughter. All alone. Then he thought of his late wife's last moments.

What was she thinking? Was she praying? He hoped she hadn't been alone, trapped in part of her office, cut off from everyone else. He hoped someone had been with her.

He pushed the thought from his mind.

Let's get to Lauren. To keep her alive was to keep part of Elisabeth alive.

The LCD screen on his visor showed he was half way there. Closer and closer.

Reznick swam on. The shoals of fish were swarming all around in an algae green world and he wondered if this would attract some sharks. He'd always had a deep fear of sharks. As a boy, he had witnessed a porbeagle, a cold-water shark, circling him and his friends for nearly half an hour as they swam in Burnt Cove in Maine. And that incident had always stayed with him down the years.

Suddenly, without any warning, Reznick gulped down a lungful of what he imagined liquid draino would taste like. He felt himself choking and coughing through his bailout regular, which he was wearing necklace style on a loop of surgical tubing. He needed to bail out. Quick.

His lungs burned and filled up with seawater. Throat burning with the chemical substance. He coughed and swallowed more water. He fought against hyperventilation.

What the hell was going on? What had he done wrong?

He forced himself to inhale slowly. Gradually, he began to regain his composure. He was still breathing. He checked the night vision computer readout as he rose to the surface, yard by yard.

When he got to the surface, he ripped off his mouthpiece and mask and gulped in the fresh air. An inky black sky overhead, stars as far as the eye could see, choppy seas lapping his face. He turned and saw the silhouette of his boat and swam back nearly five hundred yards and clambered on board.

Reznick slipped off his gear and gargled with fresh water to attempt to help the pain in his throat. He retched up the saltwater he had swallowed. Then he replayed the dive in his head and wondered what had gone wrong.

He took the rebreather below deck and switched on a desktop lamp. It all seemed fine. Then he went across to the small galley kitchen and filled up the sink with water, before submerging the rebreather. A few bubbles rose to the surface. Reznick looked closer and saw a razor-thin quarter-inch tear in the side of the expiration bag. An inside hairline fracture had expanded with the sea pressure and developed into a tear all the way through.

"Gimme a fucking break, will you?"

Reznick's heart pounded as he dried himself and changed into a pair of cargo shorts and sneakers he'd bought from a Key West beach shack.

He needed to focus.

His options were narrowed.

Reznick went back up onto deck and peered through the night vision glasses. There was still one guy on deck. A long distance rifle shot would hit the guy. But he knew that the sound of any rifle shot would give the subject a couple of seconds to hit the deck, the guy below a chance to prepare or harm his daughter.

The second option was almost a Kamikaze option. Take the boat right up to their yacht, shoot the guy on the deck, then clamber on board and take down the other guy.

The bottom line was that he was clean out of good options. He had to take a risk if he wanted to get his daughter back.

Reznick loaded up the rucksack. The last thing he checked was the Beretta. He pulled the magazine from the handgun and cleaned and oiled the barrel. He lubed the slide rails and around the barrel. Then the top of the disconnector in front of the breach face. Finally, he eased the slide forward until it was almost into battery, and then applied lube to the barrel head. Last of all, he ran a bore brush through the barrel, content that it was good to go.

Then he racked the slide, dry firing to make sure it was working, before he wiped off the excess lube with a rag.

He attached the suppressor, screwing it securely into place.

The last thing he did was thumb the seventeen rounds out of the magazine, feeling the tension in the spring, before he pushed the magazine back into the butt of the gun.

Reznick took in a deep breath of the night air and strapped the gun to his left leg, started up the boat and headed straight for the target. The boat skimmed across the water in no time, its engine spluttering too loudly for comfort, closer and closer to the lights of the boat. He slowed down as he got within the last couple of hundred yards and he switched on the deck lights so they could see him.

He started to hear music. Muffled hip-hop music.

He was around one hundred yards away from the starboard side. He maneuvered the boat to within twenty yards and then ten yards as the man on deck stood up and stared down at him.

Reznick smiled up at the guy. The guy didn't smile back. Reznick pulled out the Beretta and fired two muffled shots straight through the man's forehead. Blood spilled down the man's face as he dropped to the deck with a thump.

Heart racing, he edged closer to the rear of the boat. Closer and closer.

Slow is smooth, smooth is fast.

Then he stepped forward onto a metal railing hanging over the side and pulled himself onto the deck, rucksack on his back. He moved quietly and cautiously round the port side, eyes fixed on the cabin door. Then he crouched down low behind a huge pile of ropes.

The music was booming out. He trained his gun on the door which led to the galley. But still no movement.

The sound of the deep bass vibrated and reverberated around the boat's teak wood.

The door opened and a black man emerged onto the deck, rubbing his eyes.

Reznick did a double tap. He shot him once in the chest and once in the head before the man could react. Blood splattered over the riggings as the man collapsed in a heap. Somehow he was still breathing, swallowing blood, eyes pleading in vain with Reznick.

Reznick stood above him and stared down at him for a moment. The man's dark brown eyes were filled with tears. He pressed the gun to the man's forehead and drilled two shots into him. Blood seeped down his oily skin.

He stepped over the body and pushed open the galley door. The smell of hash and spilled beer filled the fetid air. He climbed down four steps. A table with cards, strewn with empty beer cans. He rummaged in closets and opened doors.

Please let her be here. Please God let her be alive.

Then more stairs. Down into the sleeping quarters. Polished teaks and dark woods. Crumpled duvets. Where the hell was she?

A glint of silver caught his eye in his peripheral vision. Reznick turned and saw what looked like handcuffs below a duvet. He pulled back the covers. His daughter lay prostrate, out of it, face blue-grey, lips blue, eyes closed, handcuffed to a metal railing.

"Oh, fuck."

Reznick pulled back her eyelids. His daughter's pupils were pinpricks. Reaching over he took her pulse. Her skin was cold. But he felt a faint pulse. "Oh, Christ, no, Lauren!" He slapped his daughter twice to try and rouse her. But nothing.

He ripped opened the waterproof medic bag containing the Naloxone and syringe and needles. Then he pulled off his daughter's belt and tied it tight around her upper arm. He pulled it tighter until the veins protruded.

Then he plunged the needle and syringe into the small metal container, filling the clear solution into the syringe.

Reznick held his breath. Slowly he injected his daughter with 0.4 mg of the Naloxone. He waited a few moments before he loosened the belt and pulled his daughter close, kissing her cold, grey-blue face. "Lauren, talk to me, honey. Lauren, please wake up. Come on, honey. It's dad here. Do you hear me?"

Lauren was still motionless her breathing shallow.

"Lauren, let's snap out of this," he said, gently slapping her face. "Come on, Lauren, it's dad here."

She didn't move. He waited two and then three minutes to see if the drugs took effect. But nothing. No reaction at all.

The seconds dragged. He felt as if he was drowning in slow motion. Time seemed to have stopped.

Reznick opened the fresh packaging for a new needle and syringe and filled it with 2mg of the drug. He had to counteract the opiates. He injected her again, but this time in the other arm.

He held her left hand and stroked her soft hair. Tears streamed down his cheeks. He cradled his daughter's head in his arm and stroked her forehead. The skin was clammy, the breathing still shallow, lips still a bluish tinge.

"Lauren," he said, slapping her repeatedly on the cheek. "Lauren, it's dad!"

No response.

Reznick looked at his watch. It had been five minutes since he'd administered the first lot of Naloxone and his daughter was still not responding after the second. He needed to get his daughter to a hospital. He looked at her whey-face complexion and stroked her hair. "Don't die on me, Lauren," he said. "Just please don't die on me. Hang in there. We can do this." He squeezed his daughter's clammy right hand. "Squeeze if you can hear me or understand me."

No response.

Reznick wrapped a blanket around Lauren and bounded up the stairs onto the deck and searched the two dead bodies for handcuff keys. He found a set in the back pocket of the second man he had killed. Then he fired up the engines and lights, checked the Simrad navigation equipment including the plotter, and punched in the coordinates on the satnav so the yacht would be running essentially on autopilot for most of the journey in.

He pushed a button to pull up the anchor before he sped off back through the dark waters, eyes peeled, focussed on the night vision screen, heading back to Key West. The warm wind was whipping up, spray cooling his face and arms as he accelerated the yacht through the waters.

He was three miles out and his night vision monitor showed debris – a couple of wooden crates – floating up ahead, so he manoeuvered round them, before heading back onto the set course. Past buoys until he saw the twinkling lights of Key West in the distance.

Closer and closer. For the first time he was starting to contemplate his daughter's death. It was starting to creep into his psyche like a cancer. But he couldn't let it. He couldn't think like that.

A few minutes later he saw the marina and docked, then tied the boat up, cutting the engines and power.

Reznick rushed below and felt her brow. Clammy, shallow breathing. But she was still alive. "We're back on dry land, Lauren," he said. "Just hang in there." He unlocked the handcuffs and put her over his shoulder. Then he clambered up onto the deck and headed along the gangway.

A woman boater rushed across the deck. "What's wrong with her?" she asked again.

"You got a car?" he asked.

"Sure. What's wrong with her?"

"We need to get her to the hospital. Right fucking now."

The woman ushered Reznick to her car, which was parked close by as some alarmed tourists gasped as he barged past them on the gangway. Reznick opened the back door and laid his daughter on her side in the back seat. He climbed in beside her, holding her tight. "Let's move it!" he said.

The woman started up the engine. "What's wrong with her?"

"Just get her to the hospital. She's quite sick."

The journey took five long minutes. Reznick held his daughter's hand as he barked at the woman to floor the gas pedal. A short while later the car screeched to a halt outside the Lower Keys Medical Center.

Reznick pulled his daughter out of the back seat and carried her into the main waiting area as if she was a sleeping child. "Drug overdose," he shouted. "I need help!"

He didn't see anyone.

"Emergency!"

A doctor and two nurses ran forward and placed her on a gurney, before rushing her towards the trauma room.

"What sort of drugs has she taken?" the doctor demanded to know Reznick ran alongside the gurney.

Reznick told them about the heroin she was given and the doses of Naloxone he had tried.

"How long has she been like that?" the doctor snapped.

"I don't know. A day. A couple of days. Maybe less. I gave her a couple of shots of Naloxone about half an hour ago."

"What the hell are you doing with Naloxone?"

"I'm her father. I found her. I tried to bring her round. Can you save her?"

"Did you give her the heroin?"

"Are you fucking serious? I just want you to save my daughter."

"We'll take it from here," he said, turning away.

A nurse ushered him towards a waiting area as Lauren was wheeled through some double doors and into the trauma room. He felt helpless as he slumped down in a seat, head in his hands.

Then he closed his eyes and began to pray.

TWENTY-TWO

Just before 10pm in the FBI's office in North Miami Beach, assistant director Martha Meyerstein was observing from behind a one-way mirror as Dr Frank Luntz ate hot chicken soup and cheese sandwiches in a windowless interview room. He sat hunched at a table and had a noticeable shake. But he seemed in overall good physical health despite his ordeal with Reznick.

She had trusted Reznick down in Key West and her instincts had paid off. The powers that be within the FBI would say it was wrong to aid Reznick. She knew it was against all the rules and laws she had learned. Her father always stressed the importance of ethics, the sanctity of the law and of doing things the right way. He might have forged a reputation as a pit bull in court, but he was also a stickler for protocol.

The more she thought of it the more she realised she had crossed the line and had not acted as an Assistant Director of the FBI should. She had crossed over into muddied waters. Suddenly there was no right and wrong and there was no law. And a growing sense that she would live to regret her deal with Reznick.

She stared through the one-way mirror at Luntz. The team of doctors who had only finished examining him ten minutes earlier said he showed signs of trauma and anxiety, which wasn't surprising in the circumstances. They cautioned against pressurizing Luntz to speak. But that wasn't an option as there as too much at stake.

She needed to find out exactly what had happened and what he knew about Caan, before Luntz was handed over to Dr Adam Horowitz and his team of scientists, for a full debrief.

Meyerstein felt another yawn coming on and covered her mouth. What she wouldn't give for a good night's sleep. Even a bad night's sleep would be something.

She picked up the file on Luntz and opened it up. A recent photo his wife had taken before Luntz was kidnapped showed the scientist carefree, playing football with his children in a park.

She couldn't remember the last time she had spent quality time with her own children. She'd only managed a five-minute phone conversation with them before they caught the bus to school earlier that day. When she phoned to let them know she'd be away for at least a couple more days, her mother, who had moved down from Chicago on a semi-permanent basis since her split three months earlier, sounded stressed and Meyerstein felt guilty that she couldn't say for sure when she'd be back home. She didn't want to entrust a nanny to look after her kids, and she didn't know any of the mothers at her children's school well enough to impose. But she knew she couldn't rely on her mother forever.

The more she thought of how little she saw her kids and how little time she spent in the home, the more she realised they were becoming a distant second to her job. That wasn't right. No matter how important her job, her children should come first. They needed their mother. She missed bathing them in the evenings. She missed talking about the Chicago Bears, and how when she was a kid, she was dragged down to Soldier Field in all weathers with the rest of her family to watch granddad's beloved team. She missed her dad a lot. She sometimes wished she could phone him to talk things over about how she was feeling. He instinctively knew, perhaps that came with experience, of what to do. How far to push things. He always knew there was not just the law, but a moral code to adhere to. Lying and cheating, to him, was a sign of weakness. But she knew that even if she did speak to him, being all touchy feely and opening up wasn't his strong suit. She also missed the school plays, the soccer mom routines which most of her kids' classmates' mothers were immersed in. Perhaps most of all she missed the cuddles and kisses and sitting snuggled up on the sofa at night with them, watching a cartoon before their bath. She missed the intimacy.

She shut her eyes for a moment and imagined her son Jacob's gentle little hand tying knots in her hair. She loved that feeling. And the warmth of Cindy when she climbed into her bed during the night and cuddled into her.

Suddenly, the door behind her swung open and Ray Stamper marched in with two Styrofoam cups of strong, black coffee, snapping her out of her reverie. He looked dog-tired, top button undone. Too little sleep and too much caffeine, the same as her. He handed her a cup and she took a large gulp.

"Darn, that's hot!" she said. A jolt of caffeine hit her system.

"Just got some news from Kate down at the bio-lab."

"Shoot."

"Four guys from the Pentagon have just turned up. They say Kate has not received, and I quote, 'proper security clearance', to be shown details of the work Luntz was involved in."

"You kidding me?"

"Nope."

Meyerstein shook her head. It sounded to her like a Special Access Program. It was the name given to ultra secretive work or operations known only to a select few in the Pentagon. She knew that to get such a program off the ground, it had to be cleared at the highest level of government. "Anything else?"

"We've been talking to the staff. They said Luntz and Caan were working together on a secret project, and had been for years. And we found out something."

"What?"

"Three vials have gone missing from the lab's freezers, which were discovered during a recent inventory."

"Unaccounted for?"

"Yup."

"So, what did the three vials contain?"

"That's the thing. No one knows a goddamn thing."

Meyerstein ran her hand through her hair. "This just got a helluva lot more interesting. OK. I want Kate and her team and the WMD people to let me know the moment they find out anything else. And let's keep digging some more. We're making progress. Good work."

"So what do you propose to do with Luntz?"

"We need to get a handle on exactly what Luntz knows. We need to find out how this all came about. And with that information, we can track down Scott Caan."

"What about the Pentagon?"

Meyerstein gave a wry smile and sipped her coffee. "What about them?"

"You going to find out what they're trying to keep secret?"

"That's the plan."

Stamper gave a pained expression. "You're on thin ice making that call, Martha. The shrinks are saying to take it easy with him. Might be worth holding off."

Meyerstein felt herself grinding her teeth. This was something she found herself doing more often. "We need answers." She stared through the glass as Luntz wiped some crumbs from his face with a napkin. "We need something. Anything, from this guy."

"Shouldn't we just sit tight? Wouldn't that be the smart move at this stage?"

She took a final sip of coffee before throwing the cup in a wastepaper bin. "Maybe it would. But I think we need to get in there and find out the truth, whether it pisses off the Pentagon or not." Her cell phone rang and she blew out her cheeks.

"Martha, it's O'Donoghue. You and I need to talk. Right now."

She rolled her eyes at Stamper. "Good evening, sir. I'm just about to interview Frank Luntz."

Stamper nodded in recognition of who was on the line and left the room.

O'Donoghue sighed. "I want to talk about Reznick."

"What about him?"

"I'm hearing that you cut a deal with him. Is that true?"

Meyerstein closed her eyes for a moment, wondering how he had got to hear. "I got our scientist. I want to find out more about Scott Caan. Did you get the message that three vials are missing?"

"Yes, I just got that from Stamper's team. But answer me this. Did you cut a deal, Martha? Because that would not be good. We have ways of doings things."

"Sir, I respect what you're saying. Can we iron out any problems when I get back to Washington?"

"Martha, we cannot have people like Reznick out there, killing and destroying whatever gets in his way. And another thing. I'm not going to let this lie. There will be consequences. Do you know that Claude Merceron was a Haitian diplomat?"

"Yes, I did." She explained how Merceron had links to Norton & Weiss, believed to be a CIA front.

"Martha, we can't go beyond the law to carry out our functions."

Meyerstein sighed. "We recovered the scientist. But yes, I admit, we got our hands dirty. That didn't sit well with me."

"Martha, with immediate effect, I want you back in Washington."

"What?"

"I've just been off the phone to the Pentagon, and they're saying they want their people who have special clearance to speak direct to Luntz. This is a classified project. Special Access Program, apparently. They're flying into Miami first thing in the morning."

"Sir, this is not a good time. I am about to interview Frank Luntz."

"Are you disobeying an order, Martha?"

"Yes, sir, I most certainly am. Do what you have to do. But I've got a job to do here."

Meyerstein ended the call. Her heart was racing. She was facing an internal investigation into her conduct, that was for sure. She knew that and would have to deal with it. But to compound matters, he was telling her that the Pentagon was to take over.

What a mess.

She stared through the glass at Luntz for a few moments. "Son-of-a-bitch."

Stamper came back in the room. "What was O'Donoghue wanting?"

"Someone on our team told him about the deal with Reznick."

"What?"

Meyerstein nodded.

"You want me to find out who it was?"

Meyerstein shook her head. "I'll deal with it when I get back to Washington. We have more pressing matters."

Stamper stared through the glass. "I've got a bad feeling about this whole thing. A really bad feeling."

Meyerstein sighed. "Yeah, tell me about it."

A few moments later, Meyerstein entered the interview room and smiled.

"Assistant Director, Agent Martha Meyerstein," she said. She pulled up a chair and sat down opposite Luntz, her back to the one-way mirror. The smell of soup still in the air. Luntz managed to force a smile.

"How are you feeling?" she asked.

Luntz shrugged. "I've felt better."

"Tired?"

"You could say that, yeah."

"Look, I'm not going to take much of your time. I think you'll be looking forward to a warm bath, a long sleep and some time with your family, right?" She didn't mention that a full debrief would take place in the next couple of hours with the WMD team, before he had had any chance to sleep.

"I want to help the FBI any way I can."

"And we appreciate that, Dr Luntz, really we do."

"Please, call me Frank."

Meyerstein nodded as she noticed a slight tremor in both his hands. "OK, Frank, so you're quite happy for me to ask you some questions at this juncture?"

"Certainly. I want to help in any way."

Meyerstein leaned back in her seat and smiled. "Whenever you like."

Over the next hour, Luntz recalled in minute detail and chronological order, what happened to him. His memory was precise. He remembered the moment he left his home in Frederick with the FBI agent who was assigned to look after him until he was woken at gunpoint. All the details tallied perfectly with their timeline. Meyerstein knew he could provide the breakthrough they so desperately needed.

She knew that it was important not to convey tension or pressure. She needed to be authoritative, calm and reassuring. Like a trusted, reliable friend.

"That's great, Frank, you've got a better memory than me," she joked.

Luntz smiled as he picked at the cuticles of his bitten fingernails.

"Now, Frank," Meyerstein said. She shifted in her seat concentrating on making her voice softer and more empathetic. "Let's think back to why you wanted to see us in the first place. About your concerns on biosafety at your lab. Tell me about your work first of all. The FBI scientists, specialists in this area, will want to speak to you later. But for now, just fill me in so I'm up to speed."

Luntz shook his head. "I'm real sorry, but that's classified."

She could see how he was going to play it. "What's classified?"

"The work we were doing at the lab."

Meyerstein leaned forward in her seat, a matter of inches from Luntz, and sensed his vulnerability. "Now listen to me and listen good. We're talking a possible imminent threat to national security, if you hadn't realised that already. And I'm not going to have you hiding behind security clearance, or some other bullshit. Do you want me to spell it out to you?"

There was fear in Luntz's eyes.

"Your colleague, the esteemed Lt Col Scott Caan, has gone missing. And I'm hearing three vials were taken from the lab you were responsible for. Do you know what that means?"

Luntz said nothing, looking at the floor.

"Maybe I'm not making myself clear. That means you will be facing a near certain criminal investigation into the lax security systems you had at your lab. You have put the security of the United States at grave risk. Do you understand me?"

Luntz bowed his head and nodded quickly.

"So, I'm going to ask you again, what the hell are we dealing with?"

Luntz stayed quiet.

"It's your choice. You either tell me everything, or, you're gonna face a long, long time in jail." Meyerstein leaned back in her seat knowing she was playing a high-risk strategy. "Your choice. What's it gonna be?"

Luntz went quiet for nearly a minute, occasionally biting his lower lip. Eventually he took a deep breath and spoke, voice as quiet as a mouse. "I hear what you're saying. It's just that the project is very, very secretive."

Meyerstein smiled. "I'm very discreet. Whenever you're ready."

A long silence opened up before he spoke in a hushed whisper. "My colleague, Scott Caan, and I have been working for years trying to learn as much as possible about the origins of the 1918 Spanish Flu pandemic. It killed at least twenty million people worldwide. I was part of the laboratory team, led by Dr Jeffrey Taubenberg, who resurrected the killer flu."

Meyerstein nodded, not wanting to hurry him unduly. She fixed her gaze on him for a few moments. "I remember reading about that. Can you describe the broad-brush process to me, just so I've got a better idea what we're talking about?"

"We used a highly complex computer program which perfectly matched the Ribonucleic acid, also known as RNA – which is one of three major macromolecules that are essential for all life – and DNA structures. In effect, the complete genome of the 1918 influenza virus was known. But my work – along with Scott Caan – was in the pursuit of anti-viral drugs and vaccines as well as developing a new hybrid strain of 1918 Spanish flu."

The word *hybrid* seemed to stick in her head. "You were developing a new *hybrid* strain?" she repeated.

"This is allowed under the Biological Weapons Convention which was signed in 1972. Article 1 allows exceptions for medical and defensive purposes in small quantities."

Meyerstein nodded as the full magnitude of what she was dealing with hit home. It didn't make any sense. How could it be justified to try and recreate such a dangerous eradicated strain that could wreak unforeseen havoc if released, either deliberately or accidentally? But she knew that wasn't her concern. "Was this hybrid strain as deadly as the original 1918 Spanish Flu?"

"Four-fold. It was given the highest security classification. The Pentagon was funding the whole thing. We all had to have a higher security clearance to protect the program's highly sensitive information."

Meyerstein nodded. She knew a security clearance application would have had to be submitted to the Department of Defense for review and consideration. But she felt a growing mix of anger and disbelief that a killer virus was now out of the laboratory setting. "I see. Please, go on."

"Three months ago, we finally created this new, more virulent, strain. We'd worked for years. In the last few months, we were both working very long hours."

"Was it taking its toll?"

"We were both exhausted, but we both had a Pentagon deadline to meet. We were verifying procedures and analysing all the data. It was coming together perfectly, just as I had envisaged."

"Tell me: I guess if you're working closely with someone for so long, in such tight conditions, there must have been tensions. Did you notice anything out of character?"

"Nothing. The one thing that stuck in my mind was that he hardly showed any discernible signs of stress. He seemed to work well under pressure."

"So, there were no behavioral traits to indicate anything adverse, or out of the ordinary from him or anyone on your team?"

"He was quiet, but he had always been quiet. I'd always tried to ensure a happy and cohesive working environment, and he was very much part of that. He wasn't the life and soul of the party, but that was just him. He was a scientist."

"OK, just to clarify, Scott Caan was not acting out of character. That was his natural persona, right?"

"Indeed."

"So, what happened to make you want to contact us?"

"If I can just fill you in on the lead-up to my concerns. It was all going swimmingly. Three weeks ago or so, in late-November, we finally got preliminary results back which showed that the new anti-virals we had worked on were working with the hybrid flu we had created. It was a very satisfying moment. It means that if there is, God forbid, such an outbreak again, we would be well prepared with effective vaccines and anti-virals. And we are now starting to understand how pandemics form and cause disease." A bead of perspiration on Luntz's forehead. "But then, the Pentagon, in the middle of all this, asked me to conduct a spot check. An inventory."

"Was this unusual?"

"It was usually held at the start of each year, so I'd expected to do it in January, maybe February, so that wasn't ideal. I needed Scott to oversee this inventory, but he had called in sick. It wasn't like him. Three days later, he was still off. Ironically, some flu, or something. I tried to call him by phone, but there was no answer. So, as you can imagine, I was wondering where he was. I assumed he was in his bed. But I left numerous messages on his phone. This went on for another couple of days, until I decided to head out to his house. I had never been there before. No one had. He was very private. But still there was no answer. I thought it was a bit odd, but wondered if he hadn't just headed out for some fresh air. Later that day, back at the lab, I went to study the test results from the anti-viral test on my computer, and there was nothing there. Every computer file pertaining to our research was gone."

Meyerstein nodded. "But this was backed up to secure servers, I imagine."

"It was. But when I checked, it was all gone. Nothing on the backup. I thought I was going mad. It didn't make any sense. I couldn't think straight. This was years of work, straight down the pan. Anyway, I called his home phone but it was still ringing out, as was his cell phone. Then I decided to do the inventory myself. If nothing else, as a basic security procedure. We have tens of thousands of items stored in the freezer. And it showed a discrepancy."

"What kind of discrepancy?"

"The actual stocks didn't match the numbers we thought we had. So it all had to be counted again, for a second time. It took days. Eventually we found we were missing three vials of the hybrid 1918 Spanish Flu virus we had created, and the anti-virals and vaccine."

Meyerstein felt her insides knot. The process took days? Why so long? "Did you speak to anyone else about these concerns?"

"I called my contact at the Pentagon, overseeing the project, and he told me to contact Dr Horowitz."

Meyerstein shifted in her seat. "Horowitz? Why not the Pentagon?"

"They referred me to him because he was head of the WMD section of the FBI and had the highest level of security clearance, as he used to work within the Department of Defense."

"Adam Horowitz?"

"Yes. I sent him an encrypted email saying I needed to speak to him urgently in person on a security matter at the lab. He was out of the country and arranged for me to be seen in person by his deputy at FBI HQ. And he arranged for a Special Agent to be assigned to me overnight at the St Regis, ahead of the early morning meeting."

Meyerstein shifted in her seat. "So, you followed the correct procedure, right?"

"Absolutely."

Meyerstein felt an anger build within her. She hadn't been made aware of this by Adam Horowitz or his team. Was this because of its special access status? She gathered her thoughts. "Are there any circumstances in which Caan or any member of your team would be allowed to take three vials of the virus, anti-virals and vaccines, out of the lab?"

Luntz's eyes filled with tears and he bowed his head as if in shame. "No circumstances at all."

"Would it be stretching things too far to say the specter of bio-terrorism comes to mind?"

"I think that's a fair supposition."

Meyerstein's mind was racing. "But, as it stood, all you had was circumstantial evidence that Scott Caan might have been responsible. That's all it was."

"It doesn't end there. The final piece of the jigsaw fell into place after I discovered another anomaly."

"What kind of anomaly are we talking about?"

"A lot of scientists were in and out of the freezers where we kept the new strain of the 1918 synthetic Spanish flu virus. So, it could have been any of them. But what was different about Scott was that I found out that he had returned to the lab on two separate occasions, in the middle of the night, a couple of days before he went missing. The security guard noted it down and said Scott was finishing some vital work."

"Did you take this up with Scott?"

"I was unaware that he had even entered the lab in the middle of the night. I only found out when I checked the guard's logs. The guard didn't pass on that information to me at the time, assuming it wasn't important."

"And you're quite convinced Scott Caan is the one?"

"I believe it's him. He knew the rules of the lab. Out of hours was only in the most exceptional of cases. It had to be authorised by me. And there was no good reason he had to be in there. And it categorically wasn't authorised by me to be in that lab in the middle of the night."

"None at all?"

Luntz shook his head. "Never," he said, dabbing his eyes.

"Frank, tell me about Caan. We need to build up a profile of him. What we have so far is very sketchy. I mean, where did he come from? Where did he live? What were his passions? Did you know him well?"

The tears were now running down Luntz's cheeks. "I can't believe this is happening. You know, you think you know somebody. With hindsight, I didn't know him at all. What can I say? He was recruited direct from MIT and assigned to the project. He came on board eighteen months after I had."

"Why was that?"

"Well, first he had to get top secret clearance, and then when that came through, we had to wait for his Sensitive Compartmented Information clearance before he could begin work in the lab."

"Tell me about him. His work."

"From day one, his work was exceptional. Smartest guy MIT biological science department had seen for years. And he was one of the brightest guys in the operation. He also worked longer and harder and was more dedicated than anyone. He was always there."

"Did he socialise? What about drinks after work? Bowling?"

"He didn't drink. He kept himself to himself."

"What were his interests?"

Luntz went quiet for a few moments before he answered. "He was a keep fit guy. Ran every lunchtime. Ran to work. Guy was in good shape. Really good shape."

"Tell me, when he hadn't turned up for work, was that out of character?"

"Absolutely. He was meticulous, rarely off sick, but if he was, he'd let me or one of his coworkers in the lab know either by phone or email."

Luntz dabbed his eyes and sighed long and hard. She could see he was getting agitated.

"OK, let's just step back, if we can, for a few moments to try and get a handle on where we are. It's important that we establish the facts."

Luntz nodded but said nothing.

"What I'm looking to do is build up a picture of this guy, your colleague. You say he was quiet, kept himself to himself, workaholic, keep fit, I get all that. What I'm missing is what he was like as a person. Did he talk politics? Did he read a newspaper and discuss an article? Something on CNN or Fox got his attention, perhaps?"

"You mean was he political?"

Meyerstein nodded.

"You know, it's interesting, looking back, he never expressed any views on anything."

"No views at all? Why do you think that was?"

"Perhaps he had no views on anything going on in the world…"

Meyerstein shrugged. "Or maybe, he wanted to conceal his true views."

Luntz frowned. "I hadn't thought of that."

Meyerstein cleared her throat. "Are there any days where you know he was visiting friends, and was taking time off, or stuff like that? Did he have spats with colleagues? Things that stick in the memory."

Luntz furrowed his brow for a few moments. "Well, no… Well, now that you mention it, he didn't once mention friends or family."

"Did you never ask him about his family?"

"We all live such busy lives I never really took that much of an interest. I know he wasn't married. But I don't think I ever knew anything about his private life. I don't like to pry."

Meyerstein could feel her anger mounting at Luntz's lackadaisical approach. "What about spats?"

Luntz leaned back in his seat and pursed his lips, as if deep in thought. "You know, it's interesting. There is one thing that comes to mind. I remember a colleague getting frustrated as he was trying to reach Scott to talk about some lab results. But he wasn't around. Apparently he'd phoned in to say his flight was late."

"Late?"

"Yeah, he was late for work on a Monday morning; he said his flight was delayed. Some technical fault in the plane from New York."

"How long ago was that?"

"I remember that it was November 19th when he was late, that was the Monday morning, my sixtieth birthday, not long before he went off sick and then went AWOL."

"How long was he away for? Do you know who he visited?"

"I'm guessing he left on the Saturday, November 17th, as he was in work on the Friday. But I don't have a clue who he met."

Meyerstein scribbled the details on a pad in front of her. "Tell me, what security measures do you have in place at the lab to ensure that the correct people enter the lab."

"Primarily, it's a retinal scan, which as you'll know is a biometric technique, widely used in government agencies."

"Frank, I'm going to take a break for two minutes, is that OK with you?"

Luntz nodded but said nothing.

Meyerstein ripped out the page from the pad she'd scribbled on and stood up, pushing back her chair. "I'll be right back." She went into the side room with the two-way mirror where Stamper was watching and handed over the piece of paper. "OK, I want Caan's retinal scan to be fed into the airport databases. Concentrate on Saturday the 17th November at

Dulles and all the New York airports. Cameras at taxi ranks. Then get our face recognition guys onto this. And run this with the biometric database we have. I want to see some results. Some footage of Caan arriving in New York. Where was he going? Who was he with?"

Stamper read the date on the paper and nodded. "I'll get on it."

"Caan had the highest security clearance, as had Luntz. I want us to get into Caan's life. Something is not right. Something is missing from all this."

"But if he's been cleared through the Single Scope Background Investigation for Top Secret clearance and then by a higher clearance through the Pentagon, surely they've gone through all his life with a fine toothcomb; where the subject has lived, gone to school, interviews with persons who knew him, criminal records, qualifications, previous employment, and all the rest."

"We're doing it again. Check to see if Caan ever failed a polygraph test. Foreign travel, assets, character references, I want us to go over this one more time."

"That's going to take up a lot of resources, Martha."

Meyerstein sighed. She had learned from her father the importance of not taking established facts without scrutinising them one more time. Her team thought she was obsessive with her attention to detail. And Stamper was no different. "Put my mind at rest, Roy. We can't afford not to be meticulous. That's our job, after all. So, let's do it all again."

Stamper shrugged. "OK, whatever you say. It may take time looking into his background. These security clearances can take up to eighteen months."

"I want it all done in eighteen hours."

"Jesus H Christ, Martha." He cleared his throat. "Before I forget. We've been looking over Caan's house. He hasn't lived there in weeks, according to neighbors, maybe longer. The house had been cleared out. Not a thing. Was rented out to a guy called Raymond Baker."

Meyerstein stared through the glass at Luntz. "This is so fucked up it's not real, Roy. There are more questions than answers."

"How do you think he's holding up?"

Meyerstein sighed. "It'll probably hit him in a week. If he's lucky." She had seen dozens of cases, people kidnapped or who underwent a traumatic event, who later crumbled.

Stamper said, "Don't push him too far, Martha. Easy does it. I meant to say, do you want me to speak to Horowitz about this? I can't believe we've been kept out of the loop."

"This is a Pentagon project, which he is assigned to. He wouldn't acknowledge it, even if you brought it up."

"Are you letting it go?"

"For now. I have more pressing concerns, as have you."

Stamper shrugged as if it wouldn't have been the way he'd have done it.

Meyerstein smiled. "It can wait, Roy. We can have the inquiry once this is over." Still smiling, she went back into the room with Luntz. She took a seat and fixed her gaze on the government scientist. His eyes were black, dark rings underneath. "Frank, you've been very helpful," she said. "And we appreciate that. But we have got a major problem on our hands. We need to find Scott Caan. We have checked his home in Frederick, and it turns out no one lives there. The rent was paid, but no one actually lived there since a guy rented it out by the name of Raymond Baker. Does that name mean anything to you?"

Luntz shook his head. "I don't understand. So, where did Scott live?"

"That's just the problem. The place he said he lived, he didn't."

"What do you mean?"

"It means, Frank, that Lt Col Scott Caan has been living a lie. We can't speak to neighbors about him. We don't have cell phone details. We can't find out what was on his laptop. The question is, why has he been living that lie, and who has helped him live that lie? The questions just kinda mount up..." She let the comments just hang in the air.

Luntz bit his lower lip. "I'm at a loss. Truly I am. He seemed..."

Meyerstein leaned over and held his hands. "Frank, we've got to assume the worst. I need to know if you can recreate the anti-viral drugs and vaccines."

Luntz ran his hand through his grey hair and blew out his cheeks. "It would have to be from the notes I kept. I think we could have something in a couple of weeks, best case scenario."

"I'm sorry, but that won't work. We're gonna need something within the next forty-eight hours max."

"That's not realistic. I must test and retest the possible drugs."

"I appreciate that, Frank. But we need a vaccine and anti-virals at the very earliest opportunity. Something that has a good possibility of working. And I want you to work with my colleague, Dr Adam Horowitz, a bioweapons expert."

"I'm sorry, it can't be done within that timescale."

"We will give you whatever resources you want. Money, scientists, that is not an issue."

"I'm sorry, but that's unrealistic."

"Are you going to help us or not?"

Luntz bowed his head. "This is my fault, isn't it?"

"Let's forget recriminations. We need to focus. So, are you going to help us or not?"

"I'll do whatever I can."

TWENTY-THREE

The clock in the ICU room showed Reznick it was 1.47am. He felt helpless as he sat at his daughter's bedside knowing she was fighting for her life. She was only eleven years old. A child. The only sounds were his daughter's shallow breathing and the constant beeping of the ventilator, keeping her alive.

Reznick leaned forward and squeezed her clammy hand. He knew that his daughter should have responded before now. The doctors were also concerned about the fluid on her lungs. The prognosis was bleak.

She showed classic symptoms of an opiate overdose. Eleven breaths a minute and miotic pupils. The machines around Lauren were taking her blood pressure, pulse, respiration and heart rate. The intravenous fluids were pumping in dextrose to her blood. But none of it was making a bit of difference.

He looked at the tubes coming out of her mouth and nose, concealing her flawless, beautiful face. His mind flashed back to the last time he saw her, in late summer, back home in Maine, before she was due to head back to Brookfield. Her face was tanned and her blue eyes had never looked so much like her mother. The way she smiled was just the same. Even the way she laughed.

A sharp knock at the door jolted Reznick out of his reverie and a doctor entered the room. "There's someone here to see you. Assistant Director Meyerstein from the FBI."

Reznick couldn't be bothered speaking to anyone. He only wanted to sit by his daughter's side. He watched her chest rise and then lower, painfully slow. But he knew the FBI weren't going to go away.

He sighed. "Show her in."

The doctor nodded and left the room. A few moments later Meyerstein appeared with a nurse, who checked Lauren's vital signs, noting it down on Lauren's chart, before she left.

Meyerstein shut the door quietly and pulled up a chair beside Reznick. She looked exhausted, dark rings around her eyes. She sat down and sighed. "I'm so sorry," she said.

Reznick stared at his daughter and said nothing.

"The doctors are doing everything they can for her. There's still hope."

Reznick turned and faced Meyerstein. Her eyes were moist. "I hope you're right." He closed his eyes tight. "Christ, I wish I could turn the clock back."

"We all do, Jon." She cleared her throat.

Reznick was suddenly aware of how close they were sitting together.

"Jon, I can see how much you're hurting. Look, I'm so sorry what's happened. No one deserves what you're experiencing."

"Don't they?"

"No, of course not." Meyerstein held his gaze for a moment too long.

Reznick looked down at the floor. "You're wrong. I deserve this. This is entirely my fault."

"You can't talk like that, Jon. That'll not help her."

Reznick closed his eyes, not wishing to open them again. He felt Meyerstein's soft hand on his.

"I got some questions to ask you."

Reznick extricated his hand. "This ain't the time."

"Maybe not. But I'm still going to ask them."

Reznick said nothing.

"They relate to national security. Jon, I'm going to level with you, there is the distinct possibility that many lives could be at risk. Many lives. We talked of that before."

Reznick sat in silence and stared at his daughter.

"There are people pulling the strings, behind the scenes. I want to ask you something, Jon. Does the name Brewling mean anything to you?"

"Like I said, this ain't the time."

"Not an option. Sorry. Jon, I need to know if the name Brewling means anything to you. Was he your handler?"

Reznick sighed. "No."

"You're one hundred per cent sure of that?"

"Absolutely."

"Look, Jon, this guy Brewling… You can't go after him. Is that what you're thinking?"

"I don't even know who this guy is, so how the hell can I go after him?"

"Listen, you've got to allow us to deal with this from now on. I can't allow you to head off and shoot up people all across Miami. We're drawing a line in the sand. Are you clear?"

"So, who is this Brewling?" he said. "What is Norton & Weiss Inc? Are they working for the Agency?"

"I can't talk about that."

Reznick blew out his cheeks and bowed his head. A headache was developing, throbbing deep inside his brain. He put it down to exhaustion.

"I'm curious, Jon."

"Curious about what?"

"How you get into the line of work you do. When you left Delta, I mean."

"I got a call from a man. He knew a lot about me. Then he asked me nicely if I wanted to work for him."

Meyerstein was shaking her head. "As simple as that?"

"Pretty much. They pay me a lot of money. And I sure as hell don't get asked dumb-ass questions."

Meyerstein sighed but said nothing, waiting for him to fill the silence.

He sighed. "You still trying to figure out why a guy like me is involved in this?"

Meyerstein shrugged.

"Quite simple really. It's called plausible deniability. No direct link to the American government. That's what this is all about. I don't exist in their eyes. But we all know that's a lie. Everyone and their dog know that assassination is part and parcel of who we are. It keeps us on top of the bad guys, and to hell with the law."

Meyerstein nodded. "I appreciate your candour." She smiled at him. "Look, Jon, I've gotta go. Is there anything else you need from us?"

Reznick caught a whiff of her citrus perfume again. "There is something."

"What?"

"I need to get my daughter out of here."

Meyerstein said nothing.

"This place is wide open. She's a sitting duck."

Meyerstein sighed. "I've raised this with my superiors, but this isn't going to be easy."

"Make it happen. I don't know how you do it, but just do it. Whoever is behind this will want to teach me a lesson. They'll be crazy that I have my daughter and you have the scientist."

Meyerstein ran a hand through her hair. She looked tired.

"I need my daughter to be somewhere they'll never get at her. I'll speak to your guys, whatever you want. But I want my daughter at least to be protected. Just make it happen."

She went quiet for a few moments before clearing her throat and getting up from her seat. "Leave this with me.

I'm going to make a call." She left the room, closing the door gently behind her.

Reznick sighed long and hard.

Lauren stirred slightly.

When Meyerstein returned, she shut the door quietly behind her and sat down beside him. "OK, here's what we've got," she whispered. "We're rolling. I've just spoken to the head of emergency medicine at the Naval Hospital in Pensacola. They've agreed to admit your daughter. And I can assure you, security won't be an issue there."

Reznick nodded. "Thank you. But I need to go with her."

"That's a given."

Reznick took a deep breath and then exhaled slowly. "I owe you."

Meyerstein's gaze lingered for a few moments. She smiled sympathetically. "There will be two special agents with you. My guys will want to know the chain of events that brought this about. They'll be babysitting you, just so you don't go walkabout. And you still need to answer for Merceron."

Reznick looked at his daughter. Her face was pasty, breathing still shallow. "I don't care about that now. Get my daughter to Pensacola and get her well."

Meyerstein smiled at him.

He sensed her empathy, but could see it was cloaked in steely professionalism. "Why did you do this for me? You didn't have to. You could've hauled me in. Couldn't you?"

Meyerstein's face was impassive. "Yes, I could've hauled you in. But we'd never have seen Luntz again."

"But I could've lied to you."

Meyerstein shook her head. "I can tell when people are lying to me, Jon. You don't strike me as a liar. A tough son-of-a-bitch, maybe. But never a liar."

Suddenly the door opened and two FBI agents walked in. "Are we good to go, ma'am?" one of them said.

Meyerstein nodded, pushed back her chair and stood looking down at Reznick. She handed him her card. "If there's anything else I can do, Jon, for you or your daughter, don't hesitate to contact me. This has got my cell number on it."

Then she walked out of the ICU room and past the two Feds, as the door closed behind her.

TWENTY-FOUR

Thomas Wesley was already awake when he heard the sound of cars pulling up outside his home. As his wife slept soundly beside him, he leaned over and checked the luminous dial on his bedside alarm clock. It showed 3.03am. Strange. It was unusual to hear anything in his quiet cul-de-sac after nightfall.

The most noise came when there were Independence Day barbecues being held on front lawns, or leading up to Halloween, when the kids from around the block would go door-to-door, trick or treating. Most, if not all, families worked during the day and by eight pm the oak-lined street was dead.

He got out of his bed and peered through the slats of the wooden blinds. Two Suburbans were blocking his driveway. Four men in dark suits walked up his garden path. Then his bell rang.

Who were they? Cops? Feds?

His wife stirred and switched on her bedside light looking confused, rubbing her eyes. "What's going on, honey?"

Wesley pulled on some sweat pants over his boxer shorts, put on a T-shirt and his slippers. "We've got company."

Three sharp knocks on the front door followed by the ringing of the bell again.

"Thomas, what's going on?" she said, pulling on her dressing gown.

"I don't know."

Wesley headed downstairs followed by his wife. The chain was on the door. He turned the key and slowly cracked open the front door a few inches.

An imposing man wearing a dark suit flashed a Department of Defense Special Agent badge in his face. "DCIS." Then he handed Wesley a typed court order with a red wax seal on it through the space in the door. "Thomas Wesley?"

Wesley scanned the court order and shrugged. "Yes, that's me. What's this about?"

"We have issued you a warrant to search the premises, Mr Wesley. Open the door immediately. I believe you know what this is about."

Wesley took the chain off the door and the man brushed past him as three other men followed. He stared at the wax seal as his mind raced, trying to take it all in. He knew the DCIS were the Defense Criminal Investigative Services. In essence, they were the criminal investigative arm of the Office of the Inspector General, US Department of Defense. He also knew they had full federal law enforcement authority and carried firearms.

He shut the door as three of the men fanned out throughout the house. Two downstairs and one upstairs. The lead investigator remained in the hallway with Wesley and his wife.

His wife held her hand to her chest. "Thomas, what's this all about?"

Wesley reached out and held her hand. "I don't know," he said. He turned to the lead investigator, a tall, swarthy man, with well-cut suit and black shoes. "Am I under arrest?"

The lead investigator: "Sir, we hope you will come with us and answer some questions."

"Regarding?"

The man sighed. "Regarding the possible mishandling of classified information."

••••

It was a forty-five minute journey down MD-295 South. No one spoke to Wesley. No small talk. Nothing. He sat and stared out at the headlights of the passing cars. Had Lance alerted them? Surely not.

The more he thought of it the more he wondered if he hadn't miscalculated by going straight to Lance. After all, he was a powerful politician with a growing reputation. Had he passed it on to the Department of Defence?

He felt isolated in the car. The smell of one of the men's cologne was sticking to the back of his throat, making him nauseous. The tension was palpable, not helped by the silence.

When they drove along Army Navy Drive in Arlington – very close to the Pentagon – Wesley assumed they were taking him to the DCIS HQ. But instead, they passed a sign on the right at an underpass for the Army Navy Country Club, and then it was a left and a left again, past some nondescript office buildings and down a ramp into a near-deserted basement garage.

Armed guards with semi-automatic rifles patrolled the garage leading to the elevators. What the hell was this?

The car stopped next to the elevator and the lead man got out and came round and opened Wesley's door.

Wesley stepped out of the car. "Where are we?"

"Don't worry. It's just routine."

The man led Wesley to the elevator as the three men followed close behind. The five of them got in the elevator and descended in silence to a sub-basement. Then he was led down a series of narrow corridors and finally in to a windowless room.

A mirror on one wall. They were watching him.

"Sit down, Thomas," the lead investigator said. "This is not a court of law. We're just wanting to talk to you, get to know you a bit better, and see what we can do to help you."

Wesley sat down and said nothing.

"You want a coffee, glass of water, Coke, anything?"

"I'm good thanks." Wesley was trying to show he was relaxed and not frightened.

"My name is Carlos Rodriguez," the lead investigator said, pulling up a chair opposite, "senior investigator in matters pertaining to the NSA." Rodriguez shifted in his seat. "I've just been reading your file."

"Sorry to interrupt, but I was expecting to be taken to 400 Army Navy Drive. What's this place?"

"Satellite office. It's crammed where we are."

"And the guys with the guns?"

"Heightened security after a recent internal audit."

Wesley nodded.

"OK, Thomas, I appreciate this must all be very unnerving."

Wesley forced a grin. "You got that right."

"But I want you to know that we're here to help. We don't want to point fingers. We just want to try and understand what has happened. But I'll be honest, we need answers." He went quiet for a few moments. "You see, what I can't get my head around, is how someone like you, a smart guy, would want to jeopardise American security by stealing and then leaking classified documents."

"Hey, let's not get ahead of ourselves. I don't believe I have ever jeopardised American security. I am a patriot."

"OK, we'll leave that aside just now. Would you like to talk about a conversation you had with Congressman Lance Drake, an old friend of yours from way back?"

Wesley said nothing. So, it was Drake. Son-of-a-bitch.

"Isn't it true that you passed to him an alleged decrypted conversation of a top secret military intelligence nature?" Rodriguez leaned back in his seat and shrugged as if waiting for an answer.

Wesley sighed. "Do you know why I did that?"

"I was hoping you would be able to help us with that."

"I had no other choice. I went through the system, and

no one wanted to know. I was in their bad books because I decrypted a conversation that linked a White House adviser to the Chinese military. I was sidelined as the adviser was well-connected. No one wanted to listen to me. They thought I was an embarrassment."

Rodriguez frowned and bit his lower lip. "So, you alerted the Congressman because you thought as he was an old friend, he might get something done?"

"Precisely. I wanted someone who had the clout, to ask the questions. I didn't want to go to the papers. What the hell was I to do when the established avenues are shut down?"

Rodriguez leaned forward and stared at him long and hard. "So, you're saying you admit leaking this information, is that right?"

"Only to Lance. I thought I could trust him."

"Have you leaked this to anyone else?"

"Of course I haven't. I understand the seriousness of this. The ramifications."

The agent said nothing.

Wesley said, "Have you listened to it?"

"Yes, it was intriguing. Our guys are currently working on the embedded message it contained. Did you manage to crack it?"

"Nope, but not for want of trying."

"So let's be clear, you didn't uncover the message, if indeed it does contain some form of data communication?"

"Correct."

The guy cleared his throat and smiled.

Wesley sighed long and hard. He was tired and wanted to go home. "Look, can we hurry this along a bit?"

"All in good time, Thomas."

"Have you guys established the identities of those on the tape?"

"We have a very good idea."

Wesley clenched his fist. "Well, thank God. At last someone gets it. And you guys have passed this on to the Feds and the NSA?"

"It's all in hand, Thomas."

A sense of relief swept over Wesley, glad the right people now knew the threat to the country. "Finally, at long last…"

"It's a stunning piece of work, piecing this together, I've got to say."

Wesley felt his cheeks go red. "I started getting goose bumps when I started to unravel this. The raw intercept was just audio of a pop song. The Bangles or some crap from the eighties. But then I stripped all that away and got to an encrypted conversation. It took a long time to decipher, but eventually I got. I ran the programs to see if it matched anyone on the NSA files, and it brought up a perfect match and a near-perfect match."

The agent shifted in his seat as one of the other agents left the room.

"Don't get me wrong, I thought the exact same thing as you guys. But it's a very convincing bit of voice morphing. I'm assuming you got right down to the authentic voices, right?"

"Tell me how you did it."

"Well, initially, I thought it sounded like a former senior CIA agent and the recently retired head of Mossad. You came to the same conclusion, right?"

The agent nodded. "Did you discuss who was on the recordings, when you spoke to the Congressman?"

"No, I wanted him to listen to it first, and then speak to me. He probably doesn't know who the hell it is."

"Getting back to your initial assessment…"

"Yeah, well it seemed on the surface, like a slam dunk. Two perfect matches. But they weren't. One was one hundred per cent perfect – the former CIA spook – the other was a ninety-nine point three per cent match. And that's what intrigued me. I'm a perfectionist. I delved deeper into the voice. Analysing it. I examined waveform graphs for hours at a time."

"What's that?"

"Waveform graphs? Well, they show detailed information about the environmental noises in the background, clicks. Sound depth. And I saw a couple of anomalies that pointed to highly sophisticated, state of the art, voice morphing."

"You better try and explain, in layman's terms, what exactly the hell voice morphing entails."

Wesley blew out his cheeks. "Voice morphing technology was originally developed at the Los Alamos laboratory in New Mexico. In effect, an expert can, in *real-time*, clone speech patterns and develop a near perfect copy." He felt himself getting excited talking about it and how he had cracked it. "In this digital morphing world, nothing is as it seems. And that includes voices. I am convinced the voice of the Israeli intelligence guy is fake. A quite brilliant fake. It's near-nigh impossible to detect, it's that good."

The agent leaned back in his seat and bit the end of his pencil. "That's intriguing."

"Once I'd stripped away the voice morphing and reduced it to the genuine conversation, it wasn't long before I had figured it out. I now knew who the other guy was. And it wasn't a member of Mossad or former member of Mossad or any Israeli."

"So, who is it, Thomas?"

Wesley was about to answer when it suddenly struck him that he'd been the one doing all the talking. The one detailing all his work and analysis he had carried out. He looked around as the impassive cold faces of the men in suits scrutinised him. He didn't know why, but he started to feel uncomfortable. Not overly uncomfortable. Just a feeling that something wasn't right. "Look guys, I've been very open with you, and given it to you straight. I need a break, if that's OK. I'd also like to call my wife. She'll be worried."

"That'll be arranged. But let's talk about the other voice on the recording."

"Listen, I want to speak to my wife."

"She's back at the house. Don't worry about a thing."

Wesley said nothing.

"Thomas, can you tell me just now if you have a definitive version of the conversation of the two original voices? Because, I think we need to know about that before we go any further with this."

"I need to speak to my wife."

The agent got up and smiled. "Not a problem. I'll go and speak to my boss. Probably have to wake him up. You can have a break and call your wife."

Wesley sighed in relief. His imagination had begun to get the better of him.

"Can I get you a drink? A water? Soda, perhaps?"

"Black coffee would be great."

"You got it."

The agent disappeared with his colleagues. Wesley turned and looked at his reflection in the mirror. He looked haggard. Eyes bloodshot.

A few minutes later, the door opened and a young female agent walked in. She wore a dark blue suit, white blouse and was carrying a mug of coffee. She looked in her mid-thirties and was very attractive. "Milk or sugar?"

"It's good as it is," Wesley said.

She handed him the mug and smiled, before leaving the room.

Wesley sighed and closed his eyes for a few moments thinking of his wife. She'd be worried sick. He lifted the mug to his mouth and took a couple of gulps of the strong coffee. He tasted the strong flavour that he enjoyed. Then all of a sudden, he felt a tingling feeling rush up his arms and to his head. The coffee mug fell to the floor.

Then blackness engulfed his world.

TWENTY-FIVE

The sun was edging over the horizon when the twin-engine Cessna air ambulance landed on runway three at Forrest Sherman Field, the naval air station in Pensacola. Reznick helped the doctor and two nurses lift the gurney, with his daughter strapped to it, from the plane and into a waiting ambulance. He sat beside her and held her hand, as they sped off on a seven-mile journey, lights flashing, to the Naval Hospital, and waved past the armed guards at the back gate security checkpoint.

Two feds travelled in a car following close behind. The ambulance pulled up outside the eight-storey hospital and Lauren was rushed straight up to the intensive care unit on the fourth floor.

Reznick could only watch as Lauren was hooked up to another ventilator. Nurses and a couple of doctors took her vital signs and talked about the risks involved in giving a higher dose of Naloxone, as if Reznick wasn't there.

A doctor pulled back the left eyelid and shone a penlight in her eyes. "That's interesting. Slight dilation." He did the same for the right eye. And then repeated it. "Dilation confirmed."

Then the doctor checked her arms and legs for track marks. "Lauren, can you hear me?" he said. There was urgency in his voice. "Lauren, wake up."

But she didn't respond.

After what seemed a lifetime, one of the doctors finally approached Reznick. "I believe you are the father, sir," he said.

Reznick nodded.

"Come with me," the doctor said.

He led Reznick out into the corridor and headed up the stairs to his office. He swiped his ID badge at the side of a door with the sign "Dr Jerry Winkelman". A beep. "Please come in," he said, as he pushed the door open.

The doctor sat down in a black leather chair behind his paper-strewn desk and leaned back in his seat. "Take a seat," he said.

Reznick sat down opposite.

"Lauren, as you've just seen, is seriously ill. To say otherwise would be misleading and wrong. But she did respond to the light, which might give us a bit of hope."

Reznick nodded.

"But her age is adding to our concern, and the length of time she has been in this heroin coma. We're going to give her an extremely high dosage of an antidote, which we think has to be administered right now, if we are to have any hope of bringing her round."

Reznick felt disassociated as if the doctor wasn't talking about his daughter.

"We believe that the marks on her arm were caused by skin-popping, where the needle is sunk into any bit of skin, not direct to the vein. And this may be the thing that will save her, although we can't say for sure. Your daughter's case is very similar to one I dealt with earlier this year. A thirteen year old who'd tried shooting up with his friends, and had been skin-popping. He recovered despite slipping into a coma for twenty-four hours."

When they returned to the ICU room, Lauren was again unrecognisable, tubes coming out of her nose and mouth, as the machines kept her alive.

The doctor said, "She's on a ventilator because of the low respiratory rate. And I've been told that the blood gases were shown to be hypoxic. We will monitor your daughter before, during and after this treatment process, keeping a close eye on temperature, pulse, urine output, electrocardiography, and O2 saturation."

Reznick stared down at her.

The sound of the beeping from the ventilator was the only response.

The doctor said, "Sorry, but you're going to have to leave, at least for now," he said "We need to begin her treatment. Why don't you go to the Rest Room and get some sleep. It's for the parents of patients. You look as though you need it."

The doctor called over to a nurse and asked her to show Reznick to the Rest Room.

Reznick took one long final look at his daughter. She looked as if she was just sleeping. Out in the corridor, the two Feds were waiting. They followed Reznick and the nurse along the corridor to the Rest Room without saying a word.

The nurse showed him into the large room with wooden blinds, TV on the wall. "If you need anything, just pick up the phone on the bedside table and this will take you straight through to reception."

Waves of tiredness washed over Reznick. The last two days had been insane. "Thank you."

The nurse turned to leave and Reznick noticed the two Feds were pulling up chairs outside the room to babysit him. The door slammed shut.

Reznick closed the blinds, took off his shoes and lay down on the bed. He closed his eyes. But he couldn't get the picture of Lauren – covered in tubes and hooked up to the ventilator – out of his head.

His mind drifted as sleep beckoned. Need to be strong for Lauren. There were already signs she was fighting back. He would also dig deep. He was going to will her back to him.

He had done all he could. Her life was now in the hands of the doctors and the Lord above. His shattered mind tracked back to when she was a ten month old baby. He was in Bahrain when he got a call. "Lauren has pneumonia," Elisabeth had said, voice riven by anxiety. She said Lauren's little chest was rapidly rising up and down, struggling for breath. He felt sick. Helpless. But Elisabeth had told him that Lauren was a fighter, just like her dad. And over the coming days, as he conducted a surveillance operation on an Islamist leader in one of the most Godforsaken countries he'd ever had the misfortune to visit, his daughter slowly fought back to health. But what she faced here and now was different.

The more he thought of her predicament the darker his mood. Her innocence had been taken. She had been defiled.

Reznick felt his eyelids becoming heavy. He felt himself falling. Deeper and deeper. Waves of tiredness swamped him. Then he was gone. The sky was a perfect blue. He was standing on a beach. He saw Lauren in the distance, aged around eleven months, paddling in the cold summer ocean, recovered from her pneumonia. Her cheeks were red and she was laughing and splashing in her pink bathing costume. It was late-August 2011.

He tried to shout and warn her of the breakers crashing onto shore. But his voice was lost in the roar of the water and howl of the wind, as the waves rolled up the sand. He shouted again, but still she didn't hear. Then Elisabeth appeared from the water and took Lauren by the hand, leading her to safety.

Suddenly he was cloaked in darkness. The smell of acrid smoke filled the air. The sound of sirens. He was running through a tunnel. Heart pounding. Darkness all around. Then he was out of the tunnel. Skyscrapers everywhere. He was in the city. Manhattan. And the sun was shining. A perfect sky.

He looked up. A tiny figure high up in the burning building, waving a handkerchief. Tower One. "Jon! Jon! Please come and get me! Jon! Jon!" He tried to move, but he was paralyzed. He willed himself to move. But he was frozen. All of a sudden an ominous thunderous roar and the tiny figure was swallowed in a cloud of dust and ash as the building descended at free fall speed, the smell of burning fuel thick in the air, the screaming unrelenting.

Reznick sat bolt upright in the bed, bathed in sweat and struggling for breath.

TWENTY-SIX

The *Gulfstream* was en route to New York, cruising at thirty-five thousand feet, as Meyerstein held a progress update meeting with senior members of her team. She was in full flow when the phone on her armrest rang.

Meyerstein sighed and picked it up. "Assistant Director Meyerstein," she said.

"Martha, it's Freddie Limonton in Washington." He was the FBI's top computer guy working at HQ. He had been seconded from the FBI Forensic, Audio and Image Analysis Unit (FAVIAU). "We've run face recognition scanning and retinal scans into the system for Scott Caan in New York for November 19th."

"I'm listening."

"We got something. We have picked him up from a scan at JFK."

Martha clenched her fist. She felt herself flush at the display of emotion in front of her team. They just shrugged wondering what she'd been told. "Good work."

"I've just emailed you an edited three minutes and twenty-five seconds we have of Scott Caan. It's been pieced together from countless cameras around Terminal 5. The first piece of footage comes in at one minute and twenty-two seconds, as he walks through the terminal."

"You got his flight details?"

"JetBlue from Dulles. The second lot of footage was taken in Tribeca, Lower Manhattan. Corner of Duane and Greenwich is where he gets out. The footage should be with you now."

"Lower Manhattan?" Meyerstein scanned her inbox and saw there was one new message. "OK, Freddie, I got that. But I need another favour."

"You don't ask much."

"I know, I know. Listen. Same guy, I want his image ran through every CCTV database we can get our hands on, especially government buildings and trains in New York City in the last month. But also in businesses in the Tribeca area. What was he doing there on November 19? We need to try and get a handle on his movements. Where has he visited? You know the drill."

"You want footage of every surveillance camera database to be scanned in the last month? Whoa, Martha, are you serious?"

"Absolutely."

He sighed long and hard. "That's a huge trawl. That could take–"

"Then you better get started. You need extra resources. You got it. He's out there somewhere."

Meyerstein double clicked the file and a frozen still of Caan automatically appeared on the large screen. He was strikingly handsome, high cheekbones, dark hair, dark eyes and clean-shaven. She pointed to the remote control that was on a table where Stamper was sitting. "OK, Roy, let's run this straight through first. This is the first visual of Caan since he went missing from the lab. Taken on November 19."

A few murmurs from her team.

Stamper rolled his eyes. "A month ago? That's a lifetime."

"I know, I know. But it's all we've got so far. Let's run it."

Stamper pressed the Play button and the image of Caan came into view. He strode past the huge windows of Terminal

5, which overlooked the runway. Then past the Lacoste shop. He wore a pair of faded jeans, Timberland boots and a dark coat.

Meyerstein said, "Very cute. He doesn't stand out at all. Blends in real nice."

Stamper stared at the screen. "It's no wonder this guy hasn't come up on anyone's radar. He looks like an ordinary Joe just visiting the Big Apple."

They watched as the lean Caan ambled past the shops in the terminal before he stopped to look in the window of the Ron Jon Surfer Shop.

Stamper said, "Counter surveillance measure, what do you think, Martha?"

"Well, he sure as hell wouldn't be surfing in New York in November, that's for sure."

The footage, spliced together from numerous cameras in the terminal, switched angles as he meandered past the shops, carefully avoiding the hundreds of other passengers with huge bags and suitcases. He walked past a Japanese restaurant, then a silver jewelry shop and out to a long line of yellow cabs outside.

"Freeze that, Roy!"

Meyerstein pointed at the screen. "Excellent. Now run the plates of that cab, Roy."

Stamper scribbled the details and handed it to one of his team.

Meyerstein said, "OK, Roy, let's roll the footage to Lower Manhattan."

The footage picked up Caan as he got out of the same cab. "OK," Meyerstein said, "This is Caan arriving in Tribeca. Kinda upscale these days. Let's pay attention."

The footage showed Caan carrying a holdall walking across the street at the corner of Duane and Greenwich. "Freeze that, if you will," she said. She turned to look at her team. "He is carrying a bag. Go back to the airport footage, Roy. I'm sure he wasn't carrying anything."

Roy rewound the footage. It confirmed that Meyerstein was right. No holdall.

"Where did the holdall come from? Was this placed in the taxi for him? We need to know, people."

Meyerstein faced the freeze-framed screen showing Caan at the airport. "Go back to Tribeca." She shifted in her seat aware she was snapping at her team. She needed to calm down.

They watched Caan again emerge from the cab in Tribeca. "I want our guys in New York to swamp the area around Duane and Greenwich, and start asking questions. I want every resident within one block of there to be shown a picture of Caan. Do they know him? Have they seen him out and about? Was he staying there? Visiting someone? Check all the hotels within a mile. I want to know the instant we have a breakthrough."

Stamper groaned. "This footage is a month old, Martha."

"It's all we have. It's a start."

Meyerstein wasn't as pessimistic as Stamper. He viewed himself as a realist and a pragmatist. And it was true. But sometimes he didn't view small breakthroughs in the same light as she did. To her it was concrete proof that they were on the right track. She learned that as a child watching her father in his studying. The forensic way he pieced together the smallest facts, and constructed a rational and plausible case as part of his preparations. Nothing was too small to overlook. She was doing the same. The FBI now knew Caan had visited New York and when. They had something to work with, even if it was one month old.

Meyerstein sank back in her seat. She was so tired she couldn't sleep. It was pure adrenaline that was keeping her going. She was certain her heart rate was constantly beating faster these days.

She looked around at her team again. Exhausted faces, all running on empty. "We're getting close now. I want every FBI field office, police force and all government agencies to be made aware of Caan and his image. I want every avenue explored, and leads followed up."

Roy gave a wry smile from his seat in the opposite aisle and got up, before taking a seat beside her. He leaned in close. "Martha," he said, his voice low, "you need to ease up. You're gonna give yourself a heart attack."

Meyerstein nodded, knowing he was right. She needed to slow down. Maybe even take time off. But that wasn't a realistic option until the investigation was concluded. Too much was at stake. "The bastard is out there. We'll get him. Make sure the New York field office has the footage. I want to know what the hell he was doing in Manhattan. Was this reconnaissance? Meeting with people who may have conceived of a bio-terror plot?"

"They know what to do. We're getting there. We'll find the son-of-a-bitch."

The team started firing out instructions via secure email and encrypted phones.

Within five minutes, Martha had Tom Callaghan, the Special Agent in Charge of New York City, on the phone.

"Where's this come from?" Callaghan asked.

"We got lucky. It's footage from CCTV taken at Terminal 5 at JFK on November 19. Have you watched the footage?"

"My guys are watching it just now."

"We need to throw everything at this, Tom. He was in Tribeca."

"Leave it with me, Martha. You en route?"

"I'll be with you in under an hour."

Meyerstein and five of her team took the elevator to the twenty-third floor of the FBI's New York field office, located in a monolithic forty-one storey glass-walled slab in Lower Manhattan. She had visited numerous times and was always impressed by the high quality of the Special Agents.

In a conference room, she joined nine of the Joint Terrorism Task force – including Tom Callaghan – around the table for an emergency meeting, and once again hooked up with the high-tech operations room at the National Counterterrorism Center in McLean, Virginia for a secure video teleconference. She brought everyone up to speed. On the plasma screen she could see four men and a woman at the NCTC.

"OK folks," she said, "we're all coming at this from a multitude of angles. But we need to focus on not only tracking down Caan and trying to establish where he went in Lower Manhattan, but what the possible targets are."

Callaghan piped up, "My team are swarming all over Lower Manhattan as we speak. But this ain't gonna be easy."

Meyerstein looked up at the screen, which showed the counterterrorism experts staring back at her. "These images are from a month ago, but I believe that Caan is a serious threat. Potential threats don't always originate from outside the US. We only have to think back to spring 2010, to remember the bombing in Times Square. The threat was from within. The fact that these devices have been planted in a government protected building, housing numerous agencies, may indicate the militia movement. We all remember Waco. The Oklahoma bombing, by Timothy McVeigh. However, we most certainly can't rule out the possibility that Caan is receiving help, either from inside or outside the US. I've got to be frank with you, this investigation is morphing into something much more significant and potentially much more catastrophic than I could have imagined."

On the screen from the NCTC, a middle-aged grey-haired man, Principal Deputy Director Arthur Black, put up his hand. "If I could just inject here, Martha. I just want to say that in all my years in this business, I think the way this is developing is very unsettling. This all points to a mass terror attack. And I think none of us should be in any doubt about the changing face and increasing complexity of modern terrorism. But Caan, to me, doesn't add up. Army government scientist. Has he gone rogue? For whom? Who's behind this? This clearly is not just a lone man with a grievance. My question is, Martha, why do you think he was in New York on 19 November?"

Meyerstein nodded. "I don't think anyone could say for sure, Arthur, but if pressed, I would say that Caan was doing reconnaissance, perhaps acquainting himself with a target or targets. As we are all acutely aware, New York City is the number one target for terrorists. There have been nine known plots involving targets in New York unearthed since 9/11, including a couple in the last three months. They included plans to detonate fuel tanks at JFK, plant explosives in the Holland Tunnel and several plots to attack subway stations. You can take your pick. If we also factor in that it is the largest city in the United States, not to mention a global financial and media center, you can see why it is like a magnet for terrorists."

Black and his NCC colleagues nodded, as did those round the table in New York, acutely aware of Manhattan's position as the number one target in the country.

A sharp knock at the door and Roy Stamper popped his head round the conference room door, face drawn. "Excuse me, ma'am. Freddie needs to speak. It's urgent."

Martha leaned back in her seat. "Roy, we're in the middle of a video teleconference, can't it wait?"

"Afraid not."

Martha looked around the table and then up at the faces on the huge screen. "Sorry," she said, "I'll be back with you in a couple of minutes. Take five."

She went outside. "This better be good," she said, as Stamper held the phone.

"He says it can't wait."

Stamper handed Meyerstein the phone. "Yeah, talk to me, Freddie."

Simonton was breathing heavy down the phone. "We've been running the software on Caan, face recognition, retinal scans, trying to track his movements over the last month," he said.

"What've you got?"

"Two things. Firstly, we've got a perfect match on Caan on November 19th from cameras outside The Food Emporium, nearby. And we've pinpointed a location."

Meyerstein clenched her fist and grinned at Stamper who shrugged his shoulders. "What was the second thing?"

A long sigh. "He's been here in New York in the last couple of days."

"What?"

"I've just sent you a picture. He's dressed as a maintenance man and is carrying a bag."

Meyerstein went over to her temporary desk and sat down and pulled up the image from her laptop inbox. She scanned the picture. He was the same man who was walking through Terminal 5 of JFK a month earlier. He had an easy smile, olive complexion. "This is him?"

"Perfect match."

"So, where was this taken?"

He let out another long sigh. "Martha, this picture was taken by a surveillance camera outside 26 Federal Plaza, as he entered the building you're in."

"Right here?"

"That's not all. I've just sent two images of him taken on hidden surveillance cameras by a cleaning company who service most of the building. Have you got them?"

She scrolled through her inbox, but nothing. "It's empty."

"Martha, I'll resend them."

"Goddamn, what do they show?"

"He's placed devices in the air vents all over the New York field office. The goddamn office you're in. Get yourself the hell out of there."

Meyerstein had to move fast. She gave the evacuation order after speaking to O'Donoghue and the head of the New York field office. The reason cited to evacuate and relayed to other government agencies working in the building was that there was a bomb scare. Hundreds streamed out into the plaza.

The White House, the Pentagon, and the Office of the Director of National Intelligence were all briefed.

Then she took a call from the head of the FBI's counterterrorism analytical branch, Simon Bullard, whose team had concluded that Caan was receiving outside help, and wasn't acting alone. When Meyerstein asked if there was any hint of foreign involvement, he said ominously, "It can't be ruled out."

The more she knew about Caan and the emerging threat, the more chilling the scenario became. America was under threat. But it wasn't just Caan. Who else was involved? What foreign government, if any? Was this Iran? Syria? They had numerous links to terrorist groups. What was the motivation of Caan? The questions kept on mounting up as the pressure on her and her team intensified.

Meyerstein and her team immediately headed to an FBI safe house in a suite of offices in the Upper East Side to remotely view the work of a Hazmat team scouring the air vents of the building in New York, whilst on another screen they reconvened the secure video teleconference with the National Counterterrorism Center on huge plasma screen TV.

This time, the FBI Deputy Director, Bill O'Donoghue, was sitting in. She hadn't heard anything since she flat-out refused to obey his order to stand aside.

"Martha," O'Donoghue said, leaning back in his seat, "I'm glad everyone got out safe. OK, what's the latest?"

"Thank you, sir." Meyerstein felt a headache coming on. She let out a long sigh. "Sir, we're searching an apartment in Tribeca as we speak. This is an emerging threat."

"Is this some an anti-government thing? Are we talking militia?"

"We can't rule anything in or out at this stage, sir. The questions keep mounting up. How could this have been allowed to happen?"

O'Donoghue was nodding.

"Caan has, in effect, wandered into a highly guarded government building and possibly planted biomaterials. It's appalling. We could be talking about worst case scenarios."

O'Donoghue was scribbling some notes. "Go on, Martha."

"Look, sir, we still don't know what the risks are as we haven't established what has been planted. Secondly, if this is a real bio-threat, under current guidelines, we do not instigate panic. Telling the public there are bio-bombs would turn New York into anarchy. But what I would say is that this threat is far too sophisticated to be just one lone nut. I'm not buying that."

"What are Counterterrorism saying on this?"

Meyerstein reiterated what she had been told. "And it raises the spectre that he is receiving outside help."

O'Donoghue leaned back in his seat and pulled off his glasses and pinched the bridge of his nose. "I've got to say, whilst we are behind the curve, I'm impressed that we are on this. So what are you saying? Is this a network?"

"Very much so, sir. I think they are clearly a sophisticated and powerful network. And I don't just mean some dangerous amateurs. I'm talking about an individual, in this case Caan, who may be working in cahoots with, or under direct orders from, a nation state, we just can't rule that out."

Meyerstein saw on the big screen that the NCTC people were nodding at her comments.

Principal Assistant Director Arthur Black put up his hand to speak.

"Go right ahead, Arthur," she said.

"Thank you. America has many enemies. But I don't think it's helpful to speculate as to who could be behind this at this stage."

Meyerstein nodded. "I agree. But I think we have to assume the worst, that Caan has planted devices within these air vents. The motivation? We just don't know."

A man on the screen from the National Counterterrorism Center piped up. "Hi, Martha, Ray Malone, of NCTC. I hear what you're saying, Martha, but haven't the FBI got a moral obligation to let the people of Manhattan know what it is that's inside the vents?"

"The last I checked the FBI rulebook, we serve the people as a federal investigative body and an internal intelligence agency. We have investigative jurisdiction over more than two hundred categories of federal crime. We have no moral obligation, other than as parents to our children. Look, we're expecting a *real-time* feed from the Hazmat team working in the air vents in the next five minutes. I think until then, this is all speculation."

She pressed a button and the screen went black, the video teleconference over.

She stared out of the window at the Upper East Side skyline. Meyerstein reconsidered the thrust of where the complex investigation was heading. She heard behavioural scientists, profilers, psychologists and a whole host of others outlining what sort of person Scott Caan was.

His medical records were subpoenaed. He was in excellent health. The apartment was being worked over by forensics. The profilers said that there had been myriad reports into the psychology and sociology of terrorism. And there weren't any detectable personality traits to allow the FBI to identify a would-be terrorist. The average terrorist is also not mentally ill, although they are, to a greater or lesser extent, deluded by ideological or religious beliefs. They went on to say the potential terrorists who show signs of mental illness, or have noticeable behaviour traits, are not likely candidates to be chosen by those behind a terrorist attack.

The more she learned, the less she understood about Scott Caan. It was strange that there was no more footage of Caan in New York. Why was that? "Someone is shielding him. This is not the sort of thing that's dreamed up on the spur of the moment. So, where the hell is he?"

"God only knows," came the muted reply from Ray Stamper, staring at the live news feed, which had flickered into life from Lower Manhattan.

TWENTY-SEVEN

Reznick was floating in a sea of darkness, a black sky above. The sound of humming like a chopper blade and then an incessant beeping. He opened his eyes and found he was sitting by his daughter's bedside, still holding her hand. He sat up and stared at her.

Her eyes were closed, face pained. She didn't look peaceful. She made the occasional moan, as if riven by nightmares in her deep sleep. He wondered if she would ever wake up. But even if she did, what state would she be in?

The sound of footsteps approaching out in the corridor. A sharp knock at the door and a nurse entered the room. "Excuse me. There's a call for you at the nursing station."

Reznick shrugged. "Did they give a name?"

"Said they were calling from Miami. Said you were a friend of his father."

Reznick wondered how Ron Leggett knew where he was. His gut feeling told him something was wrong. Surely the Feds hadn't passed on the information? "OK," he sighed. He followed the nurse out of the ICU room and headed to the nursing station halfway down the corridor. The two Feds followed.

A receptionist pointed to the phone on the desk. "There you go, sir," she said, flashing a white smile.

He picked up the phone and turned his back to the woman before he spoke, the two Feds watching him close by. "Yeah, who's this?"

A long silence on the line. But he knew someone was there. "Who's calling?"

A long sigh came down the line. "I'm very disappointed, Jon." It was the electronically distorted voice, which had instructed Reznick to head down to Miami "You didn't keep your side of the bargain."

Reznick's insides tightened and heart beat faster. He turned and snapped his fingers, signalling to the Feds. He covered the mouthpiece of the phone and whispered to one of them. "Do a trace on this call. Right now."

The Fed nodded and took out his cell phone to make the call.

"What do you want?" Reznick said.

"Did you think you could move Lauren without us knowing about it, Jon?"

Reznick felt the anger build deep inside him, gnawing at his chest. He wondered how they knew where his daughter was.

"All you had to do, Jon, was deliver the scientist, and you daughter wouldn't have been harmed. But instead, you decided to take matters into your own hands. And now look at Lauren. Do you feel guilty, Jon? Do you wonder if you made the wrong call?

Reznick said nothing.

"I don't think she's gonna make it, Jon."

Reznick could see it was mind games.

"We're not going to go away, Jon. When this is over, we're coming after your little girl and you."

"You finished?" Reznick said.

"No, quite the contrary, Jon. I'm only beginning. You see, Jon, we have plans in place. Plans like you wouldn't believe.

This ungrateful, bloated, filthy country, which you profess to love, is going to feel what real pain is. What real loss is like."

Reznick kept quiet, wanting him to do the talking.

"You disrupted our plans, Jon, I'm afraid to say. Plans which took us years to put into place. You and Lauren will pay for that."

Reznick closed his eyes.

"You see, Jon, America is going to suffer, and it's going to suffer a bit earlier than we planned."

The line went dead.

Reznick put the phone back down on its stand, ending the call. He looked across at the Feds who were looking grim-faced, one still on his cell. "Any luck?"

"I don't think so."

Reznick shook his head and walked back into his daughter's room. He stood at the window and looked down on the flowerbeds in the hospital grounds, a riot of colour in mid-December. He thought back over the chaotic last forty-eight hours. He thought of Lauren and the terrible last moments before Beth was killed. His mind flashed to seeing Leggett's body slumped in the shower. The nightmare had all been caused by his refusal to kill Luntz. He knew Lauren would never get peace. He had to end this. It was never going to stop until he neutralised the people behind it.

"There you are." The voice of one of the Feds snapped him out of his reverie. He walked across to the window and stood beside Reznick. "We couldn't trace the call. They were bouncing the signal off here, there and everywhere. Very sophisticated."

"Forget that. I want to speak to Meyerstein."

"Now?"

"Right now."

The Fed let out a long sigh. "I'll see what I can do." He left the room for a couple of minutes. When he came back, he handed his cell phone to Reznick. "Assistant Director Meyerstein for you."

Reznick took the phone. "How the hell can you guys not get a trace?"

"We're still working on it."

"Bullshit. They're running circles round us. How the hell did they know Lauren was here? Can you answer me that?"

Meyerstein sighed. "I don't know, Jon. Honest to God, I wish I did."

"He knows Lauren was moved and knows her condition. Is there a leak in your team? What the hell is going on?"

"OK, Jon, let's back up for a moment. They, whoever they are, might know where you are, but they can't get to your family."

"I don't think you're listening. These are no ordinary Joes you're dealing with. These guys are serious. How many times do I have to tell you?"

"Trust me, your family is safe."

"You don't know that. Look, I want in."

"I beg your pardon?"

"I want to be part of your investigation team. I want to help you get these bastards."

"That's not gonna happen, Jon."

"You're not listening, Meyerstein. These people are very, very serious. And when I mean serious, I mean, they are not going to go away. I want to help you."

"Jon, you need to back up and leave this to us."

"Listen to me very closely." Reznick lowered his voice. "He said they had plans in place and that America was going to feel what real pain was."

"He said that?"

"What, do you think I'm making this up?

Meyerstein let out a long sigh.

"He also said they were going to bring their plans forward."

A long silence opened up between them. Eventually Meyerstein spoke. "Jon, you need to let this go and leave it with us. Lauren needs you now. I also want you to know that I'm going to be thinking of you and your daughter, and praying she pulls through this."

Reznick didn't respond.

"Do you believe, Jon?"

"I don't know. Sometimes I pray. Pray for my daughter. Pray she can open her eyes and I can see her smile again."

"You did all you could do, Jon. You got to her. You... You found her alive. That in itself is a miracle."

"Maybe."

"Look, I need to go."

"Where are you?"

"What, just now?"

"Yeah."

"Why do you want to know that?"

"Curious, I guess."

"Manhattan, if you must know. Satisfied?"

"Sure."

"Look, I can't talk now..." A long pause as if she didn't want to hang up. Eventually she broke the silence between them. "Try and move on, Jon. Lauren needs you."

The line went dead and Reznick handed the cell back to the Fed, who left the room. When he had shut the door, Reznick went across and sat down at his daughter's bedside. He held her hand and stroked her soft hair. Then he leaned in close and whispered in her ear. "Lauren, I love you so much, honey. But I've got something to attend to. It means I'm gonna be away from you for a little while, honey. The doctors are going to take good care of you. But when I come back, this will all be over, one way or the other, I promise you." He kissed her clammy cheek, visible through all the tubes. "Love you forever."

Then he closed his eyes and said a silent prayer as the beeping of the machines filled the terrible silence.

TWENTY-EIGHT

The FBI's three-storey safe house on Manhattan's Upper East Side had fallen quiet as they listened to the phone conversation – retrieved minutes earlier by the NSA – between Reznick and the electronically distorted voice.

Meyerstein stood in the briefing room, hands behind her back, and stared out of the window over the houses of East 73rd Street's Historic District. More than one hundred experts from the NSA, CIA, Homeland Security, National Counterterrorism Center and, of course, the FBI, were all trying to track down Caan and the identity and location of Reznick's caller.

She was feeling the pressure like never before. The stakes were impossibly high. But she knew that cold logic instead of raw emotion was required.

She turned around and looked at the eerie *real-time* pictures from the cameras of the Hazmat team in Lower Manhattan. The night vision pictures were from a camera fitted to Special Agent Kevin O'Hare's bio-suit as he headed along an aluminium duct of the building's central air conditioning system.

Another plasma screen showed her team at the FBI's HQ in Washington, seven members round a small conference table.

Meyerstein stared up at the screen to the team in Washington. "OK, let's get started. I want to know more about this call. It's exactly half an hour since we got working on this. What are NSA saying about it?"

Gary Clark, an NSA computer and telecommunications specialist, said, "The GPS showed that the call to Reznick originated from Grand Cayman. But we've done our calculations, and it's not possible. It's a false location. Classic GPS spoofing, bouncing off hundreds of locations."

"OK, interesting. What else?"

"We are ninety two per cent certain that the call was made from a moving car. We're still working on cleaning up the voice, though. They're very good."

Meyerstein sighed. "Clearly. Any further details about the phone?"

Clark cleared his throat and leafed through a pile of papers in front of him. "Pay as you go serial number, originally part of a consignment for a store in Miami."

"Now we're getting somewhere. What about voice analysis?"

"It's gonna take time. There are so many overlays; it's a highly sophisticated operation we're dealing with."

"What about Caan? Do we have anything on him?"

"He seems to have disappeared off the radar, ma'am."

"Are we scanning all cellular traffic? He must be communicating with someone. This is not a lone wolf. The level of expertise tells us this is something entirely different."

"Fort Meade is scanning telephone, fax and data traffic, including encrypted emails, across the world."

Meyerstein knew they had a database containing hundreds of billions of records of calls made by US citizens from the four largest telephone carriers.

"Our analysts are using the extension Caan used at the lab, his home number and cell, although both haven't been used in months."

"It's beginning to sound more and more ominous."

"Look, we're throwing everything at it. We're using link analysis software and neural network software to try and detect patterns, classify and cluster data. We've also got a speech recording he made at a conference last year, and we're using advanced speech recognition software to find him. But to answer your question, nothing so far."

"OK, Gary. Get back to me as soon as we have something."

Meyerstein cut the link to Washington. Then she called up the communications link to Assistant Director of the Weapons of Mass Destruction Directorate, Professor Adam Horowitz, down in Lower Manhattan, and the National Counterterrorism Center in McLean, who were monitoring events as they unfolded. "Adam, it's Martha. I'm looking for an update, if that's possible."

A loud groan as if it was the last thing he needed to hear. "We have located ten aerosol devices, all throughout the air ducts, and we have managed to disable eight of them with jamming using extra directional antennas, but two of the devices have still not been deactivated. And that's worrying."

"So, what do you surmise is causing the problem?"

"We don't know is, the simple answer. Kevin is in the duct, as you can see. He is going to use another antenna, hoping to bounce off a second and third antenna in the duct, to jam the damn things."

Meyerstein stood, hands on hips, shaking her head in frustration. "You're saying we can't deactivate two of them? I just don't get it."

"Martha, there are a lot of factors at work here. It may be the building's design and the precise location where the devices have been placed. We've pulled apart one of the deactivated devices. And it came back positive."

Meyerstein's insides went cold. "Look, we're very concerned that this call to Reznick might mean this guy or this group, will try and advance the timers on the remaining two devices. They know we're onto them."

"We're working as quickly as we can, Martha."

"I appreciate that, Adam. Can you tell how far Kevin is from these devices? He looks real close. Isn't it possible to manually deactivate?"

"This is delicate. We've got to be very, very careful."

"Adam, I understand that." Her tone was calm, not wishing to instil anxiety into an already tense situation.

"As it stands, we don't know how this device is set up. We reckon he is eight yards away, or so. But he's got to be cautious. A movement sensor may set them off. And to compound matters, both devices are located at the opposite side of the ducts. Twenty, maybe thirty yards apart."

Meyerstein said, "OK, we'll keep this link open. Best of luck."

Horowitz sighed. "We're gonna need it."

Special Agent Kevin O'Hare could hear the conversation through the earpiece of a two-way radio fitted into his Hazmat suit. Crawling through the air duct, the light on his helmet strafed the darkness. A tiny camera was fitted to the light and beamed back pictures to the FBI safe house in New York. He edged closer to the first of the two aerosol canisters, attached to the side of the aluminium duct.

He felt slightly claustrophobic wearing the fully encapsulating bio-suit with a full face piece, self-contained breathing apparatus and bacterial spore detector. It offered the highest level of protection against any gases, vapors, mists, particles, or spores. But that didn't make it any less uncomfortable under all the protective layers.

The heat was intense. Each movement was such an effort. He felt sweat beading on his forehead. But it was the least of his worries.

He knew the risks when he volunteered as the most experienced member of the team to head down the duct. Severe to fatal, if this was indeed the hybrid version of the

Spanish Flu 1918. His suit would protect him; at least it would in theory. But what about any bacteria seeping through the vents into the packed streets of Manhattan outside? His wife worked in a deli only three blocks away. She was four months pregnant.

O'Hare's breathing was getting more laboured as he edged closer to the device. He heard the voices of his instructors down the years. There must be focus. There must be patience. The whole scenario was something he had trained to do for nearly twenty years. He had done numerous training simulations and had been involved in a handful of incidents down the years, mostly involving anthrax spores. But this was major league stuff.

"OK," he said into the two-way radio, "located the first of the devices. Looks like they are indeed attached. Magnet."

O'Hare opened up the sealed pack attached to his suit belt and pulled out a directional high-grain antenna, hand-held LCD display and a military-grade signal jammer. He screwed in the antenna to the iPod-sized jammer and flicked on the switch to activate the device. It was slow work with his protective gloves on.

The green light came on. He was in business.

The frequencies it covered were beyond ordinary cell phone jammers and were intended to combat all radio frequency threats, not just cellular activated weapons.

The jammer worked by preventing radio signals from reaching the radio receiver used to detonate a device. He knew the jammer he was using broadcast interference on multiple frequencies. And in theory, all known threats should be thwarted. But it was sophisticated enough not to affect his two-way radio.

He glanced at his LCD fast-scanning receiver display, which showed that the signals from the bio-bombs were frequency hopping.

"Yeah, as I thought, they're frequency hopping, do you copy?"

A voice at the other end said, "Yeah, copy that, Kevin."

O'Hare rechecked the LCD display again. The two signals would only appear for a few milliseconds on a particular frequency before hopping on to the next.

What the hell was this?

The system he was using should have detected and jammed the frequency hopping. It should have received and instantaneously processed a wide bandwidth of radio frequency spectrum. Then it should have detected short duration signals such as frequency hopping and burst transmissions. And then automatically jammed the signal.

So, why the hell wasn't it? This was not good. Not good at all.

O'Hare felt hot and his breathing got faster as the seconds ticked by. The more he thought of it, the more he wondered if someone wasn't using state-of-the-art jammers against them and rendering his device ineffective. But only a handful of countries – American allies – had access to the US Sincgars system whose frequency hopping mode hops one hundred times a second.

This was no ordinary terrorist group. This was a government.

"Sir, I think we've got a problem," he said, crouching within a few inches of the device.

"Yeah, I'm listening, Kevin," said Professor Horowitz.

"As you can see, I'm inches from the devices. But the jamming is still not working. I repeat: the jamming is still not working."

A beat. "That is impossible."

"I think we've got to be thinking that this is a military grade frequency hopper, evading our jammer."

"We should still be able to jam it, shouldn't we?"

"Ordinarily, yes, sir. But a foreign government who has got our level of technology may have implemented modifications, neutralising our efforts."

A long sigh. "That's not possible. Can you get up close and give us a handle of what we're dealing with?"

O'Hare peered closer to one of the devices. Welded to the side of the aerosol device was what looked like a small metal box. A whitish plastic sheet covered a Fresnel lens. It was a sensor. His blood ran cold. It was a passive infrared sensor triggered by body heat. He knew that inside would be two infrared-sensitive photo diodes or phototransistors. They would be bonded to a piece of metal to ensure that their temperature and sensitivity were about the same.

He knew that passive infrared sensors (PIRs) reacted only to drastic changes in levels of infrared radiation omitted in the surveillance area, usually caused by the movement of a person or person. The PIRs were popular amongst insurgents in Iraq and Afghanistan who used them as motion triggers for roadside bombs.

"Sir, we've got another problem." O'Hare relayed the bad news.

"Kevin, get back from there, do you hear me? Do you copy?"

O'Hare's heart began to hammer. "Sir, please, someone needs to try and disable this. Let me keep on trying."

"Kevin, get the hell out of there," Horowitz said. "We need to seal this vent up."

Suddenly there was a flash of white light and an almighty explosion that deafened O'Hare. He was in a world of silence. Then a white powdery cloud filled his vision.

Meyerstein was watching, transfixed, the *real-time* feed from Special Agent Kevin O'Hare's camera. Her team stared in disbelief and shock as events unfolded. Puffs of what looked like fine dust filled the plasma screen.

"Adam, speak to me," she said. "What are the readings?"

"Hang on a few moments, Martha…the readings from Kevin's bacterial spore detector are just coming in. Now…

Shit, his alarm's going off! Martha, it's gone off! One of those devices is spraying out the spores right now."

Martha and her team could only look on aghast. Then phones began ringing. A sense of foreboding swept the room.

"We will need fifteen minutes to confirm if this is indeed the virus. We have to use sampling and analysis such as colony counting and polymerase chain reaction."

Meyerstein said, "I think we've got to assume the worst. We must prevent widespread contamination, Adam."

"I'll let you know as soon as we have something."

Then the line went dead.

Fifteen minutes later, the phones were still ringing like crazy. Meyerstein had just come off the phone after a terse conversation with the President's National Security Adviser when Horowitz called to say that the substance had tested positive. There had been a confirmed biological attack on New York City. But it had been contained, the air ducts sealed off, the building evacuated.

As she struggled to come to terms with the enormity of what had happened, a live feed from the FBI HQ came through. The welcome face of Special Agent Stephanie Carlyle, was staring back at her, surrounded by the rest of the team on the fifth floor.

Meyerstein said, "I'm hoping for good news, Stephanie."

"We have something which appears linked to our investigation," she said. "We're putting this into the system as we speak."

"What have you got, Steph?"

"We've been speaking to the wife of a former NSA contractor, Thomas Wesley. This guy gets a knock at the door in the middle of the night. It's the DCIS and he's asked to go with them for questioning. But this is where it gets interesting. His wife calls the family lawyer to get Wesley representation.

When the lawyer calls DCIS, they didn't know anything about it. The wife is very concerned, naturally, and contacts the FBI."

Meyerstein sighed. "Steph, what's this got to do with our investigation?"

"Wesley used to have the highest clearance, so had access to all categories of information the NSA gathered, until they sacked him after he made a big faux pas, and subsequently lost his security clearance."

Meyerstein rolled her eyes and shook her head. "Enough of the background. Will you please get to the point?"

"We have two of our guys in Maryland speaking to the wife. Wesley recently met with an old friend of his, Congressman Lance Drake, about a decrypted intercept call that had alarmed him, and no one was taking seriously. His wife said shortly before he was dismissed, he was working on an intercept call, which apparently he had decrypted. He continued working on it in secret at home. But here's the kicker: he believed he'd decrypted something about some kind of threat against America."

Meyerstein felt a growing sense of excitement. "What kind of threat?"

"We don't know. But she said it had become an obsession, and he had bombarded Congressman Drake, imploring him to listen."

"Why don't we know about this?"

"His wife said he tried to contact the NSA, but no one would listen to him."

"This is a goddamn huge red flag if ever there was one." Meyerstein thought back to all the missing pieces of the jigsaw, which could have prevented the 9/11 attacks.

"Wesley's wife said he broke down one night, said he was scared. He wanted people to listen; he was talking about a terrorist attack, but no one wanted to know. Eventually he decided to speak to the Congressman."

Meyerstein felt her heart begin to beat faster. "What about Wesley's computers? Laptops? Cell phones?"

"They were all taken away last night."

"Goddamn."

Meyerstein considered her options for a few moments before she spoke. "I want the two best computer specialists we have over to Congressman Drake's office. And I want two more at his home. Roy will get this legalled. We need to find out if Wesley sent any emails to Drake. And I want everything we can on Thomas Wesley. Get back to me as soon as you possibly can."

She paced the room and looked out of the window at the skyscrapers on the Upper East Side. The smart apartments, the glass towers, only yards from Central Park and hundreds of miles away from her family in the Washington suburbs. She missed her children. She wondered what they were doing at school at that moment. She closed her eyes. She wanted to hold her children tight to her chest. She wanted to know they were safe. She knew they were, but she just missed that intimacy.

Her mind flashed back to the hospital room in Florida, Jon Reznick's daughter fighting for her life in a coma. She felt guilty. She couldn't possibly comprehend what he was going through. She imagined having to face such gut-wrenching agony Reznick was facing, watching helplessly as your child's life lay in the balance.

She pushed the negative thoughts away and focussed on the investigation.

Where the hell was Scott Caan? What was he planning next? Who was pulling the strings? Now decrypted messages. Thomas Wesley. A Congressman. More and more questions.

She knew, as assistant director of the Criminal, Cyber, Response, and Services Branch, she was under the spotlight both from within the FBI and outside. People would be analysing the way she was leading the investigation. It added to the pressure, which seemed to be mounting. Slowly. Inexorably. A notch at a time. She also knew the National Security Branch, which included the Counterterrorism Division and Weapons of Mass Destruction Directorate, would also be under immense pressure. They all were. They knew what was at stake. But she also knew that with the full might of the FBI – including its resources, reach and expertise – they would unearth whatever conspiracy was under way.

Only time was against them. The clock was running down, and still Scott Caan was out there.

Less than an hour later, the link to the Strategic Information Operations Center buzzed into life. The face of computer specialist Special Agent Johnny Lopez was on the screen.

Meyerstein said, "OK, what have your team got?"

"The personal laptop of Congressman Drake has just been analysed by us. The emails sent by Thomas Wesley I've just forwarded to you. They were heavily encrypted, but we've decrypted them all, hundreds of them."

"Good work." She turned and looked over to one of her colleagues who gave the thumbs-up sign as he studied the emails from Thomas Wesley. "How did Congressman Drake react when you guys turned up and said you'd need to scan his computers?"

"Smug, pain in the ass, if you must know, talking about infringement of civil liberties, you know the spiel."

Meyerstein looked at the emails on the laptop in front of her. "Gimme a few moments," she said, as she speed-read them. "The conversation Wesley claimed he had decrypted mentions a threat to national security."

She looked up at the screen and saw Agent Lopez grinning from ear-to-ear. "You have something else, don't you?"

"I've left the best till last. We have a clean recording of the decrypted conversation Thomas Wesley gave Congressman Drake."

Meyerstein clenched her fist. "That's what I want!"

"It was on an iPod and our analysis shows that the voices have been demorphed. This Wesley is a genius, stripping it right back."

Meyerstein felt elated. "Get this to me right now."

Lopez nodded. "Look, we're still working our way through the emails, but he doesn't name names. Wesley has simply given the recording of the decrypted conversation to Drake, but doesn't indicate who is talking. We're still working on it ourselves. Freddie Limonton and his team are also involved."

"I want that voice identified. Check and double check and then check it again, before you speak to me. I don't want ninety per cent certainties. I want one hundred per cent or nothing. Do you hear me?"

"You got it." He paused. "There's something else."

"What?"

"Freddie is analysing the audio signal. He says there are discrepancies which he hadn't spotted earlier."

"What kind of discrepancies?"

"An embedded message."

"Who's working on this?"

"We've got the best steganalysts working on it right now. But it's proving a tough nut to crack."

"I don't want excuses, I want answers."

Then she ended the *real-time* feed.

Meyerstein stood and stared at the eerie pictures beamed back from lower Manhattan. Clouds of powder still floating in the aluminium duct. Her blood pressure hiked up a notch as she thought of what the embedded message contained. A final target? Was that it?

She looked around at her team. "Where is Thomas Wesley, people? Who were the guys who took him from his house? I want answers, people."

TWENTY-NINE

Thomas Wesley came to in darkness. He tried to open his eyes and realised he was blindfolded. He tried to move his hands but felt tight leather straps cut into his wrists. He ached all over. He slowly realised he was tied to a chair. Hands behind his back and ankles strapped tight to the legs of the chair. A wave of anxiety swept over him as he wondered what was going to happen to him. He struggled hard to get free, but the straps only cut deeper into his wrists.

His heart was pounding and he felt as though he was going to hyperventilate. He took deep breaths and tried to control the panic that was spreading through his brain. His lips were parched and there was a chemical aftertaste in his mouth.

"Thomas," a man's voice echoed, from somewhere behind him. It sounded like the man from the Defense Criminal Investigative Services who had interviewed him before. "I'm sorry it's come to this, really I am. All you have to do is tell us who knows about this, and you'll be free to go."

"Who are you? Where am I? Please, I just want to go back home to my wife."

"Thomas, I can only help you so far. We know that you've given details to Congressman Lance Drake. But I can't believe that's the only person you told. That's not a realistic proposition. What I'm saying is that there must be others who know about this. Friends, perhaps. Your wife."

"I swear, it was only myself, the NSA and Lance. But I didn't tell them the full story. Only the gist of it."

"I find that very hard to believe, Thomas."

The man's voice now had a harder edge. He sensed the man was standing in front of him. Wesley smelled the man's cologne mixed with stale cigarette smoke and he felt sick to the bottom of his stomach. What the hell was going on? Who were these guys?

"Who else in the NSA knows about this?"

Wesley sighed. "The Inspector General. One or two others. But they didn't listen to what I had."

A long silence opened up.

"What about your wife?" the man asked.

"What about her?"

"I can't believe for one minute that she doesn't know about the recording and who's on it."

"Listen to me, she doesn't know."

"Thomas, nothing would make us happier than if you could just go back home. Go back to your wife. But you've got to look at it from our point of view. It doesn't look good. We're talking national security. This is not a fucking game."

Wesley said nothing.

A deep sigh. "Thomas, I'm a regular guy, just like you. I'm a Midwestern boy too."

"Where you from?"

"Not far from where you grew up in Galena, Illinois. Small town boy, same as you. Same good American values. Hard work, honesty. We both love our country, right, Thomas?"

"Absolutely."

"So let's just try and get along, so we can both get back to our families. Now, I feel like I'm repeating myself, but I need to clarify your position, Thomas. Who else knows about this apart from Lance Drake?"

"NSA and Lance and myself, and that's it. And they don't know who's on the tape. That's the God's honest truth. And it doesn't matter how many times you ask that question, I'll still give you the same reply. I can't say something that isn't true."

A long sigh from the man. "You're not making this easy for yourself. I'm sorry you've not been more forthcoming, Thomas. Really I am. You seem like a decent enough kind of guy. Smart. But there's only so much time I can spare before I have to hand you over."

Wesley smelled the man's sour breath close to him as if he was stooping down beside him.

"What do you mean hand me over? Who are you? You're not DCIS!"

Wesley struggled against the straps, but after a few seconds he didn't have the energy to continue and his body slumped back in the chair. He broke down and wept, unable to stop the long, deep sobs. "Please, let me go home to my wife."

"I'm sorry, Thomas. We need answers. A colleague of mine is in the next room. He's not an understanding kind of guy like me."

Wesley felt sick. A sense of dread swept over him. He now began to feel what real fear was.

"Our man next door, he likes to be what some just think of as... thorough. Do you know what I'm talking about?"

"Who the hell are you? You aren't DCIS."

"I'm going to–"

"I'm an American. A patriot. You can't do this to me!"

A prolonged sigh followed. "Thomas, do you know how easy it is for people to disappear? To appear to kill themselves for no apparent reason?"

The words were spoken in a gentle manner, as if from a life coach. But to Wesley, they struck terror in his heart. He didn't dare think about what was about to happen. "I've told you what I know. I can't tell you anything else."

"You are in a basement, with very thick walls. No one can hear any screams. Nothing. The sound just echoes around the room. It's a little while since we've used this room. Do you know what happened to the last person we brought down here?"

Wesley felt nauseous and light-headed, hot and anxious.

"They tell me he went mad." He let the words hang in the air, as if for effect.

The sound of the man's footsteps across the concrete floor, opening the heavy door, and then slamming it shut, before it was locked.

Wesley was alone in the pitch-black room. A sense of dread and terror entered his soul. Terror of the unknown. He had heard stories about unlisted sites where high value detainees were taken; tortured until they were broken, where no one knew they were there. Then they disappeared. His mind was racing. But he was an American. Why was this happening? What had all that to do with him? Who were these guys?

A few minutes later, the sound of the door opening and softer, muffled footsteps as if the person was wearing rubber soles. The lights went on again.

He jerked around and struggled feebly against the straps. "Who's there?"

He felt a sharp jab in the back of his neck.

"What the hell are you giving me?" He struggled again and clenched his teeth, desperate to escape. He inadvertently bit his lip and tasted blood. Suddenly he felt a tingling run up and down his arm and then up his neck. His heart pounded hard. Then he felt a surge of adrenaline and struggled wildly against his restraints. But he was trapped.

Fluorescent strip lights were switched off and a moment later the blindfold from his face was ripped off. He was in suffocating darkness. He squinted as his eyes took a few seconds to adjust and he could make out a silhouetted figure in front of him. The figure turned and left the room and the door slammed shut.

The minutes went by in the still, black, basement. Then suddenly the fluorescent lights flickered to life, flooding the room with a harsh white glow. Wesley screwed up his eyes. It took him several moments before he could see properly. He looked around. Whitewashed walls of a windowless room. The metal chair he was strapped to had been welded to a metal plate on the floor. The wrist and ankle straps were thick, brown leather. The floor was concrete.

He felt completely at their mercy.

Had they just given him a sedative? Perhaps a relaxant? Perhaps LSD? He waited for the effects of whatever drugs he'd been given to take hold.

Then slowly, almost imperceptibly at first, he saw flakes of white paint fall from the whitewashed wall. Then a pulsing sound emanated from the cracks in the wall. It got louder. And louder. The deep bass sound of hip hop.

Military loud. Assailing his senses.

Wesley felt as if his eardrums were going to explode. The hypnotic and terrifying beats were cranked up a notch for several moments. The flakes of white paint became like snow, falling from the wall. Underneath, from the cracks in the bricks, emerged insects.

He watched transfixed as dozens of beetle-like insects emerged. Then scores. Then hundreds. Swarming out of the bricks.

He shut his eyes tight to block out the image as his heart pounded faster and harder. He felt liquid dripping onto his face. He forced his eyelids open and looked up to the ceiling. Blood was dripping through the ceiling and down onto the chair and onto him. He looked down at his feet. Maggots swarming all over.

He looked at his hands and saw worms emerge from his cuticles.

Wesley started screaming as the lights were switched off. He saw snakes crawling in the bloody darkness, circling him.

Dark, whispered voices in his head. He felt sick and his insides moved. Dark sick spewed from his mouth down his front.

The sour smell made him cry. He sobbed as rats squeezed through the cracks in the walls and swarmed all over him. They were chewing his ankles and neck and he felt their sharp piercing bites sink into his skin.

He screamed and screamed as he was swallowed up in the darkness.

Wesley was aware of leaves blowing through the trees as he was walked through a darkened wood. He tried to open his eyes but couldn't. He heard them talking about the canoe. It would be found at the same time. Step by step. Legs heavy, brain woozy.

He tried to open his eyes again. Murky darkness. Blurred rocks and fast moving water. He wanted to struggle, but nothing happened. He felt a jab in his neck and he collapsed in the mud. He tried to move but he couldn't. Paralysed.

He thought of his wife and saw her smiling eyes. He was sure he could hear her talking to him. Hold on, my darling. I won't be long. I'll get you out of there.

Her voice echoed in his head like an angelic whisper. He wanted to see her face, but he couldn't see a thing. Then he forced himself to open his eyes. Standing above him, blurred, was the man who had interviewed him. His face was partially hidden in the shadows from the trees. Then he felt the water lapping around his mouth and into his lungs.

He felt himself floating on the black water. On the far shore, he saw the blurred silhouettes of two men walking back through the woods.

THIRTY

The sun streamed through the wooden blinds as an exhausted Meyerstein finished briefing her team in the operations room of the FBI safe house on the East Side. She yawned and realised she was running on empty, sleep deprived and grouchy. What she wouldn't give for a long, hot bath and a great sleep. But that would have to wait. She wasn't the only one. Many of her team – including Stamper - had gone without any serious sleep – apart from naps – as they strived to make the vital breakthrough, as they sifted reams of data that was flooding in from all corners of the intelligence community. Her father only needed four hours sleep a night and chided anyone that needed more as "weaklings".

A plasma screen showed a feed from the FBI's New York field office showing WMD agents in Hazmat suits scouring the air ducts for other lethal weapons. It never ceased to amaze her how brave and selfless her colleagues could be. The public didn't know the half of it. Another screen had a Fox News anchorman speculating that the building may have been leaking dangerous asbestos. But she knew that line or any line could not stand up indefinitely.

Hundreds of special agents across America were trawling numerous encrypted calls and emails and security video footage culled from the NSA. A specialist team worked on Thomas Wesley's recordings. Meyerstein was focussed on two objectives: tracking down Scott Caan and identifying the two people talking on the tape.

An image showing Freddie Limonton, the bureau's top computer expert in Washington, came up on one of the huge screens. He looked bug-eyed as he tried to hook up to the teleconference facility.

Meyerstein had known him since she'd joined the bureau in the early 1980s. At the time, the atmosphere of sexism and racism were still ingrained from the Hoover generation of special agents. A world where the white Anglo-Saxon man was king. Limonton was always a loner, didn't enjoy the locker-room atmosphere, and just got on with his job. He was Jewish, like her, and was often the butt of anti-Semitic jokes from a hard-core few from the old school. When cartoons of hook-nosed money lenders were taped to his desk or computer screen, he just shrugged his shoulders and smiled. Meyerstein fumed, but as the years went by, the culture began to disappear, as a new generation of smarter special agents emerged, changing the FBI for good.

Limonton cleared his throat on the screen.

"Freddie, can you hear and see me?"

"Loud and clear."

"OK, you guys have been working on this a helluva long time, Freddie. This better be good."

Freddie remained stony-faced. "I've had my best guys working on this flat out, Martha, gimme a break."

"What have you got?"

He let out a long sigh. "We've been trying to figure out why we can't get a location trace with our face recognition software. It's the best there is. But we've had nothing. A few close things, but nothing concrete."

Meyerstein looked at her watch, which showed it was 7.09am. "You wanna get to the point. I'm due to hook up with the Director in six minutes precisely."

"You need to know how cute this guy is. Martha, we ran numerous programs and variations of the program, checking for faces, but nothing. That hasn't happened to us since we got this new package. But then we started working the problem. What we needed was to pull a face out of the crowd, and compare it to all the stored images we have, alright?"

Meyerstein wanted him to hurry up, but she knew Limonton didn't know how to cut to the chase.

"Every face has numerous landmarks, as they're called."

"Unique to that person."

"Absolutely," he said, nodding slowly. "Now, there are peaks and troughs that make up everyone's facial features. These landmarks are known as nodal points. And each human face has around eighty nodal points. You with me?"

Meyerstein felt her foot tapping against the desk.

"Distance between the eyes, width of the nose and depth of the eye sockets. The length of the jaw line. These nodal points are measured."

"And this produces a numerical code, right?" she said, trying to hurry him along.

"You got it. Known as a face print. But we've been using biometrics, to check skin texture, and still we haven't come up with any trace of this guy, Scott Caan."

Meyerstein looked again at her watch. "Tell me there's a point to all this, Freddie."

Freddie smiled, panda shadows around his eyes and stubble around his chin. He pressed a button and a profile of what looked like a youthful middle aged man with longish hair appeared on one of the big screens.

Meyerstein took a long, hard look. "Don't tell me you think that's him, as it sure as hell isn't."

He tapped another button and it zoomed into the bridge of the nose. "We created a new program. The program allows for changes to the face within one point five per cent or less." He grinned. "Check out the bridge of this guy's nose."

Meyerstein stared at the image. She thought the nose was broken, like a boxer's. "What's your point?"

"Check out the left eyebrow and compare it to the right. Notice how arched they are." Then he clicked another couple of buttons which showed a picture of Scott Caan on the right and the long-haired man on the left. The long haired man looked more youthful, fresher even, and his nose was more crooked.

Meyerstein stared at the two images on the big screen, as Limonton leaned back in his seat on a third screen. "The guy with the long hair doesn't look anything like Caan. His face looks different. Puffier."

"Precisely."

Slowly it dawned on Meyerstein what Freddie Limonton was going on about. "Goddamn son-of-a-bitch." She stared long and hard at the image. "What are we talking about? Some form of facial surgery, is that it?"

"Dead on. Within the last forty-eight hours. But of the non-invasive variety."

"I'm not an expert in that area, although I could probably do with the same sort of work." Her self-deprecating humor made Freddie smile.

"We've talked to two Beverley Hills plastic surgeons and sent them the photos, before and after. They both came back with the same analysis. Caan has had three bits of work done. Firstly, a nose job, non-surgical rhinoplasty, which only takes about an hour. A soft-tissue filler is injected in small amounts under the nasal skin, to change the shape and contour of the nose. Typically it is used to straighten a crooked nose, but the opposite has happened here, and that would throw off the readings in the central region of the face. Secondly, there was a browlift and eyelift, created by Botox. It has, as its name suggests, the effect of raising the brows and lifting the eyelids, favored by middle aged Hollywood stars, especially women."

Meyerstein nodded, seeing how the changes had affected the contours and profile.

"I'm told it can also remedy a fleshy brow or one that is naturally lined. Compare and contrast." He clicked another button. "It showed noticeable differences between the forehead area before and after. The third thing is the cheekbones. Collagen filler. Changes the shape of the face, don't you think?"

Meyerstein walked up to the plasma screens and took a closer look. "Son of a bitch."

"The cumulative effects of all these small changes on Caan's face have, in effect, fooled our best face recognition systems. I'm telling you, this guy is good."

The conference room door behind her opened and Special Agent Tom Jackson shouted across, "Director's on the feed in the briefing room across the corridor, and wants you now, Martha."

"Tell him I'll be there in a couple of minutes."

"I can't say that, Martha."

"I will speak to him in two minutes." Her tone was cold.

Jackson blushed and nodded, before he disappeared again into the briefing room.

"Now listen to me, Freddie, is this a true match? I can't afford any errors at all. I need to be certain that this is Caan."

"It's him. We checked out the changes, and realised immediately why the face recognition was not finding him. Then we ran this face." He clicked another button. A long-haired man wearing glasses descends the stairs of Penn Station in downtown Manhattan, caught on camera. He freeze-framed the image. "This is our guy. One hundred per cent match."

Meyerstein's heart was beating harder as she stared at the image. "Train station. You must have his destination."

He clicked another button which showed the back of the long-haired man boarding an Acela Express to Washington DC. He clicked another button and the long-haired man emerged from the train onto the concourse of Grand Station, Washington DC.

A few moments later, Meyerstein was in the briefing room across the corridor and flicked a switch to commence an emergency video teleconference, which included the Directors of the FBI, SIOC, NCTC, The White House Situation Room, and Langley. "OK, Assistant Director Martha Meyerstein here, I'll lead, if that's OK."

The Director spoke up, his voice gravelly and strained. "You gotta development, Martha?"

"We most certainly have, sir. Caan has changed his physical appearance. The still images from Penn Station are being sent to you now."

The Director cleared his throat. He stared at the image that had just appeared on his monitor. "Good God."

"This man, ladies and gentlemen, is Lt Col Scott Caan. We have reason to believe he smuggled out three vials of a hybrid virus from the bio facility in Maryland. We believe he is an integral part of a highly sophisticated operation to attack America and we believe he is in Washington DC, intent on recreating what has happened in Manhattan."

A silence opened up between them for a few moments as if everyone was letting the information sink in.

O'Donoghue spoke first. "So where do we go from here? The National Counterterrorism Center didn't see this coming. They've been blindsided."

"We've all been blindsided, sir."

"Tell me about Thomas Wesley? What the hell was going on there?"

"What, indeed? It's a mess. The NSA claim they know nothing about any decrypted intercept. We have people working on the recording given to Congressman Drake. We hope to identify the two people by the end of the day."

"You hope? Is that what we're relying on?"

"We have our best people on it, sir."

"What about Wesley?"

"DCIS deny taking him out. He's disappeared off the radar."

"What about Luntz?"

"The latest I have from Dr Horowtiz, is that Luntz is working on anti-virals with every available scientist at our disposal. But this is gonna take time, something we don't have."

O'Donoghue shook his head. "So where does the investigation go from here? I assume there's full inter-agency cooperation?"

"Across the board, sir. The investigation's focus is now on Washington. It makes sense from a terrorist's point of view. The seat of government. The advice I'm getting is that Caan didn't use all the virus in New York, and we're assuming Washington is his next target."

O'Donoghue scribbled on a pad, nodding quickly.

"But we need to keep this very, very tight. Circulate the photo we have. Working his new image into Washington transports hubs and shopping malls, to try and get a position on this guy. He must be staying somewhere. So we have all the hotels, hostels, guest houses, you name it, having their surveillance footage scanned."

O'Donoghue looked up. "We've got to be cautious that we don't alert Caan or cause any panic amongst the public."

"Absolutely, sir. We're just informing each hotel's head of security, usually someone who is former military, Fed, or police, and there is no problem."

The Director leaned back in his seat. "You got the scientist for us, Martha. That was terrific work. And now we've got a city for Scott Caan. But we're still missing the end game location, Martha. We're playing catch-up."

"I'm well aware of that, sir. Our best analysts are going through everything we have. Email traffic, hidden files, but it's tightly encrypted. We're also scouring all the electronic devices and computers owned by Norton & Weiss in Miami. We're leaving no stone unturned, I can assure you, sir. It's just a matter of time."

"Something we don't have, Martha."

A knock at the door and Roy Stamper walked in.

Martha turned round and glared at him. "Middle of a video teleconference, Roy."

"They've just dragged a body out of the Potomac. A man in his late thirties. Near the Chain Bridge on the Virginia side. He had a suicide note wrapped in cellophane in one of his pockets."

"Who is it?"

"Not one hundred per cent, but it looks like Thomas Wesley, the missing former NSA analyst."

The mood amongst Meyerstein and her team as they were driven to the 34th Street Heliport was of quiet determination. She wanted to exude a quiet authority. No one was getting unduly rattled. It was important to remain focussed.

She checked via a secure iPad to monitor real-time events in downtown Manhattan and a feed to SIOC on the 5th floor at FBI HQ.

The cold realisation that a bio-terror attack might be in the offing in the nation's capital made her think again of her children. Their school was in Bethesda. Her gut instincts were telling her to call the head and get her children back to the sanctity of their house. But she knew that would be against all protocols and would also jeopardise the news blackout, especially if the head teacher suspected something was amiss.

A few minutes later, two choppers whisked them out to Newark, New Jersey, in seven minutes. Then they transferred to the *Gulfstream*, which was already waiting for them. Within moments of the plane taking off into the bright winter sunshine, climbing steeply as they headed south to Washington DC, Meyerstein's phone on her armrest rang.

It was from one of the SIOC team in Washington, Reed Steel.

"Martha," he said, nearly out of breath, "do you want the good news or the bad news?"

She sighed. "With the day I've had so far, gimme the good news first."

"The good news is that we've just had an update from the hospital in Pensacola. Reznick's daughter has opened her eyes. She's emerging from the coma. And she's fine."

Meyerstein smiled as she felt her throat tighten. "Well, thank God."

"Now, for the bad news. You're not gonna like it."

Meyerstein cleared her throat. "Try me."

"It's Reznick."

"What about him?"

"He's gone missing."

"What are you talking about? He's in a goddamn naval hospital. Two of our guys are babysitting him for chrissakes."

"Calm down, Martha."

"No, I won't calm down. Tell me what the hell happened."

He sighed. "After Reznick spoke to you earlier, he complained of being unwell. Dizzy. Nauseous. The doctors examined him. They said he was mentally and physically exhausted. Traumatised by what he'd been through. They prescribed a couple of sleeping tablets so he could sleep the rest of the day."

Meyerstein closed her eyes for a moment and groaned.

"It appears Reznick went for a lie down in a quiet room. But when someone went to check on him a short while ago, they found out he was gone."

"Well, that's just great. You wanna explain how he's gone?"

"I mean he pushed back some ceiling tiles, and escaped out of the main part of the hospital. A soldier's civilian clothes are missing from a locker along with his car. We think Reznick just drove out the front gate."

"You better be kidding me, Reed."

"Afraid not. It's a fuck up, I know."

"I'll deal with this later. Alert the team about Reznick."

"What do you think he's gonna do?"

"I just hope he stays in Florida. I've got enough on my plate to last a lifetime."

She ended the call. Almost immediately the phone rang again.

"Martha, we got something else." It was Freddie Limonton. "We've cracked it!"

"Give me what you've got."

"We've analysed the conversation decrypted by Wesley. We've gone over every word, every phrase. Then gone over it again and again. We missed it at first."

Meyerstein groaned as Limonton talked around the subject as usual, instead of getting to the point. "Go on."

"It's an embedded message within the audio signal."

Meyerstein felt her stomach tighten. She knew how good Freddie Limonton and his team were. "What does it contain?"

"The conversation is banal. The sort of conversation which no one would give a second thought to, right?"

Meyerstein ground her teeth in frustration as she waited for Limonton to get to the point. "Could this have been intended for Caan?"

"You got it. Caan is super bright. If he had a decoder and the cell phone number of the guy who made the call, with his knowledge, this is a serious possibility."

"OK, explain."

"This is classic stuff. When we were running the tests for the voices and the conversation, we found that there was a short data message hidden within the conversation Wesley had decrypted. Data hiding in audio signals is incredibly challenging as it covers such a wide range."

"I need to know what it contained, Freddie."

"I'm getting to that. Martha, I've just been told you're on your way to Washington, right?"

"That's right."

"The embedded message was hiding a target address in Washington."

"Where?"

Limonton let out a long sigh. "Two South Rotary Road."

"Where the hell is that?"

"It's the postal address for the Pentagon Metro station."

A short while later, as the Gulfstream headed south en route to Washington DC, the most senior officials from each government agency were on the secure video conferencing facility. The bank of TV screens in the plane came on, showing the dark-panelled White House secure videoconference center, which was located on the ground floor of the West Wing. It showed the Joint Chiefs of Staff, the CIA Director and the National Security Adviser among others. Separate screens showed her team within the SIOC command center on the fifth floor at the FBI HQ in Washington.

Meyerstein took a deep breath to calm her nerves.

Richard Blake, the chair at the White House secure video conferencing center, spoke first. "Let's begin. We'll do this in crisis mode. So, keep your microphones off unless you're speaking. If you want to speak, simply raise your hand. Let's not talk over each other. OK, Assistant Director Meyerstein has a critical update for us. Martha, we're all yours."

"Thank you, Richard. OK, let's start with the facts. There has been one partially successful bio-attack in the evacuated building in lower Manhattan, which housed the New York field office. If we hadn't got there, if there had been no evacuation, if the ventilation system had been on, we would have been looking at thousands of casualties, spreading this virus like no one's business. As it stands, one guy in a bio-suit got it straight in the face. But we shouldn't be complacent. Now, we are looking for a Scott Caan. If you check your monitors, you can see the before and after pictures we have of him. He has undergone non-invasive cosmetic surgery."

Blake put up his hand as others scribbled notes.

"Yeah, Richard, go right ahead."

"Why are we so off the pace, Martha? It's like we're chasing shadows."

"I'm well aware of that," she said, brushing aside the thinly veiled criticism. "But we are where we are. We found our scientist who may be only a matter of hours from recreating the formula for the anti-viral drugs and a vaccine. We have Caan's new identity and we have his destination. Thanks to some brilliant decryption and computer specialists and an ex-NSA guy – Thomas Wesley – who gave his life trying to alert the authorities, we have made a major breakthrough. Ladies and gentlemen, we believe that there is going to be a biological attack on the Pentagon Metro station in Washington DC."

An audible gasp could be heard from the video conferencing facility at the White House followed by a show of hands.

"I'll deal with queries in a moment. Now, as you'll know, this metro station is adjacent to the Pentagon, underground. But whilst there used to be a direct and secure entrance from the Metro to the Pentagon, that obviously changed after 9/11. Access to the Pentagon is from a new secured entrance above ground near the bus depot. We believe Scott Caan is planning to release this virus in the Metro. She saw Dr Horowitz's hand was up and she pointed at him. "Adam, go right ahead."

Horowitz sighed heavily. "My team has talked through the scenarios until we're blue in the face. Bottom line? We believe Caan may change tack. Whilst he used aerosol devices in the air ducts, I believe that if the Pentagon Metro station is the target, and he's mobile, he'll be carrying the virus in small lightweight containers. I think he'll release the virus on the train tracks or on to an escalator leading to the Pentagon concourse, perhaps a crowded carriage. He'll either discreetly smash the containers or simply open them to release the bio-material."

A ripple of turbulence shook the plane as Meyerstein nodded. "The rushing trains would help keep the virus aloft and efficiently spread the bacteria around the platform and it would take the virus right into the heart of the Pentagon unseen by its thousands of employees, right?"

Horowitz nodded. "That is the scenario my analysts and I envisage."

Meyerstein had read about the scenario. She cleared her throat before she spoke. "As some of you may know, this scenario mirrors a secret military experiment in 1966 – which no doubt Caan would have been aware of – when a seemingly benign virus…"

Horotwitz interjected. "Bacillus subtilis var niger 3. This was meant to simulate Anthrax spores which were dispensed throughout the New York City subway system. This was done ironically by army scientists – just like Caan – who dropped light bulbs filled with a harmless bacteria through ventilation grates onto the tracks to see how easy it would be to expose large number of strangers to a lethal germ."

Meyerstein put up her hand and Horowitz went quiet. "If this virus was allowed to escape in the carriages and tunnels of the Metro, and infect the Pentagon workers riding the Metro, then, unbeknown to them, they are potentially infecting each and every person who works at the Pentagon. Within a matter of days, the Department of Defense HQ may be wiped out. Nearly twenty-three thousand staff."

Blake leaned back in his seat and shook his head. "In the name of God."

A few moments later, once the enormity of what they faced had sunk in and everyone had composed themselves,

Horowitz answered a few more technical queries about the virus and when the anti-virals and vaccine would be ready, Meyerstein took questions for another fifteen minutes, most focussed on the whereabouts of Scott Caan. The tone was business-like and brisk. No one was panicking or pointing fingers. It was just a matter of let's find this guy, let's neutralise his threat and let's destroy the organisation and people behind this attack. A media blackout was agreed, as no one wanted widespread panic.

"One final thing," Meyerstein said. "We need to shut down the Washington Metro system. We can blame electrical faults. But we've got to close it down until this threat has passed."

Blake shook his head. "That's not gonna happen, Martha. If we closed it down the word would leak out why the whole Metro had ground to a halt. You could guarantee it. And then all hell would break loose."

"I'm sorry, sir, and with respect, but we cannot have people riding the Metro until this threat is over."

"The Pentagon is of the belief that if this gets into the hands of the transport authority, then it will definitely leak out. Mass panic guaranteed."

Martha struggled to contain her fury. "Then it should be on a need to know basis. We need the cooperation of the Metro Transit Police. But we need to close down this threat."

"Martha, the decision has been made. Fine, let one person at the transit police know. The chief. He'll cooperate. He's ex-army. But the Metro has to stay open or this whole thing will come out."

"You can't think about it like that. The risk of people being infected is huge. And the personnel within the Pentagon. You can't risk this."

"Martha, the decision's been made. Let's find this Scott Caan and neutralise him now."

••••

After the Gulfstream landed at Dulles, Meyerstein and her team were whisked the short distance to Arlington and then underground into the Pentagon Metro Station. She saw plain clothes FBI Special Weapons and Tactics operatives in evidence on the platform as she was taken to an office, which overlooked the platform.

A burly man stepped forward. It was Lester Michaels, chief of the Metro Transit Police. "What the hell is going on?" he asked. "I was told you might have answers."

Martha stared back at him. "I've checked your resume. You have classified clearance, you're former army intelligence; you know the drill, right?"

"That's right."

"If this leaks out, you will be hung out to dry. Do you hear me?"

"Do you mind telling me what the situation is?"

"The situation is, we believe a man with bioweapons is planning to release them at this very station. We don't know when. Or even how. Now, have I got your attention and absolute cooperation?"

Michaels just nodded, expression neutral. "Most certainly. What do you want from us?"

"I believe you have counterterrorism officers on your team?"

"Twenty."

"I want them all assigned to only the line through Pentagon Metro. I want them to work alongside the FBI on this very sensitive operation. Can you do that?"

"I can do that."

Meyerstein handed him a printout of Scott Caan, before and after. "This is the guy. He's white. In his thirties. Has had non-invasive surgery in the last forty-eight hours."

"What the hell is that?"

"Botox injections, collagen filler around his cheeks, nose job. Should be noticeable, although he might be wearing a hat, maybe a wig, makeup. We need to neutralise him. He may be carrying containers of biomatter which he intends to release in carriages, perhaps on the station concourse."

He looked at the photos and shook his head. "Is this for real? This ain't some dumbass training exercise is it?"

"Sadly, this is as real as it gets."

Her cell phone rang interrupting the conversation and she signalled that she needed to take the call. "Yeah, Meyerstein speaking?"

"How are you?" It was Reznick.

She placed a finger in her ear to block out a train pulling up. "I'm sorry, this isn't a good time." A rumbling sound in the background. "Jon, where are you?"

"In Washington, the same as you."

Meyerstein froze. "What are you talking about?"

"Why don't you come out and ask me?"

Meyerstein looked at a monitor showing the platform and gasped. Staring back up at her was Jon Reznick, cell phone pressed to his ear.

THIRTY-ONE

Two Feds both sporting dark overcoats walked up to Reznick as a phalanx of officers surrounded Meyerstein. The taller of the two Feds stood in front of Reznick. He had to be at least six nine and weighed over two hundred and twenty pounds.

"We need to search you," he said.

Reznick put his hands on his head. "Go right ahead."

The man expertly patted the angles and rifled through Reznick's jacket pockets. He produced the miniature GPS receiver and the cell phone. He handed them over to his colleague who bagged the items. "Now, I'm going to search you once again for hidden weapons. Are we OK with that?"

Reznick nodded but said nothing.

Again, the man patted the angles and rifled the jacket pockets, patting around the ankles for knifes. Then he patted the chest and back for hidden guns. But Reznick wasn't packing.

The huge Fed turned around as Meyerstein approached. "He's clean."

Meyerstein brushed past her colleagues and stood staring at Reznick. "I thought we were done."

"So did I."

"You mind explaining why you're here?"

"Does it matter why I'm here?"

"Jon, let's quit playing games. How the hell did you find me?"

Reznick shrugged. "It's no big deal."

"No big deal? Trust me, it is a big deal. So, you wanna explain yourself?"

Reznick said nothing.

Meyerstein stepped forward, her face within a few inches of Reznick's. The smell of her fresh perfume again. "Look, either you tell me how you found us or you'll be hauled away in handcuffs, your call."

Reznick let out a long sigh. "You have a secure cell phone, right?"

Meyerstein nodded.

"It also has GPS. I know a guy who provides a service to private detectives. If he has a cell phone number, he can pinpoint a cellular call to within a twenty-five metre to a hundred metre radius of the caller. He just pings the cell phone. Even secure cell phones. Should try it some day."

Meyerstein stood, face impassive. Nonplussed, big time. He found her very attractive. Her simmering anger was controlled, which he liked. And he could see she wasn't scared of him. He liked that. A lot. "I assume you know that is illegal."

Reznick said nothing.

"Look, Jon, I'd have thought you'd want to spend time with Lauren."

"There's nothing more I can do at the hospital. She's coming out of the coma."

"Don't you want to be there for her?"

"It's not a question of wanting to be with her now. It's a question of making sure she has a safe future. You heard the threats against my family. Well, I want to try and help you. In any capacity I can."

"Jon, that's not going to happen. This is not your fight."

Reznick stared back at her. "That's where you're wrong."

Meyerstein stared him down.

"Do you mind if I put my hands down?"

Meyerstein nodded.

Reznick lowered his hands and felt acutely conscious that all eyes were on him.

"Look," she said, "we are dealing with a very serious situation here, but it's all in hand."

"Is it? I'm offering to help in any way I can. Advice, situational awareness, you name it."

"We have our own experts, Jon. Besides, the FBI has rules."

"You know the first rule I ever learned when I joined Special Forces?"

Meyerstein shook her head.

"The first rule is that there are no rules. You've got to use your initiative. Like you did down in Key West. Don't be restricted by some dumbass rules and regulations. Are you serious about finding the people behind all this?"

"Jon, look, I don't have time for this." Meyerstein signalled to the huge Fed to take Reznick away. The guy reached out to grab Reznick's arm, but he easily shrugged him off.

Meyerstein nodded to the Fed to hold off.

Reznick said, "OK, answer me this. Did you manage to trace the guy who called me on the hospital phone?"

Meyerstein shook her head. "We're working on it."

"What about the bio-terrorism threat? They're targeting Washington, aren't they? You're trying to track them down, right here and now. Is that it?"

"Look, I can't say any more."

"You don't have to. I can help you."

Meyerstein let out a light sigh.

"Look, I handed over the scientist to you. And you let me get my daughter. But don't shut me out now."

Meyerstein looked at him long and hard as if trying to figure him out. "Jon, I have specialist FBI units who train for this kind of thing."

"You don't think I know that? You wanna know who trains them?"

Meyerstein said nothing.

"Guys like me. I've trained countless teams at Quantico or down at the Farm down the years. I've trained SWAT teams, you name it."

Meyerstein's cell phone rang. "Don't move," she said, and walked towards the rest of the Feds on the platform. She put her cell phone into an inside pocket and was handed another cell. She nodded as she listened to whoever was on the line and glanced round occasionally to check on Reznick. Five minutes later, he heard her say, "Yes, sir, right away."

She handed the cell phone back and approached Reznick, flanked by four Feds.

"There are two ways we can work this," she said. "The smart way or the dumb way. The smart way you go with my men to an FBI mobile command *center* in the parking lot of the adjacent mall. The dumb way... The dumb way, well, let's not go there, Jon, what do you say?"

Reznick said nothing.

"Look, this isn't your fight, Jon."

"Isn't it?"

Meyerstein ran a hand through her hair and he saw the steely expression on her face. "I don't know if you're just nuts or what."

"I aced all my psychological tests. I work better than almost anyone on the planet under extreme stress. Look, any fucking malcontent can kill or pull the trigger. But it takes a certain type of person with real expertise to make sure you get the right target. Can't you see what I'm saying? I can help you."

"Goddamn, what's wrong with you?"

"What's wrong with me? I don't know when to quit, that's what's wrong with me. Never have. And not when my family's involved."

"This is personal now with you, isn't it?"

"Someone kidnaps my daughter and you ask if it is personal. What do you think?"

"I'm having a real bad day, Jon. This doesn't help me one iota. It's only given me another headache."

"Look, I didn't come all this way just to kick my heels. So, do me a favour. Let me in."

Meyerstein shook her head and smiled. Then she turned and walked away as her team of Feds surrounded Reznick.

THIRTY-TWO

It was a seven-minute drive under leaden December skies from Arlington across the 14th Street Bridge to the FBI's HQ in downtown Washington. Meyerstein sat up front in the passenger seat beside the experienced driver, Will Collins, with the three of the most senior members of her team, including Stamper, crammed in the back. No one spoke during the short journey and Meyerstein welcomed the quiet time to think through the fast-moving investigation. She thought of Caan. Then she thought of Reznick.

They were nearing the end game and Caan was somewhere in America's capital city. She knew her team were closing in. But she couldn't help wondering if they had covered all the bases.

She noticed her hand, which was resting on her lap, shaking, but maybe that was down to caffeine and lack of sleep.

The traffic was bumper-to-bumper as they crawled through the downtown traffic. Eventually they pulled up at the security booth at the entrance to the FBI's parking garage. She flashed her plastic ID badge to the armed security officer who scanned it with a mobile reader. Then the rest of her team did the same. A beep from the reader confirmed their identities and they were waved through to her designated parking space.

Meyerstein and her team took the elevator straight down to the command center on the fifth floor. The air of tension was palpable. Ninety per cent of the team were on the phone, some were ringing unanswered, printers churning out the paper, updates being shouted across the room, tasks being given, TV stations on the news channels.

"OK, people," she said, clapping her hands to get their attention, "let's try and keep it down. We need to focus. First, can we bring up the map of the Washington Metro network on the screens?"

A Metro expert, James Handley, who'd been brought in, clicked a computer mouse and it duly appeared.

"OK, James," Meyerstein said, taking her seat. "Gimme an overview and we'll take it from there. And keep it broad-brush."

Handley got to his feet and pushed back his chair. "The Metro network includes five lines, eighty-six stations and one hundred and six point three miles of track. The system makes extensive use of interlining – running more than one service on the same track. There are five operating lines and one line under construction."

Meyerstein interjected. "And we're not just talking about one jurisdiction, right?"

Handley nodded. "There are forty stations in the District of Columbia, fifteen in Prince George's County, eleven in Montgomery County, eleven in Arlington County, six in Fairfax County, and three in the City of Alexandria. About fifty miles of the Metro is underground."

"How many stations are underground?"

Handley cleared his throat. "Forty-seven of the eighty-six stations. Track runs underground mostly within the District and high-density suburbs. The Metro system is not centered on any single station, but Metro Center is the intersection of the Red, Orange and Blue Lines, the three busiest lines. The mezzanine level of the station contains side platforms for Red Line trains traveling towards Glenmont and towards Shady

Grove. Orange Line and Blue Line trains traveling in both directions share a center platform on the station's lower level."

Meyerstein stood up again. "OK, that's enough, thanks. So, the Metro Center is the hub. That may or may not be important." She turned and looked at the screen showing the network layout. "Bring up Metro Center, facts and figures and maps, entrances, whatever." She scanned the details and something jumped straight out at her. "Hang on, hang on." She focused on the Metro Center layout on the huge screen, in particular an adjacent area of the building's plans showing a hotel. Her twenty-five years within the FBI had honed her analytical skills. But there was something else. Intuition, perhaps. Then again, maybe it was just a hunch.

Handley asked, "What is it?"

Meyerstein looked around at the group and pointed at the map. "This is The Grand Hyatt. A rather nice hotel in the Penn Quarter. A rather nice hotel with…" She let the words hang in the air.

A few puzzled faces again.

"What's so special about the Hyatt? Haven't you been there, guys?"

A few shrugs and pensive faces.

Meyerstein looked around the group and smiled. "the Grand Hyatt, apart from being a rather upscale, also has…" She again let the words hang in the air. "Come on, people."

Stamper put up his hand. "The Grand Hyatt has lobby access to the Washington Metro system."

Meyerstein nodded. "That's absolutely correct. You can enter the Metro direct from the lobby of the Hyatt." She pointed across at Freddie Limonton. "Run the face recognition program for the cameras in and around the Hyatt. How long will it take?"

Freddie punched in some keys on his laptop and nodded. "If he's been there, a few moments." The few moments seemed like a lifetime to Meyerstein. "OK, we got something." He pressed a couple of keys and three images appeared on the screens.

A casually dressed man with collar length blond hair wearing a button down pale blue shirt, slacks and tan shoes, a brown satchel slung over his shoulder, and carrying a quilted navy jacket. He clicked another button for a close-up shot.

"Scott Caan, leaving the Hyatt, forty-two minutes ago."

Meyerstein felt herself grinding her teeth. She moved closer to the screens to get a better look. "Shit, he's on the move, people! Get this image out to all our guys. He's probably wearing the navy coat." She looked across at Freddie. "Get on to the Hyatt. What name has he been signed under? When did he arrive? We need to search his room. We need a team on the ground at the hotel now. OK, run this image for all stations on this line."

Freddie punched a few buttons. A minute later another image appeared on the screen. "This is Scott Caan getting off the Blue Line train at Crystal City."

Meyerstein stepped within a few feet of the huge screens, the image of Caan looming large over her. He was now, as she thought, wearing the blue jacket and still carrying the satchel. "Damn. That's two stops further down the track than the Pentagon Metro. What the hell is he playing at?" She turned and looked round at her team. "Crystal City is home to numerous defense contractors and satellite offices of the Pentagon. Is that what this is about? Is this a stopping off point? A base camp. Let's open this up, people. I want your take on why Crystal City. Are we missing something?"

Jimmy Murphy, a senior all-source analyst, who analyzed threat information from multiple sources spoke up. "Well, as you'll know, a lot of Crystal City is underground. They've got a huge underground mall. Look, this guy is going to extraordinary lengths. He's having his face changed. He's got a new look. Maybe he's done the run through of the station. Is he checking that there's nothing out of the ordinary en route? This is meticulous detail. Does he suspect a tail?"

"Good points. But why Crystal City?"

Murphy cleared his throat. "I think he's being real cute. Perhaps he wanted to flush out any tail as he passed the Pentagon Metro."

"Definite possibility. This would mean that there might be someone else with him. The purpose being to have a wing man."

"In case Scott Caan is taken down. That would make perfect sense."

Meyerstein looked around at her team. She could see the focus and resolve on each and every one. "OK, people, get the word out." She turned and pointed to the image of Caan on the screen. "This man must not get on a train under any circumstances. He has to be apprehended, taken down, whatever it takes."

THIRTY-THREE

Reznick was sitting in the back of a Suburban with three Feds heading for Crystal City Mall, tapping his foot the whole way, his mind racing. He was wired after discreetly popping the last two Dexedrine pills he had hidden in the seam of his collar. He sat in silence, not wishing to engage the Feds in small talk or any talk. He scanned the Glock 22s that they were packing and felt envious. He felt naked without a gun.

He had been allowed onto the team and had been briefed. He was going to be an "eyes and ears" guy on the ground. It felt good to be involved, even in a peripheral capacity. He had the before and after images of Caan imprinted on his brain. The plethora of small cosmetic changes had radically changed his face. It was bizarre. His face looked more swollen despite looking younger. But both pictures still showed the same cold, dark eyes.

The more he thought of Caan the more he could feel his training kick in. He was in the zone.

They parked alongside other government vehicles next to the entrance of a suite of administration offices within the Crystal City mall. Then they headed through some doors to an elevator where they were met by two armed Metro cops who took them to an arcade-level conference room.

Meyerstein was already there as were three other Fed teams. It would be four groups of four. She looked around at the group for a few moments before she spoke, quietly exerting her will over the guys on the ground. She exuded gravitas just by the way she scanned the group. Her gaze stopped at Reznick for a brief moment before she went round the rest of the team. "OK, this is what we've got. The Crystal City shops span nine blocks. In effect, it's a network of tunnels and walkways. There are numerous exits and entrances. It's like a warren. But that's just the arcade. There are shops and offices on the higher floors. Three teams will concentrate on the arcade level and in and around the station and one team will work the upper floors. OK, first thing's first. I want the Red team assigned to the platform with me, and that includes you, Jon, OK?"

"You got it," Reznick said.

"Service frequency just now will be every three minutes. They come thick and fast and platforms get crowded."

Everyone nodded.

"Any train to the Pentagon goes from this side of the platform. This is the Blue Line. The electronic boards on the platform show when a train is heading for Largo Town Center Metro. Each train will have six carriages and can cope with up to twelve hundred people. That's a helluva lot of people. Keep alert. You know what you've got to do. We have the Blue team and Green team heading down the mall from the far side. The White team's gonna do a walk-through sweep of the upper levels. Red team, spread out on the platform, no bunching up. This is a big, big area. But if we squeeze from both sides, we will get him. It's just a matter of time. Any questions?"

Everyone shook their head.

"OK," Meyerstein said, "Let's do this right. Stay sharp."

They were each given up-to-date color pictures, and reminded that the facial recognition computer team were scanning the platform and the mall for the first sign of the guy and any update would be sent to their earpiece.

As the teams filtered out to the lower level platform and into the mall, some taking elevators for the higher floors, Meyerstein pulled Reznick aside. "OK Jon, here's how it's going to work. You will follow my direct orders or Roy Stamper's. I've put my neck on the line for you, do you understand?"

Reznick nodded.

"You will respect my authority. If this gets out, your involvement will be denied. You don't exist as far as we're concerned. Do you understand?"

"Is this a shoot to kill op?"

"It is. But not for you, Jon. Your job will simply be as an extra pair of eyes and ears."

Reznick nodded again but said nothing. He wanted a gun bad. But he was just glad to be involved at any level, on the ground.

"Look, we don't know for sure, but there may be a wingman. And before you ask, we don't have an ID on him. There might not be one. We don't know for sure. But you need to be alive to that possibility. Do you understand?"

"Absolutely."

"You will stay on the platform. Your job is to assist any requests from agents on that platform. It's the last line of defence. We must assume this is the day and this is not a dry run. He must not get on a train. Instructions will go to and from the operations center at FBI HQ to us on the ground."

Reznick nodded.

"Remember your earpiece and microphone. Everything you say will be fed back to HQ. Bear that in mind."

Meyerstein led the way as the Red team – including Reznick – followed. He saw the way she commanded the utmost respect among all the agents. She was in control of her side of the operation. But she carried herself in a most feminine way, no easy feat in such a macho world.

They took the stairs down to the track level and fanned out along the busy platform. The curved roof was like a concrete honeycomb. Diffused lighting came from recessed lights. On the platform, around fifty or sixty people milled around.

He scanned looking for the image that had been printed out in the back of the SUV and was now scorched into his brain.

Reznick knew the drill. He kept a neutral expression and began to mingle with the rest of the passengers. Occasionally he glanced at his watch or the electronic destination board.

The voice of Stamper could be heard in his earpiece. "OK, guys," he said. "The cameras are trained on you. Nice and easy, Jeff, cover the entrance, lean against the wall. Excellent. Jon, you're right in amongst the throng, just stay there. Scratch your head if you heard that, Jon."

Reznick duly scratched his head.

"Good."

Reznick knew what to look for. He had been specifically trained by Israeli counterintelligence in the early 1990s to identify suspicious behaviour in mass transit situations. But as this planned attack seemed to be at an advanced stage, the prep work would have been done. The note taking, photographs, working in groups, would have all been completed weeks ago, maybe months. But this was imminent.

What he was looking for were demeanour indicators. Nervous tendencies. The physiological dimension. Perspiration, fidgeting, repeatedly touching the face, continuously scanning the area, exaggerated yawning, pacing. Then he had to consider indicators of deception. Fast eye blink rate, sweating, stammering, clearing the throat excessively and avoiding eye contact.

He knew that nervous tendencies tended to increase in close proximity to police or security of any sort. But there were other signs.

The bulky, inappropriate clothing in spring or summer, perhaps to hide semtex or in this case, biomaterial, could be a sign. A stiff, robotic walk was another. Some of the Islamic fanatics he'd had to deal with were high. They were in the last moments of their lives, out of their minds. They knew they would soon die.

The stress would show. Breathing sped up, perhaps even hyperventilating. Another sign was staring. Those on a suicide mission were focused on a target and stared straight ahead. Some said it was tunnel vision. But the closer to an attack, the more of a likelihood that the terrorist would suddenly change appearance – as Caan had already done – to fool cameras and surveillance teams.

Reznick was on the look out for the brown satchel Caan had walked out of the Grand Hyatt with. But he also knew that it would be easy to switch that to another bag or holdall.

"Panhandler at three o'clock, Jeff." Stamper's voice was strident, almost aggressive.

Reznick stole a glance at a dishevelled old black guy rummaging on the ground inside a filthy paper bag. Almost immediately two burly Metro cops approached the panhandler and got him to his feet.

"OK, stand easy, guys," Stamper said.

They hustled the guy away from the platform as they watched and waited. The seconds became minutes and the minutes dragged. Slowly, almost imperceptibly, more and more people joined the platform. Reznick felt himself getting pressed up against other people.

The rumble of an approaching train got people jostling for position, before the doors opened. A tannoy announcement echoed around the enclosed cavernous space. Reznick scanned the faces all around him. Some people seemed more stressed than others. But that was natural in a hectic Metro, packed with men, women and children, each using up each other's oxygen, getting in their space.

Most of the passengers averted their eyes. It was a common and understandable reaction in an urban American city. Actually, he'd found the same reaction in any big city in the world. London, New York, always the same. People not wishing to engage with fellow human beings, not knowing or caring who they were. For all they cared the guy in their midst was a diseased non-person. He had to be avoided.

"Young, maybe Hispanic looking guy, brown satchel, looking suspicious, nearing the platform," Stamper said in the earpiece. "Actually, perhaps Middle Eastern, hard to say."

Reznick turned and saw a guy with an olive complexion and sharp goatee beard, reddened eyes darting from side to side. The guy didn't get on the train; he just looked from side to side. Occasionally, his head was nodding as if in time to music. His eyes were still darting from side to side. Something was making him agitated.

Maybe drugs? Maybe something to hide? Maybe just a guy with mental health problems who hung around public transport systems.

Reznick was within five yards of the young man. He could almost smell the sweat beading on his brow. Suddenly the young man turned and looked straight at Reznick.

"What you looking at, huh?"

Stamper whispered, "Jon, he's gotta knife. I repeat, he's gotta knife. Back pocket right. I can see it."

Reznick pressed his earpiece tight into his ear and wondered if the young man was a diversion or just a dumb low life encountered every day on metros and buses across America.

"Stay away from me," the young man said and pulled out a knife.

Reznick said nothing, not moving to inflame the man.

"What the fuck do you want? I ain't got no fight with you, man. I don't want any trouble. Just back the fuck up, man."

Reznick showed his palms.

"I don't know who you are, but just back the fuck up. You a cop?"

Reznick shook his head.

"I just want to catch a train, OK?"

Reznick said nothing.

He sniffed hard and waved the knife around. "You better back the fuck up or you'll be sorry, do you hear me?"

A couple of Metro cops approached the man from behind, their guns drawn, as they edged closer.

"Put it down," one of the cops shouted.

The kid began shaking as he stared at Reznick.

"Put it down!" the cop shouted again.

The kid stared wild-eyed at Reznick as he moved the knife from hand to hand. He suddenly lunged forward at Reznick who sidestepped the knife. The cops jumped on the kid as he fell on to the platform, dropping the knife. Then they grabbed the kid's arm and twisted it behind his back tight, before they cuffed him and led him off the platform.

Reznick mingled back in with the crowd who looked on as the screaming kid was led away.

A few moments later, Stamper came through the earpiece. "Goddamn immigration letters. The kid's an illegal."

The platform incident only heightened the tension. Reznick scanned the handful of passengers still boarding the train. He noticed Meyerstein twenty feet away deep in a cell phone conversation. A moment later, she put away her phone and approached him.

"You OK?" she asked.

"I'm fine. What about you?"

"What about me?"

"Something's bugging you. I can tell."

Meyerstein stared at him long and hard. "It's all in hand."

"It's not all in hand. We haven't had a sniff of Caan or any accomplice. We've got face recognition software scanning all the cameras. What the fuck?"

Meyerstein sighed waiting for some passengers to walk on by her. "We've got a problem. Six of the cameras in and around this station and mall are either out of action or being repaired."

"So, we've lost him?"

"Not necessarily."

"What do you mean?"

"I think he's still here. If he had headed out onto the street, there are numerous cameras that would have detected him. But they haven't. I think he knows the cameras are out of action. He is still here. I know it. And he is waiting for the right moment."

Reznick nodded but said nothing. He knew the pressure she would be under from the FBI Director. Her eyes were hooded and sad. But he also noted the tightness around the mouth showing her determined character.

Meyerstein's cell phone rang. She looked at the caller display and turned her back to Reznick. "Talk to me, Freddie. This better be good." She nodded her head a few times. "Who knows about this?" Then she nodded again. "Let Roy know and the command center. Top priority, do you hear me?"

She ended the call and stood, shaking her head, her back still to Reznick.

"What is it?" Reznick asked.

Meyerstein turned and faced him. "We may have a handle on who's behind this."

"Who?"

"Get back to work, Jon."

"Who the hell is behind this?"

She held his gaze for a fleeting moment. Then she turned and walked away, headed out of the station with two Feds in tow.

THIRTY-FOUR

Lt Col Scott Caan was chewing a codeine tablet to numb the pain of all the Botox and collagen injected into his face as he headed along one of the climate-controlled underground walkways on the periphery of the Crystal City shopping arcade. His quilted navy jacket was zipped up to the collar as he gripped the brown satchel tight. He headed along more zigzagging subterranean passageways past fashionable boutiques, a modern art gallery, hair salons, gift shops and a plethora of restaurants among the one hundred and thirty businesses in the underground mall. The air was heavy with the smell of pizza and fries.

He couldn't abide the ersatz 1970s architecture. It was like America. Soulless, empty, a monolithic creature.

A group of uniformed military with ID badges walked by, easygoing smiles, on their break from their Pentagon desk or some other subset of government.

Caan avoided eye contact as he walked on. Up ahead he saw the huge white clock outside Starbucks. But instead of stopping for a double espresso and granola bar like he sometimes did back at his local coffee shop in Frederick, he took an elevator to the eleventh floor. He stepped out of the elevator and walked past Ruth's Steakhouse and on for another fifty yards until he got to a suite of offices. He swiped a card and went in, the door locking softly behind him.

Caan looked around. Beige Axminster carpets throughout, rudimentary office furniture, no pictures on the wall. No computers, files or anything. It was the first time he'd visited the inside of the office. He had scouted out the mall and acquainted himself with the shops and the layout. But they didn't want him to go near the office in case it blew the whole operation.

They were concerned that the one-year lease could be traced to a fake travel agency in Grand Cayman. The cover was in place for a reason.

He pulled down the blinds. A few moments later, his cell phone rang.

"The GPS says you've arrived," an unfamiliar man's voice said.

"This very minute."

"How do you feel?"

"I feel focussed. Fresh. I'm ready."

"We know you are. But no doubt you will be looking forward to your well-deserved vacation."

Caan felt his stomach knot. He had been given the go ahead with the operation. *Well-deserved vacation.*

"We're sure it will be most memorable. Is there anything you still require?"

Caan sighed. "I have everything I need." He felt a lump in his throat. "I'll send you a postcard."

"That would be great. Take care. See you soon."

The call ended.

Caan went to the bathroom, stripped off his clothes, removed the blond wig and took out the blue-coloured contact lenses, dropping them on the floor. He scrubbed his face clean and dried it with a small towel. Then he unpacked the fresh clothes from his bag. He pulled on the grey Abercrombie & Fitch sweatshirt, faded jeans, old Nike sneakers, and carefully placed the new brown tortoiseshell-framed glasses on the bridge of his broken nose. He reapplied some cover cream over his face and neck, concealing the redness from the Botox injections, but also lightening his skin tone. Then he brushed back his short, newly dyed brown hair.

Caan closed his eyes for a few moments to compose himself, taking long, deep breaths. He'd been practicing breathing exercises for months, inducing the calm-like state that he needed. He felt sharper and more assured than ever.

Slowly, he opened his eyes.

The man staring back at him in the mirror looked a complete stranger. That was good. That was very good. He thought he looked like his father had when he had arrived in America as a young man and wondered what his father would make of what he was about to do.

Would he understand why he had to do this? The answer was: most certainly not.

The riches and accolades of America had seduced his father. Caan saw it differently. He saw what America really was. He saw the voracious monster, which polluted, corrupted and violated peoples and nations. He saw it tried to remake them in its own image. No matter the cost. It was all about spreading liberal democracy. But that was phoney. The real reason was resources. Oil, land, people. America's interests were corporate interests. The Pentagon called the shots. The countries they had defiled, the millions they had killed, be it Vietnam or Central America, had been terrorised into servitude. It wasn't about stopping Communism, but in getting access to resources and cheap labor, where American corporations could stride in and open up sweatshop factories and resell products at one thousand per cent mark-ups. They would spread the homogenous artificial world of Mickey Mouse and Hollywood to new and emerging markets. But Caan also saw, like millions of others did, the crusade to wipe out *his* people. The true believers.

His father preferred the easy cynicism and atheism of the metropolitan left. But he didn't live to see a new generation emerge.

A generation like his son. A generation that was about to throw off the shackles of the West. It was 9/11 that had been his wake-up call. He saw it for what it was. The call to arms. He began to read about the real American Dream. Turning countries to ashes. And he realised they were embarking on a crusade to wipe out as many Muslims as they could. He saw it so clearly now.

Caan was from a new generation. He was born in America, but his bloodline was Mujahedeen. His blood brothers were being slaughtered each and every day by pilotless drones. He had watched the videos again and again. He saw what American freedom really meant. He saw women and children mown down in cold blood. Screaming all around.

He would avenge. He would avenge them all. He was going to make his own history. This was their time. Their place. Their future.

Caan snapped out of his thoughts and went through to the office and into the adjacent kitchen. Inside the top cabinet was a biometric safe. He pressed his thumb against the scanner and after a couple of beeps, the safe opened. Inside was a black water-resistant travel bag. He unzipped it and saw a clear plastic box with two satin white Christmas baubles adorned by gold glitter.

This was it. This was everything he had prayed for. The time had come.

Caan zipped up the bag and slung it over his shoulder. Then he checked himself in the mirror one last time. His eyes were sparkling, face impassive.

He was ready.

A short while later his cell phone rang again. This was the final call before his mission was due to commence. It was from a private residence at the foot of the Margala Hills in Islamabad.

A Pakistani man spoke in Pashto, "Can you remember that verse from your favourite book?"

Every soul shall taste of death, and you should only be paid fully your reward on the resurrection day; then whoever is removed far away from the fire and is made to enter the garden he indeed has obtained the object; and the life of this world is nothing but a provision of vanities.

Sacred words from the Quran he had been taught to memorise until it became engrained on his mind.

Caan spoke in English. "I know the words by heart. They will always be with me."

The Pakistani man sighed. "I'm glad you enjoyed it. Until the next time…"

Then the line went dead.

Caan closed his eyes and began his breathing exercises for several minutes. When he opened his eyes he realised he was smiling.

Until the next time.

Caan walked out of the suite of offices, which automatically locked behind him and headed towards the elevator. He rode it alone to the arcade level, his heart rate quickening as he descended.

The world was going about its business oblivious to what he was about to unleash. He afforded himself a self-satisfied smile and headed straight for the Metro.

THIRTY-FIVE

The tension in the crammed investigation room within the Strategic Information Operations Center on the fifth floor of the FBI's HQ was palpable as Meyerstein walked in. Stamper was on the phone hunched at a paper-strewn desk. She noticed all available workspace was used up by analysts and special agents seconded to the investigation. Six plasma screens were showing *real-time* feeds. The largest showed the White House Situation Room as another two screens relayed live pictures from the platform at Crystal City Metro. She caught sight of Reznick and the Red team mingling with the commuters and wondered if she would come to rue the decision. Two other screens were showing Fox News and CNN. But Meyerstein's gaze was drawn to the sixth *real-time* feed showing a fresh-faced white kid with foppish brown hair staring out of the screen.

The kid was a computer genius the FBI had recruited from Brown University after the head of the computer science department – a former military man himself – let his old bosses at the NSA know about the research fellow's ability. A short while later he was leased out to the FBI.

His name was Brandon Lally and he was on the real-time feed from the second floor office of Congressman Lance Drake in the nearby Rayburn House Office Building in Washington DC.

Stamper put down a phone and looked across at her. "Need a couple of minutes, Martha."

She walked up to his desk. "Real quick, Roy."

"You asked us to look into Scott Caan's life."

"So, what've you got?"

"This Scott Caan is something."

"How so?"

"Martha, he has concocted a fantastic cover story."

"Cover story?" Her gaze was drawn again to the real-time feeds.

"You gotta listen to this. He was born in Syracuse. That's all been verified. He's an American. His father registered his name four days later. On the surface, all well and good."

"I don't see where this is going, Roy."

"I've not finished. Then we started digging into his father's past. The records we have show his father was also born in Syracuse. But I did some more digging. Turns out his father's name was changed forty-six years ago."

Meyerstein's interest was piqued. "What do you mean changed? Changed by whom?"

"The father himself. Here's the kicker. You wanna know where he was born?"

"Is he a foreign national?"

"You're gonna love this. Caan's father became a naturalised American, although our records show that he was born here. We don't know how the system shows this, but it is incorrect. The guy was born in Karachi. You believe that?"

"Bullshit."

"I kid you not. You wanna know the father's real name?"

"Spit it out, Roy."

"The real name of Scott Caan's father is Mohammed Khan. Spelled K-H-A-N. How cute is that?"

"How did we miss this?"

Stamper lifted up a copy of the original document from his desk and handed it to Meyerstein. "The father's story reads like something out of the American dream. He was an immigrant. Came to the country in 1955. He used to work as a political cartoonist. Hence the reason he left. Moved to a small town in upstate New York and became a successful syndicated cartoonist. Winner of the National Press Foundation's 1994 Ravelston Award. Also scooped the 1995 Best American Political Cartoon Competition. Truly bought into the American Dream. So much so that he changed his name. He Americanised it. And he became Caan. We're still checking, but I'm being told by Freddie that from what they've seen so far, the computer records of Caan's father have been altered by a third party. We're still trying to verify if and when and by whom."

Meyerstein's brain was racing. There were so many strands to the story. But the link to Karachi had opened up what country was likely to be behind this. "OK, this is top priority. Circulate this immediately to the team, all intelligence agencies, and the White House."

"You got it."

She clapped her hands and looked up at the screens. "Brandon, can you hear me?"

"Sure, coming in loud and clear."

"Look, there are a lot of people waiting to hear about a breakthrough. I want to find out if there was anything on Congressman's Drake's computer or the Wesley recording. Any progress?"

He nodded. "We're still piecing this together, but we have finally got something."

"Gimme what you've got."

"The guy that decrypted the original conversation – Thomas Wesley – is either a genius or a lunatic. He stripped this down to the real voices, but I don't know if he knew who the two guys were."

"Brandon, cut to the chase."

"We've run this through numerous voice analysis tests, checked and rechecked with the NSA – who're freaking out that they seem to have missed this. The problem was that the voice in the conversation Wesley intercepted had been voice morphed. They wanted us to think, if this was uncovered, that it was the Israelis. But it wasn't. We are now one hundred per cent certain of the voice. A perfect match."

"Tell me for Christ's sake," she snapped.

Brandon pressed a button on the laptop in front of him and a grainy colour picture came up on one of the huge plasma screens. The pictures showed a handsome Asian man in his late fifties with short hair wearing a military uniform adorned with medals.

Meyerstein's blood ran cold as a ripple of excitement ran through members of her team. She knew the man. They all knew the man. "Major General Muhammad Kashal. Are you sure? This is the number two in the ISI."

"One hundred per cent, ma'am. No doubt about it."

"What about the other guy?"

"No question about it, this is retired senior CIA officer, Vince Brewling. He works at Norton & Weiss in Miami."

Meyerstein was speechless for a few moments as she absorbed the information. She couldn't believe how this was playing out, the various strands concealing the true motive; a terrorist attack on America. "Brandon, stay on the line."

Meyerstein took a few moments to compose herself before she turned to face the senior military men and women staring back at her from the feeds from the White House situation room and the FBI's National Counterterrorism Center in McLean, Virginia.

"Ladies and gentlemen, Assistant Director Martha Meyerstein, FBI. I've got a critical update you all need to be aware of."

Richard Blake in the White House situation room cleared his throat. "Assistant Director, we're all ears."

"I think we've been blindsided all down the line. I have to inform you that we believe this is either a sanctioned or a renegade Pakistan terrorist operation currently in progress, as we speak, in the United States, aided and abetted, perhaps unwittingly, by a senior CIA officer."

Audible gasps from the feed.

Meyerstein said, "Within the last few moments, we've just had confirmation that Scott Caan's father's real name was Mohammed Khan. Spelled K-H-A-N."

Richard Blake leaned back in his seat and shook his head. "I always envisaged an Islamist threat to us on home soil from Iran or Syria. Are we absolutely sure this comes through Pakistan?"

Meyerstein composed herself and continued, aware of all the people hanging on her every word. "One hundred per cent. Scott Caan is a sleeper. I repeat, this is a sleeper. Scott Caan is an American. But his background, his deep background, hasn't been checked properly. Someone has fucked up way down the line, many years ago at the bio-lab. Maybe immigration, I don't know. There are preliminary indications that immigration files pertaining to Scott Caan's father have been altered to show he was born in the US."

Blake said, "Who's the Agency guy?"

"Vince Brewling. His part was to hire someone to neutralise Frank Luntz. We believe he hired Reznick. The analysis is still to be done, but Brewling was probably kept in the dark about the bio-threat to America."

For a few moments no one talked.

Meyerstein looked up at the screens. "This is a huge breakthrough."

Richard Blake whispered in the ear of the chairman of the Joint Chiefs of Staff, before he spoke. "Martha," he said, "what is your current assessment of where we are?"

"My view would be that there were two separate aspects. The first part was assassinating Dr Frank Luntz. Jon Reznick got that job through a CIA front organisation. We now know Brewling ran this. The law firm and its operations may or may not have had special access program status. We're still checking. The planting of Scott Caan is a long-term plan by the ISI or factions within the ISI, to infiltrate the highest echelons of our bio-security. The proof? An embedded message, which was hidden within a decrypted telephone call. This is as serious as it gets. And the ramifications are, of course, profound."

Blake said, "This is very grave. We have proof that the number two of the ISI, who I know personally, is behind this, and I can say without fear of contradiction, the fallout will be considerable. The fact that the NSA didn't pick this up is also very troubling."

Meyerstein said, "I must correct you, sir. The NSA did pick this up. Thomas Wesley alerted them. The problem was that no one listened. Sir, what also concerns me, is who were the people who took Thomas Wesley away? Was it the ISI operating with impunity on American soil?"

Blake said, "Look, I don't think we can assume this was a sanctioned ISI operation."

"With respect, sir, whether this was sanctioned or not, their fingerprints are all over this. The number two ordered this. The last briefing I read on Pakistan, which came out only last week, claimed the CIA had an agenda to get the Pakistan military to dismantle the ISI. We're all over them and they don't like it. They don't like what we're doing in the tribal areas of Pakistan, Afghanistan, and they don't like our developing links with India. And they sure as hell don't like the fact that we tracked down Bin Laden to their back yard, and took him out."

Blake shifted in his seat. "I can't possibly comment on such talk."

"We can't deny that there are influential people within the ISI who want America out of their backyard, sir."

Blake stared down from the screen, face reddening. "There is a significant minority within the Pakistani military who are very hostile to any interference in their affairs. They continue to fund the Taliban. And I know Kashal was very involved with helping the Taliban during our proxy war with the Soviet Union. And he is against any American involvement in Pakistan affairs. Drones and such like. We've asked for him to be replaced on at least three occasions. I believe, also, just to compound matters, a cousin of his was killed at a wedding by a drone a year or so ago."

Meyerstein said, "We can also point to the killings in Lahore by Raymond Davis, whose diplomatic status was disputed by the Pakistanis. They claim that he was a CIA operative."

Blake said, "I don't want to comment on the Davis case. Besides, the families in Lahore agreed to take the blood money."

"Look, if that's all, I need to get back to work."

"Most certainly. Look, the President and the National Security Council need to be told right away. But for now, the FBI needs to find and neutralise Scott Caan."

"Very good, sir."

Then the screen went blank.

Meyerstein gulped down another coffee and paced the fifth floor conference room for the umpteenth time. She watched three separate feeds, which were focussed on the Crystal City platform. The first screen showed Reznick and the Red team milling with passengers, scanning the crowds. "Get the feed up for our lead guy down at the Crystal City Metro."

A few moments later, the face of Special Agent Doug Hammett, appeared on the middle screen, coming from the command center vehicle down at the Metro.

"Doug, I'm watching the feeds come through from the platform, and all the time we're running the face recognition program, but still nothing. What about your guys on the ground?"

"There are more than one hundred agents scouring nine blocks, with more than one hundred shops, thousands of people moving to and from the Metro, and there are numerous entrances. We have the latest image of this guy, I know. But he could be anywhere."

"Doug, listen to me, I want to remind you that there may be a wingman involved. We have got no ID. So this obviously complicates things."

"Martha, all my people are fully briefed."

"Know what worries me, Doug?"

"What?"

"That he's slipped away. I can't believe that we haven't managed to track this guy down. Unless…" She let the words hang in air.

"Unless what, Martha?"

"What image do you have of Caan?"

"The one we just got. A casually dressed white guy with long blond hair, brown satchel and quilted navy jacket. It's very distinctive."

"What if we're looking for a guy like that, but… Doug, what if Scott Caan has changed his appearance again, fooling our guys on the ground?"

"But wasn't this image taken from the Metro Center a couple of hours ago?"

"Doug, remember the Dubai job which we analysed? Remember we ran through the scenarios, the identification problems."

"You talking about the Mahmoud al-Mabhouh's assassination?"

"Precisely. Didn't the Dubai CCTV footage show one of the assassins disappearing from the view of the cameras in a hotel lobby as a bald man in a suit, before reappearing with thick black hair and glasses?"

"You think Scott Caan would go to such lengths in such a short space of time?"

"Doug, this guy is, we believe, planning to launch a bio attack two Metro stops away, striking right at the heart of the American military. Wouldn't you – knowing there were countless cameras around – ensure you weren't stopped in the final stages of the operation?"

Meyerstein was aware of a phone ringing in the background, which was not being picked up. She turned round and glared at one of Stamper's team, a young man, who picked up the ringing phone red-faced.

She faced the screen again.

"Doug, what if there has been a switch? A last minute change. To throw people off the scent just as a precaution?"

A long sigh as he shook his head. "Martha, we need to shut this whole Metro and complex down, until we find him, that's the only way."

"I've asked for that. But sadly, that's not an option, unfortunately."

"Martha, so what are we looking for? Any six foot plus blond guy, carrying any sort of bag?"

Martha stared at the screen as her stomach tightened. "Doug, get your guys to start asking for ID. Now, I know that Caan and any accomplices may be carrying professional IDs. But they may not."

"What about body searches? Pat downs?"

"That wouldn't work. We're looking for tiny vials, which might be disguised in another less obvious form. It would mean airport style scanning. We've got to just roll with it and try and use our eyes and ears."

"This is insane, Martha."

"Tell me about it. If anyone acts up, get them out of there."

THIRTY-SIX

The sound of two chimes echoed around the platform before a station announcement. A woman's voice boomed over the station tannoy. *"See it? Say it. The Metro Transit Police would like to remind you if you see something out of the ordinary to please call the Metro Transit Police at 202-962-2121."*

Reznick watched the passengers thronging the Pentagon Metro platform. The smell from a cheeseburger being eaten by a young woman wafted his way. He felt sick at its odor. His nerves were jangling as he checked his watch. Where the hell was Caan? Had he escaped the Feds' dragnet?

A buzzing noise in his earpiece.

"OK, people," Stamper said. "We're just being told that no man or woman is being allowed onto the platform without ID being checked, body searched and bags scanned. "Just so you know. Keep alert. And let's keep our focus."

Reznick knew from working with the Israelis that a cursory check of bags was pointless. It was all about profiling. While the Americans look for weapons, the Israelis look for terror suspects. Highly trained screeners interrogate El Al passengers at length as Israeli police watch for suspicious behaviour. But the Israelis follow this up with computerised passenger profiling, which checks for anomalies in a passenger's travel plans, finances and profile.

The passengers on all El Al flights have to answer questions about why they are making the trip, where they are coming from and their occupation.

The chances of staying calm under such pressure were low.

Reznick scanned the platform surreptitiously and wondered what Scott Caan was thinking at that moment. If this indeed was a prelude to an attack, he would be wired. Psyched. But what were his motives?

The cameras, which were working around Crystal City, had not flagged up anything to the Feds' face recognition software. Was Caan still in Crystal City? Had he slipped through the net? Shit, the guy could be anywhere.

His Red team was well spread out across the length of the platform as the rumble and roar of trains came and went. The pale red lights at the edge of the platform came on when a train arrived. The familiar two chimes echoed as passengers disembarked to the stairs and then the escalators. He could see crowds were bunching up as they came down the steps to the platform. The security checks were fraying nerves.

"What the hell's going on?" a passing black man asked to his partner.

The crowds began to swell the platform, some people being squeezed up against the concrete pillars. The numbers kept on rising. Seventy, eighty, one hundred, two hundred and then well over three hundred.

A guy from behind him jostled Reznick. He spun around and a portly man in a suit was showing his hands. "Excuse me," he said, blushing.

He had to push past a black woman with two children in a double buggy as the roar of a train sparked more jostling and pushing.

"Jon, let's just ease up," Stamper said.

Reznick didn't feel like easing up, but he said nothing. He nodded to show Stamper that he had heard him. He had learned from his father that restraint was admirable and it was essential to think of the consequence of your actions.

The train approached the platform and screeched to a halt. The two chimes and the tannoy blared out instructions for the crowds to stand back as the doors opened. Hundreds of passengers streamed out into the large crowd of people gathered on the platform waiting to board the six-carriage train. Women in business suits talking into cell phones, a man chewing gum looking dead in the eyes with his sports bag over his shoulder, a couple of college kids wearing Georgetown sweat tops, talking and laughing loudly, blue collar guys, perhaps heading to or from their shift, soccer moms with their kids in tow.

Reznick took in each and every one in a microsecond whilst keeping one eye on those boarding. He tried to weigh up the way they carried themselves, how they related to other passengers, all in the blink of an eye.

The person who was attracting most of his attention was the young man wearing a white button down shirt, jeans and sneakers, chewing gum with a sports bag, standing at the far end of the platform. He had just got off the train and was lingering. Checking his watch. Twice. Thrice.

"Jeff," Stamper said into his earpiece, "guy in the white shirt with the sports holdall. You got him?"

Reznick saw Jeff nodding.

"We have close-up cameras showing him looking highly agitated. His expression is changing from pained to paranoid, eyes darting real crazy. Escort him off the platform and find out what the hell is wrong with him. Something not right there."

Jeff replied, "I'm moving in." He stepped towards the well-built young man who looked around one hundred and eighty pounds, six foot plus, muscular build.

Reznick kept an eye on the guy as he glanced at those still boarding.

Stamper said, "He's got a glazed expression, Jeff, what the hell is wrong with him? Get him out of there."

Suddenly, the man groaned loudly and collapsed in a heap, clutching his chest, convulsing violently on the ground.

"What the hell..." Stamper said as Jeff crouched down to tend to the man.

"Call 911," Jeff shouted as he saw a metal dog tag around the young man's neck. "He's epileptic. This man needs an ambulance."

Slowly a crowd gathered round the man on the ground.

Reznick turned his attention back to the people boarding. It was at that moment that Reznick caught sight of something out of the corner of his eye. A fraction of a second, if that.

A passenger with a black leather travel bag emerged from deep within the crowd, about to embark. The man studiously ignored the throng around the collapsed man and stepped onto the packed waiting train. It was a split second moment. Dark hair, Nike sneakers, jeans, grey hooded top, tortoiseshell glasses, carrying a bag. None of it matched the description they were given. But the way the man had glided past the concerned crowd without ever looking at the collapsed man grabbed Reznick's attention.

Instinctively Reznick pushed through the waiting crowds before his earpiece crackled into life. "Jon! Jon! Guy wearing the grey sweatshirt. Recognition confirmed."

"I got him."

The doors began to close as Reznick shoved past the throng. Anguished shouts of protest. Four foot open, three foot open, two foot open, one foot.

The doors slammed shut.

"Goddamn," Reznick said. He frantically pressed the button for it to open, but it stayed resolutely closed. He pulled out a slim flick knife he'd earlier hidden and jammed it into the doors. He worked it like he was working a lock. The passengers on the train looked horrified, some trying to get away from the doors. Reznick clenched his teeth. "Open you fucker!" he said. He felt some give. A centimeter. Then an inch. He managed to get his hands around each side of the door and pulled with every fiber of his being until he prized open the doors and stepped onto the train. He closed his knife and put it in his back pocket as alarmed passengers stared and the doors shut tight behind him.

The train pulled away and Reznick squeezed his way past the passengers around the doors and headed towards the next carriage up. But the passengers were packed in like sardines. The sound of banging on the window and he caught sight of Jeff running alongside, banging the glass as the train departed the station.

"Jon! Jon!" Stamper snapped.

"I'm on board."

"Jon, you have no authority! I repeat, you have no authority."

"I'm eyes and ears, remember?"

Stamper's voice was crackling with tension. "Jon, can you eyeball the guy?"

Reznick looked down the carriage and squeezed past the standing passengers. "Negative. I'm in the sixth carriage, right at the back. I think he's at the front."

"Shit. Did you see him getting on the train?"

"Affirmative."

"Eyes and ears, Jon. Do not approach Caan. We have two guys on this train and we have a reception party at the next stop, Pentagon City."

Reznick ignored the instruction as he squeezed past more passengers and entered through into the second rear carriage of the train. He was sure the target had got on near the front of the platform, perhaps the first and most forward carriage. "Out of my way!" he roared, and he pushed through the throng again, but he wasn't making the progress he needed.

The smell of strong cologne mixed with oil from the tracks lingered in the air as the train hurtled through the tunnel at breakneck speed. Deeper and deeper into the tunnel, closer and closer to the destination.

The seconds were fast disappearing.

Reznick rammed through the passengers into the third carriage from the rear, pushing and shoving anyone and everyone.

Three more to go.

He was only halfway through the third carriage as the train began to slow down.

Not going to make it.

He began to physically push passengers aside as he barged into the next carriage, the second from the front. He was stopped in his tracks. There were a hundred or so people standing in his way. The operator's voice over the tannoy announced, "Pentagon City Station. We will shortly be approaching Pentagon City Station."

The train's brakes began to screech.

He pushed past a few archetypal military types wearing ID badges, some holding briefcases. They were going to get off at the Pentagon Metro, the next stop but one. No question. "Negative."

The darkness of the tunnel seemed to go on forever.

Reznick's mind went into tight focus mode. He was still in the third carriage and once the train stopped at the next station there would only be a minute till the target destination. He wondered if he shouldn't just get out of the emergency doors in the middle of the second carriage and out onto the platform, and enter the first carriage from the platform. But the throng inside was too much. Besides, there was no guarantee he would get into the first carriage with hundreds of people from the platform possibly trying to get onto the train.

He had to push on through.

"Out of my fucking way!" he said.

A huge white guy stood up and blocked his way. Short haircut, smart suit, and shiny black shoes. Pentagon type.

"Hey, buddy, you wanna try and cool it down," he said. "There are women and children in the carriage if you hadn't noticed."

Reznick pushed past him but felt himself being pulled back by the collar. He swung round and kicked the guy hard between the legs. The man groaned and scrunched up his face in agony. Then he crumpled in a heap on the carriage floor as a couple of women began screaming.

"What the hell is that?" Stamper asked.

Reznick ignored Stamper and brushed past more people. "Out of my fucking way!" he shouted again. Twenty or more people were between him and the doors to the first carriage.

"Jon, what the hell is going on?"

Reznick moved forward. As he made it to the door of the first carriage, he heard a man shout, "FBI, freeze, put your hands in the air!"

Reznick stood still. All around shocked and scared faces. Time seemed to slow.

Then the sound of semi-automatic gunfire and screaming rang out, as mayhem ensued.

THIRTY-SEVEN

Meyerstein and her team stood and listened in horror as the intermittent bursts of gunfire and high-pitched screaming from the Metro train cut the air like a knife as it sped towards Pentagon City Metro. The real-time feed from inside the carriages had gone down and the screens were blank.

"OK, talk to me people, who's doing the shooting?" she asked, looking around at her team. "I need a visual from the carriages. All we have is audio. What the hell has happened to the on-board feed?" She pointed across to the IT specialist. "How close are we to getting the on-board video feed back up and running?"

The senior FBI computer guy, Gus Shields, punched in keys as he tried to get a connection to the feed.

Meyerstein turned and looked across at Roy Stamper. "I'm staring at static and listening to gunshots. Do we still have people on that train? I specifically said I wanted two people per carriage. And what has happened to Reznick's feed? Goddamn it!"

Stamper pressed his earpiece. "Hold on, Martha." He shook his head and looked across the room at Martha as he received an update. "Martha, this train was delayed from starting on the Blue Line. The guys we have riding on the trains were placed there within the last hour. We have only two agents on this train."

"But I asked for two per carriage. What the hell happened?"

"Christ knows."

"Who are our guys on the train?"

"Special Agents Jacobsen and Meigle. They're relatively inexperienced. ID'd the target shortly before the feed went down."

Meyerstein pointed at a female IT specialist. "Play the last sequence we have of them. I can't believe they gave a verbal warning, what the hell were they thinking? We are facing an imminent threat. Didn't they have full authority to use deadly force, Roy?"

Stamper nodded, grim-faced. "They were all given specific instructions to use deadly force."

The young woman punched in a few keys on her desktop. Then the sound boomed out across the investigations room. "Jacobsen, here. I got a visual. I repeat, I got a visual. Front carriage."

Meyerstein began to pace the room. "Talk to me about the video feed. Do you think the signal is being jammed? Have our guys been taken out?"

Shields shrugged. "Ma'am, we're trying to get an override feed in. Gimme a couple of minutes."

"Soon as you can."

"Working on it," he said, frantically punching away at the keys of his laptop.

The shooting had stopped, but the panicked screams and shouting continued. The sounds from the carriage added to the febrile atmosphere in the conference room. She sensed it and felt all her team were locked in that moment as the train hurtled through the tunnel. A couple of phones started ringing as Stamper barked out orders telling the FBI's SWAT team to hold fire.

Meyerstein zoned out the noise and adjusted her headset. "Special Agent Jacobsen and Special Agent Meigle, do you read me, this is Assistant Director Martha Meyerstein, do you copy, over?"

High-pitched screaming from a woman on the train pierced the chatter in the command center.

"Jacobsen and Meigle, do you read me, respond urgently, what is going on? Jacobsen and Meigle, this is the command center, do you read me, over?"

Meyerstein stood shaking her head, hands on hips. She looked over at the computer guy. "We have an audio feed, so why can't I hear my two Special Agents in the first carriage?"

Suddenly three of the plasma screens came into life. The room fell silent for a few moments. Half a dozen men and women and a couple of children were writhing and moaning in agony. A couple of tiny bloody hands moving at the edge of the picture. Blood splatter on seats and floor. Abandoned bags and coats strewn over seats.

Slowly, the camera panned around. The slumped bodies of the two FBI agents sprawled on the floor of the carriage, blood and grey brain matter all around, some smeared on the windows.

"Oh my good God," Shields said, wincing in horror. An audible gasp went round the room as some covered their mouths at what they were witnessing.

Meyerstein felt her stomach churn. "Oh shit, Roy, are these our guys?" She turned to look at Stamper whose eyes were dead.

"Affirmative, Martha. That's them."

"OK, we need to concentrate, people. We've got a job to do." She pointed to the screens. "Top right, behind the operator's compartment, that's Scott Caan, staring out of the window, his back to us. Middle left there is a guy with a gun. Could this be the wingman, people?"

Stamper just nodded. "Has to be."

"Freeze the camera right there!" she shouted. "And run the face recognition software."

Shields nodded. "I'm on it."

"Roy, alert the three teams on the platform at Pentagon City Metro right away. OK, computer guy, let's pan around the rest of the carriage." A few moments later they saw that around a dozen terrified passengers were huddled, some seriously injured, a couple not moving, some still screaming, squashed in the corner. "We've got to predict what Caan's next move will be. And we also need to get those people out of there."

Stamper adjusted his headset, "Martha, SWAT team leader is just waiting for the green light to go in."

"This has to be about containment, just now."

"Martha, we need to get these people off the train!"

"Roy, they are not top priority. We can't risk them releasing material. We've got to watch and wait. We've got to think of the big picture." She turned round and looked across at the SWAT expert, a former Marine, Eric Holden, who was nodding. "Eric?"

"If we go in, we'll free most of the hostages from the rear of the train. We could set off a flash bomb and stun grenades and recover the passengers, no question. But the situation is all wrong. I say the same. Watch and wait."

Meyerstein felt her heart racing. "I also want to know where the hell Reznick is. Where is he when all this is happening?"

Everyone began to talk at once.

Meyerstein held up her hand. "Can we shut down that train? I need an answer?"

The Metro specialist shook his head. "The trains are controlled in two separate ways. The cab signals to protect the trains, and a centralised speed-control system."

Meyerstein shouted above the rising din. "Can we get the cab system to pull up a stop signal?"

"No can do. The cab signal system is not centralised. And the centralised speed control is only about slowing down or braking."

"Right, we want this train to stay where it is and not move."

"Can we get a message to the driver? A simple yes or no!"

"Yes."

Meyerstein pointed at Shields. "You've got access. Get a message to the operator. Tell him, this is an emergency. Stop the train!"

Shields nodded and punched in the keys. A few moments later he shouted, "Done!"

"OK, we don't know what's gonna go down. Let's try and work this problem."

Stamper said, "What if our guys try and flee this train, here and now? What if they decide to pull the plug now and release the contents down in the Metro?"

Meyerstein nodded. "It's a possibility. But I think as they're so close to the target area, they'd want to do everything in their power to release it at the target destination to cause maximum impact to the American military, and those working inside the Pentagon."

A WMD expert Dr Lorna Renwick was nodding. "If the material is released a station early, our computer modelling shows that we might only be talking a few hundred casualties. The next stop down, and there would be a significant risk that it would spread inside the Pentagon. We don't believe they want to give us a metaphorical bloody nose, they want to bring us to our knees."

Meyerstein nodded. "OK, let's pull up the map and find possible exits out of Pentagon City Metro. I repeat, Pentagon City Metro. And Roy, I want a lockdown on the Pentagon, right now! Have you got that?"

Stamper shrugged. "The whole Pentagon?"

"Yes, the whole Pentagon. This train is still more than one stop away. But no one gets in or out of the Pentagon. I don't give a damn if it's a four star general or a cleaner, no one gets in or out until I say, got it?"

Stamper punched in a secret Pentagon number and relayed the message.

"Also, I want the air con shut down until further notice."

Stamper nodded as he spoke on the phone.

A few moments later a detailed Metro map appeared up on one of the huge screens.

"OK, let's figure this out. Firstly, how many exits are we talking about from the Pentagon City Metro, people?" she asked, looking around the room. "And remember the target destination is still one mile away, the Pentagon Metro."

Jimmy Murphy, the all-source analyst who was an expert of seeing the big picture piped up. "The way I see it, they have one obvious route when the train pulls up. Namely, getting off the train and out of the Metro. I disagree with Lorna. I reckon they would release the bio-material if they felt they were cornered."

Meyerstein strode across to the screens and picked up a pen to point at one of the maps. "What is this? A walkway?"

Murphy nodded. "That is a pedestrian tunnel under I-395 connecting Army Navy Drive to the Pentagon's south parking lot. You get to it from the Hayes Street parking lot, which is directly opposite the parking lot at the Pentagon City Mall. That's doable."

Meyerstein's mind was whirring. "Roy, let the Pentagon know everything. Are they on lockdown yet?"

Stamper had just come off the phone. "As we speak. Team heading down the escalators of Pentagon City Metro right now. Do the SWAT guys have a green light to storm this train when it arrives?"

Meyerstein paced the room again as her options narrowed. "No. It's containment just now. Besides, who would bet that they wouldn't empty any bio-materials out into the tunnel here and now?"

Renwick nodded. "The dispersal pattern of the virus in an enclosed space as a rushing train goes past would be their ideal scenario."

Stamper relayed the instructions on a headset.

"There's something we're forgetting, people," Meyerstein said. "What about if they decide to go on foot, direct to the target from Pentagon City?"

Jimmy Murphy said, "I thought I covered that?"

"I'm not talking about that route. What if they decided to run direct to the target, through the goddamn tunnel?"

Stamper turned and looked at her, ashen faced. "Shit."

Meyerstein snapped her fingers. "OK, let's keep them on this train. And they don't get off. No point taking out a wingman if the main man survives and pulls the pin."

Shields stood up and shouted across the room, "I think I've got something." He turned and looked across at Meyerstein. "It's Reznick, ma'am. His audio feed is back up and running."

"Are you sure?"

"Damn straight. Reznick's still in play."

THIRTY-EIGHT

In the panic following the gunfire, Reznick had squeezed in amongst around a dozen terrified passengers, sobbing and crying together in the rear left of the front carriage. A few feet away, three men and two women lay dead. They were spread-eagled on the floor, blood seeping from head wounds, as if they'd tried to flee for their lives.

Reznick's left cheek was pressed to the grey rubber floor and he saw four dead bodies further up the carriage. Blood spattered glass against two window seats, ten feet away on the opposite side of the aisle. A few cell phones strewn in the panic. Then he saw the crumpled bodies sitting in their seats and he assumed they were Feds, heads blown apart. Brain matter on the seats.

The vibration of the hurtling train was hurting his face and sounded like a high-pitched scream.

Reznick adjusted his body position and slid a few inches forward, keeping low, as he peered further down into the first carriage, towards the operator's cab. Then he craned his neck to the right and saw one of the bad guys. A smart-dressed clean-shaven man, with sunken dark eyes and a pale face, stood pointing a Beretta 9000S. It was a compact semi-automatic. The kind Reznick liked.

Where were the Feds' guns?

Reznick glanced at the man with the gun to make sure he hadn't noticed his movement. The man's eyes were black,

346

highly agitated and the awkward way he was holding the gun indicated that he was clearly not a military man.

Reznick was straining his neck as he scanned the floor as the passengers around him whimpered and wept, clutching at each other, shaking like mad. He saw pools of blood, discarded coats and dropped books and newspapers strewn around. Then he noticed something, sticking out from behind the leg of a seat, eight feet or more away.

It was the butt of a gun. But it was out of reach.

Fuck.

Reznick adjusted his position slightly and looked to the opposite side of the aisle and saw a guy wearing a grey sweatshirt. It was the same clothes as Scott Caan. But something about the man's posture didn't chime with Reznick. Slightly hunched, not quite the right build or the right height.

Was this another wingman? Was this a move to confuse? He needed to be sure.

The screech of the train's brakes as it slowed.

Suddenly, the earpiece crackled into life.

"Jon, it's Meyerstein. We have the video feed back up and running. Listen, the guy with the gun is Faizan Agha, a Pakistani national, studying at Georgetown University. He is the wingman. Tap on the earpiece: once for yes and twice for no."

Reznick said nothing and discreetly tapped once on the earpiece.

"The guy in the grey sweatshirt has to be Caan, but we haven't ID'd him with the face recognition software as his back is to the camera. Can you ID him?"

Reznick tapped the earpiece twice.

The train slowed down and Reznick looked up out of the window. The lights of a deserted Pentagon City Metro came into view. But Reznick knew that while the Feds were out of sight, they would be all around the station, locking the whole thing down.

The deafening sound of two gunshots rang out further down the first carriage, near the operator's cab. Suddenly people were screaming, fighting and falling over each other as they retreated away from the rear of the first carriage and scrambled into the second carriage. Reznick did the same.

A few moments later, "Jon, do you read me?"

The passengers who escaped the first carriage ran towards the rear of the train. Only Reznick was in the second carriage, alone.

Meyerstein sighed. "Jon, do you read me? The driver has just been shot. Point blank."

Reznick didn't understand that move. Why would they kill the guy who could move the train to their target destination? He craned his neck further and peered through into the first carriage, a handful of people still lying on the ground, either dead or too badly injured to move. "I can't see the shooter. Where the hell is he?"

"Jon, the shooter has now entered the operator's compartment. He's fiddling with the controls."

It was then that Reznick saw another man, at the edge of the carriage, spread-eagled on the floor, talking into a cell phone, clutching a black travel bag.

It was him.

He wore a grey Abercrombie & Fitch sweatshirt, faded jeans, Nike sneakers, and brown tortoiseshell-framed glasses on the bridge of his broken nose. The hair was short and died brown.

"There is a third man in the first carriage, do you copy?"

The man with the grey sweatshirt adjusted his position on the ground slightly and Reznick caught sight of his profile. The broken nose, the strange tight look round the eyes and puffy cheeks.

"Jon, can you repeat that, over?"

"There is a third man. He fits the profile. Abercrombie grey sweatshirt, brown glasses. He's got a damaged nose, the cosmetic changes and he's clean-shaven. He's hiding on the goddamn floor. And he's got a black bag."

"Jon, I can't see him. Are you sure?"

"You must have a blind spot. I can see him clear as day. He's talking into some phone."

"Christ," was all she could say.

The man scrambled across the floor to the other end of the cab clutching the bag, near the operator's compartment.

A few moments passed without any chat from Meyerstein. "We got him. Son-of-a-bitch."

"What's our next move?"

"As it stands, it's contained within the train. We've switched the lights to red, so they can't move. The train is in automatic mode."

"But can they override it?"

Suddenly the train jolted forward, giving him his answer.

"They're trying to move the train."

"We cannot allow that."

The train jolted again for a couple of yards and Reznick could hear the passengers way back at the rear of the train scream. "I can see the guy trying to move the lever. But they're all spread out. As it stands, I could try and take them out."

"With what?"

"Don't worry about that."

Reznick thought about the Fed's gun under the seat.

Meyerstein paused for a moment. "You have no combatant role to play. You can only observe. We're in charge. Do you copy?"

"That was then. This is now."

"We have this contained. Do you–"

"It is just a matter of time before they figure out how to manually operate the train. And then we will be in shit. I need you to cut off the train's power and put the train into darkness, do you copy?"

"Are you serious?"

"Make it happen. And I'll bring them down. It'll give me the cover I need."

"Jon, that's absolutely not going to–"

"Make it happen! Right now!"

THIRTY-NINE

Meyerstein stood and stared at real-time images of the screaming passengers, including some children, huddled in the rear carriage of the Metro train, some trying to smash windows. The nightmare was slowly unfolding before her eyes. The killing of two Feds in cold blood and the dead and injured passengers had left everyone in shock. It was almost like nothing could be done to stop the chain of events. And to compound matters, there may now be a three-man operation and she had Reznick on board with no authority, no gun, and calling for a blackout so he could try and bring Caan and his accomplices down.

She knew they were nearing the end game. And everyone was watching what her next move was going to be. How was she going to call it? She knew that one slip-up and God knows what would befall America. Failure was not an option.

Meyerstein let out a long sigh and took a few moments to appraise the situation. She knew in her guts that Reznick was right. Attack, and the biomaterials would be released. But they were nearly out of time and in danger of letting the whole scenario unfold without armed intervention.

She turned and looked across at Jimmy Murphy, the all-source analyst who was studying data on known Islamic terrorist tactics. "What's your take on this, Jimmy? A Metro blackout? High risk strategy?"

"For sure it's high risk," he said. "But so is a full assault on the train. Reznick is the best, least-worst option."

Meyerstein stared back at Murphy.

"Look, every permutation is high risk. These guys don't know Reznick is among the other passengers. That's one good thing. They think they've dealt with the threat on the train."

Robbie McVivar, another all-source analyst who had been drafted in from Homeland Security, was scribbling some notes. "I concur with Jimmy. They think they've got all the cards because they have the bio-material. Ordinarily we would have got the negotiation team in, maybe storm the train, but these are a unique set of circumstances. This is about disarming the terrorists. And to do that, we need to get in close. Perhaps we need to be unorthodox. Render the terrorists unconscious."

Meyerstein felt herself biting her lower lip. "You mean like a gas?"

Jimmy Murphy shrugged. "Perhaps. Consider this. Confined space might give us a chance to pump in fentanyl or something equivalent, incapacitating everyone inside."

"Fentanyl?" Meyerstein said. "You're talking about the drugs the Russians used to flush out the Chechen terrorists during the Moscow Theatre siege."

Murphy cleared his throat. "Very controversial, I know. But if it was pumped in via the ventilation system, we would certainly incapacitate them."

Meyerstein felt a headache coming on.

"The downside is, that, according to official figures, if I remember correctly, one hundrd and twenty-eight out of the one hundred and twenty-nine hostages died as a result of the gas, but so did most of the terrorists."

Meyerstein said, "But not all the terrorists." She looked at Stamper. "Don't know about you, but this sounds like a slow death for all concerned. It would give them time to release the bio-materials."

Stamper nodded. "No question."

A WMD expert Dr Lorna Renwick put up her hand. "I concur. Gassing them wouldn't knock them out instantly. So, that wouldn't solve the release of the virus."

Meyerstein looked at Stamper. "What do you think, Roy? Should we cut the power?"

He looked ashen-faced. "You have to. End of story."

"OK, let's do it."

Within a minute, Meyerstein had convened an emergency teleconference with the military in the Situation Room at the White House, the National Counterterrorism Center in McLean, Virginia and Dr Horowitz and his WMD bio-team in New York. She relayed the full story as succinctly as possible to the military and intelligence experts up on the huge screens. She felt all eyes on her.

"You want us to out the power?" the chair of the Joint Chiefs of Staff said.

"Absolutely, sir."

"There will be no air conditioning, everyone will be in darkness, is that what you're saying?"

"Sir, with respect, it's a risk and not something I take lightly. But we are looking at a bio-terrorist attack in the offing. Their killing of two FBI Special Agents and members of the public means we can't just sit back and react to the situation as it develops. We have to do everything in our power to stop this train reaching its target destination. We pull the power, the train will be unable to move. We will have confined the threat, and we can focus on taking down those responsible inside the train."

Professor Horowitz appeared on another screen from New York, still dealing with the first incident. "Can I say something?"

The chairman nodded. "Go right ahead."

"Assistant Director Meyerstein's analysis is sound. We need to stop this train from getting into the tunnel and to the

Pentagon Metro where I believe they will release their bio-material. And the consequences will be devastating, until we find an antidote and have the vaccine."

The chairman stared out of the huge plasma screen and said nothing.

"Sir, we're wasting valuable time. We need to do this. We haven't got the luxury to debate this at length."

"You'll need to run this past Homeland Security."

"Sir, we need a decision right now!"

"I said, run it past Homeland Security."

Meyerstein wanted to curse him for his timidity, but instead she let out an exasperated sigh. "Of course, sir. If you give the go ahead, I can speak to them in a matter of seconds."

A long silence opened up as he considered his options.

Meyerstein glanced at the clock, the seconds ticking by. She glanced at the *real-time* feed from the Metro carriage. It showed hysterical passengers at the rear of the train, jolting violently as the terrorists tried to get the train moving again. "Sir, they are trying to get the train into gear as we speak. Now this is not something that we should drag our heels on. This is not time for a discussion. I need a decision."

The chairman sighed. "Do you think this will work?"

"It'll have to."

"Then do what you have to do."

The seconds ticked by on the SIOC Command Center clocks showing the time in the major cities around the world, as Meyerstein was put straight through to Sarah Harper, Under Secretary at the Department of Homeland Security's National Protection and Programs Directorate. Meyerstein skipped the pleasantries and went straight to what she needed.

Harper sounded officious. "I'm in charge of the Office of Infrastructure Protection. We're supposed to reduce the risk to our critical infrastructures and key resources during any acts of terrorism. Isn't that exactly the opposite of what you're asking me to do?"

Meyerstein felt her blood pressure hike up a notch as she watched the train's CCTV. "Listen, I don't want to hear your bullshit. We need to shut down a small segment of DC and we need to do it now. If we don't, we'll all be plunged into darkness if this attack is successful."

"You can't seriously expect me to–"

"Listen to me, this is not the time for a lengthy discussion. Here's the choice. You either make that decision right now or I'll be on the phone to the Secretary of Homeland Security, your boss, who reports direct to the President, demanding to know why you are obstructing this critical request."

A beat. "Are you threatening me?"

"You're damn right I am. Either you speak to Pepco and pull the plug on the Pentagon City Metro or I'll drag your bony ass out of there and do it myself."

She let out a long sigh. "OK, leave it with me."

"I didn't ask to leave it with you. You do this now, or you'll be facing Federal charges, do you understand?"

"I'll do it right now."

Then she hung up.

Meyerstein slammed down the phone on the desk and began to pace the operations room. She adjusted her headset, needing direct contact with Reznick in this critical phase. A few moments later a phone rang and Stamper picked it up. He nodded then hung up.

"Ten seconds to blackout."

Meyerstein turned and stared up at the huge screens. She couldn't believe what she was seeing. The train was moving into the tunnel.

FORTY

The train lurched forward as it headed into the tunnel and Reznick was thrown to the floor.

"Jon, I'm giving you the full authorisation," Meyerstein said into his earpiece.

Reznick crouched down low as he peered into the first carriage. Dead bodies, glass strewn everywhere, pools of blood on the floor, bodies of two dead Feds and innocent passengers. At the front of the train, he saw one of the bad guys at the controls in the operator's cab and the man with the gun barking instructions. But he couldn't see Caan. "What about the lights?"

"Jon, five seconds till the power goes down. Do you copy?"

"Affirmative."

"Jon, you must stop these guys at any cost, do you understand?"

"Leave it with me."

A click signaled the conversation was over.

Reznick was on his own. He peered through into the first carriage. The man with the gun was still shouting instructions. Time slowed as he heard his heart pound.

Suddenly, they were plunged into darkness. Muffled screams from the rear carriages and terrible wails as the train ground to a screeching halt.

Reznick crawled fast towards the first carriage. Head low, body low, flush with the ground. The military low crawl was perfected in muddy trenches under barbed wire, battle-hardened Marines screaming abuse. Stay low or get hit.

Closer and closer. Inches.

He now saw three separate silhouettes. Two in the driver's compartment and one up in the far right of the carriage.

He crawled on into the first carriage and he felt thick fluid on his hands. Blood. To his right were the dead FBI men lying slumped. He felt in the dark through the men's clothes, and took out a handgun magazine from an inside pocket which he put in his back pocket. Then he groped around on the floor until he felt the cold metal gun.

He pulled back the slide and focused on the guy at the far right.

Shoot, move, communicate. The soldier's mantra.

He edged a few inches closer. Then he aimed and squeezed the trigger. Flashes of fire spewed out of the gun illuminating the darkness around him. The figure collapsed in a heap. Reznick rolled sideways and aimed at the tallest man in the operator's compartment. He fired off two shots and the bullets tore through the glass and into the man's head. The fire from the gun lit up the blood-spattered shards of glass. The smell of cordite and smoke heavy in the air. But the third man had disappeared.

Had he hit the ground? Had he been hit by a ricochet?

"I've hit two of them, both down!" he shouted. "Can't see the third."

Reznick crawled fast down the first carriage, keeping his head low. He moved past the slumped body of the first man he had killed. The sound of broken glass crunching as he crawled through on his hands and knees, ignoring the searing pain as the glass cut into his skin.

Then he pointed his gun at the remaining glass in the operator's compartment and fired off the rest of his magazine. Glass shattered. The sound was deafening in such an enclosed space. His ears were ringing. In the distance he heard a scream.

Reznick got up and kicked in the operator's door. The slumped body of a man in uniform, drenched in blood, glass covering his body, and Caan's second accomplice. Then he saw a floor panel had been lifted.

Caan had escaped.

"Our guy has gone! I repeat, he has gone."

"Get after him!"

Reznick ejected the magazine from his gun and slid the new magazine until it locked into place. He pulled back the slide and tucked his gun into his waistband. Then he lowered himself down onto the tracks and crawled out from underneath the train.

Further up the line, in the tunnel, the sound of crunching footsteps on gravel.

"He's on the tracks heading towards Pentagon Metro station! I'm on it, over!"

"Take him out, for chrissakes!"

Reznick sprinted along the wooden beams along the tracks and headed deep into the blackness of the tunnel. He reckoned Caan had a one hundred yard start. Maybe more. His brain went into overdrive. The seconds seemed to slow down.

His blood was pumping and his heart pounding as he gave chase in pitch darkness, all senses switched on. He made the calculation. Caan was barely one hundred yards into the tunnel. It was a mile or so or one thousand seven hundred and sixty yards. Therefore, just over one thousand five hundred yards until the target reached the Pentagon Metro station.

On a running track it would take around four and a half minutes. On this terrain, nearer six.

He pumped his arms harder as he went deeper into the darkness of the tunnel. Up ahead on the right, he saw a pale blue light. He knew that would be an emergency call box. The smell of dirt and damp and oil pervaded the musky air. But the ghostly light gave Reznick the first glimpse of the running silhouette.

The guy was fit. And he had a bag slung over his shoulder.

"He's got to be stopped. And quick. We're checking the train as we speak for any other bio-materials, but nothing so far."

Reznick knew a headshot still wasn't possible. His mind raced, scenarios running through his brain. He had to stop him now, in his tracks. But a shot to the back – the best target area – might inadvertently pierce the bag as well, and release the bio-contents, releasing them into the tunnel.

Reznick was gaining on him. The silhouetted man – Scott Caan – weaved and bobbed along the tracks. Then he disappeared from sight.

"Fuck!"

Reznick slowed down to gauge where Caan was.

"Reznick, talk to me!"

Up ahead the sound of heavy panting and stones crunching told Reznick that Caan was still on the move, but perhaps struggling with the terrain or conditions.

Reznick picked up the pace. He felt the sweat sticking to his shirt, beading his forehead.

"Reznick!"

His breathing was getting harder. He didn't need distractions. But he didn't want to pull out the earpiece or lapel microphone. They needed to know what was happening. He stopped for a moment, panting hard. He turned his head slightly so the peripheral vision could kick in better. He knew that the human eye has rod cells – sensory cells at the back of the eye, apart from the center, opposite the pupil – meaning peripheral vision is better in low light and detecting movement.

Reznick looked down in the pitch-black tunnel and saw two tiny pale yellow strips. Rear reflective strips from Caan's trainers.

He locked onto the tiny yellow dots in the distance and began running along the concrete ties, which ran down the track. Faster and faster, gaze fixed on the yellow strips, moving up and down like pistons, as Caan kept running.

A couple of hundred yards up ahead a soft red light. Not a train signal, but like a road sign.

Reznick's eyes were getting more accustomed to the pitch dark. The light bathed the track in a soft red glow. The silhouetted figure was heading straight for it.

Suddenly the figure stopped and turned. A glint of metal and a flash before a deafening bang and what sounded like a ricochet.

A searing pain tore through his right shoulder as if it was on fire. Reznick gritted his teeth as the pain threatened to overwhelm him. It was like a hot poker pressed into an open wound. He stared into the suffocating darkness and tried to pinpoint the whereabouts of Caan as sweat dripped from his brow. He tentatively touched the wound. Superficial graze, albeit painful.

"What the hell is going on down there?" Meyerstein said. "Jon, I need you to speak to me."

Reznick ground his teeth against the pain. His mind flashed back to the deranged pain of Delta's vomit-inducing forty mile cross country movement with a sixty pound rucksack and weapon. Staff sergeants just looked on. No interaction. They didn't give feedback if you were doing bad or good, or going too slow. It screwed a lot of guys up who could not adjust to it. It was all about self-motivation. Who had the will to dig deep without any help? He had to push through the pain and psychological barrier himself, time and time again. He taught himself to love the pain. Pain is your friend. Suck it up and see.

The sound of running up ahead on gravel echoed around the tunnel. Caan was on the move.

Reznick willed himself to ignore the pain and head down the tracks again into the blackness, only the palest of red lights for guidance. Up ahead the sound of a metal door screeching open. A sickly yellow light spilled out illuminating Caan for the briefest moment.

"Jon, are you alright, copy?"

"I've been grazed. I'm OK. I'll survive."

A long pause before a sigh. "Take him down with a body shot if need be, Jon. Do you copy?"

"Too risky. I need to get in closer."

Reznick felt sweat running down his face and into his ears as he pounded down the track. He felt the earpiece slipping and before he could stop it, the damn thing had fallen out of his ear. "Goddamn," he said.

He was on his own.

He sprinted onward towards the red sign. A hundred yards. Then fifty. Then he saw it was a red emergency sign glowing in the dark. Yellow marking on the metallic door. He yanked at the handle and went inside. He flinched as the harsh yellowish light burned his eyes. A discarded grey sweatshirt and brown satchel lay strewn on the ground.

He wondered if this was to change his appearance again. But he also knew the bio-material would definitely be on his person, leaving the bag behind.

Above him scuffed footsteps and urgent breathing as Caan climbed the stairs.

A surge of raw adrenaline shot through Reznick's veins. He ignored the terrible pain in his shoulder and bounded up the concrete steps two at a time knowing he was a sitting duck. But he had to catch the bastard.

Suck it up.

That's what Reznick told himself during the Delta selection process as he hit mental and physical walls. Suck it up. Enjoy the misery. It will not beat you. Nothing will ever beat you. Ever. He thought of his father wearing his medals at the Vietnam Memorial. Then he thought of Lauren in her hospital bed. But then he thought of his wife, the split second before the tower collapsed. He imagined the horror and fear that must have engulfed her as she disappeared into the dust and the concrete and twisted metal.

He had to do this. He would do this. And he would catch that fuck for all of them.

The adrenaline continued to surge through his body giving him huge amounts of energy. He heard the sound of a metal hatch creaking open. Some artificial light from the street leaked in, and the roar of traffic and peeping horns.

Reznick's stomach knotted as he climbed higher and higher and then emerged blinking onto a busy Arlington street. He was on a sidewalk. The sound of police sirens in the distance. He scanned his unfamiliar surroundings trying to get a fix on the target. The monolithic monstrosity that was the Pentagon loomed in the distance. But then he got a visual on a running figure in the distance. He was wearing a navy blue windbreaker with yellow lettering on the back.

He ran across the road as cars screeched to a halt and peeped their horns as he headed towards the Pentagon. "Hey buddy, you wanna look where you're goin'?"

Reznick kept focused on the distant figure. Through an underpass and across another road. He saw a sign for South Fern Street and then a sign for the Pentagon Metro. He was gaining ground.

Reznick saw a sign for South Rotary Road and ran towards hundreds of people milling around, police cars and FBI vehicles, red lights flashing. He saw a cordon and realised the Metro station had been evacuated.

Then he spotted Caan and what looked like an ID tag dangling from his neck. Reznick fixed his gaze on the jacket as he disappeared into the crowd. The last thing he saw was that his jacket had emblazoned on his back, *FBI* in yellow letters.

A cold finger of fear ran down Reznick's back as he ran towards the crowd staying focused as Caan made his way through the crowd.

Reznick barged through the crowds who parted, some shouting and yelling, until he came face to face with two huge cops who were standing behind some yellow police tape.

"Freeze, police!" one shouted.

Reznick put up his hands as he slowed down and walked toward the cop. He saw Caan head into the station.

"Easy, fella, keep your hands where I can see them?"

Anger gnawed in Reznick's guts. The bastard was getting away.

Reznick put out his hands as if the officer should cuff him. The cop obligingly pulled out his cuffs from his belt and Reznick kicked the gun out of his hands. Then he smashed him in the side of the face, knocking the cop out cold. The other cop went clumsily for his gun. Reznick moved quicker and kicked the cop in the guts. He fell to his knees and the gun fell from his hands.

He burst through the tape and down into the Metro. He headed down some stairs and then an escalator before he caught sight of Caan running past some automated ticket machines to the Pentagon screening area. Heavily armed Pentagon police with dogs blocked the way.

A shot of adrenaline coursed through his body one more time as one of the cops took aim and fired at him. The bullet whizzed past his head and ricocheted off some metal.

He sprinted down one escalator and then ran up another. Then another escalator.

Caan was on it. Then he was gone.

Then he caught sight of Caan running towards an escalator. Reznick closed in.

At the bottom, Caan turned round and his black eyes met Reznick's. The face was puffy, the nose broken, cheekbones high. *It was him*. He grinned and unzipped his jacket.

Reznick didn't hesitate. He pointed the Beretta straight at Caan's forehead and aimed. Then squeezed the trigger twice. The shots rang out and echoed round the station.

Caan collapsed as blood streamed from the side of his head.

Reznick ran down the escalator, gun trained on Caan. He stepped over the body and then kneeled down beside him. Pressing his index finger to his neck he felt for a pulse.

Nothing.

Then he opened up Caan's jacket and ripped open a huge inside Velcro pocket. Inside were two white Christmas baubles with a glitter pattern.

Reznick carefully closed the jacket and was about to stand up when a voice behind him shouted, "Don't fucking move. FBI SWAT."

Reznick froze.

"Drop the gun!"

Reznick loosened his grip and dropped the gun, making a heavy clunking sound as it hit the escalator.

"Turn around and take three steps backwards onto the concourse, hands on head."

Reznick turned around, put his hands on his head and took three steps back. "Don't touch the Christmas baubles in his pocket, whatever you do! Look, I'm on your side. I've just taken this guy out. He was the target. Speak to Meyerstein of the FBI."

"Shut the fuck up and listen. I want you to strip off. Top, jeans, shoes, socks. Right down to your undies."

Reznick complied, ignoring the burning pain in his shoulder. He stood in his boxer shorts, hands on head, blood dripping onto the stone concourse.

"Now slowly, turn around."

He complied and stared straight at them. They stood, guns pointing at him, their gaze locked onto his muscled torso and the red Delta dagger tattooed on his chest.

"Very slowly, very slowly, take three steps towards us and then kneel down, with your hands still on your head."

Reznick walked towards them and kneeled, hands on head. "Listen to me," he said, "do not move that guy on the ground. Do not touch the Christmas baubles, do you hear me?" He could feel himself slipping away. He fought to remain conscious. Then he looked up at the lead SWAT guy. He saw Meyerstein appear from behind. She smiled and walked towards him.

Reznick smiled back. "What the hell took you so long?"

Then everything turned black.

FORTY-ONE

The hours that followed were a bit of a blur as Reznick lapsed in and out of consciousness. He felt cold and was losing blood fast as he was rushed to the emergency room of The George Washington Hospital. The voices of the paramedics and then the doctors and nurses echoed in his head as if in dream. His every breath induced searing pain in his shoulder wound.

"Goddamn," he snarled.

Harsh hospital lights. Blurred faces staring down at him.

He felt himself drift away. Deeper and deeper into a far away land. Elisabeth's face was looking down on him. He felt her stroke his hair. "It's OK, Jon. Everything's gonna be all right."

When he came to, a young female doctor was smiling down at him, as she bandaged his shoulder wound. "Welcome back," she said. "You got lucky. The bullet narrowly missed the brachial artery. That's the main artery that supplies blood to the arm and hand. That was a real close call, believe me."

Reznick didn't feel lucky. He took a few moments to get his bearings. "I thought it was only a graze." His throat was dry and he barely got the words out.

"We've given you strong antibiotics and that will hopefully keep infection at bay. No serious tissue damage; how, I don't know. However, you'll need to rest up for a few days."

The doctor left the room and Reznick was on his own. He tried to move his shoulder and winced at the searing pain. He tried to sit up straight, but his head felt light. Damn.

Reznick looked around his room. It was all hospital fresh and white. The smell of disinfectant in the air.

His eyes felt heavy and he drifted off to sleep. He dreamed of Lauren. As a baby. As a toddler, walking on the beach, as he held her hand. And he dreamed of her as a young woman, talking about college. Talking about her mother late into the night. He dreamed of his wife on *that* day. It was the same dream. Before the towers fell. Then he was back home alone. The smell of the salt air and all before him the cool blue waters in the cove.

When Reznick came round again, he had been asleep for fourteen hours straight. He was aware that someone was in the room. He struggled to open his eyes. In his peripheral vision he saw Stamper and four unsmiling Feds. One was holding up a navy single-breasted suit and black Oxford shoes. Reznick turned and looked across at them. "What's all this?"

Stamper was chewing gum. "You're coming with us."

"Not until you tell me how my daughter is."

Stamper smiled. "She's opened her eyes."

Reznick closed his eyes as relief flooded through his body. He realised how close he'd come to losing her.

"You wanna get ready, Reznick?"

"Are we going on a date, Roy?"

Stamper shook his head and grinned. "You're crazy, do you know that?"

Reznick eased himself out of his bed and winced. His shoulder was heavily bandaged. His hands were cut from the shards of glass, but the wounds had all been cleaned up. He put on his shirt, taking an age to button it up. He got on his suit, and tried to tie his shoe laces, but couldn't manage it. Stamper kneeled down to help.

Reznick looked in the mirror. It didn't look like him. He looked like a stockbroker. He was wearing an expensive navy single-breasted suit, white shirt, pale blue tie, black Oxford shoes. He couldn't remember the last time he had felt the need to wear a suit.

He was signed out and escorted to the elevator. Inside, Reznick turned to Stamper. "How did you know my size?"

Stamper chewed his gum and tried to stifle a smile. "We measured you up when you were unconscious, tough guy."

Reznick shook his head and smiled. "So, are you going to let me know what this is all about? Where are we going?"

"You'll see."

It was dark when they left the hospital's staff entrance to go to a waiting car in the basement garage. He was strapped into the back seat and they drove off. The DC traffic was a crawl, despite it being evening. He stared out at the passing people driving past, going about their business, unaware of what really happened down in the Metro. His thoughts were scrambled. He thought of Lauren way down in Pensacola, safe and alive, and for that, he was truly thankful. But he also thought of Maddox and wondered what his role was in the whole operation.

A short while later, Reznick caught a glimpse of the Hoover building – FBI HQ.

"What's going on, Roy?" Reznick asked.

Stamper shook his head as they drove towards a basement garage and IDs scanned in an electronic reader. He was marched into the building and taken up to the seventh floor. They got off the elevator and he was escorted along a corridor to the executive conference room. The FBI's most senior executives, including Meyerstein – clapped him in.

Reznick felt light headed as he was introduced to the Director and was toasted with single malt, thanking him for his efforts. A letter was read out from the President. Reznick felt embarrassed at being the *center* of attention.

He shrugged off his natural inclination to avoid such gatherings and knocked back the amber liquid, feeling a warm glow inside. The morphine combined with the whisky also took the edge off the pain. After several minutes of excruciating small talk with some FBI executives, and a rambling speech from the Assistant Director about "the American way", Meyerstein asked Reznick round to her office.

"Take the weight off," she said, sitting on the edge of her desk, hands folded demurely.

Reznick slumped down and took a few moments to take in her office. The shiny mahogany desk was uncluttered, a gold-leaf-framed black and white photo of Meyerstein with her kids, playing in a park. On the wall to his left, a huge plasma screen, showing a *real-time* feed from Lower Manhattan. Opposite that was a wall covered in awards and a few pictures of Meyerstein with the Director and the President.

She shifted on the desk and looked at him, face impassive. "How are you feeling?"

"I've felt better."

"Well, for what it's worth, you scrub up well."

"Jon Reznick, style icon, what do you think? Front cover of GQ, right?"

Meyerstein smiled and edged off her desk, before sitting down in a black leather seat behind her mahogany desk. "What I'm going to say does not go beyond these four walls, am I clear?"

"I'm listening."

"This didn't happen. None of it."

"I understand."

"The incident is going to be described as an undercover surveillance operation and a gunman killing a couple of Feds. Then he was cornered and shot. There shall never be any reference to bio-materials or any foreign governments or their operatives by you to anyone, ever. This never happened. Are we clear?"

"Whatever you say."

Meyerstein looked at him with her cool blue eyes and smiled. "We are in your debt, Jon. But I think we rode our luck, don't you?"

"Sometimes you make your own luck."

"I can't remember when I had so many hard calls to make. But I guess, sometimes, the rule book is just a guide, right?"

"The first rule is that there are no rules."

Meyerstein smiled. He liked her smile. "You might be interested to know that preliminary tests show that the two baubles recovered from Caan here in Washington contained the same virus as the batch used in New York City. Our scientists say that the contents of two vials were found in the baubles. The aerosol containers in New York were estimated to have contained the contents from one vial. But thankfully, unlike New York, there was no release here in Washington. There are no traces. And we've now accounted for all the bio-material stolen from the lab in Maryland."

"What about the guys behind it?"

"What about them?"

"I assume you know who was responsible?"

Meyerstein steepled her fingers on her desk. "I can't say anymore."

"Can't or won't?"

"Let's just say we're dealing with this in our own inimitable way." She shrugged. "Is the inquisition over?"

"What do you know about the two people who visited the small hotel in Washington where I took Luntz? Are you at liberty to say who they were?"

"French contractors who were born in Algeria. We believed they killed our Special Agent at the St Regis, and then were ordered to the small hotel to kill you and Luntz. But they've disappeared off the planet. We're using diplomatic channels to try and find out where they are."

Reznick felt his eyes getting heavier. He looked at Meyerstein and she looked washed out. "When was the last time you slept?"

"That bad, huh?"

Reznick gave a rueful smile.

"I can't remember the last time I slept."

Reznick smiled. "What about Luntz?"

"What about him?"

"How is he?"

"He's doing well, thank you. I'm told an antidote and vaccine is being rushed into advanced trials in the next twenty-four hours."

"Pass on my regards."

"I'll say you were asking after him. But I think he'll need counselling for the next ten years after what happened to him."

Reznick laughed.

Meyerstein shifted in her seat. "Do you mind me asking something?"

"Sure."

"Why did you trust me down in Key West? I mean, I could've doublecrossed you, couldn't I? It would've been easy for me not to keep my side of the bargain."

"Gut instinct. You have a face I can trust."

Meyerstein blushed. "Yeah?"

"Oh, yeah. I've enjoyed working with you, Meyerstein."

"My name's Martha. Do you think you'll remember that being so doped up and all?"

"Sure. Martha. I like that."

Meyerstein ran a hand through her hair before she stifled a yawn. "It's been an experience, that's for sure."

Reznick felt a burning twinge in his shoulder and winced at the pain.

"You OK?"

"It's nothing. Tell me, what about the guy down in Miami pulling the strings?"

Meyerstein shrugged. "What guy?"

"Brewling."

"Ah, him. We believe he has been professionally disappeared."

"Meaning?"

"Meaning, he is being protected by some of those behind this plot. But we'll find him. I personally think he was being played as well."

Reznick said nothing.

"But we have had some progress. We have already intercepted and decrypted a conversation he had with the President of a Swiss bank where he holds five separate accounts, via an NSA operation. We believe it was made on-board from a private jet flying over the Mediterranean."

"You mind if I hear it?"

Meyerstein arched her eyebrows. "And why may I ask would you want to know the sound of his voice? I can't allow any spill out from this, do you understand?"

Reznick nodded. "Just curious."

She picked up a remote control and pressed a couple of buttons. The speakers on the huge TV came to life. Then the voice of Brewling. "Are all my assets liquid or will I have to wait to transfer them to the Caymans? I need this situation to be resolved right away."

The glass of whisky and the morphine had dulled Reznick's brain. His exhausted mind was trying to process the voice. Something about it seemed vaguely familiar.

The voice spoke again. It was cold. Chilling. Mechanistic in its delivery.

The voice was familiar. Eerily familiar. Slowly it dawned on him.

"You OK?" Meyerstein said. "You look as if you've seen a ghost."

Reznick forced a smile, eyes heavy. It was a ghost. The voice was of the man he knew only as Maddox. He had been played from the moment the call was made to his cell phone at his home in Maine. He felt waves of anger run over his body.

"You OK?"

"That voice, are you sure that's Brewling?"

"One hundred per cent."

"Well, I'm not an expert in voice analysis, but that sounds a helluva lot like my handler. But I knew him as Maddox."

Meyerstein leaned back in her seat, face impassive. "Maddox. Thanks for that. I'll pass that on. But we'll find him, don't worry."

Reznick smiled and got up from his seat and reached over to shake Meyerstein's hand. She stood up and smiled as he gripped her soft hand tight.

"Nice working with you," she said. Her hand felt warm. "Look, we can move you to a safe house, until this is resolved."

"Don't worry about me. My only concern is Lauren and she is safe."

"I understand. Before I forget, you wanna know the latest news on Lauren, as of fifteen minutes ago?"

"How is she?"

"She's now fully conscious and has made a remarkable recovery over the last twenty-four hours. Jon, they've done all the diagnostic tests, and they're satisfied your daughter is not damaged in any way."

Reznick looked at Meyerstein who smiled back at him. "I owe you one."

"You don't owe me anything."

He let out a long sigh. "Look, I gotta go."

"Where are you going at this hour?"

Reznick smiled. "I'm going to see my daughter."

FORTY-TWO

The Feds offered to fly him down in the morning, but Reznick needed to be alone. He was provided with a black BMW X5 and he started the brutal one thousand mile journey through the night. It would be the best part of fifteen hours.

It would give him time to think. He wanted the open road.

Reznick stared out at the oncoming lights as he sped down the freeway and his thoughts ran free. His shadowy world had been visited upon his beloved daughter. His decision not to carry out the assassination had brought those consequences to his door. But although he'd have to live with that, it was his daughter who would ultimately pay the price.

Would she be visited by nightmares? Flashbacks? Perhaps she would.

The more he thought of it the more he seethed.

He thought of Maddox – the pseudonym for Brewling – and he was engulfed with hatred. He wanted to wipe him out. It was Brewling all along.

The car ate up the miles. On and on, deeper and deeper towards Pensacola. He drove I-66 west and crossed into Virginia, before heading down I-81 South through Tennessee. The wee small hours passed slowly, Alabama talk radio hosts banging on throughout the night about Obama and the Tea Party.

By the time the sun edged over the horizon as he drove through the Deep South, his shoulder was burning like hell.

He stopped for a breakfast of pancakes, maple syrup and a couple of painkillers, washed down by two black coffees.

He felt better as he drove through southern Alabama. The sky turned blood red, the fields a reddish brown.

With daylight, the dark thoughts seemed to dissipate. The road was bringing him closer to his daughter.

Reznick thought of his daughter's future. College. Falling in love. Having a family. A career. The usual obsessions of Middle America. When he edged across the Florida state line, the flawless morning sky was cornflower blue.

Reznick pulled up at the security gates of the Naval Hospital in Pensacola just before 10am. He flashed a special pass the FBI had given him. The soldier checked his list and ushered him through.

He signed in at reception, before he was escorted to the ICU. A doctor was waiting for him just outside her room. He stepped forward and shook his hand. "Dr Todd Frith, I'm a neurologist here at the hospital. Can I have a few minutes before you see your daughter?"

Reznick's heart sank fearing the worst. He nodded and followed the doctor into a side room alone.

"Please, take a seat, Mr Reznick," Dr Frith said, pulling up a couple of seats.

Reznick sat down, hunched forward, clasping his hands.

He let out a long sigh. "Your daughter has emerged unscathed from this coma. I've carried out a series of tests and a full neurological examination. MRI, CAT scans, everything, to test her functionality. She is perfect. I carried out more tests just over an hour ago, and she is well on the road to recovery. But she is now under sedation, as we feel she needs some proper sleep and rest. So, five minutes with her, if that's OK."

Reznick smiled as relief flooded through his body. "Thank you."

His mind flashed back to when Lauren was a child. Playing in the rock pools down on the beach in the cove with her mother, a few months before she died. The smell of the salty air and the biting chill of the wind, as they ran and played and fooled around, before enjoying a picnic. It was their private beach. Their own world. Enclosed. Safe.

His abiding good memories of Elisabeth were on the beach, smiling, not a care in the world.

The doctor asked, "Mr Reznick, are you OK? You look quite pale."

"I'm fine. I'd like to see my daughter, if that's OK."

"Of course."

The doctor got up and shook Reznick's hand as his pager bleeped. "Excuse me, I've gotta go. Nice talking to you."

Reznick stood outside Lauren's room for a few moments. He had doubted this day would ever come. He gathered his thoughts, composed himself before he gently pushed open the doors to her room. His daughter was no longer hooked up to the machines. No beeping.

He stood and looked across at his daughter. Her golden hair was tousled on the starched white pillow cloth. His thoughts were scrambled. Part guilt, part elation, part exhaustion. He sat down at her bedside and leaned over and stroked her silky hair. She was in a peaceful sleep, breathing calmly.

He touched her face and she stirred and slowly opened her eyes. A flicker of recognition and then a huge smile as she reached out to take his hand.

Reznick squeezed it tight. He thought his heart was being ripped out at the roots. He wiped the tears from her face and kissed her softly on the cheek. "You're safe now, honey."

She looked up at him for what seemed like an eternity before she smiled. "I always knew you'd come and get me, Daddy."

Then Reznick pulled her close and hugged her tight, neither one wanting to let go.

EPILOGUE

Six months later, Reznick was sitting alone on his deck – the house to himself – nursing his second bottle of beer on a balmy early summer evening in midcoast Maine. The last remnants of the sun had turned the ocean a burnt orange, the tops of the old oaks on fire. He felt at peace for the first time in months.

His daughter, Lauren, had moved to a new school in upstate New York. She emailed every day with boundless optimism, talking about walks with her friends in the rolling hills, upcoming school visits to Central Park, art galleries, museums and a whole bunch of wholesome stuff.

He was missing her, but the dark days of last winter had passed.

Reznick didn't venture far. He had hung around the Rockland area most of the time. He walked past the abandoned sardine packing plant his father used to work in. He tried to imagine how hard it must have been for his dad to do a job he loathed, memories of Vietnam burned into his mind. He took long walks on the beach, did the garden and took time to watch the flowers grow. He occasionally sat on the beach in the cove and thought of his wife and daughter, when she was just a baby all those years earlier, playing on the same sand, laughing and joking. He imagined what his life would have been like if his wife had survived. He wondered if they would have had more children. When he closed his eyes and listened to the water rush up the sand, he thought he heard their laughter and voices hanging in the breeze.

The rest of the time he tended the trees his father had planted. This was his home. The clapboard colonial his father had built with his own hands. The oak floors, the crafted shutters and beige and ocean blue walls.

When his phone rang, he saw an unfamiliar number on the caller display. He let it ring and ring. Eventually he picked up.

"Yeah?" he answered.

"Sorry to bother you, Jon." It was the soft voice of Meyerstein.

Reznick sat up straight, rubbing his eyes. "Hi. Long time no hear."

"Indeed. How are you, Jon?"

"I'm fine. What about you?"

She let out a long sigh. "Working. You know how it is."

"Do you guys ever take a vacation?"

"Not as often as I'd like. Look, I'm just calling to check on how Lauren is. I believe she has now moved to a new school."

"She has. And she is good. And for that, I'm truly grateful."

"Look, Jon, I have some news."

"What kind of news?"

"Jon, I think from this moment on, Lauren can sleep securely in her bed. It's all over. The job is done."

"I'm sorry, how do you mean?"

"Turn on the TV. CNN."

"Why?"

"Just do it."

A long silence opened up on the line.

Reznick went inside still holding his bottle of beer in one hand, the cell in the other. He put down the bottle of beer, picked up the remote and switched on the TV, channel surfing till he came to CNN.

"And the breaking news this hour," the male anchor in Atlanta said, "is that the second in command of Pakistan's intelligence agency, the ISI, has been blown up by a car bomb in Islamabad."

Reznick stared transfixed at the screen.

The anchor continued, "Pakistan military sources tell us that Major General Muhammad Kashal's car may have been followed by two men on motorbikes from his heavily-guarded compound, before the remote detonation took place. Pentagon sources said that Kashal's loss was a blow in the fight against the Taliban both in and outside Pakistan."

A picture of a smiling general in full military regalia appeared in the top right hand corner of the screen.

Reznick stared at the picture and realised what Meyerstein was saying. This was the mastermind. They had got him and someone else was getting the blame. A black flag operation if ever there was one.

The anchor continued, "And in a bizarre twist to this story, a former American military adviser was in the car with Kashal and died in the explosion. Sources say Vince Brewling had previously served as the CIA station chief in Islamabad in the 1980s, and is believed to have been good friends with Major General Kashal when they worked together to oust the Soviet Union from Afghanistan. Sources are reporting that Mr Brewling was paying a private visit to Kashal and was not on US government business."

A picture of a whey-faced man with mottled skin, rheumy blue eyes, was shown in the top left hand corner of the screen. Brewling? So this was the man he knew only as Maddox.

Cold justice had been served.

Reznick stared at the picture on the screen before finishing the rest of his beer. He switched off the TV, and went outside.

"It's finished, Jon," she said. "But I've got a proposition."

"And what's that?"

"I'd like you to work with us."

"For the FBI?"

"On a consultancy basis, so to speak. Certain situations might arise where a man of your talents–"

Reznick sighed. "I'll think about it."

"How about I call you in the morning?"

Reznick stared up at the billions of stars in the inky black sky, as the roar of the ocean echoed deep down in the cove.

"I said I'll think about it," he said.

ACKNOWLEDGMENTS

With deepest gratitude, I would like to thank the following people for their help and support:

Many thanks to my editor, Emlyn Rees, and everyone at Exhibit A Books, for their hard work, enthusiasm and belief in this book. Thanks also to my agent, Sam Copeland.

Special mention must go to Angela D Bell, FBI, in Washington DC who assisted my numerous questions with good grace and impeccable professionalism. Many thanks also to the FBI field office in Miami.

I was very fortunate that Larry Vickers, formerly of 1st Special Forces Operational Detachment – Delta, commonly referred to as Delta Force, was another who gave his time and expert technical knowledge freely.

During research, I found *Delta Force: The Army's Elite Counterterrorist Unit* (Avon Books) by Charlie Beckwith and *Inside Delta Force* (Bantam Dell) by Eric L Haney really useful books.

I would also like to thank Ash Swanson in Miami Beach for helping out with South Beach research.

Last, my family and friends for their encouragement and support. And, most of all, my wife, Susan, who was with me every step of the way, as each draft developed, offering brilliant advice, coupled with no small amount of patience.

ABOUT THE AUTHOR

J B Turner began his writing career as a journalist. His news stories and feature articles have appeared in the *Daily Mail*, *Daily Telegraph*, *Daily Express*, *The Scotsman* and *The Herald*. He is married and has two young children.

jbturnerauthor.com
twitter.com/jbturnerauthor

A Victorian mystery.
Murder. Vice. Pollution. Delays on the Tube. Some things never change...

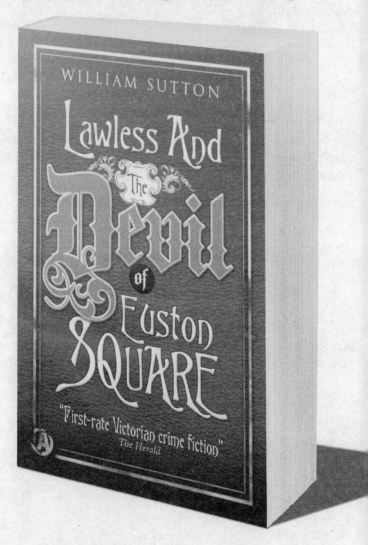